KATE MCMURRAY

What's the Use of Wondering?

"This is a beautifully done, sweet, sexy, romantic, true love tale! Highly recommended to bring a smile to your face!"
—*Divine Magazine*

"...a sweet coming of age/transitioning to adulthood story."
—Jessie G Books

There Has to Be a Reason

"...a beautifully written story. Very realistic. Definitely a book I would recommend to others."
—Gay Book Reviews

"...I really enjoyed this. I had never read this author before but will definitely read more of her work."
—Night Owl Reviews

The Boy Next Door

"The story was unique and not something I've read over and over, which is refreshing!"
—Alpha Book Club

"I was completely captivated by this book."
—Inked Rainbow Reads

By KATE MCMURRAY

Blind Items
The Boy Next Door
Devin December
Four Corners
Kindling Fire with Snow
Out in the Field
The Stars that Tremble • The Silence of the Stars
A Walk in the Dark
What There Is
When the Planets Align

DREAMSPUN DESIRES
The Greek Tycoon's Green Card Groom

ELITE ATHLETES
Here Comes the Flood

THE RAINBOW LEAGUE
The Windup
Thrown a Curve
The Long Slide Home

WMU
There Has to Be a Reason
What's the Use of Wondering

Published by DREAMSPINNER PRESS
www.dreamspinnerpress.com

KATE MCMURRAY

HERE COMES
the FLOOD

DREAMSPINNER
PRESS

Published by
DREAMSPINNER PRESS

5032 Capital Circle SW, Suite 2, PMB# 279,
Tallahassee, FL 32305-7886 USA
www.dreamspinnerpress.com

This is a work of fiction. Names, characters, places, and incidents either
are the product of author imagination or are used fictitiously, and any
resemblance to actual persons, living or dead, business establishments,
events, or locales is entirely coincidental.

Here Comes the Flood
© 2020 Kate McMurray

Cover Art
© 2020 L.C. Chase
http://www.lcchase.com
Cover content is for illustrative purposes only and any person depicted
on the cover is a model.

Mass Market Paperback ISBN: 978-1-64108-183-2
Trade Paperback ISBN: 978-1-64405-344-7
Digital ISBN: 978-1-64405-343-0
Library of Congress Control Number: 2019916129
Mass Market Paperback published May 2020
v. 1.0

Printed in the United States of America
∞
This paper meets the requirements of
ANSI/NISO Z39.48-1992 (Permanence of Paper).

PROLOGUE

Two years ago

Olympian Gets DUI

RALEIGH, NC, July 18—Retired Olympic swimming phenom Isaac Flood was arrested Thursday for driving under the influence after a night out at Mercury, a dance club in Raleigh. Police pulled Flood over after swerving across a yellow line. He had a blood alcohol count of 0.15, just under twice the legal limit.

Flood is one of the most decorated Olympians of all time, winning a total of nine medals in three Olympic Games. He retired two years ago, after his last Olympics, and has since cultivated a reputation as a party boy....

Olympic Diver Comes Out in Video

BOULDER, CO, August 2—Olympic gold medalist Timothy Swan announced he was gay in a video he posted on his website last night. In the video, Swan, 22, stated he's dating Patterson Wood, an actor on teen soap *Oak Hills*. "I've never been in love like this before," Swan proclaims on the video, with Wood sitting beside him....

January, this year

"WHAT THE hell was that?"

Adam stared down at Isaac as he treaded water. Isaac found Adam's stare unnerving. He was tempted to dunk his head back under to avoid it.

Instead, he grabbed the edge of the pool and kicked his legs out. "What the hell was what?"

"Your flip turns. You're doing this weird thing with your kick. I think it's slowing you down."

"Oh." Isaac tried to mentally replay what he'd done. He didn't think he'd changed his kick.

"I don't know how I never noticed it before. Have you been doing it this whole time? Jesus. Okay. So, when you flip, straighten out your legs right away to push off. None of that fluttery stuff."

"I'm doing fluttery stuff?"

Adam sighed. "Think about it this time instead of going on autopilot." He took a step back from the pool. "Do it slow so you can think it through. Don't worry about your time. I'm gonna watch on the camera, okay?" He picked up his tablet from where he'd left it on a chair near the side of the pool.

"Okay."

At the ripe old age of twenty-nine, after being out of competitive swimming for three years, Isaac's body didn't function the way it used to. In a lot of ways, swimming felt like habit, as easy as walking. But in others, it was entirely new. He couldn't just hop in a pool and swim speedy laps the way he used to. So Isaac swam slowly, mindful of his strokes. He got to the end and did the flip turn, and thought about where his legs were as he came out of it. He returned to Adam and lifted his head out of the water. "Did I fix it?" he asked.

"Yeah, that was better. But let's try it again. Get out."

Isaac pushed himself out of the pool and got back up on the block, knowing what came next. Adam said, "Do it at speed now. Same thing. Straight legs. No fluttering."

Isaac waited for Adam to get his stopwatch ready. When Adam blew his whistle, Isaac launched himself off the block. He put everything into his strokes, thought about the flip turn, came back. He grabbed the edge of the pool and looked up at Adam expectantly.

"You shaved six-tenths off your one-hundred-meter time. Do it again."

Isaac climbed out of the pool.

An hour later, once Isaac's limbs had turned completely to jelly, he was headed toward the locker room when a guy in a polo shirt snagged him. The insignia on the breast of his shirt indicated he worked for the U.S. Anti-Doping Agency.

Drug test. Great.

Not that Isaac had anything to hide. His heart rate spiked just the same.

"Test his BAC too," Adam said.

Isaac gaped at him. "Coach."

"It's for your own good."

Isaac frowned. Did Adam not trust him? "I've been sober for eleven months and eighteen days."

Adam patted Isaac's shoulder. "I know. We're going to prove it."

The anti-doping guy held up his case full of testing equipment and pointed toward the locker room. Isaac let out a sigh and followed him, resigned. This was his life now, an endless series of tests to prove that he'd dried out and gotten his shit together. No one would ever believe or trust him on that score again, which he supposed he deserved.

Luke Rogers—another swimmer Adam coached, one Isaac considered his chief competition for a spot on the Olympic team—stood near the entrance to the locker room, looking at his phone. "You see this bull-shit?" he asked.

"What bullshit?" Isaac said, scrubbing his hair with a towel, still annoyed about the test.

"That gay diver, Timmy Swan? Apparently he and the actor from that CW show got engaged."

"And I care because…?"

Luke shrugged. "I don't know. In case you thought you were the only aquatics athlete who could snag gos-sipy headlines."

"Apparently not."

"Jealous?"

"Not even a little." He pointed at the anti-doping guy. "Come on. Let's get this over with."

TIM SLID into the shimmery silk robe. It felt strange on his skin, not like the old terry cloth robe he wore at home. "Are you sure about this?"

"Of course, babe," said Pat, who wore a pair of pajama pants made from the same fabric.

Tim didn't know how to articulate how deeply uncomfortable this whole production made him. He'd never been a big fan of having his picture taken, let alone in these ridiculous clothes. And he didn't like that everyone on set was staring at him, and the whole boudoir theme made it feel like they were inviting the entire world into their bedroom. On top of that, he was missing practice—crucial with the Olympic Trials just a few months away—in order to do this dumb photo shoot.

"It's romantic!" Pat insisted.

Tim sighed. He didn't think there was anything romantic about a froufrou photo shoot for an LGBT magazine. He tugged on the cuffs of the robe. "I feel so naked."

"Really, Timmy? There are literally hundreds of photos of you on the internet wearing nothing but a tiny Speedo. You're more covered up now than you are when you compete."

Tim wanted to make an argument about context, but he knew it would be futile. "Fine. Let's get this over with."

They were on a set dressed to look like a bedroom, and everything was gray. The photographer had insisted all the gray made the bright green color of their silky pajamas pop.

"This is good visibility for us," Pat insisted, positioning himself on the bed. He motioned for Tim to sit next to him.

Tim crossed his arms over his chest. "Who cares? Whether or not people know my name won't affect my chances of winning a gold medal. It won't help me do three and a half somersaults off the platform."

Pat rolled his eyes. "Don't be a pill. Come here."

It all felt like a mistake. Just a week ago Pat had come to him with a ring box containing two platinum bands, and Tim had felt so overwhelmed by the gesture that he'd said yes. Every time he looked at the ring on his hand now, though, all he felt was uncertainty. Tim was only twenty-four. Pat was his first boyfriend. He loved Pat, but it felt like this was happening too fast.

He needed more time to live his life, to work on his diving, and he wanted to do that outside of the spotlight. Marriage felt like a period at the end of a sentence Tim wasn't ready to finish—a sentence in giant type on a billboard on a major highway that everyone saw on their way to work. And now Pat wanted to do this splashy photo shoot, showing off their love to the world, but Tim only wanted to vomit.

Still, he slid onto the bed next to Pat and let Pat hug him from behind. He closed his eyes, savoring Pat's touch, his big hands, his warm skin.

Then he saw the flash from behind his eyelids.

"That's beautiful," said the photographer.

Tim barely managed to stop himself from running away.

June, two months before the Olympics

Transcript from TBC broadcast of USA Swimming Olympic Trials

DAVIS: I'll tell you, Jim, I never expected to see Isaac Flood again, at least not in a pool.

O'TOOLE: I agree, and yet here we are. For the last eighteen months, Flood has been working with coach Adam Vreeland at the Southeast Aquatic Center in North Carolina. He's coming out of retirement, but I gotta say, he looks better than ever. His strokes are cleaner, he's in great shape. I think he's got a solid shot at making this team.

DAVIS: All right. Well, here we are at the start of the 400-meter freestyle final. There's Flood in Lane Three.

O'TOOLE: And they're off. Flood is off to a little bit of a slow start. There's Reggie Stevens in Lane Eight. He's always fast out of the gate. And then in Lane Four, right next to Flood, is Luke Rogers. Luke is the favorite to win this event at the Olympics. He's the reigning world champion and has been swimming at world-record pace all season. There, Rogers is pulling ahead. Here they are at the turn. And… Rogers is ahead with Stevens right at his tail. But look at Flood!

DAVIS: This is really a remarkable race.

O'TOOLE: Hard to say how it will shake out. These guys aren't going to put their all into it until the end. But oh, Flood is pulling ahead of Rogers. I don't believe it!

DAVIS: Fourth turn. If you see the line, you can see that Flood and Rogers are both moving ahead of the world record set by Rogers last year. I don't believe it. How great does Flood look?

O'TOOLE: It's a remarkable story. I don't believe it either.

DAVIS: Does this change the makeup of Team USA?

O'TOOLE: I think it might. I didn't think Flood had a chance, but now…. Last turn! And here's Rogers. And Flood. They're neck and neck in the last stretch. Who knew Flood could do this anymore? Rogers is in the lead, but oh my God, Flood is gaining on him again! And it's…. Flood wins the race! I don't believe it!

DAVIS: Well, there you have it. Isaac Flood is headed to his fourth Olympics. And he looks thrilled….

Transcript from the TBC broadcast of USA Diving Olympic Trials

GREGORIUS: Timothy Swan will perform a back three-and-a-half pike, an incredibly difficult dive.

MICHAELS: He's made quite a few headlines lately.

GREGORIUS: True, but not for his diving.

MICHAELS: Still, he's one of the most beautiful divers in the world. He's been doing well in international competition, but there's a lot of competition, especially from the Chinese and Mexican divers.

GREGORIUS: Do you think he can repeat his gold medal from four years ago?

MICHAELS: Not sure. He really came out of nowhere to win that gold medal. No one expected him to even be in the running. He just had a great day. It remains to be seen if lightning can strike twice. But he's my favorite of the American divers to do well in Madrid.

GREGORIUS: And he's a favorite of the tabloids too.

MICHAELS: A very public breakup will do that.

GREGORIUS: Not to mention he's one of the few out gay Olympians. That's gotta be tough for him.

MICHAELS: Let's watch him dive. And… beautiful! Just beautiful.

GREGORIUS: I only hope he can keep his personal life out of the news going into the Olympics. I'd hate to see that affect his performance. Otherwise, he's guaranteed a spot on the team….

CHAPTER I

August, five days before the Olympics

ISAAC HAD done this three times before, so it probably shouldn't have surprised him that his room in the Olympic Village remained unfinished. It smelled of fresh paint and plaster, the bedding had been left in a haphazard pile on the bare mattress, and the bathroom had neither a shower curtain nor any paper products.

The previous Olympics had been this way too, although that building had also featured shoddy construction. Everything here at least seemed structurally sound. Just... not quite ready for people yet.

He sighed and dropped his luggage on the bed. As a senior member of the American team, he'd managed to score his own room, due to his need for quiet and focus or whatever bullshit Adam had fed the US Olympic Committee. Singles were rare; Luke had told him on the plane that his jealousy was intense because he'd be bunking with a wide-eyed nineteen-year-old new to international competition. Isaac had laughed.

But the joke was on him. This room was a shithole. Bare white walls, a single dresser that seemed to be made of particleboard, a thin mattress on a cheap frame, and the most bare-bones bathroom he'd ever seen. Although maybe the other rooms weren't much better.

His phone chimed with a text from Adam: *Pool time in 30 mins.*

And that was another thing. He'd been in this godforsaken city all of an hour, and Adam wanted him in the pool already.

At least the location itself wasn't so bad. Madrid boasted a certain Old World beauty as the host city. Isaac had never been here before; the only city in Spain he'd ever visited previously was Barcelona. This, at least, was not one of those countries with an authoritarian regime that didn't care much for—or actively condemned—men such as himself who occasionally liked to be with men.

A headache blossomed behind his eyes. Probably dehydration.

He dug his water bottle out of his backpack and walked over to the bathroom sink, only there was no water when he turned the knob. Of fucking course.

The Aquatics Center would have showers, though. Isaac quickly moved stuff around in his bags, changed into warm-up pants and a T-shirt, and hoisted his duffel bag onto his shoulder.

When Isaac walked into the Aquatics Center a few minutes later, an unholy racket echoed through the whole interior. "What the hell is that?" he asked Adam, who stood near the entrance of the locker room.

"They're screwing the chairs into the stands."

"Oh good God."

"You stop noticing it after a while. I have your suits. USOC apologized about thirty-six times for the delay."

Isaac grimaced. Officially sanctioned team swim-suits irked him. Usually they were state-of-the-art, so he shouldn't have complained. But new racing suits were so… confining. Still, all kinds of ridiculous things could shave tenths of a second off his times, so he'd take whatever advantage he could get.

When he'd shown up at the Trials, he'd only been hoping to prove he could still swim well enough to make this team. But now that he was here, in the actual Olympic venue, he suddenly realized he wanted to win.

The competitive spirit still burned in him, it turned out. Clawing his way out from the bottle had been one of the greatest challenges of his life, and he'd been tell-ing himself for weeks that he didn't *need* to win. He just needed to prove to himself that he was still vital, that he could still do the thing he'd been training his body to do for more than two decades. Everyone in his life had been treating his making the Olympic team as a miracle. That he stood here in Madrid should have been enough.

But no, he needed to win. He'd gotten this far, hadn't he? Why not push himself to be more, to be better?

Adam handed him a duffel bag. "Try the new suits. There are two of each style in there, plus the warm-up suit you have to wear during all broadcast races—which is all of them, basically. I do not care even a little which suit you wear as long as you're comfortable. Lane Four is yours after you change. Luke's got Lane Five."

"Thanks."

Isaac supposed official gear wasn't so bad. He'd been seated behind a couple of synchronized swimmers on the plane, who had told him their official suits each had hundreds of Swarovski crystals sewn on. "That's ridiculous," Isaac had said. One of the gymnasts told him to shut up, but the other had nodded gravely.

He changed into a new suit and pulled on the waistband. It was snug, but not problematically so. He walked over to a mirror and examined himself. He'd had his whole body waxed the previous day, but he'd likely have to do some touch-up work before his first race.

He'd let his hair grow wild during his brief retirement. It had felt odd. Unnatural even.

He ran a hand over his smooth chest. He turned sideways in front of the mirror and admired his body. He didn't look half-bad for a recovering alcoholic. He was thinner than he had been four years ago, and not as muscular. Sleeker, maybe. Adam had put him on a tough diet, making the legitimate argument that he no longer had the metabolism of a twenty-two-year-old.

Isaac walked back out to the pool. Adam made him do some warm-up stretches. He closed his eyes and listened to his body as he moved.

The thing was, he felt good. Better than he'd felt in a long time. Four years ago he'd shown up expecting to win, as if it was his due. He'd reigned as the best swimmer in the world. He had nine Olympic medals and twenty world championship medals. He was the most decorated swimmer since Michael Phelps. He'd walked into the previous Olympics expecting them to drape medals around his neck. And he'd won a silver medal in the 400-meter freestyle with almost zero prep. He'd swum the 4 x 100 relay with a hangover.

He'd been a cocky asshole. And he'd felt like shit the whole time, physically. Constantly nauseous and achy. Not to mention, everyone kept telling him it was over. He wasn't as fast as he'd been at seventeen, at twenty-one. This would be his last Olympics. It was time to figure out what he was going to do with the rest of his life.

That was where his trouble began.

But now that trouble was behind him. He was here. He was in the best shape of his life. He was still swimming. He was sober. He felt good.

"Get in the water," Adam said. "See how you feel."

Isaac dove in and swam four laps without putting a lot of oomph into it, just to get used to the water temperature, the chlorine levels, the feel of the swimsuit, the peculiarities of this venue. He liked this pool. He could feel himself slicing through the water. He caught Luke slipping by him in the neighboring lane out of the corner of his eye and didn't care. He did his flip turn, the way he'd practiced a thousand times with Adam, and he swam back again.

"Good," Adam said when Isaac popped his head out of the water. "Get up on the block. On the clock this time."

TIM WORE sunglasses on his way into the Aquatics Center, because even though most of the press had yet to arrive in Madrid, he'd grown accustomed to the paparazzi following him, and he'd grown fucking tired of it.

Tim found Donnie, his coach, standing at the base of the platforms. Donnie stared intently at a clipboard, and without even looking up, he said, "Suit up. I'll get you in the rotation."

"All right."

A half hour later, Tim stood on a platform, ready to do the only thing he ever really wanted to do. Tim loved diving. He loved the thrill of it. He loved the physicality of twisting his body and making it conform to his will as he somersaulted through the air. He loved flying. He loved the sensation of entering the water just right.

Up here on the platform, no one knew who he was. No one else was here. So no one cared that he'd broken off an engagement right before the Trials. No one knew that Pat had seen Tim more as a meal ticket than a lover, that Pat had been mooching off Tim since his show had gotten canceled, that Pat had hoped being seen as an adoring partner in the audience at the Olympic Games would somehow revitalize his career.

Tim had left him as soon as he figured that out.

His heart still ached sometimes. The only time it didn't was when he hurled himself off a diving board and into the waiting pool below.

So he dove. An easy one first. A simple forward pike. He jumped off the board, folded his body in half, and unfolded gracefully before entering the water.

When he got out of the pool, Donnie said, "Good. Keep your form tight. Your knees were a little bent on that one."

Donnie got gruff when he was nervous, which was almost always the case when Tim or one of his other divers was about to compete. Tim embraced it, relished it, was glad to be critiqued on his dives and not his personal life choices.

Six dives later Tim felt invigorated more than tired, but his practice time was up. He retreated to the locker room, deciding to take a shower now, given the unlikelihood of having running water in his room.

Then a flashbulb popped in his peripheral vision.

Tim didn't even stop to look at who'd snapped the photo or what the target had been. He'd been through this enough in the past year that he knew better than to look. Instead, he put his head down and beelined into the locker room.

As he headed to the showers, he nearly collided with a broad swimmer's chest.

"Hey, whoa there." The man before Tim put his hands out and clasped Tim's arms.

"Sorry. Wasn't paying attention."

"Hey, you're Tim Swan, aren't you?"

Fuck. The guy had an American accent too. Tim didn't want to look up, but he did slowly.

Isaac Flood.

They'd never actually met, despite being on the same Olympic team four years before. Not for any particular reason; their paths just hadn't crossed. Well, and the swim team was super cliquey and tended not to mingle with the other athletes.

"Hi," Tim said. "Yes. Sorry."

"Don't apologize. You were lost in your own head. I get it."

Tim took a step back and tried to get his bearings. Good God, Isaac Flood was a big man. He had to be six three or four, with wide shoulders and arms that seemed three miles long. He had a broad chest and pale skin. His rich brown hair was tousled from being under a swim cap. He had gorgeous, depthless blue eyes. Tim had long thought Isaac Flood was sexy, but seeing him now, he realized he'd had no idea.

Tim took a deep breath. "Yes. I was lost in thought. Sorry for bumping into you. You're Isaac Flood."

"I am indeed."

Tim nodded. "Maybe you're the best person I could have run into. I mean, because you get why...."

That is, you get so much media attention that you....
See, there was a photographer near the pool and...."

As Tim stammered, Isaac lifted an eyebrow.

"Forget it," Tim said.

"You're hiding from the media."

"You could say that."

"Dude, I know exactly what that's like. I spent four weeks in rehab. The press wasn't allowed within a certain radius of the facility, and I still spent all four of those weeks looking out for reporters hiding in bushes or whatever."

Tim let out a breath. Of course. Isaac Flood, of all people, would know how Tim felt. "I wish I wasn't so jumpy. I'm trying not to let it affect me."

Isaac tilted his head. "So, what? The media is following you because you're engaged to some actor. Who gives a shit?"

"Actually, we broke up six weeks ago."

"Oh. I'm sorry."

"Please don't be. And I don't want to talk about it. All I know is that even the color commentators seem more interested in what I do with my dick than what I do when I dive. And frankly, I'm sick of it."

Isaac pursed his lips and looked at Tim for a long, unnerving moment. He glanced around. They were essentially alone. Water ran in the shower area, behind a partition Tim couldn't see around, so he assumed men were showering. But otherwise no one stood in eye- or earshot.

Isaac said softly, "Because you're not returning Olympic champion Tim Swan, you're gay diver Tim Swan."

"That about sums it up, yeah."

"And I'm not four-time Olympian Isaac Flood, but alcoholic fuckup Isaac Flood."

Tim knew Isaac had an alcohol problem, because he lived in the world. Probably only one other aquatics athlete got as much attention as, if not more than, Tim, and that was Isaac. Because Isaac had been to three previous Olympics. Because he'd been a cute kid once. Because he'd been on a Wheaties box. Because all of his endorsement deals had been pulled after he'd gotten the DUI.

And yet, here Isaac Flood stood.

Maybe Tim could learn something here.

"You coming or going?" Tim asked.

"From the shower? Going. Just finished. I figured I'd get one in because the water's not running in my room."

"Same here. I'm headed for the showers, I mean. But, uh, I hope we run into each other again."

Isaac smiled. "Yeah. Me too."

CHAPTER 2

AT HOME Isaac had a personal chef who prepared most of his meals. He'd been on a heavy diet of leafy greens, whole grains, and lean protein since he'd started training again. He'd resisted the diet change at first and found it hard to follow—too many rules, too few cupcakes—but he'd adjusted. And he couldn't deny that the changes had made him feel like he was back in fighting form.

But the Olympic Village was sponsored by a fast-food chain, and they had outposts peppered throughout the area. Isaac hadn't eaten a hamburger or anything fried in eight months, and he wasn't about to start during competition. Especially not first thing in the morning.

"My kingdom for a green smoothie," Isaac muttered to himself.

He had to ask three people for directions, but eventually he found himself in a cafeteria that at least had a station where he could get some eggs. He texted his chef to see what would be the best thing to eat, given the options, but then remembered the time difference. Tony would most certainly still be asleep. Still, within a few minutes, Tony texted back a potential menu.

Tony was worth every penny of his hefty salary. Isaac filled a plate.

Isaac found Luke seated at the end of a table, clearly flirting with Katie Santiago from their swim club, who was a bit too young for him. Isaac considered butting in and joining them, but then he saw Tim Swan sitting at a table by himself.

Little Timmy Swan. That's what they'd called him four years ago. Isaac vaguely remembered that Team USA had been very excited about this diving phenom. Tim wasn't *that* little, it turned out. He was shorter than Isaac, sure, but most people were. Tim was maybe five nine or five ten, and all lean muscle. While he wasn't as bulky as most of the swimmers, Tim was svelte like a diver. Undeniably strong but… beautiful too.

Isaac's libido had stood up and taken notice the moment Isaac had put his hands on Tim the night before in the locker room. He'd only done it to keep the kid from injuring himself, but then, *pow*. Tim had tan skin, hair so dark it was nearly black, and dark eyes that belied a certain amount of intelligence and thoughtfulness. And he was gorgeous—one of the most beautiful people Isaac had ever encountered in person. The lines of his body were masculine but finely drawn.

That all pulled Isaac right in.

Plus, he'd recognized in Tim a kindred spirit, someone who'd been in the spotlight and despised the glare.

So Isaac walked over to Tim's table and slid his tray onto it. "This seat taken?"

Tim looked up, seeming startled. "Oh! No, please sit."

Tim's gaze remained on Isaac as Isaac sat in an appallingly uncomfortable plastic chair. He adjusted his seat, trying in vain to make his butt conform to the seat, and felt Tim's gaze on him the whole time.

"I thought the swimmers had their own little breakfast club," Tim said.

"Eh. I mean, Luke is the team captain, and he's been saying that for team unity or whatever the fuck, we should eat all our meals together. But he's clearly trying to get into Katie's bikini bottoms right now, so I figured I shouldn't interrupt him."

Tim tilted his head. "Team unity? It's not like you're a soccer team."

"I know. But Luke gave a whole speech last night about how we're better together than apart." Isaac shrugged. He thought a lot of the rah-rah team stuff was bullshit, but he played along because he didn't want to ruffle feathers. This included making a spectacularly stupid video in which he lip-synched to a pop song about partying from a couple of years ago, which all of the swimmers participated in. According to Isaac's mother, the TV station airing the Olympics in the States had already shown the video about seventeen times.

Isaac had come here to win. He'd have fun after his races were over.

"It's not that I'm not patriotic," Isaac said. "And I like my teammates. Even the cheerier ones. Hell, Luke is one of my best friends. We train together at home. So I'm not saying I'm a lone wolf. I'm just trying to stay focused, that's all. And some of the nonsense is distracting."

"I understand. The diving team is a lot smaller than the swim team, but we had to do all these photo shoots and stuff before we flew out here. Honestly? I hate photo shoots."

Isaac laughed. "Yeah? But you're so photogenic."

Tim rolled his eyes.

Isaac hadn't been joking, though. He'd seen the photos Tim had done with his actor ex when one of the girls Adam coached brought the magazine to practice. Tim had looked hot as fuck. Hotter than the actor. He'd been all tan skin and abs for days.

Isaac took a bite of his eggs and mentally chastised himself for getting turned on by his new friend. Such things would only be a distraction. He needed to focus.

"That's a lot of food you've got there," said Tim.

"I eat six thousand calories a day."

"Jesus."

"I burn it all off in the pool. I ate a lot more when I was younger, but it tends to stick around more now."

"Where? Do you have a single ounce of body fat?" Tim made a show of looking around.

Isaac grinned.

Tim rolled his eyes again.

ISAAC FLOOD had an unselfconscious air about him that Tim couldn't help but admire. It wasn't so much that he didn't know how hot he was, but that he did and didn't think it mattered.

As they walked out of the cafeteria together, Isaac lifted the edge of his shirt and used it to wipe sweat off his forehead. "Dear God, it's hot."

"Only in the sun. It's breezy in the shade."

"Uh-huh."

Being this close to Isaac's body was a little intoxicating. Isaac's skin looked smooth and soft—not a hair anywhere—and his sinewy frame was clearly strong. His body was a little freakish, granted—built like an inverted triangle with a ridiculously exaggerated wingspan—but Tim thought it perfectly made. Tim was strong and worked hard to keep lean enough to be able to throw his body around in the air, but he didn't have a swimmer's body. Tim wondered if Isaac had been born with that physique and realized he was well-suited to swimming, or if he'd carved his body to be a machine in the water. Some of both, probably.

"Aren't you from one of the Southern states?" Tim asked. "It gets pretty hot there."

"North Carolina. Yeah. Well, I'm from Florida originally. It gets really fucking hot there. I'd move north if I could. Minnesota. Somewhere it snows a lot in the winter."

Tim laughed. "Summer Olympian loves the winter."

"Don't knock it. I hate being hot."

The unintentional double entendre made Tim laugh, but he didn't want to call attention to the fact that he thought Isaac was hot. In trying to hold back the laugh, he snorted. Then he gave up and laughed easily.

Isaac laughed too. "I just heard what I said."

"It's such a burden, being attractive."

Isaac giggled—actually giggled!—and then said, "Yeah, well. I haven't seen a lot of action since I got sober."

The laughter died then. Tim had never been much of a drinker, but he could imagine craving the kind of oblivion that would come with consuming too much. He'd almost canceled the trip to Madrid on several occasions, not wanting to face the media, not wanting to be "that gay diver," not wanting to think about Pat or any of the mess that had been their breakup. If there was some elixir, some pill he could swallow to make it all go away… well, he wouldn't because he loved diving too much, but he could certainly see the temptation.

"How long have you been sober?" Tim asked quietly. Because of course everyone knew about Isaac Flood and his DUI and his comeback.

"Eighteen months, six days."

"That's good."

Isaac grimaced.

"What?" asked Tim.

"Usually when I say that, people are skeptical."

"Really? They don't believe you're sober?"

"I fell off the wagon once after rehab. Honestly, just that one time. At New Year's I was feeling sorry for myself, and I let a friend talk me into a party at a bar. The mere presence of alcohol proved to be too much of a temptation. It was awful. It was a mistake. But now it's like everyone is waiting for me to do it again."

"Do you still want to drink?"

Isaac did not look amused by this question. "I'm an alcoholic. I want to drink all the time. But I want to swim more."

A woman with long, wavy hair suddenly jogged over. "Isaac!" Then she deepened her voice and said, "Here. Comes. The Flood!"

"Hi, Melissa."

"Buenos días. Who's your friend? Oh, wait, you're Tim Swan, aren't you?"

Dammit. "Yeah. That's me."

"Melissa Murphy, at your service. Once and future Olympic gold medalist." She threw her hand at Tim.

Tim shook it. "Swimmer?"

"Did you not see all puff pieces they did about me at the last Olympics?"

Oh, this girl annoyed him now. He'd been enjoying talking to Isaac, even if the topics were heavy. Then this Melissa barged in, intruding on what had been a nice postbreakfast walk. "Sorry," he said. "Too busy winning diving medals."

She huffed. "Of course. Well, look out for me Monday. That's my first race."

"Okay," Tim said, not wanting to argue about it.

"Melissa is kind of the swim team's one-woman pep rally. She was the mastermind behind that karaoke video we all did."

Tim had seen it. He nodded.

"You know a thing or two about viral videos too, huh?" Melissa said. "I mean, ours didn't get as many hits as *yours*, but it was still pretty good."

"What video did you do?" Isaac asked.

"I assume she means the one I made when I came out." And if there was a single thing in his life that Tim had the most mixed feelings about, that was it. It was important to come out publicly, but he hadn't anticipated how much attention he would attract.

How much attention Pat brought to them.

It had been Pat's idea to do that video, and Tim had been so deliriously in love, he'd gone along with it. But now everyone knew his business. Tim would bet no one in the media even knew if Melissa was dating anyone. But everyone knew that Tim was gay and that he'd recently ended an engagement.

Well, except Isaac, who didn't seem to know about any of it.

Isaac was squinting when Tim brought his attention back to the conversation. "Yeah, I guess I remember that. The coming-out-video thing."

"It sucks about your breakup with Patterson," said Melissa. "Was it, like, a fame thing?"

Tim's pulse kicked up and his stomach flopped. "A what?"

"Melissa…," Isaac said, a warning in his voice.

Which she apparently didn't hear. "It's, like, how Hollywood marriages never last? One partner gets more famous than the other, and then there's all this jealousy and drama and blah-blah."

"I'm not an actor." Tim looked at Isaac for help, but Isaac seemed engrossed by something on the ground.

"No, but you're a household name."

"No, that wasn't—fame had nothing to do with the breakup." At least, not in the way Melissa implied. Pat hadn't resented or been jealous of Tim's fame; he'd thought Tim was his ticket to *more* fame. Pat wanted the pair of them to make headlines in the tabloids, which Tim had no interest in. Pat could keep his fame. Tim just wanted to dive.

Melissa held up her hands. "All right."

"This ex-fiancé of yours is an actor," said Isaac, his tone flat.

"Um, hello? What rock do you live under, Flood?" asked Melissa.

Isaac shrugged. "I mean, I knew that. He's on some TV show I don't watch."

"Not anymore," said Tim.

"Oh, yeah, I heard it got canceled," said Melissa.

Tim was losing patience. Not only had Melissa interrupted Tim's nice conversation with Isaac—a guy he admired, who was, incidentally, smoking hot—but she was dredging up things Tim would rather not think about. He had no interest in reliving the last few months. He wanted to put it all behind him and focus on the Games. "I have practice scheduled soon. I better go."

Isaac looked up, concern on his face. "You want to, I don't know, get a meal or something later?"

Tim glanced at Melissa but focused his attention on Isaac. "You have your phone on you?"

Isaac nodded and pulled it out of his pocket. He handed it over, and Tim programmed his phone number into it.

"Text me later."

"I will."

Melissa raised her eyebrows, probably assuming that since Tim was so publicly gay, he was hitting on Isaac, even though he wasn't. Isaac was a good-looking man—no, he was ridiculously hot, in point of fact—but Tim needed a friend more than he needed a boyfriend. Especially a friend who understood how oppressive the spotlight could be.

"Have a good practice today, guys," Tim said. Then he left.

CHAPTER 3

ADAM FROWNED. "You're in the air too long."

Isaac nodded as he pulled himself out of the pool.

But Adam was still talking. "You gotta get into the water faster off the block. You're hanging too much. Don't show off, Isaac, just get in the water."

"What was the time?"

"Three forty-five. You're probably going to need to shave a second off that to get past the preliminary heats."

Isaac grunted. The 400 free was his event to lose. He was the returning Olympic champion, and he'd held the record time for five years, until some young whippersnapper had broken the record at Worlds earlier that year. A time of 3:45 was embarrassing; he routinely swam that race four or five seconds faster.

"In the water faster," Isaac said.

"And tighter turns. MacLean from Australia does turns better than you. Rolls sooner, gets off the wall smoother."

Isaac rolled his shoulders but didn't respond.

"And Hiroshi's strokes are longer," Adam continued.

"Are we done cataloging my faults?"

"Come on, Isaac. This is the Olympics, not a pleasure cruise. You came here to win, right?"

"Yes."

"You're too tight. Go take a breather. We'll do it again in thirty. Get in the water faster, use your whole body, get longer strokes, make your turns tighter. You absolutely have it in you to win this. I've seen you swim better than this."

"Yeah. Sorry." Isaac stretched his arms above his head, then shook out his body. He *could* do this. Why was he so tense?

Because he couldn't lose this. He could *not*. Sobering up and getting his body back into fighting form had been the most difficult thing he'd ever done. And he hadn't worked that hard just to lose.

"Don't be sorry. Calm down, loosen up, and do it better next time. I want to do some sprints too. Ryan and I are trying to work out who to put in the relay final. If you can get your hundred meters below forty-eight seconds, you're in."

Isaac went back into the locker room, pondering the relay. He generally preferred middle distances over sprints, but he always had fun at the relays.

But now he just wanted to find a quiet spot to sit, put on some music, and mentally fix his 400 free.

So, of course, Tim Swan, wearing nothing but the tiniest of swimsuits, stood right there in the middle of the locker room.

"Oh, hey," Tim said as if he weren't practically naked.

"Practice?" Isaac asked.

"Yeah." Tim stretched his arms. "Springboard yesterday, platform today."

Isaac nodded. "How are you feeling?"

"Great! I mean, I'm worried about the Chinese divers because they fly through the air like gymnasts, especially Liu, but if I maintain my form and don't make any major mistakes, I've got a good shot at a medal. You?"

"I suck, so...." Isaac shrugged.

"Get out. You do not suck. What makes you say that?"

"I've been turning in slow times all day." Isaac sighed. "I'm too tight. I have to figure out how to loosen up."

"Are you nervous?"

"No. Well, maybe a little. I'm putting a lot of pressure on myself. Which is making it feel like all my muscles are tied in knots." Isaac rolled his head and shook out his shoulders.

"Sit." Tim pointed to the bench in front of the row of lockers.

Unsure, but willing to go along with it, Isaac straddled the bench and sat down.

Tim moved behind him. "May I?"

"Do what you will."

Tim put his hands on Isaac's bare shoulders and just rested them there at first. Then he rotated his thumb and dug into Isaac's tight muscles. He gradually increased the pressure.

"I know the swim team has been playing around with some Chinese medicine techniques," Tim said. "Cupping can get the blood flowing back into your muscles if they feel tight, but I like this better. There are acupressure points in your back, and stimulating them locally can help relieve pain. But if you work out how all the points in the body are connected, I can actually put pressure elsewhere and have it give you

relief where you need it. For now, though, how is this?"
Tim dug into a spot near where Isaac's neck met his
shoulder.

Isaac groaned involuntarily, but the pressure from
Tim's hands seemed to make the muscle pop, and tension flowed out of it. "That's good."

"Yeah?"

"Yeah. I don't know jack about Chinese medicine,
but keep doing that. I think it's working."

"I mean, the main goal is to get your blood flowing.
That's the purpose of this pressure." Tim pressed the
heel of his hand into the space between Isaac's shoulder
blades, and it hit Isaac right where he needed it. "You
want to get your blood circulating. That will help ease
the muscle tension. Although, also, you could relax."

Isaac laughed. "How do you know all this?"

"I studied sports medicine in college. I thought
about going to med school for a while, but I decided to
keep diving instead."

Tim's hands spread out across Isaac's back. Those
hands felt huge, despite Tim's relatively small frame.
Well, Tim wasn't small so much as smaller than Isaac.

"God, that's good," Isaac said with a sigh.

Tim chuckled. "It's like you've never gotten a
massage before."

"I usually wait until after the meet is over."

"So how do you relieve tension before a meet?"

"Sex."

Tim's hands froze on Isaac's shoulders. Isaac realized what he'd said, so he backpedaled. "Not so much
anymore, but when I was younger, I'd go out the night
before a meet if I was tense and find a distraction."

"God, really?" Tim resumed the massage, digging
his fingers into the base of Isaac's skull. The pressure

there seemed to loosen something up in Isaac's lower back. Tim's hands were magic, relieving tension wherever they touched. A shiver went up Isaac's spine; it had very little to do with the massage itself and everything to do with the potential of how that touch could go further. Perhaps while they were both horizontal.

Isaac cleared his throat. "Really. I know. I used to get hammered the night before meets too. I won a lot despite myself. I thought I was untouchable. Top of the world, right? Isaac goddamned Flood. Legend. Best swimmer since Michael Phelps. Did you know two of the world records I set are still mine?"

"So basically what you're telling me is that, because you're Isaac Flood, you goofed your way through meets. Did you do that your last Olympics too?"

"Yeah. Pretty much. I can't do that anymore, though, and not just because I'm trying to hang on to my sobriety. I'm not as fast as I used to be. My body is different."

"You really were the best, then, if you could get drunk and have anonymous sex and still win gold medals."

Isaac groaned. "I'm not the best anymore."

"Is that why you're so tense?"

He thought back on the last Olympics and all the squandered potential. He'd had dozens of opportunities during those Games to train and learn, but he'd partied instead. Would he have won more medals if he'd been sober? Probably. "I want to do this right. I don't want to just go through the motions. I want to put my all into it this time around. Go out on a high note, not as a has-been."

"You are doing it right."

Isaac closed his eyes and leaned back a little, into Tim's hands. Tim's fingers dug and poked into Isaac's muscles, but in the most delightful way. Isaac's skin seemed to come alive under his touch; it ached and tingled. Tim's hands were warm and smooth, arousing Isaac's muscles, soothing his old aches. If it wouldn't have been wholly inappropriate, he would have thrown his head back and moaned, because while Tim's touch was clearly meant to be therapeutic, it was nearly sexual too. How easy would it have been to turn around, to bury his face in Tim's hair, to hug him and massage him in the same way, to grope and touch each other and get off right here in this locker room? After all, Tim was all but naked, sitting behind Isaac, massaging his back. Isaac was suddenly very conscious of Tim's nudity.

"Lean forward," said Tim, so matter-of-factly that Isaac figured he couldn't be as turned on as Isaac was. "This might hurt a little."

Isaac leaned forward. He couldn't see what Tim was doing, but he sure as hell felt it when Tim put pressure on the knottiest muscles in Isaac's shoulders. Isaac cried out, because it hurt like a bitch, but when Tim began to rub the muscles more gently, some of the tightness leaked out.

"You're good. I'm hiring you as my personal masseuse."

Tim laughed. "No such luck, big guy. I have to go climb up to ridiculous heights so I can jump and do three flips before I land in the water."

Tim stepped away, so Isaac stood and took stock of his body. A lot of the tension had eased. "Still," Isaac said, turning around. "You're a goddamned miracle worker."

Tim smiled. "I try. You better now?"

"Holy hell. Yeah." Maybe the distraction of sexual arousal had helped ease his tension as much as anything else, though clearly Tim knew some things about the way muscles functioned if he was able to relax Isaac's with only his hands. Good Lord. Isaac's whole body sang. He felt like he had the power to do anything now. "I'm gonna go swim around the warm-up pool, and then I'm going to finish the hundred meters in forty-seven seconds, and I'm gonna anchor that goddamned relay if it kills me."

Tim laughed. "Sounds like a solid plan." His gaze settled somewhere near Isaac's collarbone. "If the tension comes back, talk to the team doctor. See what they can do to help loosen those muscles. Acupuncture might work for you too."

"Like, with the needles?"

"Don't knock it. I see my acupuncturist once a week. There's actual science that supports its therapeutic benefits." Tim glanced at the clock in the corner. "Crap, I gotta go. Take care of yourself, all right?"

Isaac watched Tim go, momentarily distracted by the way Tim's muscles rippled in his back as he moved, the way his round butt filled out his swimsuit. Thinking about the massage again, mentally picturing Tim nearly naked and sitting behind Isaac, his hands all over Isaac's bare back, had Isaac's skin tingling again. He grabbed a water bottle from the cooler in the corner and poured it over himself, trying to stave off an embarrassing situation.

But good God, he wanted Tim.

For months Isaac had tamped down the part of himself that wanted anything except to win swim races. He'd seen plenty of people—male and female—to whom he'd been attracted, but none that he'd wanted as viscerally as he wanted Tim Swan.

And if he was not mistaken, Tim wanted him right back. Maybe he could engineer a naked encounter before he flew home in three weeks.

So resolved, he pushed it all aside and walked out to the warm-up pool. He dunked himself in it and swam around a little before walking back out to the main pool. Adam was yelling something at Luke but looked up when Isaac approached.

"Luke's in the relay," Adam said. "As are Conor and Randy. Do you want that fourth spot?"

"Yes, Coach," said Isaac.

"Forty-eight seconds."

Luke stepped back. He didn't say anything, but he crossed his arms over his chest. Isaac got up on the block and got himself into position. Adam got out the stopwatch and said, "Ready? Set. Go."

Isaac shifted the angle of his entry and got in the water immediately, with very little time spent in the air. He felt good in the water, like he easily sliced through it. He put a conscious effort into tightening up his flip turn, then tore up the water on the way back—back straight, fingers together and pushing through the water like paddles, head straight. He caught the fifteen-meter mark out of the corner of his eye and felt good about his laps. He touched the wall and lifted his head.

Adam grinned. "Forty-seven point six. Hot damn."

Luke slapped Isaac on the back as he got out of the pool. "Welcome to the relay team."

TIM'S SYNCHRONIZED diving partner, Jason, was already standing at the ladder to the platform when

Tim got to the diving pool. Jason's dark skin seemed to glow under the bright lights of the Aquatics Center as he surveyed the platform. "We only have thirty minutes," Jason said as Tim approached. "Water polo practice is happening after that."

Donnie walked over. "Are you boys ready?"

Isaac still filled Tim's head; all Tim saw was his broad back. Tim could still feel how warm and smooth his skin had been, still hear the groans Isaac had let out as Tim worked his muscles. They'd shot to Tim's groin as if they were making out, and Tim had forced himself to think of math problems and dive codes to get his body to calm down.

Now he shook his head and tried to focus on Donnie and Jason and diving.

"I want you to watch this," Donnie said, pulling out his tablet. He cued up a video and hit Play.

The Chinese team.

There were so many variables in a dive—how hard you pushed off the platform, how far out from the platform you jumped, the rate of your rotations, whether you positioned your body vertically as you entered the water. Two divers in a synchronized pair could each execute a dive perfectly but still look different from each other. However, the Chinese divers were so in sync, they practically moved as one. The camera angle in Donnie's video made them seem like they *were* one, because Tim could only see the diver in the foreground.

"Here's what we're going to do," Donnie said. "You guys had this in practice at home, but now your synchronization is off. I don't know if it's nerves or what. All week Jason has been jumping farther off from the platform and Tim is starting his dives a fraction of a second sooner, which means you guys sometimes don't complete the rotations together. This one's from yesterday."

Donnie played another video—less professional, clearly shot with Donnie's phone—showing Jason and Tim, and he was right. Jason jumped a little harder, got out farther from the platform, and as a consequence, hung in the air a half second longer than Tim did before he moved his legs into the tuck. Tim completed the dive a hair sooner. And that meant their synchronization was off enough to be noticeable.

"So," Donnie said. "Calm down and ignore the change in venue. It's a platform, right? Just like the one we train on in Colorado. Got it?"

Jason nodded. "Just a platform."

Donnie made eye contact with Tim, so Tim nodded too.

"Now I want to try this two ways. First, Jason, ease off and don't jump out so far. Then we'll try it with Tim jumping out farther. Tim, count out loud if you can and shout when you start rotating. We'll tweak it until you're back in sync."

Six dives later, Donnie finally seemed satisfied, so Tim and Jason cleared out of the area to let the Spanish water polo team take over the pool for practice.

Back in the locker room, Jason chattered about the other medal contenders—the British team and the Italian team seemed most likely to be fighting for podium space with Tim, Jason, and the Chinese divers—and Tim half tuned him out. Then Jason said, "But, man, I can't get over how beautiful everyone is. You know? There's this British swimmer who is so gorgeous, I get totally tongue-tied whenever I get near her. Her eyes are green, and her body is… wow!" Jason looked dreamily into the distance.

Tim smiled as he fished his street clothes out of his locker. Tim couldn't disagree; an overwhelming number of people in peak physical condition walked around everywhere Tim had gone since arriving in Madrid. Of course, this was why athletes were handed a pile of condoms with their welcome kits when they checked into the Olympic Village.

"Have you talked to her?" Tim asked.

"Yeah, kind of. I mean, I said hello and introduced myself. I don't think she's interested."

"Why not? You're a good-looking guy." And Jason was cute, although he wasn't really Tim's type. He was a little too willowy, but he had a nice square jaw, close-cropped black hair, and of course, a diver's body. Like Tim, Jason was biracial, something they'd talked about a fair amount in the past. Jason's mother was white and his father was African American, giving Jason beautiful brown skin. Tim was half-white and half-Filipino, which mostly just made people ask him "What are you?" a lot.

Jason shrugged. "I guess I'm all-right-looking. What about you? You got your eye on any ladies?" Seeming to catch his error, he stopped and his eyes went wide. "Any guys, I mean. Yikes. Sorry."

"It's fine," said Tim. "And I'm focusing on the dives. I don't want any distractions."

"Oh, yeah. Sure. Me too."

Tim smiled. He and Jason had become close friends in the time they'd been diving together. They had to trust each other in order to perform those dives in perfect harmony.

Tim put on his warm-up pants and a T-shirt, intending to get in some time at the gym before he took a shower, when he heard Isaac say, "The Russian team always puts Mozorov second. He's great at the longer distances, but he's not the fastest sprinter. If I can get out there and swim a forty-eight-second split, I'll open up a big lead for us."

Some other voice said, "But the French will put LeBlanc third. He'll make up the time. Maybe you should swim anchor."

"No, you want Conor as the anchor. That's non-negotiable. So I think we do Randy first, then me, then you, then Conor."

"But we put Greg and Hunter in the prelim."

"Yeah. I can't swim the prelim. I mean, I will if that's how it shakes out, but I'd rather get the rest."

Tim and Jason rounded the corner. The other guy was Isaac's training partner, that guy Luke. He was arguing with Isaac, but Tim didn't hear what he said, because Isaac made eye contact with Tim, and Tim thought he might spontaneously combust.

So much for keeping cool in Isaac's presence. This could become a problem.

CHAPTER 4

THE DAY before the Opening Ceremony, Tim woke up to a text from Isaac asking him where his room was. Tim looked at the other bed; Jason was gone—he'd made up his bed, in fact—so he'd probably left for breakfast and the gym long before Tim had even stirred. So Tim texted Isaac his room number.

I'll bring breakfast, Isaac texted back.

Only when Tim let Isaac into his room did he make the connection between the man he was ridiculously attracted to and the fact that they'd be near a bed.

Isaac held up a brown paper bag. "Sorry. I couldn't deal with people this morning, but I didn't want to eat alone. Is this okay?"

"Yeah," Tim said, closing the door. "But that doesn't make sense. Am I not a person?"

Isaac grinned. "No, you don't count as people. I actually like you."

Tim smiled back, unsure of what to make of that.

"Two more days before this shit starts for real," said Isaac.

"Are you swimming today?"

"Yup. Pool reservation's in two hours. So I have plenty of time."

"Same. I mean, my coach has the platform reserved for Team USA in about an hour and a half."

"I have breakfast sandwiches. Egg whites and turkey sausage on whole wheat flatbread, but I got the chef to throw a slice of cheddar on each. Lean protein is all well and good, but a sandwich is not a sandwich without cheese."

As if it were Mary Poppins's carpet bag, Isaac opened the paper bag and pulled out two of what looked like softballs wrapped in tinfoil—the breakfast sandwiches, presumably, probably with extra sausage patties—a Styrofoam bowl that probably held potatoes, and two paper coffee cups. "I didn't know how you like your coffee, so there's sugar and those little creamer packets in here."

"No sugar," Tim said.

"Right. Gotta maintain your beach body."

Tim gestured at Isaac, whose hard muscles were evident even under a loose white T-shirt and the basketball shorts he wore. "Again, I ask where this mysterious body fat you think you have might be hiding."

"You should talk."

Tim looked down. He hadn't gotten around to changing out of his sleep shorts yet. He ran a hand through his hair, which was probably also a disaster, and he hadn't shaved in two days. "God, I'm a mess right now, aren't I?"

Isaac doctored his coffee. "Mess is relative."

Tim laughed and shook his head. "Says you."

"Okay, first of all, you're an athlete at the Olympics." Isaac held up his thumb. "You're going to spend half of your time over the next week in or near a pool. More than half, probably. You're going to be wet and sweaty. As an athlete, your performance matters more than your appearance. Well, unless you're a female gymnast." Isaac grimaced. "I mean, they're great athletes too, but with makeup and glitter and everything."

"I get what you mean."

"Nothing against gymnasts."

Tim laughed. "No, of course not."

"I mean, that one male gymnast? What the hell is his name? With the floppy hair. Uh, Jake… something Polish or Russian or something, right?"

Tim shook his head. "What are you talking about?"

"One of the Team USA gymnasts is, like, the poster boy for the network coverage of the Olympics. His name, I want to say, is Jake something. And now I'm mangling this. My point is just that he's really hot. I'm showing my appreciation for gymnasts."

Tim giggled, then put his hand over his mouth because he couldn't believe he'd giggled, and finally just let himself laugh. "What I hear you saying is that there's a gymnast you have a crush on."

Isaac groaned and ran a hand over his face. "No, I… I made a joke about gymnasts, but they are all super strong. I think the makeup-and-glitter thing the women gymnasts do is fucking ridiculous, and it kind of minimizes how strong they are, but male gymnasts are… oh, forget it."

"No, finish the thought." Tim grinned, giddy now.

Isaac rolled his eyes.

"Why, Isaac Flood, do I detect an attraction to male gymnasts?"

"Fine," Isaac said, holding a hand up. "I'm bisexual. Cat's out of the bag."

For whatever reason, that made Tim giddier. "I was just giving you a hard time. I know exactly who you're talking about, and he is smoking hot. Good jawline. And arms. He's got great arms."

"Yeah. I like that too. Swimmers are so weird to look at, you know? Wide necks, the lot of us." Isaac held up his hands as if he was going to choke himself, but then he dropped his arms. "Lot of my teammates would be super hot if their chins didn't fade into their necks."

Tim snorted. "Well, whatever. I think swimmers are hot."

"Yeah?"

"Yup."

And then they seemed to arrive at an impasse, because Tim wasn't quite ready to admit he thought Isaac was hot.

On the other hand, Tim wanted something to happen here, especially now that he knew Isaac wasn't straight. But how did one make a move? Before Pat, he'd only had a couple of random hookups to his name, and those were all guys who had approached him. And with Pat, well, Tim couldn't even remember how that had gone anymore. They'd met at a bar or something, hadn't they?

Then again, Pat had probably manipulated all of it, so if there'd been some sweet meet-cute at the beginning, who knew how genuine the moment had really been?

Fuck Pat sideways. Tim still got mad thinking about it.

Pat had left Tim a twenty-four-year-old man with very little romantic experience who couldn't figure out how to hit on a man he found ridiculously attractive.

"What are you thinking about so hard?" Isaac asked, handing over a breakfast sandwich.

Tim hesitated, at first intending to lie and say he was thinking about twists and somersaults. Then he decided to go for it, figuring he'd never get anywhere if he didn't say how he felt. "Honestly? I was working out how to hit on you."

Isaac paused in unwrapping his sandwich. Then he half smiled and nodded. "Not what I was expecting you to say, but all right. I'll tell you, though, I could use a friend right now, more than a good lay."

How should Tim have taken that? Was Isaac turning him down gently? Although what Isaac probably needed was something deeper than a quick fuck. "I can do that too. Just, you know."

Isaac looked up and raised an eyebrow. "What do I know?"

Mortified now, heat flushing Tim's face, he said, "You know how hot you are."

Isaac laughed. "That is not a thing I know."

Tim wanted a hole to open up under his chair. "Whatever. We can be friends. Forget I said anything."

Isaac still laughed as he grabbed a chair, flipped it around, and straddled it backward, facing Tim. "I don't want to forget it. But I do want to be clear about something. Because I think we get each other. Like, you're dealing with a media spotlight that makes you uncomfortable. Something bad happened to you, but you don't want that to define your Olympic experience. I can't escape it either. Poor Isaac Flood, right? He was a legend until he became an alcoholic. Then he showed up at Trials, and suddenly he's qualified for another Olympics! It's a goddamn miracle." Isaac shook his head. "I just want to swim, you know? Of course you know, because you just want to dive. You don't want to be the athlete who dated a movie star. You don't want to be the gay diver. You want to be an athlete, period. God, that's us both, for different reasons."

"Yeah," Tim said, unsure of what Isaac was trying to tell him.

"I showed up in Madrid expecting to get in there and get it done. To be my own man and swim my races and maybe win something. But since you and I started talking to each other? I realized I don't *want* to do it alone. I mean, yeah, I've got my coach and my teammates. My mother and my sister are flying in tomorrow. But I just...." Isaac looked up. "No one understands. Adam, my coach, has been amazing, he knows what my goals are. My family has been sympathetic and supportive. But no one gets how hard this is. No one understands how badly I need this. Except, I think, you. And talking to you has been the best part of my Olympic experience so far."

Tim's heart broke for Isaac. The alcoholism, that was harder to relate to, but needing a win? Needing to do it for himself, spotlight be damned? Yeah, Tim understood that.

"For me too," Tim said softly.

Isaac reached over and ran his hand along the side of Tim's face. "I like you a hell of a lot. I don't want to fuck this up. Because I think we're going to need each other for the next sixteen days."

That was likely true. Tim didn't want to put their budding friendship in jeopardy either. He found himself leaning into Isaac's touch anyway. He looked up and met Isaac's gaze.

Tim couldn't help himself. Sitting like this, they seemed almost the same height. Tim leaned over and pressed his lips against Isaac's.

Because yeah, he needed Isaac's friendship. But he needed this too.

Isaac groaned and shoved his fingers into Tim's hair, holding him there while they plundered each other's mouths. Oh, Isaac was a good kisser. A great kisser. A tremendous kisser. The pressure of his firm lips felt strong and exciting against Tim's. His tongue snaked out to run along Tim's teeth. He tasted of toothpaste and coffee. And merely by being there in that room, Isaac made Tim's heart pound and his skin tingle. But now that they were touching, Tim worried he might go up in flames.

But he couldn't stop. He reached out and ran his hands along Isaac's arms, feeling all that warm, smooth skin. He'd heard people ragging on Isaac's looks, calling his body freakish because his proportions were so odd, but to Tim, he was perfect.

When they pulled apart, Tim had a moment of worry, thinking Isaac might be angry or reject him again. Maybe kissing Isaac had been a stupid risk.

But Isaac smiled. "I suppose we could be the sort of friends who make out sometimes."

Tim laughed. "That sounds good to me."

ISAAC SWAM laps in the warm-up pool because it was the only way he could think of to shut off his brain.

He couldn't get Tim out of his thoughts. They hadn't done anything after the kiss besides eat and then walk down to the Aquatics Center together. But that kiss was very much still on Isaac's mind. Because while he'd been completely honest with Tim, and he needed an ally more than anything else, he wanted Tim too.

He'd really only wanted to have breakfast away from other people this morning, but he'd wanted to see Tim too, so he'd texted. He hadn't intended to do or say anything in particular. But Tim had the whole of it now. And he still wanted Isaac anyway.

So this could happen, whatever was going on between them. Isaac wanted it to happen. But he didn't need a distraction right now.

He hauled himself out of the pool and went to find Adam. It was early still. Official swim heats wouldn't begin for two more days. There were a dozen other swimmers practicing in the pool, but Isaac knew from experience that it would be much worse this afternoon.

The diving pool sat on the opposite end of the Aquatics Center, which was a massive complex that housed four pools and was the main venue for all swimming, diving, and water polo events. So the diving pool was far enough away that Isaac could barely see the people congregating at the base of the dive tower.

As Isaac stood near the blocks and waited for Adam—who was engaged in what looked like an intense conversation with Luke and Katie—he watched the divers, but he couldn't see much besides when a diver jumped off the platform. Even then, the diver looked like a stick. They were too far away to be distinguishable. But Isaac liked to think he could see Tim, and that Tim was the best one.

God, what was happening to him? When had he last even had these kinds of feelings for someone? Not since before rehab, he knew that much.

Isaac shook out his arms. Adam walked over and said, "All right, Luke, Isaac, and… where'd Randy go?"

"Sorry, Coach," Randy said, walking over sheepishly.

"Did Conor ever show?"

"He was in the warm-up pool a few minutes ago," Isaac said.

"I want to run through the relay and practice exchanges. Luke and Isaac are probably fine, but Randy and Conor could use some practice. Katie, would you go fetch him? And remind me later to buy that kid a waterproof watch?"

Katie ran off.

Adam was rarely a difficult taskmaster, but he tended to get snippy during high-stakes meets. And it didn't get any higher stakes than the Olympics. Adam had been appointed one of three official Team USA coaches, due to his long history of coaching gold medalists, even before Isaac became his star pupil. Other swimmers were allowed to bring their own coaches, so there were a dozen of them milling about, working with forty athletes in all. In other words, Adam had a lot of personnel to manage, and he looked visibly more stressed than usual.

Adam pulled out his stopwatch as Katie returned with Conor in tow. "All right. Since we're practicing exchanges, the order is Luke, Randy, Conor, Isaac. I'm going to time you, though, so don't slouch. I'd like to get the final time around 3:12, so let's see if we can do that. I think we're going to need 3:10 to win. Each of the other teams has a weak link, but you never know what might happen. Up on the block, Luke."

Isaac got caught up in relay practice, in looking at the time and critiquing the exchanges, until his turn up on the block, waiting for Conor to touch the wall. Then he just swam, not thinking about anything except his form in the water and how fast he could get down the pool and back.

After he touched the wall, he popped his head out of the water. Adam frowned. "That was a forty-nine-second hundred meters, Isaac," he said. "Whole relay took 3:15. We can do it faster."

Isaac wanted to tell Randy and Conor to ignore Adam, because these practice times were never as fast as the real thing. No one was willing to push his body to the limit yet, and there was no roaring crowd, no guy in the next lane about to touch the wall sooner. Swimmers did extraordinary things in competition.

Conor, in the midst of his first Olympics, seemed more in awe than upset, though. He looked around the Aquatics Center as if he'd just stumbled into a dream. So Isaac kept his mouth shut, letting the kid have his moment, while Adam told them to take five so he could run drills with Katie. "But we're going to run the relay again, and it *will* be faster," he threatened as they left.

"Didn't see you at breakfast," Luke said to Isaac as they walked back to the warm-up pool.

"Got a breakfast sandwich to go."

"I know you think the team unity thing is bullshit, but it would be nice for the younger guys to see you're a team player. On nights you're not swimming, unless you really need the rest, you should be up in the stands cheering everyone else on."

"I know, Luke. And I do want to encourage everyone. I'm also scheduled to swim six races, possibly as many as nine, if Adam and Bob decide to put me on all three relay teams. So cut me a little slack if I want to sleep in."

"You didn't sleep in. I saw you leave your room at eight. What's going on, Isaac?"

Isaac and Luke had known each other since they were kids. Luke knew about all of it. Luke had taken more drinks out of Isaac's hands than anyone else in his life, had watched Isaac puke enough times that he deserved a medal, and had been the first one to encourage Isaac when Isaac said he wanted to get back in the pool. They were old friends. Isaac didn't need to lie, even if he did resent Luke keeping tabs on him, at least a little.

"Well, if you must know, I'm not loving the way everyone stares at me when I go to eat, so I had breakfast with a friend in his dorm room."

"A friend you're sleeping with?"

"No. A friend I have meals with. You'll note I left my own room this morning."

"Keep it in your pants until you're done swimming. Sex screws with your focus."

Isaac sat at the edge of the warm-up pool. "No, sex screws with *your* focus." No one else was in earshot, except Conor and Randy, who were already swimming slow laps. "Should I be giving you this same lecture about Katie?"

"Katie and I have an understanding."

"That you'll bone as soon as you're both done swimming."

Luke grinned. "Hey, I like Katie. We both know this is her last Olympics. She's great at the middle distances, but she doesn't have the speed she used to. Hell, this could be my last Olympics too. So we've decided to celebrate once it's all over."

"How long have you been seeing each other? Isn't she kind of young for you?" Isaac asked, reading between the lines.

Luke sat next to Isaac at the side of the pool. "She's only six years younger than I am. And I dunno. We've been dating three months? Give or take? I really like her. I mean, I've always liked her, but I don't know. We went out to dinner after practice one night and got to talking. We've been friends for a million years, and now we might be more."

"Well, if you're happy, I'm happy for you."

"This breakfast friend of yours. Is it someone you plan to, uh, celebrate with?"

"Maybe," Isaac admitted. "Still deciding."

"Do I know this person?"

"Uh. Not sure. Probably not personally, but if I told you, I'm guessing you'd know who he is."

"He?"

Isaac shrugged.

Luke slapped his back. "As long as it's not a beach volleyball player. I hate those guys."

"No. Not beach volleyball." Isaac laughed. It felt like some kind of truce had been reached. "Look, I'll support the team in any way I can. But you know I'm not very good at the rah-rah-cheerleader bullshit. I'll cheer everyone on during their races. I'll be there for anyone on the team who needs something. But that's all I can do. The shared meals and the viral videos and all of Melissa's insanity? That's not me."

"I know. Just don't be an asshole. That's all I ask."

"I can do that."

"Did you see that Pearson dyed his hair green?" Pearson was an Australian swimmer, Isaac's chief rival in the breaststroke races.

"Did he?"

"Yep. Matches the officially sanctioned Australian swimsuits. It's a trip."

Some commotion caught Isaac's attention, and he looked up in time to see Randy and Conor goofing around at the far end of the pool. Luke shook his head. "Come on, old man. Let's swim some laps."

CHAPTER 5

ISAAC HAD the official Ralph Lauren ensemble hanging in his closet, but he didn't want to put it on. What he wanted was a drink. The craving was intense and had been since he'd spotted the Spanish volleyball team passing around beers a little while ago. Well, the craving was always there, an itch in his chest he couldn't scratch, the need to just make everything go away. His body ached from training, he missed the familiar comfort of his apartment in Raleigh, and his anxiety about the beginning of preliminary swim heats the next day ran high. He did not need to put on boat shoes and a blazer. He needed to figure out how to calm his nerves enough to swim well tomorrow.

And that reminded him of that massage he'd gotten from Tim. Maybe he needed a distraction after all.

Instead of changing into the costume and heading to the stadium for the festivities, Isaac put on pajamas, grabbed the fleece blanket he'd packed, and walked down to the lounge at the end of the hall to watch the Opening Ceremony on TV.

A few of the other swimmers popped in to say hi. Most of the athletes competing the next day—which included a good third of the swim team—were not attending the celebration, opting to rest up instead. The male gymnast Isaac thought was hot—his name *was* Jake—also popped in to watch the ceremony for a few minutes. Isaac tried not to let the guy's arms distract him, but this guy was jacked, and his broad shoulders pulled at his T-shirt. He walked into the room as if he had no idea how attractive he was.

"I gotta sleep," Jake said, "but I'm too wound up."

"I know what you mean. I'm Isaac, by the way."

"I know. Everyone knows who you are, Isaac Flood. Wheaties box and all that."

Isaac sighed. "Right."

"I only bring it up because I'm jealous. I want a Wheaties box. This is my second Olympics. Everyone's all Jake Mirakovitch, he's the one to beat this year, but I'm terrified. I've been nailing every one of my routines in practice, but I did four years ago too, and we all know how that went." He shook his head.

"I don't know how that went," Isaac said.

Jake grimaced. "Probably best not to relive it. Let's just say, the team was a mess. First place going into the team final, and then we all choked. Me especially. I fell off the pommel horse. Whiffed one of my release moves on the high bar. Tenths of deductions here and there add up if you make enough mistakes. We were the gold-medal favorites, but we came in sixth. Sixth!"

"I'm sorry." Isaac knew well what the weight of all that pressure felt like.

"Qualifiers tomorrow, and I want to make at least two event finals and qualify for the all-around. Because the women's team has been raking in medals for years, but the men's team is a joke."

Isaac laughed softly. "Aren't you supposed to be all 'We're the best! We're gonna win gold!'"

"Publicly, sure. But you get it, right?"

"I do. Nothing you can do, man, but your best."

"Yeah. How do you prepare for a race?"

"What do you mean?" Isaac glanced at the TV. Dancers with colorful flags pranced around the arena. He looked back at Jake, who was clearly not asking about Isaac's workout regimen.

"I mean, how do you keep from choking when the spotlight is shining on you?"

Isaac wasn't really in the mood for a philosophical discussion. He pulled his blanket tighter around him. "It helps when everyone has low expectations."

Jake scoffed. "When has anyone had low expectations of you?"

Now, Isaac wanted to say, but he shrugged and said, "Fair. But swimming isn't a team sport. I'm only letting myself down."

"But what about swim relays? That's a team thing."

"I don't know. I mean, it's different. There's some strategy, but at the end of the day, it's about who swam the fastest. If I'm doing a relay, I push as hard as I can for my team. What else can I do?"

Jake nodded. "Sure. Gymnastics is an individual sport too, but we have this team vibe. We got through the last couple of years of competition and injuries and Olympic Trials together, like we're brothers-in-arms, you know? I don't want to let them down. I guess it adds to the pressure."

Isaac let out a breath. "I don't know what to tell you. It's the Olympics. This is the pinnacle, right? I mean, there are world cups, national championships, all that, but the Olympics is the thing everyone watches.

Instead of letting that pressure get to you, you need to focus on yourself. It's not about proving yourself or whatever. It's about pushing your body to the limit of what it can do. Right? If I'm in a final, I push as hard as I can. I move my arms faster, harder. I put my all into it until it feels like my body is on fire and I have to throw up. I race until I can't breathe anymore. Because it's not about being safe and comfortable—it's about doing the absolute best that you can."

And that really summed up the whole philosophy of why Isaac came here. It was how he'd won all the races he had in his career. Because when the time came to race, all of the other bullshit fell away. He didn't think about the pressure, about where he'd get his next drink, or even much about gold medals. His singular focus was on swimming as fast as he fucking could.

Jake nodded. He seemed thoughtful now. "Okay."

So Isaac pushed on. "I don't know a lot about gymnastics, but the whole evolution of the sport is figuring out what the human body can do, right? Each Olympics, the sport advances. Sixty years ago, maybe you could win a gold medal by doing a cartwheel over the vault horse. Now you gotta flip in the air three times, right? You want to win, of course you do, but the thing to focus on is your training, your practice, doing the best you can within your ability. If you're nailing those routines in practice, they're yours. You know you can do them. So you don't blink, you don't falter, you push the nerves aside. It's a big stage, yeah, but it's also just a meet, you know?"

His own pontificating surprised Isaac, but Jake was practically eating his words up with a spoon. "You're totally right. It's just a meet."

Since Jake seemed to be hanging on Isaac's words, Isaac tried to think of what advice he'd want if he were freaking out before a race. "Don't worry about what the Chinese or the Russians or... who the heck is good at gymnastics? The Brits, the Japanese, whoever. Don't worry about what they're doing. You can't control how well they perform. But you can control yourself. And if you're good, that medal's yours. You nail your routine in the meet, it's yours."

Jake nodded. "I never really thought about it that way. I mean, I completely understand what you're saying. But my coach is always, 'You need to do this, Jake, you need to do that.' Hosuke from Japan does this triple layout dismount from the high bar, so I have to do it higher, more perfect. Boskovic from Russia does this pommel horse routine that he once scored a sixteen with, so I have to make mine more difficult."

Isaac agreed. There would always be a faster swimmer than Isaac. At this Olympics, there were likely many, particularly younger guys whose bodies hadn't been ravaged by age and alcohol. This made Isaac burn with the desire to swim well, because he loved his sport. He loved it so much, he sometimes ached when he was out of the pool. So he asked Jake, "Do you love gymnastics?"

"Huh?"

Isaac considered. "If you know who I am, you know what happened. And my life, it's all swimming. I love swimming. I love the feel of the water on my skin. I love the thrill of racing. I'd spend most of my life in a pool if I could. I got back into swimming after rehab because it made me feel sane again. Anyone at this level has to love their sport. Do you love gymnastics?"

"Of course," Jake said. "I see your face, but I do love it. I love tumbling. I love that thrill of flying over the high bar. Of sticking a landing. And I… I like the burn when I push my body as far as it goes."

That was the key. Isaac nodded. "Get that burn back. That's the ticket to winning. Forget about everything else."

"You're one hundred percent right."

Isaac smiled. "And if you lose, you lose. What happens? The TV network talks about how disappointing it is—and it is disappointing to lose—but whatever, you'll be back in the gym in two weeks, doing what you love again, and that's all that matters. I mean, really, fuck everything else. Fuck the gold medal, fuck the Wheaties box, just get out there and do the goddamn best you can do. If anyone thinks it's not good enough, fuck 'em."

Isaac closed his eyes and let that truth wash over him. He was convincing himself as much as Jake, at this point.

Jake laughed. "So that's how you became the second-most-decorated swimmer of all time? 'Fuck 'em.'"

"Pretty much."

"I'll keep that in mind. It doesn't make for a good postevent sound bite, though."

Isaac held up his hands in a "so what?" gesture. He hated doing those interviews anyway.

Jake and Isaac watched the pomp on TV for a minute before Jake gestured at the screen and said, "Does it go on like this for a while?"

"The host cities are always trying to outdo each other. Tonight we'll see hundreds of years of Spanish history distilled into one flourish of artistic expression."

"You know, I think I can sleep now."

Isaac laughed.

THERE WAS a vending machine somewhere in the building that housed Team USA that had protein bars, but Tim couldn't remember where it was. So far he'd found a soda machine and a machine full of chips and candy that looked like no one had touched it. Tim wouldn't let himself have any junk food until after his events, but after an hour at the gym, he could have used a snack.

Thinking maybe the protein bars were in the lounge, Tim stuck his head inside. There was only a soda machine, and Isaac Flood, curled on the sofa and wrapped in a blanket, staring at the TV. He was alone.

"Hey, Isaac."

Isaac lifted his head. He met Tim's gaze and smiled. "Hi."

"You're not going to the Opening Ceremony?"

He shook his head. "I'm swimming tomorrow. I'd rather rest. Not to mention, a bunch of the track-and-field guys were smuggling booze into the stadium. I didn't want the temptation."

Isaac's candor warmed Tim. He was glad Isaac felt comfortable enough to cut to the chase. Tim wanted to ask Isaac what had driven him to drink, if it was bad wiring in his brain or if he'd had a real problem he'd needed relief from. Probably both. At least he knew himself well enough to avoid situations that could get him in trouble.

"You're not going?" Isaac asked.

"I still might. I'm on the fence. But I got a little woozy after the gym, so I'm trying to find something to eat."

Isaac lifted one of his hands out of the blanket. He held up a protein bar, which he then threw at Tim. Tim caught it easily.

"Thanks."

"No problem. I also heard from my buddy Dave that there are a handful of restaurants that will deliver here, if you need a real meal. This one place is supposed to have the best seafood paella in the city."

Tim plunked down next to Isaac on the sofa. "Maybe. I usually have to wait a while after the gym before I can eat anything heavy." He unwrapped the protein bar, broke off a piece, and popped it in his mouth.

"I've never been to an Opening Ceremony," Isaac said. "I usually go to the closing, but it's tough when you have to swim the next morning. A lot of the swim team is probably in bed right now, but I couldn't fall asleep."

"What event do you have tomorrow?"

"Prelim heats." He looked up as if he was trying to remember. "Uh, 200 free is tomorrow. There's a relay tomorrow too, but my coach hasn't decided if I'm swimming in it yet." He let out a sigh. "Since this is probably my last Olympics, I guess I *could* go to the ceremony. It's kind of a neat thing. I've heard."

"It's not really for *us*," Tim said. "I walked four years ago. They keep you in a room in the bowels of the stadium for a couple of hours, and then you walk out with the US delegation when the time comes. Then they keep you in a holding area while you wait for the other nations to walk out. You're right, it is kind of a big party. Someone always smuggles in booze. One of my old teammates hooked up with a volleyball player last time."

Isaac chuckled. "As you do."

Tim smiled. "But I mean, all the pageantry, it's meant for the spectators, not the athletes. You know? I think you're better off resting if you think you'll need it for tomorrow."

Isaac nodded. "When's your first dive?"

"Monday. Synchronized diving."

Isaac grimaced. "Really?"

Tim shrugged. "I prefer the individual competition, but I started doing synchro to hone my form and timing, and my partner, Jason, and I have a whole system worked out now. The Chinese divers are better than us—"

"Aw, come on. You're the defending world champion!"

"For the synchro events, they're better. The Chinese A team does dives with higher difficulty scores. I can do those dives in competition, but Jason isn't quite there yet, so our set has a lower cumulative max score. That means we have to be flawless, because it's pretty unlikely the Chinese divers will make a mistake. Then there's this team from Italy, and… well, it doesn't matter."

"Maybe I'll come watch if I don't have to swim Monday."

"You'll have to swim Monday, I'm sure. Didn't you qualify for all the races?"

Isaac laughed. He tugged his blanket tighter around his shoulders. "Not *all* of them. I'm doing the middle distances in free and breaststroke, and I'm doing the IMs, the 100 free, maybe the relays if my coach decides to put me in." He shrugged. "I am swimming a lot, it's true. I'm not going to win all those races. I probably won't make it past prelims for some."

Tim gave Isaac a skeptical look. "The great Isaac Flood? Really?"

"I'm not seventeen anymore." Then Isaac let out a soft laugh. "You know, when I showed up for the Trials, I only wanted to prove I could still do it, you know? I just wanted to swim again. To slice through the water. To feel my body burn. To get that thrill from racing. Whether I won or not didn't matter as long as I put everything I had into it again. But I've trained hard for the last year and a half, and I feel better than I have in years—in a goddamn decade. I'm healthy. I'm sober. And pretty much since the moment my plane touched down in Madrid, I've wanted to win."

Tim understood that desire, and he could feel Isaac's conviction wafting off him in waves. "You really think this is your last Olympics?"

Isaac nodded. "I mean, never say never. I'm not even that old. Four years from now I'll only be thirty-three. I might still be competitive then. But I think... I think for my own sanity, I need to find another purpose. Because I could do another Olympics, but I've got maybe five years of competition left in me at the outside before my body gives out and I won't be able to compete with the younger swimmers. My lack of a purpose got me in trouble last time. So now's the time to figure out what to do next."

"Any ideas?" Tim wanted to ask more about what Isaac meant, but didn't want to push it when Isaac seemed open to sharing. And Tim of course knew that one day he'd have to do something with his life that was not diving, but a graduate degree in sports medicine called to him when his career ended. He always figured he'd set up a practice or consulting business once he finished school. Each elite athlete had a shelf life, which Tim had known from the moment he'd opted to train instead of going to grad school. Not having a real plan? That was anxiety-inducing.

Isaac laughed. "Nope. I mean, usually swimmers my age? They get married and have kids. Family becomes their purpose. Then they get coaching jobs or whatever. Or nonswimming jobs. I know a guy who swam in three Olympics and then became a lawyer."

"Wow." That seemed so normal. Getting married, getting a nonsports job. That much normalcy felt surreal in a way, foreign from life as Tim had known it, something he saw on TV but hadn't experienced much of himself. He doubted Isaac could relate to it much either.

"Yeah." Isaac stared unfocused toward the TV. "But who the hell would marry me? A has-been Olympian alcoholic." He shook his head. "Sorry, I didn't mean to invite you to my pity party."

"It's okay." Tim searched for something to say. He had some experience with feeling unwanted. "I just mean, I don't think you're some loser, and I don't mind you saying what you feel. I've been there. I felt like the biggest idiot after I broke up with Pat."

Isaac nodded slowly. "Yeah. I can't even imagine what it must have been like for you to do that with everyone watching."

"That did kind of make everything worse."

Isaac looked off into the distance again. "I called my doctor a little while ago. My doctor from rehab, that is. I talk to him when I'm struggling. I'm happy to be here, I am, but I'm surprised by how pulled apart I feel.

I want to win, and I'm worried I won't, and that makes me want to drink."

"You drank during your last Olympics." It wasn't a question. Tim tried not to judge Isaac for it, though. He understood intellectually that Isaac had been in the grips of addiction. Isaac's honesty surprised Tim but made him admire Isaac too, for being so plain about it.

"Yeah. It's surprisingly easy to get booze in the Olympic Village."

"Did you swim drunk?"

"No. I respect the sport too much for that." Isaac let out a sigh. "Still, I felt like shit most of the time four years ago. Now I feel good, I trained right, and I'm clean and sober. If I can win a silver medal with a hangover, I should be able to do anything now."

Tim admired Isaac's determination and found himself drawn to it. He wanted to touch Isaac, to comfort him, but despite the frankness of this conversation, they barely knew each other. He shifted his weight on the sofa and his knee brushed against Isaac's.

"All that training should mean something," Isaac said.

"Yeah," said Tim. "I miss chocolate cake. I'm on a strict diet now. My chef won't let me near sugar."

"You have a chef?"

"*You* have a chef."

Isaac nodded. "I can afford one now. At least when I was drinking, I was too busy being drunk to spend my endorsement money. God knows when I'll ever get another endorsement deal."

Tim wrinkled his nose. "I hate endorsements. I shot a commercial a few months ago. Most humiliating thing I ever did."

"What was the commercial for?"

Tim held up the protein bar wrapper. "A different brand of these things. It's supposed to air during the Olympics broadcast."

"Nature of the beast."

"I shouldn't be mad. A few hours' work with some of these companies, and I've got enough money for my mortgage."

"You have a mortgage?"

"I bought a house when I left Pat. I mean, it's in the middle of nowhere and I got it for a song, but it's mine, you know? Pat and I were bouncing between Boulder and LA for a long time, but can I tell you? I fucking hate LA. I can't breathe there. So I bought a house in the mountains."

"Sounds nice."

"It is." Tim loved his little house. It was quiet and peaceful and comfortable, the best thing to come out of his breakup with Pat.

"I live in a shithole apartment in a city I don't even like that much, but I want to stay near my coach while I'm still training. Well, and my family is close by. My sister has a toddler who hasn't figured out what a loser his uncle Isaac is yet, so that's fun. And my mom's about a ten-minute drive from my place. She still makes me come to Sunday dinner if I'm in town."

"Aw." Tim had to smile at that. He'd read that Isaac and his mother were close. But he didn't want to press Isaac to talk about it. "I mean, I love the mountains, but I'm mostly in Boulder because that's where my coach is. I started working with him in college."

"Kids come to Raleigh from all over to work with Adam."

"And work with you, I'm guessing."

Isaac rolled his eyes. "I'm nothing."

"That's really not true."

Isaac sighed. "I know." He leaned back and rested his head on the back of the sofa. His blanket fell away enough to reveal that he wasn't wearing a shirt.

On the screen, the commentators announced that the Parade of Nations would be starting shortly. Tim sat up a little. Before he'd been an Olympian himself, this had been his favorite part of the Opening Ceremony. "My sister and I used to watch and critique the costumes," Tim said.

"Yeah? I've never watched the full Opening Ceremony before. I mean, the last Olympics that I did not participate in happened when I was thirteen. My mother probably made me go to bed before we got to this point."

"Ha, really?"

"Yeah. She was strict when we were kids. Especially when I started swimming competitively. TV went off at nine, I had to be in bed by ten. I didn't argue, because usually I was so wiped out from swim practice that I couldn't stay up that late anyway." Isaac wiped his face. "Your parents still together, Tim?"

"Yeah."

"My dad took off when I was three. Mom worked two jobs to pay for my swim lessons."

"Yeah, I… yeah. I was lucky." Tim's parents had a great marriage and had always been supportive. And he knew quite a bit about Isaac's family, since his mother and sister had so often been shown in the stands when Isaac had raced in previous Olympics. There had been lots of human-interest pieces during previous Olympic broadcasts. None of them had mentioned the alcoholism, though. Whether it was because people didn't know or because it didn't fit with the picture of the athlete the network wanted to portray was anyone's guess.

On the screen, the athletes from Greece entered the stadium. "What made you take up diving?" Isaac asked.

Tim smiled. He liked that Isaac was trying to get to know him. He didn't mind answering questions, especially not after Isaac had shared so much, and it was nice, sitting with him, just the two of them, as athletes from all over the world paraded across the screen. Tim's pulse kicked up at the thought of those athletes marching only a few miles from where they currently sat. It struck Tim again how incredible it was that he was *here*.

He swallowed and said, "My parents enrolled me in a bunch of activities when I was little. I started gymnastics as a toddler. I swam by the time I was five or six. Somehow my parents still found time to take me to the park near my house, which had a pool with springboards at three different heights. Mom forbade me from getting up on the three-meter springboard until I was a stronger swimmer, but that was my goal. All the kids at the pool seemed like they were having so much fun. So I worked on my swimming skills. I didn't even want to dive, I just wanted to jump off that springboard. Then, a couple of years later, I saw this thing on TV about Greg Louganis. I was maybe nine at the time."

"Sure." Isaac turned slightly more toward Tim. He smiled.

"I remember, the woman who was narrating it, she kept saying how beautiful he was when he dove. And he really was, you know? I've since studied his form, and he dove gracefully. He innovated the sport, tried things no one had done before. As I watched, something in me clicked, and I thought, 'I want to do that.'

I already had the gymnastics skills by then to do some tricks off the platform."

Isaac nodded. "Louganis was pretty amazing."

Tim scooted a little closer to Isaac. "It certainly didn't hurt anything that Louganis was also gay. I knew I was, by then. I don't think I could have articulated what it meant, and I sure as hell didn't tell anyone, but I knew. And, I mean, I can't even imagine what it must have been like for him. Being in the closet. Knowing he had HIV when he hit his head in '88." Tim let out a sigh. "That's part of why I went along with the coming-out video. I weighed staying in the closet like Louganis or being 'the gay diver' like Tom Daley. I knew the media would label me, but that seemed better to me than staying in the closet. It was more important to live authentically, to not have that hanging over me when I dove." Tim looked at Isaac for a reaction, knowing Isaac would likely understand. It was hard to sum up how agonizing that decision had been in a few words, but something told Tim he didn't have to explain himself much more to Isaac.

"Do you regret it?" Isaac pulled his blanket a little tighter around his shoulders.

"I regret a lot of things where Pat is concerned, but I do not regret coming out."

Isaac nodded. He focused on the screen, where the Belgian team walked into the stadium. Tim had just been talking; he hadn't meant to imply anything where Isaac was concerned. Tim didn't know if Isaac's bisexuality was public knowledge or not. Maybe it was, but the rest of the nonsense in his life overshadowed it.

"I got to meet Louganis at the last Olympics," Tim said, trying to blow past any awkwardness. "I almost died. He'd been hired to mentor the team. The first meeting we had, I blabbered like an idiot about how he was my idol."

"I imagine that was a lot like the time I met Michael Phelps."

"Did you pass out or what?"

Isaac laughed. "No, but I did get really nervous. Actually, the first time I met him, he was doing a product launch or something in Baltimore, and I *begged* my mother to let me go. I was… sixteen? It was before my first Olympics, for sure. My mom drove us there. Phelps signed a swim cap for me. I still have it. Then we were teammates a few times. And everyone kept saying, 'Isaac Flood is the next Michael Phelps.' I fell short of that."

"Not yet." Tim leaned closer. He wondered sometimes if the media knew how much pressure they put on athletes, how detrimental it could be. Because Isaac wasn't just being self-deprecating; he beat himself up for not rising to the bar everyone set for him.

"You know, it's funny. A few minutes ago, I told another athlete that the medals and whatever didn't matter. All that mattered is pushing your body to do what you love. And I have done that. I'm doing that this week. But I have to keep reminding myself of that, and try not to feel bitter."

Tim shifted over on the sofa, closer to Isaac. He wanted to hug the younger Isaac who felt like he didn't measure up, because of the shadow of other athletes or even just his own brain chemistry. "That's a good outlook."

"Yeah."

Onscreen, the Chinese delegation marched into the stadium. Tim and Isaac sat and watched silently as a few countries walked in the parade. Team USA would be coming in soon, since "United States of America" translated into "Estados Unidos de America" in Spanish.

The floor seemed quiet. Tim hadn't heard or seen anyone walk by in a while. Likely everyone was either sleeping, trying to sleep, or they were down at the stadium. Tim sidled a little closer to Isaac. Their shoulders touched now, and heat radiated off Isaac.

"You ready for tomorrow?" Tim asked softly.

"As I'll ever be. I should be sleeping, but I can't turn my brain off."

"Do you... want some help?" The intimacy between them had stoked the fire of Tim's physical desire for Isaac. Isaac was compelling and sexy but troubled too, and part of Tim wanted to soothe all his ruffled parts....

Isaac turned his head and met Tim's gaze. Tim slid a hand under Isaac's blanket and splayed his fingers across Isaac's chest to make his intentions clear. Lord, Isaac's chest was a thing of beauty, wasn't it? All those flat planes, broad shoulders, hard muscle, soft skin.

"You don't know how badly I want to say yes," Isaac said.

"But?"

"But I have a race tomorrow. I really do need to sleep. But you should know, I have a single room."

"Seriously?"

"Yeah. You have a roommate?"

"My dive partner, Jason."

"You do this shit four times, and your coach can pull enough strings to get you your own room. I'm just saying, if there's some night when neither of us has to be anywhere the next day, I'd love to spend a night with you."

Tim's heart pounded at the thought. "So noted."

"But I want to drag you down the hall right now," Isaac whispered. "I want to get you out of your sweaty gym clothes and into my bed. I want to fuck you until we both forget all about gold medals and dives and races and all of it."

Sweat broke out all over Tim's body. "I want that too."

"Everyone's right, though. It'll screw with my focus tomorrow." Isaac looked away. Then he seemed to decide something. "Tell you what. First one of us to win a medal names the time and place. Hell, maybe resolving the tension between us will help us relax. But for now? I've got a date with my coach at seven in the morning."

"I'm gonna win a medal, then," Tim said.

Isaac smiled. "I mean, just given the sheer number of races I'm scheduled to swim in, my odds are better than yours."

"But you're saying that if I win a medal, then I can say, 'Isaac, we're having sex tonight,' and you'll do it?"

"You know what?" Isaac paused and appeared to consider. "Yes, that is exactly what I'm saying."

"And if *you* win?"

"Then we do it my way."

Tim laughed. He curled his hand around Isaac's side and pressed his chin against Isaac's shoulder. Isaac put his arm around Tim and held him close for a moment before letting him go.

Tim said, "That's not much of a threat. I'm pretty sure this is a win-win bet. And what if you win a medal at your first race? You've still got all those races after that. Won't us sleeping together screw up your focus or something?"

"Why deny myself pleasure?" Isaac squeezed Tim's shoulders. "I figure, if I win a medal here, who gives a shit about my focus after that? I will have won a medal."

"Mmm."

Isaac smelled really good. Faintly of chlorine, but clean. He used some product, deodorant or aftershave, that was kind of piney. And his skin under Tim's hand was warm and smooth.

"You have no body hair," Tim said.

"Nope. Nada. I even get my pits waxed. I know it's insane, but hair could create enough drag to slow me down fractions of a second, which means the difference between winning and losing."

"Hey, I get my chest waxed. I get it. It's just kind of a new thing for me to feel up a guy and find him so smooth. Down below too?"

"Everything I can't shove under a swim cap."

Tim wanted to lift up the blanket and take a peek inside Isaac's pajama pants. He wondered if Isaac had tan lines.

But he had to pull away. He was hard and wrapped up in Isaac and if he didn't leave, he'd end up banging Isaac right on this sofa.

Only he couldn't pull away. He kept running his hand over Isaac's chest, and he canted his hips closer to Isaac's. Isaac moaned softly.

Then Isaac said with a bit of a groan in his voice, "If you don't kiss me right now, I'm going to go insane."

Tim tilted his head up and let Isaac come to him, which he did a moment later, crashing his lips into Tim's. Tim opened his mouth and let Isaac in, and a lightning bolt shot through his body. Isaac's mouth was hot and slick. He smelled of pine and pool, and he was all warm skin and the promise of sex.

Tim couldn't wait to get naked with him.

But he knew he'd have to. Isaac had made his feelings on the matter clear.

Tim pulled away reluctantly and said, "We should probably not get carried away."

Isaac smiled ruefully. "You're right." He glanced toward the TV. "Oh, and look, they're already on Finland. We missed the entrance of the American team."

"Worth it," Tim said, grinning.

CHAPTER 6

Day 1

Transcript: Swimming Preliminary Heats

DAVIS: Hello from the Domingo Aquatics Center. I'm Nick Davis with my colleague, veteran swimmer and gold medalist in his own right, Jim O'Toole. How are you, Jim?

O'TOOLE: I'm great, Nick. I think we're in for some incredible races this week. We've got an American team that collectively holds *six* world records. We've got superstar swimmers like Melissa Murphy, Luke Rogers, and Katie Santiago, and we've got promising newcomers Conor Smith, Randy Manning, and Jen McMahon. And, of course, we can't talk about swimming without talking about Isaac Flood.

DAVIS: I never thought I'd see this, Jim, I gotta tell you. We all thought Flood was done after the last Olympics. He retired, he partied a little too much. We counted him out. And then he showed up at the US Olympic Trials without having swum in international competition in three years. And he just destroyed everyone.

O'TOOLE: He's been back training with his long-time coach Adam Vreeland. I talked to Adam this morning, and he had nothing but good things to say about Flood. And Flood is swimming all over this program, with the potential to win as many as nine medals.

DAVIS: Realistically, what do you think his chances are?

O'TOOLE: You know, I wouldn't count him out. He has so much natural talent and a work ethic like no one I've ever seen. He's not quite as fast as he used to be, but he's got strength and endurance, and I expect he's got a good shot at a medal in the middle-distance races. But you never know. He's said he feels like he's in the best shape of his life, so let's see if that's true.

DAVIS: At twenty-nine, he's one of the older members on this team. Lot of young swimmers on Team USA.

O'TOOLE: Sure, but you had swimmers like Michael Phelps and Ryan Lochte winning gold medals at thirty-two. I don't see age as a big factor here. The three years he's had off from swimming might be. Keep in mind also, some of Flood's old rivals are back. Look for McKeown and Pearson from Australia in the breaststroke races. Pearson edged out Flood four years ago to win gold. And there are some promising young sprinters from Hungary as well that Flood is going to have to look out for. And that's not to mention his own teammates. This American field is maybe one of the best they've ever sent to an Olympics. They've trained well, they're strong, and they've got a pile of world championship medals.

DAVIS: But you like Flood's chances?

O'TOOLE: You know, I do. I think he'll be reaching for the podium in all of his races. I watched him in practice yesterday, and his times are slower than what they used to be, but his form is good. Adam Vreeland says he looks solid. And it's the Olympics. Anything can happen.

"TWO HEATS down," Adam said. "Fastest time was 4:08 so far, so these heats are slow. You have McKeown, Hsu, and LeBlanc in this heat with you, so it's going to be faster than the previous heats, but you can swim faster than 4:08 without trying that hard. So take it easy here. Swim a solid race, don't slouch, but don't feel like you have to go all out either. If you push too hard, you'll tire yourself out."

"Yup." Isaac pulled on his cap and fiddled with his goggles.

"You don't need to win your heat to make it to semis, is what I'm saying."

"I know."

"But there are six heats. Why the hell are there six heats? I didn't know there were so many IM swimmers."

Isaac had basically stopped listening. He knew all this. "Not my first rodeo, Adam."

Adam nodded and slapped him on the back. "I'm just saying, these are slow heats. Don't slack, but don't kill yourself either."

Isaac walked out of the ready room and followed the other swimmers out to stand on deck for the fourth heat.

The 400 individual medley used to be Isaac's favorite race, but he found that the older he got, the more this race punished his body. It was a tough way to get the meet started, and he'd have to swim it twice today: the preliminary heats now and the semifinals tonight. If

Adam wanted him to swim in the relay tomorrow night, that could end up being a tall order.

But no matter. He walked out to the blocks as the third heat exited the pool. The fastest time in that heat was only 4:07.85. Isaac could swim this race in 4:06 easy, 4:05 if he pushed it, and, as the scoreboard had indicated four years ago, in 4:03 on freaky days when he'd destroyed the world record.

He unzipped his jacket and glanced at the field. Hsu, a Chinese swimmer, was the reigning world champion. McKeown had been at this as long as Isaac had, an old vet but probably still a factor. LeBlanc was good but past his prime. And anyway, given how slow the previous heats had been, Isaac just had to finish in the top four and he'd advance.

He stripped to his swimsuit and went through the prerace ritual: checked his cap, tugged it over his ears, checked his goggles, adjusting them, even though they didn't really need adjusting, stretched his arms over his head, tugged on the waistband of his swimsuit, shook out his arms, bowed toward the pool, splashed water on himself, then stood back up. The ready whistle sounded. He stood beside the block and watched McKeown do the dumb prerace dance he'd been doing for fifteen years, kind of a kicky samba thing.

The whistle to get on the blocks sounded. Isaac consciously tried to shove aside the fact that this was the first swim in this Olympics. Just another meet. He had this.

"On your marks."

Isaac crouched into position on the block.

The buzzer sounded.

Jumping off the block was a Pavlovian response at this point. Isaac got in the water before his brain caught up to what was happening. Then he threw out his arms to start the butterfly. Butterfly was the hardest stroke for him, so he was happy to get it over with first; it took a lot of strength to get his upper body out of the water enough to bring his arms out and in front of him to act as paddles as he pushed himself forward in the water. But he felt good. He swam strong, he sliced through the water, and then spotted the wall. He touched the side of the pool and turned to do it again. And he flew. In no time, he reached the wall again. He flipped back, raised his arms for the backstroke. His pace was not leisurely, and his arms tingled a little, but this stroke was easier on his body. He essentially floated down the pool until he saw the flags indicating the turn was ten meters away. He flipped and did it again, looking up at the ceiling of the Aquatics Center, following along with the latticework grid of the unfinished ceiling to help keep him swimming in a straight line. Then he turned into the breaststroke, which was *his* stroke, and he found the joy of it now. He didn't look at the lanes beside him. He didn't think about semifinals or finals. He just swam the way he knew he could. He glided through the water. This was easy. This was fun. Then the final turn, and he pulled his arms into the crawl stroke, and just… went. Moved like the water was pushing him instead of working against him. He swam to the wall, flipped, and then turned it on a little, pushing himself to finish the race. He touched the wall and popped his head up.

Well, considering men were still swimming, he'd done all right. He glanced up at the scoreboard. 4:06.25. First place in the heat by two seconds.

Christ.

He treaded water for a second, trying to catch his breath. His body burned, but in a satisfying way. Hsu tapped his hand in congratulations.

He climbed out of the pool. A reporter interviewed guys as they walked back to the ready room, but Isaac ignored her. He gathered his things from the side of the pool and gave the reporter a wide berth, hoping not to be stopped. When he was safely inside the athletes-only area, Adam walked over and slapped him on the back. "You might just pull this off."

"Yeah?"

"Yeah. That was insane. Best I've seen you swim in a while. You beat the rest of the field by a body length. How much are you hurting?"

"I feel all right." He still panted, not quite having regained his breath, but his body felt good. Felt alive.

"I did tell you not to push it."

"I didn't push it."

Adam raised an eyebrow. "You mean to tell me you did the 400 IM in 4:06 without pushing it?"

"I didn't think about the time, honestly. I just swam."

Adam laughed. "Keep it up, kid."

TIM WATCHED Isaac's heat from a TV monitor near the diving pool while he waited for his practice time. In the distance, he could hear the Chinese coach yelling at his divers, which irritated Tim because they were already pushing everyone else's practice times later. The silver lining was that for lack of anything else to do, Tim got to watch Isaac swim.

The race was incredible. And it was a *prelim*. Isaac seemed to fly through the water. Tim had seen him race before; he'd watched Isaac's first two Olympics on TV. But it was a different experience knowing Isaac the way he did now and knowing what Isaac had been through.

"That's why he's the best in the world," said Jason, watching from behind Tim.

"Yeah."

"I wanted to be him when I joined the swim team in college, but I never quite swam fast enough."

"You wanted to be Isaac Flood?"

"Here. Comes. The. Flood!" Jason shouted. "Yeah, I did. That guy was the coolest, if you were a swimmer."

The Chinese team did another perfectly synchronized dive, which somehow still angered their coach, and they finally cleared off the platform.

Then a reporter showed up.

The press had been in the booth all day, watching practice dives, occasionally coming down to confer with the divers and coaches about which dives they were planning for Monday's final. A lot of the commentators were former divers and came to many of the international competitions; they had a good rapport with the athletes and also knew when to keep their distance. But this reporter was not one of the regular commentators. She immediately got Tim's back up.

"We're up," Jason said.

Tim nodded and walked over to Donnie. "There's a reporter here."

"Okay. I'll send Rudy to get rid of her. Get to the top of the platform. Let's start easy with dive number one."

As Tim climbed the stairs to the top of the platform, he heard Rudy, Donnie's assistant, arguing with the reporter.

"What does she want?" Tim asked Jason.

"No idea. Well, I mean, probably to talk to you."

"But why?" Tim knew she could want to know about what dives he had planned, but he sensed she was here to ask him nosy questions he didn't want to answer.

"Forget about it, Tim."

But Tim could still hear Rudy's adamant refusals to grant her an interview. He felt sick to his stomach as he stood at the edge of the platform with Jason. He pushed it aside, looking forward to the dive but still distracted. Donnie blew the whistle, indicating they should go. The dive was a forward pike, low difficulty level, a slam-dunk dive any novice diver could do, meant to show synchronization more than anything else. They got into position. Donnie blew the whistle again.

And Tim totally whiffed it.

He came off the platform and got enough height to pull himself into formation, but he knew his legs weren't straight, and then when he kicked his legs up to enter the water, he kicked too hard and rotated past vertical. The backs of his legs slapped the water as he entered.

Fuck.

The worst part was that the fucking reporter still stood right fucking there when Tim got out of the water.

"The hell was that?" Donnie said, seeming more mystified than angry.

"She wants to talk to me," Tim said, gesturing toward the reporter.

Donnie turned the full force of his wrath on the poor woman then. "Lady, you need to get out of here. You're distracting my divers."

"Timothy!" she shouted. "Timothy Swan. How much is your breakup with Patterson Wood affecting your performance here?"

Tim started to panic. He had to get this woman out of here. He couldn't talk about Pat. He didn't want to talk about Pat. Not here.

Diving had always been his sanctuary. On the platform, it was just him and the air and the water. It was his safe place. And this woman had invaded it.

"Have you faced any homophobia here in Madrid?" she shouted.

Tim looked at Donnie. Donnie looked just as panic-stricken.

"There's a rumor you and Patterson Wood are back together. That he's in Madrid to watch your dives. Can you tell me if it's true?"

Pat? Here in Madrid? No, there was no way. They'd been broken up for weeks. Why the hell would Pat be in Madrid?

Tim started to hyperventilate.

"Can we have her arrested?" Jason asked.

Tim's panic was so vivid, he could hear only the rushing in his ears as he struggled to catch his breath. Everything else faded as he struggled to pull air into his lungs. He became aware of hands pushing him toward a bench, and then of his head being shoved between his knees. Then a medic appeared beside him and took his vitals, and the panic began to subside.

When Tim had a handle on his breathing again, he took a few long, shaky breaths and looked around. He sat on a bench behind one of the showers. It was a spot usually reserved for coaches during the competition. He drew in a few more breaths and looked for Donnie.

"She's gone," Donnie said. "She wasn't supposed to be here. She's a reporter for one of those entertainment shows, which is doing a series of special episodes from Madrid, and she wanted to interview you for the show."

"She wants gossip on Pat."

"Looks that way. She got past security because she flashed her press credentials and they didn't know any better. I could have had her arrested, but I didn't want to make the situation worse for you. They are tightening security, though. Only reporters here for official broadcasts will be allowed in. There's a list with the names, so the security guards will check that from now on."

"Okay." Tim sighed. "I'm sorry. I didn't mean to lose it like that. But I saw her, and I couldn't deal."

"You have enough to deal with," Donnie said kindly.

"I think I'm going to need the rest of the day off. We can resume tomorrow."

Donnie nodded. "Go sleep it off. The pool will still be here in the morning. Do you want me to line up a security escort to get you back to the Athlete Village?"

Considering the reporter hadn't been arrested, and the potential for there to be more reporters, Tim said, "Yeah. Please."

When Donnie wandered off to confer with security, Jason sat next to Tim. Tim said, "I'm so sorry."

"Stop apologizing. You've been through a lot this year. You should be able to put it behind you to compete here, not deal with nosy reporters. What happened with Pat is none of her business."

"Yeah." Tim felt weary. He rubbed his forehead.

"Timmy, you're one of the best divers who has ever been on a platform. I mean that. Not just right now. Not just among Americans. But in the world, you're the best. Defending Olympic champion. World champion three times over. I'm honored to be your partner. That asshole reporter wants to make this about your personal life, but that doesn't matter at all. You're the best. Period."

"Thanks, Jason."

On the way back to his room, Tim couldn't get over the feeling that he wished Isaac was there to say something acerbic and shake him out of his funk. Isaac was likely still at the Aquatics Center, or else he was napping before his semifinal that night.

But Tim texted him anyway: *Reporter showed up at my practice and totally threw me off my game.*

It took a long moment, but Isaac texted back: *Fuck 'em.*

BEFORE HEADING back to the Athlete Village to get some sleep, Isaac climbed into the stands and sat beside his mother, Rebecca. She was a quiet type, supportive and loving but not demonstrative with her emotions. When Isaac sat beside her, she put her arm around him, gave him a quick squeeze, and then retracted it.

"You're swimming well."

"So far."

"Considering it looked like you would never swim again for a while there, I think you're doing just fine."

"You're my mother. You have to say things like that."

She laughed. "In my eyes, you're still that gangly six-year-old who wanted to take extra swim lessons. You were all arms and legs in those days. Now look at you. All grown-up."

"I just... I fucked up. And I hurt a lot of people, you included. And I recognize that winning a medal here fixes absolutely none of that, but I guess I just wanted to prove to myself that I wasn't completely useless."

"I forgave you."

"That's a very mom-like thing to do too. Abby hasn't." Abby was Isaac's sister, and she had more or less disowned him when his drinking had gotten really bad. He didn't blame her; he'd been awful in those days, drunk more than he'd been sober, wasting his money on cheap beer and bottom-shelf liquor just so he could get through each day. They'd forged a peace since he'd come out of rehab, but things were still unsteady some days.

"She's here, you know."

"She is?"

"Yup. She wasn't feeling well this morning, so she stayed at the hotel. She said she ate something weird on the plane, I think. But she'll be here to watch you tomorrow."

Isaac nodded and watched as the next heat started in the pool. Softly, he said, "I haven't really forgiven myself."

"I know. You'll get there." She sighed. "I blamed myself for a long time. Or my genes, at least. Your grandpa was a nasty drunk."

Isaac had heard the stories. Grandpa had stayed sober when his grandkids were around, and Isaac had been oblivious until the man had died when Isaac was fourteen. After the third or fourth person at the wake had called Grandpa "a real son of a gun," Isaac had asked his mother about that, and the floodgates had opened. Perhaps his death had made it okay to talk about him.

He shook his head. "It's no one's fault but my own. Maybe alcoholism is a disease, but I did some shitty things. That I was drunk at the time is a weak excuse."

"You're sober now, and that's what matters. We didn't lose you."

"I still want to drink."

"But you won't. I have faith in you."

"I appreciate that, Mom, but—"

"Focus on the Olympics. Focus on swimming. Then focus on the next thing. You'll earn your next chip, no problem."

Isaac sighed. He put his arm around his mother and leaned his head against hers for a moment. She stiffened a little—even with her own son, she was awkward when it came to being touched—but let out a sigh. The truth was that he'd focused on *her* a lot in rehab, though he hadn't wanted to say as much. But Isaac's father had never really been a part of his life, and his mother had worked extra jobs to make ends meet and bring up two kids who had caused her a lot of grief over the years, Isaac more than Abby. But after everything she'd done for him, Isaac had wanted to get better so he wouldn't throw everything she'd done for him away. "I love you, Mom."

"I know, my big boy. I love you too. Now go get some rest so you can win some medals. I've seen you do it a bunch of times, but it really never gets old."

Isaac laughed. "Okay, Mom. I'm on it."

CHAPTER 7

Day 2

TIM STOOD in the lounge, watching the TV that broadcast the American network's coverage of the Games.
And sure enough, he was making headlines.

"The other odd story of today," said a pretty
blond reporter, "is that diver Timothy Swan apparently bailed on a practice after the press showed up
yesterday."

"Turn that shit off," Isaac said, walking into the
lounge.

Tim had missed Isaac the night before. After having dinner with his parents, who had flown to Madrid
earlier in the day, Tim had holed up in his room a good
chunk of the day but emerged to watch Isaac swim on
TV before he retreated to his room again. Isaac had
swum the fastest in his semifinal heat, but he'd come
in second overall. Not that it mattered, since it was the
final he needed to win to get the medal. But regardless,
Isaac had likely still been at the pool long after Tim had
gone to bed.

But man, Tim was glad to see Isaac now.

On the TV, a woman said, "He became visibly upset. We don't really know why. He had a bad practice, that was clear. The Chinese team may have intimidated him. Some say he panicked because of pressure from his coach—"

Isaac turned off the TV.

"That's some bullshit." Tim's pulse picked up. He was angry more than panicky now, but his breath caught in a similar way.

"What happened yesterday?" Isaac asked.

"A reporter showed up at practice. She started asking questions about Pat, and I freaked."

"Ah."

Tim loved that he didn't have to explain. He turned to face Isaac. Isaac glanced behind him, then reached forward, putting his hands on Tim's waist. Tim bowed his head and pressed it against Isaac's chest. Being shadowed by Isaac's big body comforted Tim, but touching him had a calming effect too. Tim's breathing returned to normal.

Tim took a deep breath, sniffed, and stepped away. "Do you worry about getting caught? With me, I mean. It doesn't seem like you do, but I'll admit, I'm a little worried. There aren't any reporters in these dorms, but all it really takes is a gossipy athlete walking by and blabbing to someone. Then we'll be on that fluffy half-hour entertainment show that airs before the main coverage every night."

Isaac shrugged. "Fuck 'em."

"I'm serious."

Isaac let out a breath. "All right, yes, I'm a little worried. But only because I'm not ready to share this with the world yet." He reached over and ran the back of his hand along Tim's cheek. "We just met. No need to shout it from the rooftops."

"You're not worried about some of the less tolerant athletes? Bad press? Being outed?"

"Believe me, I know all about bad press. It sucks. When I was arrested, the press pored over my whole life in meticulous detail. I'm genuinely surprised none of my male exes came forward, because that little detail would have been a delicious cherry on top, right? But the thing is, it blows over. They're just words."

"So if someone saw you kiss me and told a reporter, you wouldn't care, then?"

"I'd care, but... what have I got to lose at this point? My family and friends know I'm bisexual. The DUI pretty much tanked everything else."

That gave Tim pause. "You're not just using me to go out in a blaze of glory, are you?"

Isaac looked confused by that, at least. He furrowed his brow and leaned away. "Why would you— oh. It's the defeatist attitude, isn't it?"

"It's hard to figure you out sometimes. I think you *do* care, but you think you've already lost everything. You have a second chance here, Isaac. Not many people get that. You should be making the most of it instead of assuming everything will turn out terribly."

"I should, you're right. I am. I think... I mean, I want you to know, your friendship means a lot to me. That we can talk freely with each other is so valuable. If I leave here in two weeks with no medals, I'll still have had this time with you. That's no small thing." Isaac sighed. "I want my life back. I want to feel like I own it, not that it's out of control. Getting sober was a big part of that, but if I can prove I can still swim? If I can say, hey, I'm clean now, I'm healthy? Maybe I get my career back. I can swim for a few more years while I figure out what to do next."

"There you go." Tim smiled. He was encouraged by the shifts in Isaac's attitude. "But tonight you're going to win a gold medal for me."

"I thought we agreed it just had to be a medal."

"I've decided it has to be gold."

Isaac grinned. "All right. For you? Anything."

ISAAC HAD a breaststroke semifinal the afternoon before the 400 IM final. He supposed it could have been worse; there were only three heats of swimmers, so they were foregoing semifinals, saving him from having to swim a second race that night. When he'd been younger, two medal races in one night would have been no issue, but now that he was almost thirty, he needed more recovery time between races.

So he stood in what had been designated the American Lounge corner of the ready room. Adam said he thought the time to beat in the 200-meter breaststroke was 3:45, which felt reasonable; Isaac's world record was two seconds faster than that. He'd set that six years ago, long before the DUI, but still, somewhere in his body lived the muscle memory to get that done.

One of the other coaches called Adam away—just as well, because Isaac preferred to play white noise through his headphones before a race—so Isaac sat in a folding chair, aware of the camera in the corner trained on him.

His phone lay in his jacket pocket, with the white noise app already turned on, so Isaac slid his headphones on. He closed his eyes and zoned out. He needed to calm down enough to relax.

His muscles felt good, though. He'd watched some of the other swimmers go through the cupping therapy and thought it too freaky—it involved sucking skin and muscle into a glass cup, leaving big purple bruises behind, so no, thank you—but he took up Tim's suggestion for acupuncture that morning, which had done some good. It didn't hurt, and maybe it did nothing, but having to lie still for a half hour had helped soothe Isaac's fraying nerves if nothing else.

An announcer called his heat, so he stood and followed the other swimmers out.

The camera from the American network was really up in his business, but he kept his headphones on until the last possible moment, ignoring everything that was not this race. There were a couple of swimmers in the field that Adam had thought he should look out for, but Isaac didn't know them, and he didn't much care.

Four lengths of the pool. That's all he needed to do.

He swam. He enjoyed it. He was in his element with the breaststroke. He turned on the gas a little for the last lap and enjoyed the burn in his muscles. It started to hurt the last twenty-five meters, but Isaac didn't care.

This was what he'd been put on the planet to do.

He hit the wall and didn't even look at the scoreboard for a moment. He breathed. He saw the reactions of the guys on either side of him, slapping the water and celebrating. Then he turned around.

Second place. 3:45.2. Not the best, but good enough to get into the final.

This time he zoned out and ended up getting stopped by the reporter on his way back to the warm-up pool.

"Hi, Mindy Somers, TBC Sports. You have a minute?"

Isaac sighed and nodded.

"Isaac, you've been looking really strong in your preliminary swims. You're one of the favorites to win your race tonight. You just swam the third-fastest time in the breaststroke semis. How do you feel?"

"I'm pretty good," he said, panting still.

"What's it like, being back in the Olympics again?"

Isaac breathed for a second, buying him time to decide if he should blow her off or give her a good sound bite. He settled on saying, "I'm happy to have another chance."

"You've been through so much the last few years. You came out of nowhere at the Trials to qualify for a number of races here in Madrid. What was that like?"

"Well, I've been training for a year and a half with this goal in mind."

"Do you expect to win a medal?"

God, he wanted her to go away. But he smiled and said, "I'd love to, but really, I'm just happy to be here."

Mindy Somers tossed it back to the guys in the booth, so Isaac ducked away.

After his cool-down, Isaac decided to head back to his room for a nap, but as he was changing, Tim and Jason came into the locker room.

"Oh, hey," said Tim. "How'd your heat go?"

"Good. Qualified for the final. What are you doing here?"

"Women's final is starting, so we had to clear out of the pool."

"I'm headed back to the Athlete Village. Want to go with me?" Isaac asked.

Jason seemed to take the hint. "I'm gonna try to talk the swim coaches into letting me swim a couple of laps in the warm-up pool." He hooked his thumb back toward the pool and cleared out.

Isaac knew he probably shouldn't get too used to having Tim by his side, since he'd be flying back to Raleigh and Tim back to Colorado when this was all over, but he also wanted to make the most of it now. His rehab mantra had been to take each day as it came. Tim brought Isaac more happiness than he could have expected, so he would savor it each day that he had it.

A short shuttle bus parked just outside the athlete's entrance to the Aquatics Center did loops between the venues and the Athlete Village. Isaac nodded at the driver, who leaned against the bus, fiddling with his phone.

"Ride?" the driver said.

"Yes," said Isaac.

They boarded the bus. The trip back to the village was quick. When they got off the bus, Isaac and Tim ran into a group Isaac thought might have been the American basketball team, goofing around on the giant Olympic rings near the entrance to the village.

"Hey, here comes the Flood!" one of them shouted. He hopped off the ring he'd been standing on.

Soon Isaac and Tim found themselves surrounded by a bunch of basketball players—he recognized one of them as a player for the Charlotte Hornets because they'd done some event together in Charleston a few years ago. Before the DUI.

"We're off tonight," one of the guys said, "so we were gonna come see you win your tenth medal, Flood."

"Oh, you don't have to."

"No, seriously, we are all about Team USA," said another basketball player.

Isaac laughed. "Well, sure. You're expected to run away with your gold medal."

"We have some competition," one of the guys said.

"Yeah, hell, that Serbian team is full of NBA players," said another. "And the Spanish have the home-court advantage."

"You're the best team by far," said Tim.

"Yeah, we are." A bunch of the guys high-fived each other.

"You're Timmy Swan," the Hornet—whose name escaped Isaac—said to Tim.

"Yeah."

"We'll come root for you too. When do you dive?"

"Tomorrow. Then again next Tuesday and Saturday."

"Yeah, boy. New gold medals for everyone. U-S-A! U-S-A!"

All of the basketball players started chanting, "U-S-A!" Their enthusiasm was infectious, but Isaac really wanted to go get that nap.

"Thanks, guys," Isaac said. "If I don't see you tonight, good luck tomorrow."

Isaac ducked away, and after Tim signed an autograph for one of the basketball players, he returned to Isaac's side. Tim said, "Those guys are fun."

"Yeah, but I'm glad I don't play a team sport. I like my team, but I don't want to spend all of our time together."

Tim laughed. "You're such a grump."

"What I like about swimming," Isaac said, "is that it's an individual sport. Most of the time you can't see what your opponents are doing, and if you stop to look, you lose. So all you can do is swim as hard as you can. You can't control anything in the pool except your own body. You can't control if the other swimmers in the pool are having the best meet of their lives, if someone else breaks a world record, if someone else is having an off day. All I can do is get in the water and be the best I can be."

"I get that," Tim said. "Hell, it's the same for me. Except for the synchronized events, I'm out there on the springboard or the platform by myself. I have no control over whether the other divers are good or not. I can only control myself."

"Exactly."

But Isaac was tired and didn't want to have too many more of these philosophical discussions. After he'd talked Jake off the ledge the other night, the American men's gymnastics team had indeed finished in the top spot after the team qualifiers the night before, with Jake qualifying for four event finals and the all-around. Isaac hadn't watched, but Melissa from the swim team had assured him Jake had been awesome. And hot, but Isaac already knew that.

He glanced at Tim and smiled. Jake was hot, but he had nothing on Tim.

Tim smiled back. "What was that smile for?"

"Nothing. I like you."

Tim grinned wider. "I like you too."

Someone off to the side shouted something unfriendly at them, but Isaac didn't recognize the words.

Tim apparently did, though, because his whole face crumpled.

"Come on," Isaac said, "let's get out of here."

"Did you hear that?"

"Yeah. I don't know what he said, but it wasn't friendly."

"He basically called us faggots."

"Let's go."

Isaac didn't give a shit what anyone said about him. He threw an arm around Tim because Tim was upset, and he nudged him toward the closest building, which happened to be America House.

And, of course, a whole huge group of people were sitting around and cheered when they walked in, Isaac with his arm still around Tim. Someone shouted, "Here comes the Flood!" He looked around and spotted Luke, sitting with his family near the bar. So Isaac headed that way.

"What are we doing?" Tim asked.

"Getting away from that asshole. Also saying hello to Luke."

Luke looked up as Isaac approached. "Hey, Flood, what's going on?"

Isaac finally pulled his arm away from Tim, who looked at him questioningly. So Isaac said, "Did you guys meet? Tim Swan, Luke Rogers."

They shook hands. Luke's mother gave Isaac a hug and ruffled his hair.

"Don't you have a race tonight?" Luke asked.

"I was on my way back to my room for a nap when Tim and I were first accosted by the U.S. basketball team—" Isaac stuck out his thumb. "And then someone shouted homophobic things at us in a foreign language."

"An athlete?" Luke asked.

"Yeah. No idea who it was."

"They spoke Spanish," said Tim.

"Doesn't really narrow it down," said Luke. "I was going to say, if you knew which team, you could file a complaint. Officially, the Olympics has policies about that."

Isaac slid onto a stool and said, "Are they enforced?"

Luke shrugged.

"I didn't even see what colors the guy wore," said Tim, sounding miserable. "I think he had on a warm-up suit, which probably had his country's name on it, but ugh...." Tim rubbed his head as if he had a headache.

Isaac wanted to pull Tim into his arms but didn't know if it would be appropriate.

Luke furrowed his brow. "So are you guys...?" He pointed a finger back and forth between them.

"Not really," said Tim. "I mean, we're friends, right?"

"Of course," said Isaac.

Tim nodded, satisfied. "We were coming back from the Aquatics Center together. That's all." He sighed. "It's because of me. It's because everyone knows I'm a fag."

"Don't use words like that," Isaac said. He wasn't offended—he just didn't like the self-deprecating way Tim said it. "You have nothing to be ashamed of."

"I'm not ashamed, I'm... tired."

Isaac gave in and touched Tim again then, running his hand along Tim's arm. Tim looked up and met Isaac's gaze.

"You can still file a complaint. Athletes are supposed to be able to feel safe in the Athlete Village."

Luke cleared his throat. "As team captain, I felt like it was my responsibility to know what the policies were. You are not the only LGBT member of the swim team, after all, Isaac."

Which Isaac knew. Backstroke specialist Sabrina had a girlfriend back home who had opted not to fly to Spain.

"If anything else happens," Luke said, "let me know."

Isaac nodded but was suddenly exhausted. "Yeah. Listen, I gotta go take a nap. We just needed to get away from whatever was happening out there."

"Are you all right, Tim?" Luke asked.

Tim didn't look all right. He looked shaken up. But he nodded.

"Let's get out of here," Isaac insisted.

CHAPTER 8

Transcript: Men's 400 Individual Medley Finals

O'TOOLE: Let's take a look at the contenders. In Lane One, we've got Carlo Pereira from Brazil.

DAVIS: Fifth-fastest time in the world this year.

O'TOOLE: Powerful swimmer. Not sure he has what it takes to keep up with some of the top guys in this field, though. In Lane Eight, we have Chiang Hsu from China.

DAVIS: He won the World Championships in this event last year. His prelim time wasn't that fast, so he's going to have to really turn it on if he wants a shot at a medal.

O'TOOLE: In Lane Two, one of the Americans, this is Duncan Schmidt in his first Olympics. Twenty-year-old swimmer from Cal Berkeley.

DAVIS: I like his chances here. He swam the fourth-fastest time in the prelims.

O'TOOLE: In Lane Seven, Adam McKeown from Australia. I'm genuinely surprised to see him here. His butterfly is a little slow. But he's one of the best breast-strokers in the world, though, so if he can utilize that to compensate, he might have an outside shot at a medal. I like him better for the breaststroke races, though.

Expect him to be a real challenge for Isaac Flood later this week.

DAVIS: I'd say he's Flood's chief competition, actually. Him and Pearson.

O'TOOLE: Lane Three, we've got Francois LeBlanc from France.

DAVIS: He's the reigning world champion.

O'TOOLE: He looked solid in prelims. I'd say he's the favorite here. In Lane Six, Peter North from South Africa.

DAVIS: He was the world junior champion two years ago.

O'TOOLE: Less experience than the other swimmers in this field, but he had a great prelim swim. Lane Five, David Hocking, a phenom swimmer out of Great Britain.

DAVIS: He was the silver medalist in this event four years ago. He has since hired a new coach and completely changed his training regimen, and it seems to be paying off here in Madrid.

O'TOOLE: Absolutely. And, finally, in Lane Four, Isaac Flood.

DAVIS: Listen to that crowd! They love him here.

O'TOOLE: As they should. He was one of the top qualifiers in the prelims. He looks better now than he did at the Trials even.

DAVIS: That's his mother, Rebecca, up there in the audience. And a small cheering section, it looks like!

O'TOOLE: See the *Here comes the Flood* signs? Brings you back, doesn't it?

DAVIS: No one expected him to be here, after everything he's been through. But here he is, and I think he's got a great shot at a medal.

O'TOOLE: All right. They are up on the blocks. And they're off!

DAVIS: Oh, Flood got a great start off the block. He got right off and into the water. That's what you gotta do if you want a shot against these other sprinters.

O'TOOLE: But this is really an endurance race.

DAVIS: True. Flood has always been a brilliant middle-distance swimmer. He's got a knack for timing and knows how to pace himself.

O'TOOLE: He looks great now, heading into the second turn. He's second as we move into the backstroke lap.

DAVIS: He's right there with the front of the field as it starts to separate a little. That Flood is keeping up with the leaders at this point is amazing. Butterfly is his weakest stroke. Oh, look at this!

O'TOOLE: Flood is gaining on LeBlanc!

DAVIS: And we're into the breaststroke lap.

O'TOOLE: And Flood is pulling ahead!

DAVIS: The challenge is going to be if he can hang on to his lead. If he gets tired and doesn't keep up this pace during the freestyle lap, he's done. A number of the swimmers in this field are faster freestylers.

O'TOOLE: The trick is to get a wide lead over the rest of the field now, on his best stroke, so that no one can catch him. That certainly seems to be his strategy.

DAVIS: It's a good lead he's building. About half a body length now.

O'TOOLE: I never thought we'd see this. He looks great in the water. The crowd is going bananas.

DAVIS: He's almost an entire body length in front of the rest of the field going into the last lap. Right at the world-record pace.

O'TOOLE: I don't think he'll hold on to that wide a lead in the last lap, but it's going to be an amazing finish.

DAVIS: And we're into the last lap. Flood is still ahead by a good amount, but LeBlanc is gaining on him. And here's Hsu in Lane Eight. He wants that medal too.

O'TOOLE: McKeown is falling back. He was in third going into that last turn, but he's fallen off the pace.

DAVIS: I can't believe it! Flood is still in the lead. LeBlanc is right behind him, swimming hard. He's closing up that lead, but I think it's going to be Flood as we move into the last twenty-five meters.

O'TOOLE: It's the Olympic Games! Anything is possible!

DAVIS: LeBlanc is coming up on Flood. I don't think he can catch him, though. And it's... it's Flood!

O'TOOLE: I don't believe it. Isaac Flood wins gold! LeBlanc gets the silver and Hsu gets the bronze.

DAVIS: That was amazing. Let's take another look at the start. Do you see how Flood explodes off the block? He's off and in the water almost immediately, and he stays underwater until about the ten-meter mark. You'll see, McKeown has already taken two strokes by then. Flood conserves his energy, but he still looks great in this butterfly lap. He gets his arms over his head but keeps most of his body in the water, and he's not kicking very hard.

O'TOOLE: But he won this race in the breast-stroke. That's his bread and butter. He just flies through this lap, opening up a wide lead over everyone else in the field.

DAVIS: And then he beats everyone to the finish.

O'TOOLE: Isaac Flood showed us, never count him out.

ISAAC FLOATED at the end of the pool, still not believing he'd actually pulled it off. His time, 4:05.8, was off the world record, which he remembered was 4:03-something, but that was still faster than he'd swum in practice in months. Somewhere, Adam must have been apoplectic.

He got out of the pool. He knew it would be bad form to dodge reporter Mindy Somers standing near the locker room entrance, so he let himself be maneuvered into the camera frame as the rest of the swimmers talked to reporters or filtered back to the warm-up area.

He could not catch his breath—his whole body felt like it was on fire, and his stomach was unsettled. But the burn felt good. He could still do this.

Mindy Somers was vaguely familiar, but Isaac couldn't put together if she was a former swimmer or just a sports reporter who'd been kicking around the network's pool of commentators for a while. But she was definitely American, given the network logo on her bright pink polo·shirt and her accent.

"Congratulations, Isaac. How do you feel?"

"I feel good," Isaac said. "I feel really good. That was a great swim."

"That was your seventh gold medal and your tenth medal overall. And it looks like you'll have a shot at even more medals. How do you feel about your odds here?"

Isaac hated answering these questions, and he still hadn't caught his breath, so he panted through his canned answers. "I like my odds. I've been training hard for over a year."

"And I hear you're doing a leg in the four-by-one-hundred relay."

"Yeah, they decided I should be on the team, I guess."

"That final is coming up in about an hour. Are you good for it?"

Isaac shook out his arms. "You know, I really am. I'm gonna go get in the warm-up pool to stay loose, and I should be good."

"Then I won't keep you. Congratulations again."

Isaac nodded and walked off.

When he walked into the warm-up area, the gathered American swimmers and coaches shouted and cheered for him.

Isaac lost it.

The tears stung his eyes. He ran a hand over his face to keep his emotions in check, but it was a futile cause, because as soon as he saw Adam's tear-streaked face, Isaac wept.

He'd done it. He'd hit rock bottom and then crawled all the way back. Good God, he'd won a gold medal.

"I've never fucking seen you swim that well," Adam said. "Good start, tight turns, near-perfect form." Then Adam threw himself around Isaac, pulling him into a tight hug. "We're going to do this. We really are. I'm so fucking proud of you." He pulled away and slapped Isaac on the ass. "Okay, get in the pool. You're swimming again in an hour."

A BUNCH of athletes partied in the lounge on Tim's floor in the Athlete Village. Jason was there, flirting with a pretty woman, as were most of the American dive and synchronized swimming teams, plus a bunch of people Tim didn't know. They were arranged in a crescent around the TV in the middle of the room, which showed swimming.

The words *Men's 400m Individual Medley* flashed across the screen, so Tim had made it just in time.

The screen panned across the audience at the Aquatics Center. A bunch of people in USA T-shirts were holding up signs that said *HERE COMES THE FLOOD!*

"I wish I had a slogan," someone said.

"It helps to have a punny name," said the girl Jason was flirting with.

Jason looked up. "Oh, hey, Tim."

"Like Timothy Swan," said the girl, grinning at Tim. "There's gotta be a pun there somewhere. Swan dive?"

Tim shook his head. It wasn't the first time some-one had tried to pun his name. He settled onto the floor at the feet of a couple of the female divers. One of them, Ginny—America's best hope for an individual springboard medal—rubbed Tim's shoulders and said, "Hi, Timmy."

"Hi, Ginny."

Onscreen, the buzzer sounded and the race got off. Tim spent the next three minutes anxiously watching the screen, leaning to the left or right as if that would help Isaac go faster. He felt sick in the pit of his stomach, fearing that Isaac would lose. But he wanted Isaac to win. Isaac deserved this win. He needed it.

"So let me get this straight," one of the athletes Tim didn't know said. He had an Australian accent. "Isaac Flood quit swimming."

"Retired," said Ginny.

"Fine, retired," said the Australian guy. "Then he takes up drinking instead of swimming. Gets himself arrested. Goes to rehab. Then he just comes back and wins a gold medal?"

"Proves anyone can do it," Ginny said. "Even you, Colin."

The Australian guy balked. "That gold medal has my name on it."

"Which event?" Tim asked.

"I'm diving against you, mate," Colin said. "Individual platform."

"Oh. Okay."

"Okay? That's all?"

"Tim is very low-key," said Ginny.

"Which events are you doing?" asked Colin.

"Platform synchro, and then both individual events," said Tim. "I'm stronger on platform. Just so you know."

The whole room went, "Oooh."

On screen, Isaac pulled ahead in his race. Tim had his gaze trained on Lane Four, where Isaac, in a blue cap and blue swimsuit, swam for his life.

"Look at this guy," said Artie, one of the other American divers. "I mean, Flood is amazing. I heard he won a medal with a hangover at the last Olympics."

"I think," said Ginny, "now that he's clean, he's unstoppable."

Tim couldn't really hear the commentary on screen over the chatter in the lounge, but he could hear the enthusiasm. It was like watching a soccer match in Spanish. He half expected someone to shout, "GOOOAL" when Isaac hit the wall.

Instead, Isaac touched first and the whole room erupted in cheers.

Tim's heart pounded. Isaac had won. Isaac had *won*. He had a gold medal.

Onscreen, Isaac looked up at the scoreboard and looked baffled for a moment before he lifted up and slapped the water.

"He's dreamy," Ginny said. "Anyone know what his deal is? Single or—?"

"If Isaac Flood had a girlfriend," said Ginny's synchro partner, Kayla, "I think we'd all know about it."

Tim kept his mouth shut, not the least because it had just dawned on him that Isaac winning a gold medal meant that they'd be having sex. Tim wanted that palpably. The thought alone made his skin tingle, and his stomach bubbled with anticipation. The screen now somewhat lovingly showed the whole length of Isaac's body as he got out of the pool, from his swim-cap-tousled hair to his broad shoulders, flat, muscular chest, tight abs, narrow hips, legs that went on forever. God, Isaac's chest. Tim loved it, couldn't wait to get his hands on it later. A lot of swimmers looked like that, but there was something about Isaac's particular combination of the swimmer's body, the long arms, his great height, and his movie-star face that made him particularly appealing.

"Good Lord," said Ginny, echoing Tim's thoughts.

Tim wondered, if the press was interested in Isaac enough to determine if he had a girlfriend, what would they do if he had a boyfriend? Could being with Isaac invite more of the press attention Tim wanted no part of?

Maybe he was getting ahead of himself. Likely this was an Olympic romance. He'd fly back to Colorado and Isaac would fly back to North Carolina, and they'd never see each other again. So why not have as much fun as possible in the meantime? They were relatively safe in the Athlete Village, away from the prying eyes of the media, which wasn't allowed beyond each country's designated public space. Hell, even the families of the athletes weren't allowed in the dorms.

"He's going to swim again tonight," Ginny said.

"So?" said Colin. Tim detected a little jealousy in his tone. Maybe he was sweet on Ginny.

"So, as swimmers age, it takes their bodies longer to break down the lactic acid in their system. So it's actually kind of dangerous for swimmers over thirty to sprint so close together."

"Isaac is twenty-nine," said Kayla. "He went to UNC with my sister."

"I'm so jealous of your sister," said Ginny. "Flood was really cute as a kid. But he's dead sexy now."

Colin was glaring daggers at the screen.

Tim laughed softly.

"Come on, Timmy, you have to agree," Ginny said.

"That Isaac Flood is dead sexy?" said Tim, deciding to play along. "I agree 100 percent. And now he has a gold medal, which makes him even sexier."

"Do *you* have a gold medal, Colin?" asked Ginny.

Colin looked like he wanted to kill someone. Probably Isaac. "No," he grumbled.

"*I* have one," said Tim, enjoying himself. "Technically, Isaac has seven of them now."

"Flood is a wanker," Colin said.

CHAPTER 9

BACK AT the Aquatics Center, Isaac climbed out of the warm-up pool. He felt good. A fair amount of excitement and adrenaline flowed through his system from his win earlier. Adam walked over and said, "Think you can swim a hundred meters in forty-eight seconds or less?"

"In my sleep."

"Good, you're swimming anchor."

Isaac nodded. The other guys were ready to go, standing in their coats at the American Lounge corner. Isaac located his caps and goggles, and then Adam helped him into his coat. He walked into the little holding room where the athletes had to wait until the announcer summoned each team. Isaac slipped his headphones over his ears and reached into his coat pocket for his phone, starting the white noise app. He took a deep breath and tried to calm down, to focus. It was one thing to swim his own race, but he had three other guys depending on him now.

Luckily, they all knew better than to talk to him once the headphones were on.

Adam slapped each of them on the back, and then an official gave them the signal to walk out. Luke grabbed Isaac's hand, so Isaac grabbed Randy's, and all four of them raised their hands together as they walked through the pool entrance. They were a team, the gesture was supposed to say.

They were expected to win.

Isaac tuned out the crowd noise and everything else except for the pool in front of him. The Americans were in Lane Six, which wasn't the best lane assignment, but the prelim team had qualified third overall, and this was the placement they were stuck with.

Adam had assigned Conor to the first lap, so he got ready, got up on the block, and went when the buzzer sounded. Isaac still had about two minutes to collect himself, so he kept his headphones on and took a few cleansing breaths. He shrugged out of his coat as Conor returned and exchanged with Luke. Randy walked over to the block. Isaac watched Randy as he finished stripping and pulled his second cap on. Isaac did the prerace dance as Luke and Randy exchanged. He had no notion of where the team swam in the race relative to the other teams, although now Luke and Conor were standing at the edge cheering Randy on. Isaac stepped up on the block. Isaac saw from that vantage point that Randy had a healthy lead, a good body length and a half ahead of the next nearest swimmer, although Isaac couldn't really tell who was where in the outside lanes.

Still, this should be no sweat. It was Isaac's race to lose.

Isaac told himself he could only swim his own race. He got into position as Randy approached; then he jumped into the water when Randy touched the wall.

And he swam.

He pretended it was practice, that Adam and his damned stopwatch stood at the edge of the pool and not his teammates, that he raced against the clock and not seven other swimmers. He got to the turn and didn't look. When he turned his head to breathe, he just breathed and didn't try to see what was happening in the neighboring lanes. The not-looking approach had worked for him in the medley.

He came home, threw out his hand on the last stroke, and hit the wall.

When he surfaced, his teammates were whooping and hopping up and down. Luke reached down and grabbed his hand in a manly handshake. Isaac looked around in a daze. The scoreboard showed that they'd won by almost four seconds, and that Isaac had swum that lap in forty-eight flat.

You're welcome, Adam.

Isaac was fucking tired now, though. His body ached. His limbs were jelly. His first attempt to get out of the pool ended with his arms giving out and him slipping back into the water. His teammates had to essentially lift him out of the pool.

They all got themselves collected before Mindy Somers in her pink polo snagged them. Her assistant arranged all four guys in the camera frame and gave them strict orders not to move.

"Hi, guys!" Mindy said perkily, glancing back at the camera. "Congratulations. How does it feel?"

She shoved her microphone at Isaac, so he said, "Great!" even though it took everything in him not to collapse.

Thankfully, she moved on to Luke. "This is your third Olympics, Luke. You missed the gold medal four years ago by hundredths of a second. How does it feel to be back on top?"

"Good, great!" said Luke, still panting.

"Randy, this is your first Olympics. Now you've got a gold medal. And on a team with legends like Luke Rogers and, of course, Isaac Flood."

"I watched," he panted, "the Olympics," pant, pant, "when I was a kid." Poor Randy really tried to draw in a breath, but he was also giddy enough to make that impossible. "I mean, I saw," pant, pant, "Isaac's first gold medal, you know? I was so inspired." Wheeze, pant. "And now to be here with him?" Pant, pant. "Incredible!"

Mindy turned to Conor. "When Isaac Flood won his first gold medal, you were four years old."

"Aw, don't tell me that," Isaac said.

Conor laughed breathily. "Yeah. Crazy, right?"

"Well, I have to kick it back to Nick and Dan in the booth. Thanks, guys! Congrats again!"

Isaac and his teammates stumbled back to the warm-up pool. Isaac hopped in to swim a cool-down, but he just floated there for a few long minutes as Luke swam a lap and came back.

"Are you dying now?" Luke asked.

"Pretty much."

"That was an incredible thing you just did, by the way. I don't think I could swim two final races in the same night."

"I'm pretty sure my muscles are melting."

"Come on, Flood. Do your laps, cool down your body, and try to keep upright when they put the big medals around your neck."

Isaac groaned.

"You know what else this means, don't you? Two gold medals in the same night?"

Isaac did know. Prior to his arrival in Madrid, he'd been toxic. Going into the previous Olympics, there had been glossy media profiles, interviews on all the network shows, commercials, piles of endorsement deals. His face had been in nearly every Olympics promo spot the network had done.

This year? Bupkes.

Oh, he got the gear guaranteed to anyone who made Team USA, and he wasn't alone among his teammates in not having endorsement deals or sponsorships.

But he thought about that as he swam a slow lap in the warm-up pool, willing the burn in his body to fade. Phelps had still gotten endorsements for his last Olympics, and he'd had a DUI on his record too. But Isaac wasn't Michael Phelps. He wasn't as cute or charming. He wasn't a leader like Phelps had been. Wasn't really a team player. He'd cultivated a reputation for partying hard. The Bad Boy of Swimming, they'd called him, though he hardly thought he qualified as a bad boy. Aside from the DUI, he'd never gotten in trouble with the law. He didn't have tattoos, save for the Olympics rings on his ass, something he'd done after his second Olympics, while drunk. At least no one could see that, since it was under his swimsuit. The media generally had treated Phelps well, like someone who made a mistake, but once it surfaced that Isaac had been a full-on alcoholic, it was over. Rather than partying, he'd wasted his peak years trying to drown himself in a bottle of vodka. He'd also somewhat famously taken home a one-night stand who had stolen one of his medals, although he'd gotten it back when she'd stupidly put it up on an online auction site. So maybe some of the bad press was deserved, although his mother often tried to tell him he'd gotten a bad break.

But he'd just changed everything with less than a minute in a pool.

When he climbed out of the pool, Adam and one of the other coaches were waiting for him.

"How do you feel?" Adam asked.

"Like I'm dying." And Lord, he wanted a drink.

"Here's the deal. Medal ceremonies are in about fifteen minutes, so that's how long you have to pull yourself together. Wear the warm-up suit with the red sleeves."

"I have a warm-up suit with red sleeves?"

"It's in your locker."

"Okay."

"We've gotten six media requests, but I imagine you're wiped out now, so I've put them all off until tomorrow. But your first is the morning show at nine o'clock. You have to be there at least a half hour before that."

"Oy. That's...." He glanced up at the clock. "Ten hours from now. And I still have to do a medal ceremony?"

"Well, you have to stand on the podium to get your medals."

Isaac sighed. "All right."

"And be back here tomorrow at noon to do the 400 free prelims."

"Of course."

"Sheri will put together an itinerary for you." Sheri was the assistant to USA Swimming. She generally handled logistics for the whole team.

"All right."

Adam stared at Isaac for a moment; then he pulled Isaac into a hug. He slapped Isaac's back a bunch of times. "You did good, kid."

"Thanks."

On the walk back to the locker room, he thought of Tim. Most likely he wouldn't ever be able to cross the threshold of this locker room again without thinking of Tim. And he wanted Tim here. He wanted Tim in his arms. He wanted someone to share this with. The sentiment didn't quite cancel out his desire for a drink, but it was still strong. On the other hand, he'd won not just one gold medal, but two, and he intended to make good on their agreement. As soon as his limbs started working like they were supposed to again.

He found his locker, next to Luke's, and got it open. A warm-up suit with red sleeves did indeed hang from the bar in the middle.

"Good Lord," Isaac said.

Luke slapped his back. "Welcome to the rest of your life, Flood."

TIM WAS dozing when his phone beeping startled him awake. He glanced at it.

Text from Isaac: *Twice.*

A moment later Isaac sent a photo, a shirtless selfie with two gold medals hanging from his neck.

"Oh my God," Tim said aloud.

He'd seen the individual medley, but then he'd gone back to his room to lie down for a little while, tired and irritated by the other guys crowding around the TV in the lounge. He'd completely forgotten that Isaac was scheduled to swim in the relay.

Do you plan to celebrate tonight? Tim texted.

A long delay passed before Isaac texted back. *The guys from the relay team are. I should for team unity. Then I gotta rest because I have more races tomorrow.*

Tim found that disappointing, but then, he'd also been hoping Isaac would want to spend the night with Tim to celebrate.

Miss you, Tim texted. Then he regretted it, because of all the needy, clingy things to say....

But Isaac texted back a smile emoji. Then he said, *Come to my room tonight. 308. I'll text you when I get there.*

Tim grinned at his phone. *Wouldn't miss it for anything.*

Tim hauled himself out of bed and into the shower, wondering idly where Jason had gotten to. Probably hooking up with whoever had caught his fancy this evening. Their first event was the next day, but Tim had already decided spending the night with Isaac was more important than sleep, so he'd be a hypocrite if he called out Jason for doing the same. He'd track Jason down in the morning.

About twenty minutes after Tim got out of the shower, he got the text from Isaac summoning him to room 308. It was one floor down from Tim's room; the American delegation took an entire building in the college-dorms-on-steroids complex that made up the Athlete Village. The whole building was an explosion of stars and stripes, the bland white walls of the hallways festooned with flags and posters, and more flags hanging over the balconies attached to each of the suites.

Tim took the stairs, which meant he passed two track runners who seemed to be running drills up and down the steps for fun.

He got to Isaac's room and knocked. Isaac opened the door and practically yanked him in. Then Tim found himself crushed against the closed door and kissed within an inch of his life.

When Isaac finally eased off, Tim said, "Why, hello."

Isaac smiled. "Hi."

"Um, congratulations?"

"Thank you."

"Two medals, huh? So you're an overachiever."

"Two *gold* medals. You said I only had to win *one* gold medal."

"So I did. But you're probably tired."

Tim had meant it sarcastically, but Isaac nodded. "I can barely move."

"Oh," said Tim.

"Believe me. If I thought I could muster enough energy to fuck you senseless, I'd be doing it right now. But I have to be up again in…." Isaac looked at his phone. "Six hours, Jesus."

"Practice?"

"Morning television."

Tim laughed. "Really?"

"Everyone wants to interview me. 'Swimming's bad boy wins two gold medals.' That's an actual headline."

"You're a bad boy?"

Isaac shrugged. His face sobered, and he added, "I really wanted to see you tonight, though. Is that strange?"

"No. Not at all. I watched your first race. I wish I'd been there at the Aquatics Center to celebrate with you."

Isaac smiled. "I wish you'd been there too."

"Good thing we're here together now."

"Yeah. I'm very glad you came down here. But is it okay if we just sleep?"

Tim could the exhaustion in Isaac's eyes. And it was only Day 2. "Yeah, we can sleep."

"You'll recall that the agreement was not that we'd have sex immediately, but that winning a gold medal allowed me to dictate when and where. So, basically, not tonight, but as soon as my arms stop feeling like spaghetti noodles, it's on."

Tim smiled and put his hands on Isaac's shoulders. "Reasonable."

Isaac grinned. "Glad you think so."

CHAPTER 10

Day 3

IT HAD been a while since Isaac had done the interview circuit. A couple of years of being persona non grata would do that. Sheri came with him to the Olympic Broadcast Center. The drive over was lovely—the car took them through the Salamanca district, and Isaac realized he was seeing more of Madrid than he'd seen since the bus ride from the airport.

Madrid had many sports venues peppered throughout the city, so some of the Olympic events were being staged miles away from each other. The car passed by the WiZink Center, or the Palacio de Deportes, as everyone called it, which the signage out front indicated was the home of Olympic Basketball. In a lot of ways, this section of Madrid could have been any European city Isaac had been to—London, Dublin, Paris, Berlin—but it also had some interesting architectural flourishes, from the curved balconies overlooking the street to the church-like towers atop many of the buildings. Isaac didn't really have the vocabulary to describe it all, but he liked it and thought it was pretty. If only he had a camera.

He could have turned on his phone, but since last night's medal ceremony, every time he had, it buzzed nonstop with text messages, voicemails, and social media alerts. Isaac appreciated the outpouring of love, but it was too much to deal with right now.

"They set up the broadcast center in an office building off El Retiro Park," Sheri said. "The park is gorgeous, by the way. Sort of like Central Park in New York."

"Okay."

"You should walk around a little after the interview."

"I have to get back. I have a prelim race early this afternoon."

"Right, right. Next week, then, after the swimming is over. If you need a ride anywhere, let me know. Cab fare is on USA Swimming."

"I may take you up on that. I've never been to Madrid before." Although he wondered if she'd even offer if he didn't have those two gold medals currently hanging around his neck, tucked under his official USA windbreaker, because after a couple of years of living in a shitty apartment in a shitty neighborhood in Raleigh, he was in the habit of not conspicuously displaying anything someone might want to steal.

There were some people, sports fans maybe, lingering outside the broadcast center, some of whom had posters and signs. One of the posters read *Here comes the Flood!* so Isaac supposed they had heard about his imminent arrival. Then it became clear all of the fans were there for him.

"Holy shit," he said.

"Flood! Isaac! Can you sign?"

He signed some of the things that were thrust at him, including the *Here comes the Flood!* sign, a couple of old T-shirts, and a few posters that showed his body, and then Sheri herded him inside.

All of the nations broadcasting from Madrid had different studios set up throughout the building, including the American network, up on the sixteenth floor. A PA led Isaac and Sheri into a greenroom, where a sumptuous feast was laid out. It looked especially amazing because he had only had a yogurt for breakfast, and his stomach rumbled now. Earlier it had seemed more important to stay in bed, curled around Tim, than to get up. So he'd had to grab whatever was available from the snack bar in the lobby of his dorm building.

Tim had looked so sleepy and happy that morning. His face was angelic in the early morning light. When Isaac's alarm had gone off, he'd lifted his head, smiled at Isaac, and then gone back to sleep. His body was soft and warm and fit nicely against Isaac's, so Isaac had been reluctant to leave. He'd gotten out of the building and met Sheri and her car just in the nick of time.

And, well, maybe it was time to admit that he was falling for Tim.

But that didn't matter now, because he had to talk about gold medals with the perky blond reporter who anchored the network's morning show.

Sheri sat with him on a mustard-colored sofa while they waited for his name to be called. She said, "You nervous?"

"A little," Isaac said. He wasn't "the race is about to start" nervous, but he was concerned he'd get tongue-tied or say something stupid.

"Just answer the questions. They've been briefed that they're not to ask about your past. This should be a breeze."

Well, there it was. On the one hand, Isaac didn't need his dirty laundry aired, but on the other, his alcoholism was a key part of his identity now. It should have been a part of this story, but maybe it was better not to rock the boat. The USOC and the American media wanted to keep a glossy sheen on everything, allowing nothing controversial or scandalous to grace their airwaves. He'd read that officials from the World Anti-Doping Agency had been invited to ensure there was no cheating, which struck Isaac as a lot of theater and not actually an effective way to rid competitive sports of performance-enhancing drugs. But he could play along and give a few platitudes, keep it simple and shallow, and keep the turmoil to himself, even if talking about it might help someone watching on TV. Still, talking about this with anyone made Isaac feel naked, like that cop was pulling him out of his car while he was drunk all over again. God, he hated this whole thing.

He nodded to Sheri.

Another PA escorted him onto the set a few minutes later. A monitor in the corner indicated the network was currently airing commercials, so Isaac had a minute to sit and settle on the overstuffed white leather sofa. A large coffee table loomed in front of him. A coffee cup with the network's logo on it sat on a coaster. It seemed to hold water, but Isaac would have killed for a hot, black cup of coffee. Maybe they had some in the greenroom that he could make off with.

He shook off his craving and refocused on what he had to do now. The anchor walked over and settled into an armchair perpendicular to the sofa. "You ready?" she said.

"I guess so."

"These are easy questions. Don't sweat it. Okay?"

"Let's do this."

Green lights indicated the network came back on the air, and the anchor, who seemed to assume Isaac knew who she was since she didn't introduce herself, said, "Welcome back. I'm here now with American swimmer Isaac Flood, who has overcome a great number of obstacles to win two gold medals at last night's swimming finals. One was in the 400-meter individual medley, and the second was as anchor on the four-by-one-hundred freestyle relay. Good morning, Isaac."

"Good morning."

"You get any sleep last night?"

"Some. I have to race again this afternoon. I celebrated with the boys a little, but then I went to bed."

"You're swimming a pretty intense program at these Games. How are you feeling after the weekend?"

"Pretty good."

"It must have been hard to swim that second race so soon after the first."

"Honestly? I had so much adrenaline from the first race that it carried over to the second. I felt great during that second swim. Not so great after it, though. Still, I got a good night's sleep, so I'm ready to get in the pool again."

"I bet your coach is happy to hear that. Adam Vreeland is one of three lead coaches for Team USA. He's gained a reputation for training Olympians. You've been working with him since you were little, yeah?"

"Yes, I started taking lessons with him when I was six."

"So you've been working toward this for decades, essentially."

"Yeah, I…." Isaac hesitated, not sure how much he should say. He thought he should be honest, but he didn't want to piss off anyone who might be watching. USA Swimming had his back, but would potential sponsors? Because as much as it seemed to cheapen the experience, endorsements and sponsorship were the best way to ensure he had a source of income for the foreseeable future. "I've been working at this for a long time."

"This is your fourth Olympics. Does it feel any different this time?"

"You know, it does a little. I'll be honest, I coasted on a lot of success into the last Olympics. This time it feels more like a challenge. I've been out of the circuit for a while. I don't know my competitors the way I used to. There are a lot of young guys coming up who are amazing. Strong swimmers, fast swimmers." He let out a breath. "When everyone's calling you the favorite, there's a different kind of pressure."

"So you feel less pressure now?"

"It's a completely different kind of pressure. I'm trying to prove something to myself. That I can still do this, you know? I worked really hard to get back into competitive form, and I feel great, better than I have in a long time. So, basically, I want to show that my career's not over."

"I'd say you achieved that. Two gold medals."

"There's still a lot of swimming left."

"And we wish you the best of luck, Isaac. Next up, Doug and I will be cooking up some authentic Spanish dishes. Stay with us for complete Olympics coverage here in Madrid."

"And we're at commercials," said the director.

Isaac nodded and stood, anxious to get out of there. Then a male reporter jogged over. Isaac recognized him as one of the other morning show hosts. "Listen," the reporter said. Again, he didn't introduce himself, probably assuming Isaac would know his name, but Isaac was terrible at names. "I'd like to do a more in-depth interview with you. Hopefully we can make time for it before the end of swimming so we can air it as a lead-in. I'd wanted to do the story before the Olympics, but the network vetoed it because they thought you'd crash and burn here."

And because they were off the air, Isaac said, "I'm only a human-interest story if I win medals, huh?"

The reporter shrugged. "The network controls the narrative going into the Games. You've been around long enough to know that. We're limited to doing a set number of these packages and can only do them for athletes we think will win."

"Thanks for your faith in me."

"Hey, I thought you'd do well. This is exactly the kind of story viewers love. You hit rock bottom and then climb back up to win gold? That's an amazing story."

"So if we do this, do you want to talk about all of it? The alcoholism, the DUI, rehab, the whole thing."

"We can discuss that. The important part of the story is really you making a big comeback."

Did Isaac want to talk about it on national television? Would discussing it work out for him in the long run? "Can I think about it?"

"Sure. Here's my number." The reporter handed over a card. Marcus Holt. "Call or text me and we'll set up a time."

"All right."

Isaac pocketed the card and then a PA maneuvered him back to the green room. He poured himself a cup of coffee while Sheri clucked about how great the interview was. Then she said, "We gotta get you back. You have your stuff to go straight to the pool?"

"Yeah, my bag is in the car, remember?"

"Oh, right. Yes. I'll have Raul take us straight to the Aquatics Center."

Isaac pilfered an apple but didn't have time to add milk to his coffee before Sheri led him back out of the network's offices. But coffee was coffee, and he needed the caffeine fix more than he needed to dull the harsh taste of coffee brewed in a three-gallon urn.

On the ride back, Isaac said, "Marcus Holt wants to interview me."

"Oh, that's wonderful!" Sheri's whole face lit up. "That would be great for you."

"Well, he wants to do an interview that talks about my comeback, so I'd have to get into everything. I'd have to talk about the DUI and rehab."

"Oh. What are you going to do?"

"I don't know. That's why I brought it up. I can't tell if it's a good idea."

Sheri tilted her head and appeared to think about it. "I don't think it is. I mean, do you really want to air all that? The US Olympic team has already gotten its share of negative press. Like that gay diver who was dating the actor? You don't want that kind of attention, do you?"

It looked like now was not the time to let Sheri know he'd spent the night with that gay diver. Even if they'd only slept in each other's arms, and nothing else. "No, I guess not."

"I mean, I can't tell you what to do, but my recommendation would be to keep your head down and swim. Forget about the interview. You don't need that kind of press."

Some rebellious part of Isaac that bucked at people telling him when to shut up made him want to do the interview, but he said, "Okay. That makes sense."

A FEW quick text messages led to Tim tracking down Jason. They met at the cafeteria for breakfast.

"Sorry for not coming back last night," Jason said sheepishly as they sat down with their trays. Tim had opted for a vegetarian egg white omelet that looked delicious. Jason had a plate full of what looked like a variety of breakfast meats on top of a burrito.

"It's okay," Tim said. "I'm not your parent."

"I ran into Becky Lowood last night. She's that UK diver? The one who won the bronze at Worlds last year?"

"I know who she is, yeah."

"Anyway, she came by the lounge after you went to bed. She's good friends with Ginny and Kayla. So we got to talking. And then we kept talking… in her room. I mean, nothing really happened. We made out a little bit. But we didn't, like, go *all the way*."

Tim smiled. He found Jason's little moments of immaturity charming. "It's okay, Jason. I ended up going to see Isaac after he got back from celebrating his gold medals."

"Isaac? Flood?"

"We've been hanging out. We're friends."

Jason tilted his head. "Friends or *friends*?"

"Unclear." When Jason raised his eyebrows, Tim added, "I don't know how public this is, so don't go spreading it around, but he's bisexual. I kind of thought something would happen last night, but he was too tired. Which is fine. Besides, it's probably not a good idea to get involved with someone on the night before I have to dive."

"I guess. You like him?"

"Yeah. I like him a lot. But don't... I mean, I'm telling you this as a friend. Don't tell anyone. Isaac and I have been hanging out and texting and we like each other, but I don't really see it going anywhere. We live on opposite sides of the country."

Jason grinned. "Who cares? It's the Olympics, right? Everyone here has the dating apps on their phones turned on and is hooking up with everybody else. Ginny said the rhythmic gymnasts down the hall from her have been having a grand old time with a few of the guys from the Ukrainian rowing team."

"Ha. Isn't Ukraine one of our gymnastics rivals?"

"Isn't the Olympics all about peace and love?"

Tim grinned. "I don't know about all that."

"It's cool that Isaac won two races, though. How does he feel?"

"He's doing well. He went to the broadcast center to do an interview this morning."

"God, that's so cool. Do you think we'll be on TV if we win a medal? I mean, beyond the event broadcast."

Tim had been all over the network's programming four years ago, and he'd already filmed a package about his career heading into this Olympics. So he'd be on TV plenty, which meant Jason likely would too. "Yeah, probably."

"My dad couldn't fly down here because of work, so I hope he can watch."

Tim nodded. "My parents are staying at the same hotel as most of the press. They keep running into reporters and, like, the retired Olympians who are here to do puff pieces on the news."

"That's amazing."

Tim shrugged. It was amazing, but he'd gotten his fill of the press. "You feel ready for today?"

"Oh, yeah. I feel loose. Our practice dives this week have been pretty solid, yeah?"

"We're good, yeah. I feel pretty confident. The trick, though, is to stay loose and calm. If you get nervous, you'll tighten up and make mistakes. Maybe you don't think you'll be nervous, but I can tell you from experience that the pressure of competition? With all the people watching from the stands and the cameras and the Olympic logo everywhere? It can get to you."

"I've got my headphones in my bag."

"Good. And remember to jump up, not out, off the platform so we sync up better, like we practiced the other day."

"Of course. I got it, Timmy. We got this."

Tim appreciated Jason's confidence. "Yeah. I think maybe we do."

CHAPTER II

Transcript of TBC Olympic coverage, profile of Timothy Swan

BELL (voiceover): Timothy Swan has been hailed by many as the next Greg Louganis. He's an American diver who is universally agreed to have the most beautiful form in the air. He's the first American diver in a while not to specialize but to compete in both the platform and springboard. And he's an all-around athlete, getting his start in gymnastics and swimming before focusing on diving. This diving prodigy is a hometown boy. He grew up in Brookfield, Colorado, taking swimming, diving, and gymnastics lessons in nearby Boulder, and then he attended the University of Colorado, where he won the US Diving Championships four years in a row. He continues to train in Boulder with his coach, Donald Westfield.

SWAN: I love the mountains. It's so beautiful here.

BELL (voiceover): Four years ago, Swan achieved the impossible. At the age of twenty, he performed a series of near-perfect dives and upset the Chinese divers, universally agreed to be unbeatable. But Timothy Swan was focused and flawless, and he comes to Madrid to defend his title in the ten-meter platform.

SWAN: I think I can do well on the springboard too. I missed it four years ago by a handful of points, but it's there, that podium. I think I can get to it.

BELL (voiceover): But it's been a difficult four years. He continues to rake up medals at home, but injuries kept him off the podium at the World Championships... twice. Some have questioned whether he's still good enough to compete internationally, or if that Olympic gold medal was a fluke. And then there's this.

SWAN (in an online video): This is a hard thing to do, but it's really important for me to do it. I want my fans to know the real me. So I need to tell you, I'm gay. And this is my boyfriend, Patterson.

BELL: Do you have any regrets?

SWAN: About coming out? No. Never. Even after everything that's happened... I mean, I get letters. I got one just last week, actually. This kid is a swimmer, not a diver, but he told me... he said his parents won't approve of him, but he's gay and he wants to be an Olympic athlete, and my coming out helped him think it was possible. And that's everything, you know? If my coming out inspired only that one kid, it would be important. But I get letters like that a lot, hundreds of kids, and it's amazing.

BELL (voiceover): But not everything has been amazing. A whirlwind romance with actor Patterson Wood culminated in a marriage proposal this January. It looked like Swan was on top of the world. But his happiness was short-lived. The couple split this May, mere weeks before the US Olympic Trials.

SWAN: It was hard emotionally. But diving saved me. Getting ready for the Trials and now the Olympics helped get my mind off of what happened with my relationship.

BELL: And how is training going?

SWAN: Really well. I have a new synchro partner, Jason. He's a fantastic diver. Future of US Diving. You heard it here first.

BELL: Synchronized diving is a relatively new Olympic event. It's why a lot of divers choose to specialize in the platform or the springboard. They'll do two competitions in their specialty, the synchro and the individual. But you're still doing the individual springboard event as well.

SWAN: I decided to give it a go. I did well at Trials.

BELL (voiceover): He did so well, he was the US men's top qualifier in all of the events he entered.

BELL: You're modest.

SWAN: I'm trying to be realistic. There's a stacked field. Brilliant divers from China, Japan, Italy, England, and Australia. The medals could really go to anyone. On the one hand, it's an exciting time to be diving and to realize that I can compete with all of these men. On the other hand, it's a tough field to compete against. All I can do is keep training and put my all into it.

BELL (voiceover): Swan *is* modest, though. He's an incredibly brave young gay man who is trying, at the age of twenty-four, to dive his way to another gold medal. Will he upset the Chinese again, or are they truly unbeatable? Does he have a real shot here? We'll have to watch to find out.

Transcript: Men's Synchronized Ten-Meter Platform Final

HOLLAND: Welcome back to the Domingo Aquatics Center. I'm Al Holland, and with me is Diane Bell. We're here tonight for the finals of the men's ten-meter platform final in synchronized diving.

BELL: I like the Americans' chances in this competition, I have to say. Timothy Swan is the returning Olympic champion in the ten-meter platform. You'll remember, four years ago, he gave a spectacular final dive that edged out the Chinese divers.

HOLLAND: But you have to admit, the Chinese are pretty hard to beat.

BELL: The team of Xiao and Ting are the reigning world champions, and they've been nearly flawless in the last three years of competition. I'm not sure anyone can beat them. Timothy Swan is paired up with a relative newcomer, Jason Evans. Evans was the junior world champion, but he has very little experience at this level. They could surprise us, and they've looked good all year, but this is a very deep field.

HOLLAND: In other words, you think the Chinese are going to win gold, but the Americans have an outside shot at a medal.

BELL: Well, yes. Don't forget about the pair from Great Britain, though. They're also a factor. They've looked great all year. And the Italians are also in the hunt, with the pair of Cologna and Burghini looking very good.

HOLLAND: Before we show you round two, let's go to some highlights from round one. First up are the Italians.

BELL: These first-round dives are going to have a lower degree of difficulty, but look for the difficulty and the scores to go up each round. For this first dive, it's all about both divers being in perfect sync with each other.

HOLLAND: All right. Well, let's take a look at this dive from the Italians.

BELL: That was pretty great. Not a difficult dive. The degree of difficulty is only a 2.0. But both divers are in sync with each other. They're off the platform together and quickly get into the pike position, then roll out and both enter vertically with very little splash. That's what you want to do in your Olympic final.

HOLLAND: Still a lot more diving to go. The next pair up are Timothy Swan and Jason Evans.

BELL: Their practice sessions have looked good. Swan and Evans seem like a solid pair. Swan is a little cleaner than Evans and his form tends to be tighter. He's a beautiful diver. But if these guys can demonstrate good synchronization, they have a shot at a medal. They're doing the same first dive as the Italians.

HOLLAND: All right, here we go.

BELL: Oh, that was a great dive! You'll see when we watch it in slow motion, they're both off the platform at the same time. Evans is a little farther out from the platform than Swan, but that won't affect the score. They're very well in sync, as you'll see here. Into the pike, and then they open up at the same time and they're into the water cleanly. That was a great entry by both divers.

HOLLAND: And those scores put them ahead of the Italians....

BY ROUND three, Tim and Jason were in third place, behind the Brits and the Chinese, but the margin of difference between them was small enough that if Tim and Jason kept diving well, it was still anybody's gold medal. The degree of difficulty of Tim and Jason's last dive was higher than the Brits', so they had a good chance of at least taking the silver.

Not that Tim was obsessing about the scoreboard.

Jason preferred to ignore it. Right now, he sat at the edge of a hot tub with his headphones on, bopping his head and mouthing the lyrics to whatever he was listening to.

Donnie looked grim when he walked over. "The Chinese have basically been perfect," he said. "The Italians are right on your tail, only six points behind. If you whiff a dive, you're off the podium."

Well, gee. "I know," Tim said.

"Not that I think you will! You guys looked great out there! No major mistakes. I'm really proud of you. But just so you understand the stakes...."

"I do."

Donnie nodded. "Okay. You guys are the only divers in the competition doing the double twist in the last dive, so this might be ours if you nail it. You looked great on that last dive, but Jason was a little slow. Remind him to use his abs, get his legs right into the tuck, and get past the hurdle faster. That way at least you're better in sync."

"I will."

"Okay, good." Donnie looked back at Jason. "What the hell is he listening to?"

Tim followed Donnie's gaze. Jason looked nearly ecstatic as he mouthed the words to some song. He put a hand over his ears and mimicked being in a recording booth.

"Who knows?" Tim said. "If it keeps him from getting too nervous, that's all that matters."

"Yeah. That's what's doing the Russians in. Did you see them?"

"No."

"They're very nervous. Really tight. They're not completing their rotations and are going in sideways. Same thing has been happening to that Australian pair."

"Sherman and Colin? But they're so good."

"It's the Olympics. Nothing is preordained. Keep that in mind. Don't get cocky."

"No. I don't feel cocky."

"Good."

The one thing that sucked about competition at this level was that the waiting time between dives could be lengthy. Divers dawdled at the top of the platform, trying to calm their nerves. Judges seemed to agonize over scores, sometimes taking their own sweet time to post them. A few divers had balked, getting to the edge of the platform and then hopping back as if they were suddenly afraid. While it wasn't illegal, judges tended to frown on that if the actual dive fell short of perfect. So it was a challenge to stay warm, and that was why there were showers and hot tubs near the platforms. Still, it was difficult to keep nerves in check if you had to wait a half hour between dives.

As he and Jason lined up for their last dive, Tim wondered if Isaac was watching. The prelim swimming had been wrapping up on the other side of the Aquatics Center when the diving finals began, but Tim hadn't seen Isaac since that morning. Likely he'd gone back to the Athlete Village to nap.

It was probably just as well.

They had 402 points heading into their last dive. They'd been in the second spot going into the final, so they were diving second-to-last, before the Chinese. That was good news; they wouldn't have to wait long for the final result. But they were going to need ninety points to win a medal. The Italians currently had 485.5 points and the Brits had 490.6.

At the top of the platform, Jason nudged Tim with his shoulder. "We got this."

"If we win gold tonight," Tim said, "Isaac will sleep with me. We have a deal."

"Guess we better win, then."

Jason held up his fist, so Tim bumped it. They walked forward to the edge of the platform.

The dive was ridiculously difficult. In fact, it had the highest difficulty in the competition. The Chinese had a higher cumulative difficulty score, but this dive was Tim and Jason's trump card. They'd been routinely nailing the dive in practice, but it had been shy of perfect in competition all year. They jumped backward, did two and a half somersaults in the air, then straightened out to twist twice before hitting the water. Completing the rotations and the twists took every bit of strength Tim had. That they had to do the dive at the same time in perfect synchronization made all of it that much tougher.

But this dive was in their grasp. Jason seemed more relaxed than Tim, which was a good sign. And really, Isaac was only a factor here insofar as he was on Tim's mind. Tim knew they'd sleep together before the Olympics ended, probably several times, and he was eager for it.

But now he had to dive.

He and Jason stood in position at the edge of the platform. "Ready?" Tim asked.

"Yes."

"Okay. One, two, three, go."

Then they were in the air. Tim could see Jason out of the corner of his eye, but he flew and had to maintain control. He used his core strength to pull into the tuck, hurled himself around twice, pulled out into the twist, caught sight of Jason again—who was right there beside him—sighted the water, and went in.

He'd gone in straight. The dive felt good. No major mistakes.

When he surfaced, Jason was screaming.

"Oh my God!" Jason said. "Oh, my God, we did it!"

What they'd done remained to be seen, but it seemed like they'd dived successfully. Jason knew as well as anyone that if you did it wrong, you could feel it.

They both swam to the side of the pool and got out, but Jason was still pumped, jumping up and down and shouting. He pulled Tim into a hug.

Tim slung an arm around Jason and walked him back away from the pool so they could wait for the score to come in. Donnie approached with a grin on his face. "Amazing, you guys. Just amazing. I've never seen you dive like that in competition. That's gotta get you nines, at least."

Jason turned toward the scoreboard. Tim wanted to ward off disappointment, but he turned as well.

Score for the last dive: 92.6. That put them at 494.8 for the day, which shot them into first place.

"Only the Chinese left," Donnie said.

For a brief moment Tim pictured himself on top of that podium again, someone draping that gold medal around his neck. His pulse shot up, his heart pounded, and the image was so vivid, he felt like he could have reached out and touched it.

He watched on the monitor as the Chinese divers walked to the edge of the platform. Their dive had a slightly lower degree of difficulty, but it was tenths of a point, so if they executed it better than Tim and Jason had done their dive, the gold was theirs. They also started backward, hurled off the platform, pulled into pikes, did two and a half somersaults before pulling out into a twist and entering the water. They executed the dive as if they were mirror images of each other, the most perfect dive synchronization Tim had ever seen. And they went into the water perfectly vertical with impossibly small splashes.

"They'll win the gold," Tim said, feeling a little defeated.

"But you'll win a silver," said Donnie. "That's not a small thing."

It wasn't. And when the Chinese score went up—94.5, giving them an overall score of 496.2 for the day—Tim tried to be excited that he and Jason were the second-greatest dive team in the world.

The final scores were posted, with Tim and Jason in silver-medal position, and Jason lost his goddamned mind, jumping and hopping and hugging Tim, and Tim found his enthusiasm so infectious that he forgot all about the Chinese and went with it.

He'd won a medal at the Olympics. Donnie was right; that wasn't a small thing.

CHAPTER 12

THE DIVE team seemed reluctant to party until the early hours, since the women had their individual springboard preliminary rounds the next day, so Tim called it an early night. Besides, he and Jason had to get up early to go on TBC's morning talk show. The car was picking them up at eight. Plus, now that the adrenaline had worn off, Tim was exhausted.

But when he got back to his room, he found a note slid under his door. "It's not a gold, but I'll accept it. Room 308. I'm there all night."

"Well?" Jason asked.

"I'm gonna go see Isaac."

"Good luck." Jason winked.

"You won't... I mean, if you hook up with that British diver, you won't mention this, will you?"

"My lips are sealed. I promise not to tell anyone."

"Thanks. I appreciate it."

Tim gave Jason a hug again, congratulated him on the medal, and went upstairs.

Isaac opened the door with a grin. He held the door open for Tim this time instead of yanking him in for a kiss, which was a little disappointing, except the fatigue was starting to settle in. So Tim breathed deeply and took in Isaac and the room. Isaac wore a faded USA Swimming T-shirt and a pair of blue warm-up pants. He looked good, relaxed, a little disheveled.

"Did you race tonight?" Tim asked.

"Yes, but it was just a semifinal. I'll win another medal tomorrow." He grinned. "You, however, have won a silver in an event the guys on TV didn't think you had a shot in."

Tim balked. "Really? They said that?"

"I watched the American broadcast in the lounge between sessions today. Mostly they kept pointing out that Jason was untested at this level of competition and they thought he'd get nervous and tense up."

"Somehow he didn't. I think I was more nervous."

Isaac smiled. "Where's your medal?"

"In my room... which I'll have to return to in the morning. I'm supposed to rendezvous with Jason before we go to the broadcast center for interviews."

"That'll be fun." Isaac led Tim into the room and pointed at the bed, so Tim sat. He was thankful for it, leaning back and relaxing into the mattress, willing himself to stay awake because he didn't want to fall asleep and miss a moment with Isaac.

Isaac didn't sit, though. Instead he paced along the length of the bed, hovering over Tim, and said, "Speaking of TV appearances, here's a puzzle for you. Marcus Holt wants to do an in-depth interview with me."

"The guy from *Wake Up, America!*? Does he want to talk about rehab and all that?"

"I think so. He wants to put the emphasis on my recovery, but I think it's only really worth doing if I talk about the whole shebang. I can't decide if I should, though. Like, do I talk about everything I went through? On one hand, it might be good to get it all out there.

On the other hand, all my business will be out there. I'm starting to get calls about endorsement deals and sponsorships again, and I don't want to jeopardize that. I feel like talking about the last three years will only remind people that I'm an alcoholic, and that's not exactly the guy you want repping your sports apparel brand, you know?" Isaac sighed and sat on the bed finally. "It may depend on how the next few days play out."

"Okay." Tim tried to come up with something better to say. Which path was correct? Tim could see arguments for doing the interview—being honest, possibly helping someone watching at home who struggled with the same demons Isaac had. Or staying mum—keeping the public out of his private life and earning some money. Tim's own endorsement and sponsorship money paid his mortgage because it was hard to hold down a job when he was training, so he understood why that money would be important. He shook his head, unable to come up with any decent answer to the question.

"Do you think I should do it?" asked Isaac.

"That's really up to you. I mean, I think it could be great. You could be an inspiration to someone struggling. This could be the move that makes your career. Or not. I don't really know." Tim bit his lip because he thought there were two possible outcomes to the interview: either everyone would drop Isaac like he was a toxic hot potato, or everyone would see what an inspiration he was and fully embrace him. And if the first thing happened, Tim didn't want to be the one who'd talked Isaac into doing something that ruined his career.

Isaac nodded slowly like he was mulling it over. Then he smiled. "Sorry, I don't mean to steal your thunder. You looked great today. You and Jason both, but you especially. I can see why everyone says you're so good."

"Everybody says that?"

"Yeah. Although also, you look amazing in that tiny bathing suit."

Tim smiled and patted his hard belly. "It's why I'm not allowed to eat sugar during the competition season. The men in my family tend to get doughy. I'm fighting against genetics."

"No sugar at all? Winning a silver medal has to at least deserve a cupcake or something."

"Not all of us swim enough to burn off six thousand calories a day."

Isaac winked. He seemed to be in a good mood, at least. "So how tired are you?"

Tim knew what Isaac meant, so he replied, "Pretty tired. Now that I'm winding down from the victory high, I'm getting sleepy. Winning a medal takes a lot out of you."

"I have to swim three times tomorrow. A prelim, a semi, and a final. I mean, I feel good now, but if you're tired…."

Tim laughed. "You know? There's a part of me that's like, 'Forget your exhaustion, let's just do it.' But good God, even my bones are tired."

"It's a feeling I'm familiar with."

Tim laid his head on Isaac's shoulder. Isaac slung his long arm around Tim's back, so Tim snuggled in closer. He liked being pressed against Isaac. He'd liked waking up with him too. This second night in a row spent together implied nights like this might become a habit. The bed in the room was barely wide enough to comfortably accommodate them. And though Isaac had a coveted single, the room was tiny—Tim had seen bigger closets. But it was private, and it smelled like Isaac.

Isaac kissed the top of Tim's head. "I'm honestly also a little superstitious. I can't think of a rational reason for sex to affect my performance, and yet I can't shake the feeling that it might."

"Maybe we should put it off until after you're done. That's only, what, four, five days? That's nothing."

Isaac laughed softly. His warm breath feathered across Tim's face. "Sure. Nothing. No big deal. I spent part of the afternoon watching you parade around in the tiniest of swimsuits, secretly hoping that little Speedo would slip off so I could see the goods and get all hot and bothered, fantasizing about our night together. I've been hard half the night. But okay, let's put off doing something about all this sexual tension for another week."

"Did you hook up with anyone at the last Olympics?" Tim asked. He didn't want to know the answer so much as he wanted to get to the bottom of the sex thing. Because though the fatigue was starting to really drag him down and he doubted he'd be able to get it up, let alone stay awake long enough to do much more than kiss, he wondered if there was anything to the superstition about it affecting performance.

Isaac hesitated. "Well, I did. With, uh, more than one person. Male and female. But it was after the swimming ended, and I was drunk."

"Oh."

"Not something I'm particularly proud of." Isaac looked off into the distance. "I have a lot of regrets about four years ago. But I want you to know, I have no regrets about anything that has happened between us. Your friendship means a lot to me. If we never have sex, I'm still glad I met you and that we've gotten to spend so much time together."

"Same for me."

Isaac leaned away and met Tim's gaze. "You're about to conk out, aren't you?"

"I really am. I'm sorry. I thought I could stay up late, but I don't think that's happening."

"Lie down. I'll be right beside you. Maybe I'll start the long process of dealing with all the nonsense on my phone."

"I haven't even looked at mine. I saw my parents after the medal ceremony. I'm with you now. Everyone else can wait for tomorrow." Tim yawned.

"All right, kid, time for bed."

"I should probably sleep for a little while."

Isaac smiled and nudged Tim under the covers.

ISAAC WAS still awake when he felt Tim stir. He glanced at the clock. It was coming up on two in the morning, and Isaac knew he should be asleep, but he was full of restless energy. His whole body hummed with it. He needed rest, though—the schedule for the next three days was grueling.

He'd sorted through the text messages at least. His email and social media notifications were a lost cause. He rarely gave out his phone number, though, so the text messages had been limited to the friends and family who weren't in Madrid.

His mother and sister *were* in Madrid; at least one of them had been to every swim event so far. Isaac agreed with Tim; that mattered most. He hadn't seen much of them, but knowing they were here, supporting him, helped him feel like he wasn't alone. His sister,

Abby, hadn't come to the last Olympics—they'd been on the outs at the time over Isaac's drinking—so the fact that she was here now meant a lot. She believed in him again. He held on to that as if it were something precious.

There was a text from Abby in the mix, asking him if there were bedbugs in the Athlete Village—considering his mattress had still had plastic on it when he'd arrived, he felt confident saying no—but otherwise it was all just giddy congratulations, so he responded to everyone (most with a "thanks" and a medal emoji) and was about to toss his phone aside when Tim stirred and rolled over. He got close enough to the edge of the bed that when Isaac reached out to keep him from rolling off, he became startled and woke up.

Tim settled onto his back and blinked at the ceiling a few times. He looked over at Isaac. "Hi."

"Hi. Sorry, I didn't mean to wake you up, but I expect hitting the floor when you rolled off would have been more jarring."

Tim yawned. "They should let us have bigger beds."

"The organizers probably didn't imagine a lot of sharing."

"Ugh. It's like being in college again." Tim lifted his head up and slammed it back onto the pillow; then he shifted his weight, clearly trying to get comfortable.

Isaac chuckled.

Tim rolled onto his side, alongside where Isaac sat at the head of the bed. Tim put his arm around Isaac's waist and snuggled closer. A man could get used to this.

A few moments later Tim's breathing evened out and he went back to sleep.

Isaac put his phone down and shifted on the bed a little. Tim shifted with him but didn't wake up. Isaac supposed it came with the territory; in his years of traveling to swim meets, he'd slept in some strange places. There'd been a World Championships years ago in Japan in which the housing had been nice, but on a particularly noisy street in Tokyo. Isaac had roomed with Luke, and Luke had expressed amazement that Isaac had been able to sleep at all. But sometimes an athlete needed to sleep, and Isaac had essentially willed his body to shut down.

He put his arm around Tim and held him close. They hadn't even done anything except kiss, but Isaac was drawn to this man who lay in his arms. He was glad that part of him still worked, even if the relationship was doomed because of sport and geography.

He started to drift off himself when Tim stirred again and tightened his arms around Isaac. "You'll come visit me in Colorado, right?"

"Sure," Isaac said, although it felt like a lie.

"I have a place in the mountains. Which sounds super luxurious, but I promise, it's just my house."

"I have a shitty apartment in Raleigh, so you can visit me there, but I bet it's much less nice than your house."

"You'll make money from swimming again." Tim sounded tired but certain. "A few gold medals can do a lot to make sponsors forget your past indiscretions."

"Is your implication that I'll be able to afford a better apartment?"

"Yeah." Tim propped himself up on one elbow but kept touching Isaac, running his fingers over Isaac's abs. "I can't imagine what the last couple of years have been like for you. But you can put it behind you now, right?"

Isaac wasn't so sure; so much of what he had experienced was tightly woven into who he was now. But he said, "I certainly hope so."

"You have regrets?"

"Of course."

"During my interview for the network package, the reporter asked me if I have regrets. I don't. Well, I regret that I let Pat manipulate me as long as he did, but I don't regret coming out. It's important, you know? To show young kids that they can do anything and it doesn't matter if they're gay or half-Asian or whatever."

"You're half-Asian?"

"My mother is Filipino."

"I didn't know that. I mean, I guessed you were biracial, but it felt rude to ask about it."

"I always assume my eyes are the giveaway, but you're not the first person not to realize it. I've had people guess Latino. My parents are always at my big events and get lots of camera time on the American broadcast, so I assume everyone knows, which is maybe presumptuous." Tim sighed and shifted his weight slightly. "But my point is that by coming out, I'm saying to the world, hey, I'm gay and I can do this. I'm a proud, talented man. I think the Olympics are kind of the great equalizer in that way."

"Really?" Isaac had never seen it that way. It seemed like some athletes or countries had different advantages and deficits—countries with more money could afford to provide their athletes with better training facilities, state-of-the-art equipment, and other resources—and viewers and the press made assumptions about who would win or lose. Often the press-driven narrative felt like a self-fulfilling prophecy, or that certain outcomes were preordained.

"There are, of course, some barriers to success. Some teams have more money, better training programs, a culture that supports them. Some athletes are blessed genetically. How tall are you?"

"Six four."

"Which gives you an advantage in swimming, I bet."

"It does." Isaac was a little uncomfortable with this conversation. He squirmed but didn't stop Tim, liking the sound of his voice if not what he was saying.

"I mean, the great athletes often have these advantages. The best runners have long legs. The best gymnasts are short. The best volleyball players are tall. Athletes tend to fall into the right sports for their bodies. I was too tall to be a gymnast. I always felt like my arms and legs were in the way. I was never good at the apparatuses anyway, but I could tumble all day long, so I was better suited to diving. I'm not saying it's a completely even playing field. Still, race, sexuality… none of it matters as much as being in top physical shape and performing in your sport to the best of your ability. The best time wins the race."

"That's true." And Isaac did believe that in his heart. But Tim was talking about an Olympic ideal, not necessarily the reality. Although maybe Tim had a point too. Isaac tried to relax and listen, to hear what Tim was saying without his own experience and bitterness tainting it. Tim was naïve, maybe, but he also saw the world in a way Isaac liked.

"And now all these barriers have been broken. I'm not the first openly gay athlete. I'm not even the first openly gay diver. Several came before me. But kids still look up to me. They tell me, you know, it's important to see people like themselves be successful." Tim took a deep breath and flattened his hand against Isaac's belly. "You could be that role model, you know. If you do the interview, I mean. Show that it's possible to make mistakes and make amends. That alcohol doesn't own you. That you can hit bottom but still get back up to the top."

Isaac pressed a hand to his forehead. "Jesus. I mean, I get what you're saying, but it's so hard to talk about."

"I know. You may decide it's better to lie low. But it could also be good publicity if you frame everything in a smart way. Or maybe you can help someone. Particularly athletes. We train our whole lives to reach the pinnacle of our sports. I mean, you know. How many hours a week do you spend in a pool? How hard has it been to hold down a job around your training schedule?"

"Yeah." Isaac mostly lived off his endorsement money, which was why his apartment was so sad. He trained six days a week during the swim season. He'd had a few part-time jobs, but he didn't have enough hours free to take on a full-time job. Many athletes needed endorsements and prize money to support themselves while they trained.

Tim said, "Our careers are done before we're forty. Some athletes are done a lot sooner. And if you've trained for the Olympics your whole life and not only do you not win, but your career ends soon thereafter? I bet a number of athletes have to deal with substance abuse or depression after the Games are over. Maybe you can help show them their lives aren't over when their athletic careers are done, after all."

It was a nice sentiment, but Isaac wasn't the right man to deliver that message. He wasn't noble; he didn't have a pat story he could sell in a thirty-second commercial. He was too much of a fuckup. "Shit, this role model stuff is not for me. I'm no role model. I'm an alcoholic who happened to win some swim races."

"I think you sell yourself short," said Tim.

"I'm not… I mean, Luke is the team captain. Everyone looks up to him. He's a good guy. Likes to mentor the younger swimmers."

"I don't think you have to be a mentor to be a role model."

"I'm selfish. I'm here for selfish reasons."

"I don't think you're selfish either." Tim ran his hands over Isaac's pecs, over his shoulders.

"No? Because I am. Totally fucking selfish." Isaac sensed a change in Tim's tone. The serious conversation was over.

"Maybe it depends on the context," Tim said, snaking his arms around Isaac.

"I suppose I give back in certain ways."

"I suppose I want you to give me something right now."

Isaac stifled a chuckle. God, Tim was cute. He leaned over and pecked Tim on the mouth. "Yeah?"

"Kiss me like you mean it, asshole."

Now Isaac laughed. "Sounds about right."

They kissed. Isaac thrust his fingers into Tim's hair and opened his mouth, really kissing Tim, sliding his tongue into Tim's mouth. Tim tasted like toothpaste, which was endearing. So was Tim's daring move to get something started. Isaac hesitated for just a second before running his hand down Tim's back, over his ass, and hooking his hand behind Tim's knee to pull him closer. Tim was hard under his warm-up pants, his cock pressing against Isaac's hip. Isaac's skin tingled and his own cock grew hard against Tim's belly, which Tim must have felt in return.

"Should we?" Isaac asked.

"God, I want to."

Isaac's body was here for it. His hips practically drove themselves forward as he pressed into Tim. "I want to fuck you so bad."

"I've wondered a little how bottoming would affect my diving."

That pulled Isaac out of the trance. "Oh shit, I didn't think of that. I don't want to hurt you in any way."

Tim smiled. "Tell you what. If I win an individual medal, I'm all yours. For now, though, I don't see how an orgasm can hurt anything."

Tim took the lead, pressing Isaac onto his back and straddling his thighs. Tim shimmied out of his pants, which seemed to take some effort but revealed a gorgeous, hard cock, bigger than Isaac had expected. Isaac reached for it, but Tim slapped his hand away. Instead, Tim peeled Isaac's pants down and pushed them to Isaac's knees, trapping his legs there. Then Tim shimmied forward, lined up their cocks, and took them both in his hand.

Isaac moaned.

The friction was delicious, but more than that, watching Tim writhe above him was something he'd take and hold on to for later. Tim's face was something else. His mouth fell agape as he stroked their cocks together, his brow furrowed as if he was working out a complicated math problem, and he thrust his hips forward in a way that put pressure on Isaac's balls in the most delightful way. Isaac reached up and tweaked Tim's nipples, which pulled a moan from Tim's mouth.

"This is gonna be fast," Tim said. "I've been wanting you all week."

Isaac thrust his hips up, his cock lining up better with Tim's, wrapped in Tim's warm fist. He already felt the telltale tingle. He wanted to point out that he hadn't had sex since before rehab, but he couldn't make his mouth form words. Instead he nodded, thrust against Tim, and got his own hand in the mix.

Tim hissed.

Isaac pulled him down, trapping their hands and cocks between them, and he kissed Tim hard. He was careful not to bite Tim's lip, though he wanted to—there were too many TV cameras around, too many concerned coaches. Tim had to be near-naked on TV in a few days for the individual qualifying dives, so Isaac couldn't leave marks. But he could hold Tim in his arms. And they could come together, have a messy orgasm together.

"Oh, sh—" Tim said before moan-sighing. His whole body vibrated, and then Isaac felt him come hot between them.

The sudden slickness, their hot hands, the pressure…. Isaac's orgasm felt like Tim had unleashed something in him. He threw his head back and arched off the bed, practically howling as he came. It was probably messy and loud, but he didn't care. He pulled his hand away and threw both arms around Tim, hugging him close, panting as he came back down.

This man. Isaac had never been with anyone like him. So sweet and idealistic, but smart and sexy too, with his own baggage that he could somehow move past when it counted. Isaac connected with Tim in a way he had rarely connected with anyone, something his sobriety was probably a factor in. Maybe he'd been too drunk to really be intimate with anyone beyond a quick fuck. Maybe he hadn't been ready.

Tim wriggled a little, getting his trapped hand free, and then he pressed a kiss to the space between Isaac's pecs.

"Have we just doomed ourselves to failure and obscurity?" Tim asked, also panting.

"Probably. Oh well." He pulled Tim up for a scorching kiss. If he was doomed, so be it.

CHAPTER 13

Day 4

TIM HAD slipped out of bed early Tuesday morning, but Isaac decided to linger, enjoying Tim's scent on his sheets. When he got to the Aquatics Center a few hours later, Luke was waiting for him. "How are you, old man?"

"I'm doing okay." Isaac actually felt pretty loose. Relieving some of the sexual tension with Tim likely helped with that.

"We're in the same heat for the 400 free."

"Oh. Great. Gee."

"They say the heats are randomly assigned, but I wonder sometimes if there isn't someone with a masochistic streak pulling the strings."

"Who else is in the heat?"

"Hsu. That Italian guy, Perinelli. Coreirra. Then a bunch of guys I don't know."

"Stacked heat."

"It's suspicious."

Isaac shrugged. "Happens."

"You don't seem concerned."

"I don't have to win my heat. I just have to swim the sixteenth-fastest time. Besides, if I can't beat those guys, I don't belong in the final."

For whatever reason, that finally got Luke's shoulders to drop. Luke smirked. "Think you can beat me?"

"I know I can. I routinely clocked in faster than you in practice the whole month leading into the Games."

"We'll see."

Isaac went into the locker room and changed into his suit. He did a few laps in the warm-up pool before Adam told him to get ready for the race.

When Isaac got to the ready room, Luke was already sitting in one of the uncomfortable plastic chairs, his hood over his head, his coat zipped up to his chin. Isaac pulled on the coat Adam handed to him. Isaac didn't bother to zip it, but he pulled the hood on over his swim cap and sat next to Luke. The coat kept him from cooling down too much from the air; the warmth helped keep muscles loose, but also, the Aquatics Center clearly had the AC set to Arctic.

Luke grinned and said, "First."

"Oh, you think this means something? You're ready first so you'll win the race?"

"There's an old wives' tale about children who are born early always being on time and children who are born late always being tardy. I was born three weeks early. I get to the end of the race early."

"Is this your form of trash talk?"

An official called their heat, so Isaac moved to stand up, although Luke got to his feet sooner. "First."

Isaac rolled his eyes.

He stood on the block a few minutes later, two lanes away from Luke.

And he decided he didn't care what Luke did in this race. Luke could win now for all Isaac cared. Isaac's only goal was top sixteen. He had to swim a fast race, but as Adam had told him right after his warm-up, as long as he touched the wall under 3:50, he'd be fine.

The buzzer sounded and Isaac got in the water. The start felt good, and maybe that was all that mattered. The feeling. If he felt good in the water, if he wasn't holding back, then he could do anything. He wouldn't swim all out in a prelim, and he had to swim two more races today so he needed to conserve his strength, but he wouldn't slouch too much either.

Eight laps of the pool. Isaac slid through the water, vaguely aware of swimmers in his periphery. He had the sense he kept pace with everyone until, after about the second lap, the swimmer in the lane to his left slipped away. Somewhere in the third lap, the swimmer on his right slipped away too. Swimmers in more distant lanes might have had huge leads right now, but with only five heats, Isaac felt good about his odds of making the semis.

New technology on the bottom of the pool let him know how many laps he had left, which helped because he had a moment when he doubted he was really almost finished. But it said right there on the bottom of the pool that he'd swum into his last lap, so he turned it on a little, deciding to sprint the last length of the pool. He reached his hand out, touched the wall, and popped out of the water.

He'd swum it in 3:45. He came in second, behind Luke. He'd made the semis easily.

When he got out of the pool, Luke was already waiting. "First," Luke said.

"We'll see," said Isaac.

As he got back to the locker room, though, a guy in a lab coat stopped him and handed him a cup. Adam stood next to him, looking grim.

"Sorry, Isaac."

Isaac shrugged. "It's fine. The only things I've put in my body today are egg whites and orange juice."

That made Adam's frown deepen. "You're gonna need to eat more than that if you expect to race tonight. Should I have Carl make you lunch?" Carl was USA Swimming's staff chef. Isaac hadn't even realized he'd come to Madrid, but there was an odd cabal of people following the team around, including the therapist who specialized in Chinese medicine and an aesthetician who helped with body waxing and shaving.

"I... all right. Sure. I am pretty hungry."

"I'll get you and Luke set up. Meet me at the American Lounge after you pee in the cup and change."

Forty minutes later Luke and Isaac had been herded into one of the kitchens where stadium concessions were prepared, where they sat on rickety stools at stainless steel tables.

"We were one and two overall in the prelims," Luke said as Carl slid plates in front of them. Then Carl gave a little wave and took off.

"That's good," Isaac said as he observed the calorie-fest before him. There seemed to be half a chicken on his plate as well as a shit-ton of vegetables, piled high in colorful mounds, and then a baked potato, probably because Carl knew Isaac loved a baked potato and would eat them all day long if he didn't burn off starch so fast.

Luke tilted his head. "I've never seen you so mellow at a competition."

"It's prelims, bro."

"I know, but you used to get really tense. Like, the minute we entered the arena for a meet, you'd be all business."

"Well, part of that is something I worked on in rehab. You gotta take each day at a time, right, so I approach swimming as each event at a time. I can't focus on the whole meet or I'll get overwhelmed and want to drink."

"You want to drink now?"

"I always want to drink. I know, for example, that the walk-in fridge behind you is full of bottled beer, and all I'd have to do is walk in there and take one. I won't, but it's distracting me."

Luke glanced back at the fridge. "Should we move?"

"No. I'm all right. I'm just saying."

"Is it true you used to swim drunk?"

Isaac tilted his head. Had they never had this conversation? Luke had taken plenty of drinks out of Isaac's hand and had encouraged him to go to rehab, but maybe they'd never really talked all this out before. "No. Never drunk. Hungover? Yeah. Many times."

"And you still won?"

"I won a silver medal four years ago while hungover. Although I lost some races too."

"So basically, had you been sober four years ago, we'd be having conversations about how you're the greatest swimmer of all time."

"Probably not of all time. I'd take 'of this generation,' though."

Luke nodded. "You get drug tested today?"

"Yep." Every athlete at the Olympics was subject to random drug testing, especially because the World Anti-Doping Agency and the IOC were cracking down hard. Isaac suspected the high-profile athletes got tested more often, though he couldn't prove it. "Adam makes them take my blood alcohol too."

Luke's eyes went wide. "Seriously?"

"Adam thinks it's a deterrent. I actually don't mind. If anything, I can say, hey, here's incontrovertible proof I'm sober now."

"This is apparently how it is now. Those Russian athletes got caught doping, and now we all have to get tested more often."

"Doping never interested me. I don't need drugs to win."

"Plus, I've heard some of those drugs kill your sex drive and shrink your balls. Who needs that?" Luke winked.

"Exactly. I have a reputation to maintain."

A laugh burst out of Luke. "Of course you do." He shook his head. "You know, the worst part is that the swimmers who got caught this time? They all swim far slower than you do on your worst days."

"Maybe everyone should take up drinking." Isaac dug into the meal. Carl sure could cook a chicken; it was juicy and well-seasoned.

"Hey, don't knock it. Best baseball player of all time was Babe Ruth, right? He didn't need PEDs. His whole career was fueled by booze, hot dogs, and women."

"There you go."

Luke ate a few bites, then said, "Speaking of sex, how are things going with Tim?"

Isaac didn't feel ready to talk about it, but since this was Luke and there was no one else around, he said, "Good, I think. I mean, for what it is. We both know it doesn't have a future past the Closing Ceremony."

"What makes you say that?"

"He lives in Colorado. He trains there. He'd never move."

"Why can't you move?"

"And leave Raleigh?"

Luke tilted his head. "Sometimes I can't tell if you're serious or not."

Isaac shrugged. "Leave Adam, I mean. And my mother. And you, dumbass. Raleigh is… whatever. The place I live. Also, it's the place where the best swim coach in the world trains world-class swimmers and all my family lives."

Luke leveled his gaze at Isaac. "Listen. I love you, you know that, right? You're like a brother to me. We've trained together a long time. I think you've still got a few more world championship swims left in you. But how long do you really see this happening? You've made your big comeback. You proved your naysayers wrong. So maybe it's time to think about the future. I don't know if Tim is the person you're going to spend the rest of your life with, but you know as well as anyone that life is too short not to pursue what you want."

Isaac didn't say anything, but he knew Luke had a point.

"Besides," Luke said, "they have swim coaches in Colorado. Tara and AJ both train near Boulder. George Marsh still works out there."

"It feels big," Isaac said. "First of all, I've only known Tim for a hot minute. Second, I've lived around Raleigh most of my life."

"And you hate it. I know you do. You stick around for Adam, and for your mother and Abby and that little nephew of yours. Family's important, but I know Raleigh is not exactly your favorite place on the planet."

Isaac sighed. "You mean the scene of all of my worst life moments? For example, the intersection on South Wilmington where I got arrested? Or that time I almost got arrested at Flex because I was hammered and decided starting a fight was a good idea?"

"My point was just that a change of scenery might not be the worst thing."

Isaac shrugged. He'd never really contemplated leaving Raleigh before. He didn't have a lot of love for the city, but he did love some of the people there. Moving half a world away for a man he just met? That seemed insane. "It seems dumb to switch coaches when I'm swimming this well."

"I'm not saying you have to move next week. And you know, they do have these things called airplanes."

"Gee, thanks."

DONNIE TEXTED to say the synchronized swimmers had taken over the dive pool, so Tim let his parents take him to lunch after his morning of TV interviews. Tim's father, Fred, had found a restaurant in his guidebook—which had so many little sticky flags sticking out of it, it looked like a porcupine—that probably catered more to tourists than locals, since it was actually open for lunch. Still, they had a good meal, and his parents enthused about his silver medal.

"You haven't had much time to see Madrid, though, have you?" Tim's mother said.

"No. And this afternoon I'm meeting Donnie and Jason in the gym for training."

"I like this city a lot," said Tim's dad. "We had the best dinner last night, didn't we, Malaya? One of your teammates recommended a wonderful place. Before that, we took a tour of the Royal Palace. It was really something."

"Gorgeous. And the architecture! It's a fascinating city, Timmy. You'll be missing out if you don't see some of it."

"I'll have some time next weekend," Tim said. He wondered if Isaac would want to come with him.

"We have a whole day planned tomorrow," said Tim's dad.

"Your father signed us up for one of those hop-on, hop-off bus tours. Which I think is a little tacky."

"At least we didn't have to rent a car. It's the easiest way to get around and see everything." Tim's dad turned to Tim. "We'll let you know what's worth seeing."

"Thanks."

"Maybe Jason will want to come with you," said Tim's mother. "He's a nice boy, right?"

Oh boy. "Yeah. Jason's great. But not in the way you're implying. He's straight."

"Oh, well," Tim's mom said. "I just hoped that after everything that happened with Pat, you might be dating again soon. It's been a few months since you broke up."

Tim looked around. They were in a restaurant a few blocks from the broadcast center, miles away from the Athlete Village. Tim didn't see anyone he thought might be an Olympic athlete, at least in terms of physique, but it was hard to tell. Most elite athletes had a superhuman quality to them, but then there were shot-putters or weight lifters and really, all bets were off. Still, he didn't recognize anyone nearby, and most of the tables seemed occupied by Spanish speakers. So Tim said, sotto voce, "Well, as it happens, I've been spending some time with one of the other athletes. He's not a diver, and no, I'm not telling you who he is yet. Not until I have a better handle on what's going on with us."

"Is it a gymnast?"

"Mom."

"Just curious. That one gymnast is really handsome. Jake Mirakovitch. We went to men's gymnastics the other day when you were not diving."

Tim had never met Jake, but he tamped down a spike of jealousy as he remembered that Jake was the gymnast Isaac thought was hot. He shook his head. "Mom. I only told you I'm hanging out with this guy so you don't worry I'm going to die alone, but that's all I'm saying. I mean, he lives on the other side of the country. The odds of it working out are pretty slim."

"But you like him? He treats you well?"

"Yeah, so far. I mean, mostly we've just eaten meals together and talked." And rubbed off on each other the night before, but his mother didn't need to hear that.

"Maybe that's all you need," his father said softly.

"Yeah, I…." Tim shook his head. "It's nice. He doesn't want anything from me other than for us to spend time together. He barely knew who I was when we met. I don't think he cares about fame. Of course, we only met a week ago, so I can't assume anything yet, but my instincts tell me he's a good guy."

"We just want you to be happy, darling," his mother said.

"I know. But hey, I won an Olympic silver medal. I can't be sad about that."

Tim's mother reached over and brushed his hair out of his face, just like she had when he was a little kid. Tim closed his eyes and let her, glad for this little bit of home in the sprawling city.

CHAPTER 14

BECAUSE OF the synchronized swimming practice, and after some frustration at the gym, Donnie ordered his divers to the pool late in the day. That was why Tim was still at the Aquatics Center when the swimmers started to file in for that night's races.

"You want to see if we can stick around to watch?" asked Ginny. "I'm not diving tomorrow. Are you?"

"No, not until Monday," said Tim.

"Wait here."

Ginny came back a few minutes later with Jason and Kayla in tow. "Turns out USA Swimming has a whole section reserved for friends and family of the team, and they've got some seats available if we want them."

Half the dive team wound up joining them. Tim saw that the American network, TBC, had its camera trained on them, so he knew reporters were aware the dive team sat in the stands. He wondered if Isaac would find out Tim was watching him. How would Isaac feel about that? Maybe he wouldn't like it.

Tim got cold feet suddenly, not wanting to jeopardize Isaac's performance in any way. On the other hand, he wanted to see Isaac swim in person, and who knew how many opportunities he'd have for that?

"I'm kicking out too hard," Kayla said as they settled into their seats. "That's what Donnie keeps saying. My dives at Worlds last year were almost all short of vertical, so I tried straightening it out. But Donnie thinks I've gone too far."

"So don't kick so hard," said Jason.

"I can do these dives. What is it about the Olympics that makes everything I know leak out of my head?"

"Nerves," said Ginny.

"How'd you stay so loose during the synchro competition?" Tim asked Jason. He remained impressed by how cool Jason had been under pressure.

"My music," said Jason. "Also, I never look at the scoreboard. It's best not to know where you stand and then be pleasantly surprised."

"So you didn't know you were in second place until the end?" Kayla asked.

"Yeah. I kind of thought we were in the middle of the field, like we'd end up fifth or sixth. I had no idea we were winning."

"But you knew, Tim. Right?"

"Yeah. I knew. I can't not look at the scoreboard. I get anxious if I don't know exactly where we are in the standings. But really, whatever approach you take, the real trick is not to tense up. If the nerves get to you, your body won't behave the way it's supposed to."

"Like, it's the Olympics?" Jason said. "But it's also a meet. There's more cameras and people and whatever, but it's not that different from, like, a college meet or a regional thing or whatever. The platform is the same distance from the water."

"Look at you," Ginny said. "You win one Olympic medal and suddenly you're an expert."

Jason sat up a little and pointed to his chest with his thumb. "Hey, I won the medal."

That shut Ginny down. Tim chuckled.

Isaac had said he had two races tonight. Tim glanced at his phone, where Isaac had texted *100 breast, 400 free*. He took that to mean Isaac would swim in the 100-meter breaststroke final, which was scheduled for toward the end of the night, and the 400-meter freestyle semifinal, which was happening pretty early.

"Flood is swimming," Ginny said.

"I know," said Tim.

"Twice."

"Yup."

"Who are you texting? Did the whole planet text you after you won the medal?"

"Yeah." Tim turned the screen off. "I'm still getting texts from people back home. It's been nonstop. How do I answer all these?"

"You don't. Send a mass text telling everyone you appreciate it and go back to training."

Tim nodded. "Or just shut the thing off."

"Or that."

Isaac did not swim in the first race, a backstroke semifinal, but there were two Americans in that heat. Ginny cheered her head off even though she didn't know either swimmer, so Tim got into it too. Having a stake in the race—wanting specific swimmers to win— riled up Tim, and he got tense watching. Both Americans qualified for the final.

Then an official announced the 400-meter freestyle semifinals.

Isaac wasn't in the first heat, but his training partner Luke was. So was another American, though Tim
didn't recognize the name. The swimmers came out
and fiddled with things at the blocks for a few minutes
before they were ready to race.

Luke won the first race. A Chinese swimmer came
in second and a Brazilian swimmer was third. The other
American took the fourth spot, but Tim had watched
enough swimming to know that didn't necessarily
guarantee him a spot in the finals.

Ginny had cheered for Luke, but she went full-on
bananas when Isaac came out.

Isaac took off his shoes and socks and slid out of
his warm-up pants, though he continued to stand there
in his coat for a minute. He stripped in a practical way;
his purpose was to keep warm until the last possible
second, when he'd get down to his swimsuit and jump
in the pool. His mannerisms were practiced and busi-
nesslike—but there was something sexy about them
too. Tim loved Isaac's broad chest—which he'd barely gotten to explore during their quickie the night before—and seeing it on display now, both directly next
to the pool and up on the big screen next to the scoreboard, was quite an experience.

"He's so sexy," Ginny said.

"Oh yeah," said Tim, because why fight it?

The swimmers were told to get to their marks, so
Isaac fiddled with his goggles and got up on the block.
He did some weird thing with his hands that seemed to
be more of a pantomime of getting ready to swim than
anything real. Still, he cut a compelling figure, and Tim
couldn't take his gaze away.

Isaac bent forward. "Set," said the announcer. Then
a buzzer sounded and the swimmers were in the water.

According to the scoreboard, Isaac was in fourth after the first lap, but there were many more laps to go. Tim got nervous for him, though, his gut clenching as he leaned forward.

"He's pacing himself," Ginny said. "He doesn't want to get too tired because he has to swim again later."

By the third lap, Isaac had caught up and seemed to be swimming neck and neck with the two other leaders. By the fourth lap, he had inched ahead.

He was amazing.

Tim thought he might have shouted the loudest.

Isaac finished the race second, but had a good enough time to advance. Up on the big screen, Tim could see Isaac nod as if he was satisfied with that. The swimmers patted each other on the back or gave each other high fives or back pats—it all seemed very collegial—then they all got out of the pool and retreated toward the locker room.

Tim finally breathed.

"Wow, that was tense," he said.

"I know!" said Ginny. "This is really exciting. I wish we didn't have to train the rest of the week or I'd say we should come back every day."

"We should take up one of those sports that has its whole event on the first day. Then we'd be done and could just watch other competitions," Jason said. "Like shooting or archery or whatever. Those are all done pretty fast."

"Can you do any of those sports?" asked Ginny.

"I did archery at summer camp when I was a kid," said Jason.

"That totally counts as Olympic training," said Kayla, with an eye roll.

They sat through another hour of races, with a lot of wait time in between. "It's like golf," Kayla observed after a while. "A lot of sitting for, like, three minutes of action."

At one point Ginny squealed again. Tim thought Isaac had come back out, but she was looking at her phone. "Hey, look at this. There have already been three marriage proposals at the Madrid Games."

"Yeah?"

"Yeah. The first was on Saturday. The Brazilian women's soccer team won their first game, and then the girlfriend of one of the players ran onto the pitch and proposed. The second was a fencer from Italy who proposed to his girlfriend after he secured the gold medal. And the third was a cyclist from Great Britain who proposed to his boyfriend in front of the Plaza Mayor when they went on a tour."

"Aw," said Kayla. "Something for everyone."

"It's nice that there are so many openly gay athletes," said Jason. "I mean, the media is talking about these proposals, right?"

"Yeah. It's pretty great."

Tim nodded, but he remained a little skeptical. "It is nice. But, I mean, my parents told me that there was some controversy because that one British diver's husband was in the audience during the team competition, but the American network wouldn't show him on TV."

"That's dumb," said Ginny. "What's the big deal? It should be about the divers, not their high-profile spouses."

"Well, think of it this way. If what my parents said was true, if I'd married Pat, they wouldn't show him in the audience. But they showed a whole lot of both of the Australians' wives. Like, they want to embrace the LGBT athletes but not show too much."

"Oh," said Ginny, seeming chastened.

"Sorry. I'm not bitter, I promise. And Pat's out of the picture, so it doesn't even matter. I just hope that someday, if I get married while I'm still competing, the cameras pan to my husband supporting me from the stands. Just like they'd show the spouse of any other athlete. That's all."

"Did they ever show Pat when you were dating?"

"Not really. Although Pat didn't come to a lot of my meets."

"When you blamed his schedule, how true was that?"

Tim sighed. He didn't love the third degree Ginny was giving him, but he answered, "His schedule *was* usually the reason he couldn't come. He'd be filming something and not available to travel, that sort of thing. But his schedule was more important to him than me. Some of that comes with the territory of being an actor, but sometimes he'd bail on my meets so he could get strategic paparazzi photos taken and that sort of nonsense."

"Good riddance," said Jason.

"Yeah. That guy was a tool," said Ginny. "You're better off without him."

Tim laughed ruefully. "I am. You're right."

He wondered if he was making a better choice by falling for a certain swimmer. Because he was definitely falling. But Isaac was a risky choice. The alcoholism was something he still struggled with. Did that make him a bad bet? And they lived so far apart, there was no way it would ever work.

One day at a time, Tim told himself. That's how Isaac would tell him to look at the situation.

He kept trying to frame the rest of his scheduled time in Madrid as having a whole two weeks left, but really, he only had two weeks left.

He shook his head and tried to focus on the swimming. Ginny was shouting again, so there must have been American swimmers in the water.

Tim wanted Isaac, bottom line. The question was how to make that happen past the Closing Ceremony.

"I think that's Flood's mom right there," Ginny whispered as she gestured toward the front of the section they were sitting in.

A middle-aged woman with graying hair sat five rows in front of them. Tim could only really see the back of her head, but it could have been Isaac's mom. Tim had seen pictures of her, or video footage of her cheering on her son from the stands, so he knew what she looked like. She chatted with a younger woman, closer to Tim's age—maybe Isaac's sister, because she didn't have the physique of a swimmer. And there were plenty of swimmers around them in the stands to compare with.

Finally the announcer proclaimed the 100-meter breaststroke final was next. For the finals, there was a little more ceremony. As they called each swimmer, he stepped out in front of a flashy screen that displayed his name, and he waved to the crowd.

Tim caught himself holding his breath again as he waited for Isaac to emerge. Isaac walked out a moment later, wearing the heavy-looking coat again, his cap in place and goggles on his forehead. He waved at the crowd with both hands. The applause was deafening.

Tim realized Isaac was probably the defining story of the Olympics right now. And Isaac would hate that.

Isaac went through the dance again, carefully taking off everything but his swimsuit, cap, and goggles. At the side of the pool, while everyone got ready, one of the officials fiddled with some piece of equipment, delaying the start. The longer this drew out, the tenser Tim became, watching and unable to do anything to help Isaac.

"He's better at the two hundred," Ginny said, "but the breaststroke is his best stroke."

"Do you run his fan club?" Tim asked. He hoped it didn't sound snippy, because he didn't mean it to be.

She grinned. "I just like him. I think he got a bad break. He made some mistakes, and the establishment kind of abandoned him. But here he is, winning races again. It's inspiring, isn't it?"

The racers got up on the block. One hundred meters was one lap, just down the length of the pool and back, and the whole race would take about a minute. But Tim's heart pounded.

Up on the blocks. Set. Go.

Isaac got in the water fast. Everyone seemed pretty much on pace, but the field started to spread out a little as they approached the first turn. According to the scoreboard, Isaac was third in that turn, but he caught some kind of momentum and pulled into second place once he began the back half. Tim slid forward on the seat, leaning to try to see better. Isaac came up to the guy in first place. If no one else caught him, he'd win a medal at least. But Isaac wanted the gold; Tim knew that. Isaac closed the gap in the last twenty-five meters. And then they were at the wall, but so much water splashed up, Tim couldn't see who reached the wall first.

The results flashed up on the screen.

Isaac had won his third gold medal of the Games.

"Holy shit," Tim said.

"Oh my God," said Ginny.

Everyone in the audience buzzed. The woman Ginny thought was Isaac's mom sobbed all over the woman beside her. Tim really hoped she wasn't Isaac's secret girlfriend or something. Then he shook that thought off; Isaac wasn't Pat. He could trust him. The woman was probably his sister. And when she turned and looked back at Ginny, currently screaming her head off, Tim thought he could see a family resemblance.

That had been the last race of the night, so Tim bent down to grab his bag, but Ginny said, "Let's stay for the medal ceremony and sing the national anthem like it's a pop song."

Tim thought it might be nice to see Isaac get his medal. His *third* medal this week. Jesus.

People filtered out of the stands as the athletes went to change and a crew set up the podium. The first medal was awarded for a women's event, and then Isaac and the other medalists from the 100-meter breaststroke came out to raucous applause.

The ceremony itself seemed to drag. The athletes stood on the podium, chatting with each other while they waited for the medals to be carried out. Once the woman who held the medals on a tray arrived at the podium, each athlete in turn shook hands with the other winners, stepped up to his place, and received a handshake, his medal, some cheek kisses, and the little statuette of the Madrid mascot—a cartoony bull—they were handing out instead of flowers. So it took several minutes before Isaac even stepped up to the top of the podium to receive his medal. Then the flags were lowered, and the national anthem began, and Ginny, true to her word, belted out, "Oh say can you see?"

But Tim couldn't take his eyes off Isaac. Isaac seemed somewhat overcome, his eyes a little red as he looked toward the flags, which happened to be lowered directly in front of where Tim sat. Isaac's eyes searched the crowd below the flags and his gaze seemed to settle on his mother, who gave a little wave. Then Isaac looked up. And his gaze met Tim's.

Isaac looked startled for a moment, but then his gaze locked on Tim, and they stared at each other through the rest of the anthem. By the time Ginny began to shout, "Oh say does that star-spangled banner yet wave!" Tim knew with certainty Isaac saw him there.

Tim also knew his destiny had just taken a left turn.

Because there was no way he was letting this man go when he flew back to the States.

"HALF THE dive team wound up in the audience tonight," Luke said when Isaac walked back into the locker room.

"I noticed." Isaac wanted to get to Tim more than he wanted to breathe. He'd packed up his bag before the medal ceremony, so he stopped now to fish his phone out of it, and then he hoisted his bag onto his shoulder.

"It's nice of them to be supportive," Luke said. "Katie said they cheered louder than anyone."

"We'll have to thank them," Isaac said as he texted Tim to tell him not to leave without him.

Do you care if the whole dive team sees us together? Tim asked.

Nope was Isaac's reply.

He didn't give a fuck about keeping this relationship a secret. Because it *was* a relationship. He'd realized as he'd stared at Tim's eyes during the medal ceremony that Tim was the best thing to happen to him... well, since rehab, probably. And he'd be a fool to let that go.

Isaac had a moment's hesitation wondering if he cared about being outed—he didn't. He'd survived being arrested and the shame of admitting he was a drunk. He felt no shame about his sexuality and didn't really care who knew about it, because it didn't affect how he swam, and he generally viewed it as a positive, something to take pride in. His friends and family all knew. So if he got some press for being with Tim, so be it; it could never be as terrible as the press he got after the DUI.

"Tim's here," Isaac told Luke. "I mean, with the dive team."

Luke grinned. "Go get him. You just won your third gold medal in as many days. Live your life, Isaac."

"I plan to."

When Isaac and Luke reached the athlete's exit of the Aquatics Center, Tim waited there with a few of the other divers, most of them wearing their official warm-up suits or jackets that said *USA Diving*. One of the female divers, who had red curly hair—Isaac didn't know her name—squealed when he walked out. "Oh my God, congratulations!"

"Thanks. Tim, I—"

"That was *so* amazing," the redhead said. "Nobody expected you to win."

"Uh, thanks. So, Tim, I—"

"I think you just pulled off a miracle," Tim said.

And then, because the only people standing there were three divers and a couple of the swimmers waiting for the bus back to the Athlete Village—and also because Isaac didn't really care what anyone thought anyway—he reached for Tim, grabbed his head, and pulled him in for a hot kiss. Tim went with it, hooking his arm around Isaac's, but Isaac sensed more people coming outside, so he pulled away.

"So, you two know each other," said the redhead.

"Um, yeah," Tim said.

"I did not know you were gay, Isaac Flood."

"Bisexual," said Isaac, frustrated with the girl. "Tim, I—I'm really glad you're here." He let out a breath, glad he finally got to say what he wanted to say.

"Me too."

They all boarded the bus back to the Athlete Village. Luke got on the bus shortly thereafter, and he punched Isaac lightly on the arm. "Well done all around," he said.

Isaac nodded.

Tim said, "Isaac, I—"

"Shh." Isaac lowered his voice. "You're spending the night with me, right?"

"Yeah."

"Then whatever. Bask in my glory."

Tim laughed. "Yeah, but…." Then he shook his head.

Isaac supposed it was out now that he and Tim were… doing whatever they were doing. He didn't care if the swim team knew—and they were all hooking up with each other anyway; Exhibit A was Luke and Katie, who canoodled whenever they were together—and he wondered how long it would take for this piece of information to leak to the press. He felt a pang of regret at the idea that the story would likely become "Flood is gay!" and not "Flood came back from rock bottom to win three gold medals," but Isaac could only control himself and his own happiness. Headlines would fade, the public would forget him, and some things were more important.

"Do you trust your teammates?" Tim asked.

"Sure."

"I'm just worried…. I mean, I don't mind other people knowing about us, but if it leaks to the press…."

"So it leaks to the press."

Tim let out a frustrated grunt. "If it leaks to the press, then the story stops being about gold medals. For me, it will be all gossipy stories in tabloids about how I've moved on from Pat. Or I'm dating a vulnerable swimmer who just got out of rehab and doesn't know what he's doing."

Isaac narrowed his eyes. "I know exactly what I'm doing."

"I know, but just…." Tim looked out the window for a moment. When he turned back to face Isaac, he said, "I want the story to be about what I did here athletically. Not what I did with my dick."

Isaac nodded. He did a quick inventory of the bus. There were the kids in diving T-shirts that were Tim's teammates, and there were five members of the swim team. That was it. So Isaac knelt on his seat and said, "Hey, guys?"

It was a small enough crowd that he got everyone's attention.

"Cone of silence, right? What you all saw… I mean, you know now, Tim and I are kind of seeing each other. But it doesn't leave this bus. Got it?"

There was a murmur of assent. Luke gave Isaac a thumbs-up.

"Because I trust you guys. And me and Tim just met. It's not really a thing yet."

"Understood," said one of the divers.

"Yeah, we won't say anything," said the redhead.

"Okay. I don't want to be a dick, but it's important. I trust you all. Just so we're clear."

Everyone nodded. Isaac felt pretty confident that they understood the situation. A couple of the divers looked young, so they might have been inexperienced, but they knew now. Luke had already given the swim team a "Don't talk to the press about team gossip" speech a few days before.

Isaac slid back into his seat. "Okay?"

"Yeah," said Tim. "Thanks. So we're clear, it's not shame, it's just…."

"No, I get it. Believe me, I understand how stupid the media can be."

Tim nodded. He was quiet for a moment. Everyone on the bus fell into conversations with their seatmates, and Isaac closed his eyes to savor the little bubble of privacy he had with Tim for the moment. He opened his eyes again and met Tim's gaze. They smiled at each other.

Tim reached over and fingered the medal that still hung from Isaac's neck. "This might be the closest I get to a gold medal."

"Aren't you a reigning Olympic champion?" asked Isaac. "Do you not already have a gold medal?"

"Sure, but that was the last Olympics. That medal is not in Madrid. Look how pretty this design is." Tim traced the edges of the design, a floral motif clearly inspired by the architecture and design in Madrid. It was slightly different than the pattern on Tim's silver medal. "Also, the diving competition is fierce, so I don't know if I'll ever get one of these."

"Competition, schmompetition."

Tim laughed. "You seem so mellow. You're riding quite a high right now, aren't you?"

"I feel amazing. If I come in dead last in the rest of my races, I won't even care." Isaac sighed and looked up at the ceiling. "Three gold medals. What the fuck?"

They spent most of the rest of the bus ride in comfortable silence, and they seemed to move that way through the building that housed the Americans, stopping at Tim's room briefly before going to Isaac's.

Safely in Isaac's sanctuary, Tim said, "You're incredible."

"No. I'm an ordinary man who just did an incredible thing."

"All right. Well, watching you was sure incredible."

Isaac grinned. "Do you want to make this night more incredible?"

"What did you have in mind?"

CHAPTER 15

ISAAC WORE a navy blue jacket with red sleeves—
the official Team USA jacket that was part of his medal
ceremony uniform—over a USA T-shirt and a pair of
black warm-up pants. Tim wondered if Isaac's whole
wardrobe had been supplied by the USOC. Tim had
a similar pile of clothing he'd been issued at athlete
check-in, which happened shortly before he flew to
Madrid. And just in case any athlete thought he didn't
have enough USA garb, there was more available at the
America House shop.

Tim didn't hate all the free stuff. Everything was
custom-made. His dive suits had been made to his
body's exact specifications, in part to prevent wardrobe
malfunctions.

But it was funny to watch Isaac, a guy who probably didn't have a whole lot of patriotic zeal, slide off the
jacket and tug at the hem of his star-spangled T-shirt.

"So, before we get down to business…," Isaac
said. He waggled his eyebrows and paused for Tim to
take in his meaning. "I have a favor to ask."

"All right."

"My hair's growing back. On my body, I mean.
It's sort of patchy, and just in a few spots. There's a

woman on staff who does waxing, but I only need some touch-ups. When Luke and I roomed together, we used to shave the hard-to-reach places for each other, but he's busy fooling around with Katie, so I wondered if you could help me."

"You want me to shave you?"

"Yeah. A little."

Shaving Isaac felt like a new level of intimacy, although he'd had Isaac's come smeared into his skin the night before, so maybe they'd crossed that threshold anyway. The idea of shaving Isaac excited Tim. "Yeah, okay."

"Good." Isaac reached for the hem of his T-shirt.

But Tim stopped him. He was revved up from the adrenaline of watching Isaac win and from the crazy kiss outside the Aquatics Center, and he'd been thinking about that chest all evening. "Let me."

Isaac smiled. "All right."

Tim stepped toward Isaac. He ran his hands under Isaac's T-shirt, over Isaac's abs and pecs, touching all that soft skin before he revealed it. Isaac's chest was still smooth, making Tim wonder which parts of his body needed shaving, but he savored the feel of that skin under his hands before he pulled—with some effort—Isaac's shirt off over his head.

"You're really tall," Tim said.

"That's the rumor."

Tim pressed his hands into Isaac's back and leaned in to plant kisses along his collarbone. Isaac threw his head back and put his long arms around Tim. He said, "Mmm. But there are more important matters at hand."

"What do you need shaved?"

"Well, let's take a look. The lighting is better in the bathroom."

Isaac led the way into the small room. He flipped the switch and gestured toward the razor and shaving cream he'd left on the counter. "It's mostly my legs and arms," Isaac said.

"Okay. I've never shaved another person before."

"You've shaved your own face and chest, though, right?"

"Yeah."

"Same idea. Try not to nick me."

Isaac pulled off his warm-up pants, leaving him standing there in a pair of blue briefs. He sat on the toilet and propped one leg up on the lip of the tub, then grabbed the can of shaving cream. "I had my whole body waxed four days ago. I can usually go a week to ten days without needing much touch-up, but my leg hair is stubborn. So, see, there are all these little lines of stubble?" He gestured to his shin. "My thighs seem okay, but down here by my ankles, the hair is growing back."

"This is a little weird."

"You don't understand weird until you have a swimmer roommate who asks you to shave his back hair. Because that has happened. And it's about the least sexy thing on this planet."

Tim laughed. "Okay. Lather up."

"I think I can do most of my leg, but maybe you can spot me and get anything I can't reach."

Isaac turned on the water in the sink. Then he smeared shaving cream in a thick layer over his leg and got to work. After each pass, he rinsed the razor in the sink.

"You missed a spot near your ankle," Tim said as he settled to sit on the lip of the tub, right next to where Isaac had his foot propped up.

"You do it, then." Isaac handed the razor over.

Tim worried he'd nick Isaac's skin, but he followed Isaac's lead, went against the grain, and moved the razor over Isaac's skin in the same direction Isaac had.

They managed to shave any errant hair off both Isaac's legs by passing the razor back and forth. Isaac did his left arm but asked Tim to do his right, since he was right-handed. Tim tried to apply the amount of pressure he'd need if he were ambitious enough to do this kind of hair removal. The scrape of the razor along Isaac's skin and the repetitive pattern of movement soothed Tim too, and he got over the weirdness and began to relax.

"Armpits," Isaac said, raising his arm and his eyebrows.

Isaac lifted his left arm, so Tim smeared the armpit area with shaving cream. Isaac's body was stubbly there, not super hairy, and the muscles of Isaac's arm cast shadows that made it a little hard to see. But Tim went to work, scraping the razor over Isaac's skin until most of the hair and shaving cream were gone. He wiped off Isaac's skin with a damp washcloth and inspected his work. Then Tim gave in to temptation and pressed his face into the skin there, feeling the newly smooth texture of Isaac's underarms and smelling. There was a faint sweaty scent, but mostly Isaac smelled of his minty shaving cream.

"All smooth?" Isaac asked, his tone wry.

"Yup."

Tim repeated the process under Isaac's other arm, feeling it with his face again and kissing it this time. It was strange to be with a man who didn't have hair there. Tim had liked the armpits of some of his past lovers, because their scent, concentrated there, was more intense. But being this close to Isaac was sexy too.

Isaac brought his arm down and ran it along Tim's spine. "We good?"

"Anywhere else you need shaved?"

Isaac gestured for Tim to back away slightly so he could run his hands over his arms, armpits, and legs. "You did a good job." Then he ran his hands over his chest and belly. He tilted his head as if he were deciding if more work was needed. Then he slid a hand into his briefs, pressing his fingertips to the area just above his penis. "Yeah, okay, probably the, er, bikini area too."

"Really?"

"Have you seen how low the official swimsuits ride? I can't have any hair there either."

"Do you do the whole Brazilian thing? Like, get your balls waxed and all that?"

"Yup. Hurts like a mother. Luckily I've never been super hairy down there, so I usually only have to do the whole shebang once a season." Isaac tilted his head. "How do you stay so hairless under that little swimsuit?"

"I see a lady back home who just does the parts the swimsuit doesn't cover. I've never had my balls waxed."

"It's an experience. You could help me out now and get right above my cock, the creases of my thighs, anything where there might be hair."

"So you'd have to get naked."

Isaac winked at Tim. "That a problem?"

"Not for me."

Isaac stood and slid off his briefs. The sight of Isaac's cock, which plumped up a little under Tim's gaze, momentarily mesmerized Tim. Isaac then sat back on the toilet seat and spread his legs. "Go to town."

Good Lord.

Tim took a good look first, reminding himself he was helping Isaac stay competitive and not sitting face-to-crotch with a man he really liked. Isaac's cock was right there, though, practically calling to him. Tim wanted to take it in his mouth, but instead he lifted it slightly to get a better look at where Isaac's hair grew back.

Isaac's body hair was dark, at least, and easy to spot. There was stubble above his cock, along the sides of it, at the tops of his thighs. Isaac shifted his hips enough for... Lord... Tim to see his asshole too, which seemed completely hairless. Tim slid his thumb across it.

"Woah, buddy," Isaac said with a laugh.

"Just making sure there's no hair."

"Uh-huh."

Tim grabbed the shaving cream and wiped some over the stubbly areas. He carefully scraped it away, satisfied when removing the shaving cream revealed smooth skin.

He tried to ignore the fact that Isaac was getting hard.

But by the time Tim finished, Isaac was fully erect, his cock huge. Tim took the washcloth Isaac handed him and wiped away the last of the shaving cream. Isaac looked down and inspected Tim's work, running his fingers over his whole area. Then he grabbed his balls.

"Nice job," Isaac said. "It feels good."

Tim leaned forward a little and made a show of looking close. "I mean, I should probably get a closer look."

"If it's for quality assurance purposes...."

"It is."

Tim took Isaac's cock into his mouth.

Isaac moaned and widened his legs further, then pressed his fingers into Tim's hair. He massaged Tim's scalp as Tim licked and sucked, enjoying the pressure and weight of Isaac's cock against his tongue. Then he backed off slightly but dove down to lick the area he'd just shaved. The lingering shaving cream tasted bitter and chemical, but Tim had to have his tongue against Isaac. He licked the newly smooth skin, then took each of Isaac's balls into his mouth—quality assurance, as well as making sure that pre-Games wax still served him well—and Isaac hissed and moaned above him. Then Tim dove back onto Isaac's cock, sucking it into his mouth and licking the underside.

"Good God in heaven," Isaac muttered, shifting his hips a little, lifting off the toilet seat, fucking Tim's mouth. "You're doing a good job there too."

Tim smiled at the pun but kept sucking, wanting to feel Isaac come on his tongue. He lifted his hand and fisted Isaac's cock, stroking it hard, pulling more moans from Isaac.

Then Isaac's back arched and he said, "Oh, fuck," and he came in Tim's mouth.

Tim held him there until he stopped pulsing, then opened his mouth to show Isaac what he'd left behind. Isaac groaned at the sight. Tim closed his mouth, swallowed, and showed Isaac his clean tongue. Isaac groaned harder.

"That was hot," Isaac said, panting.

Tim knelt back and grinned up at Isaac.

Isaac bent forward, cupped Tim's cheek, and kissed him hard. Tim opened his mouth, letting Isaac's tongue inside, and hoped Isaac could taste himself there.

Isaac pulled away slightly. He kissed Tim's nose. "I want to take a shower and wash away some of the shaving cream residue. Care to join me?"

"I'd love to."

ISAAC WOKE up the next morning once again curled around Tim, only this time they were both buck naked and Isaac's hard cock had wedged itself between Tim's asscheeks. He sighed happily, enjoying the pressure of Tim's soft skin against his own.

Isaac had wound up returning the favor for Tim, shaving all around Tim's cock and balls and then show-ering again, and they'd gone late into the night, playing with each other's naked bodies, washing, making out. Isaac had come three times, making his current hard-on kind of a miracle, and Tim had come that much too.

It had been awesome.

No penetration yet, but Isaac didn't want to do anything that would fuck with Tim's body more than he already had. Bottoming didn't necessarily lead to pain, but sometimes the burn lingered, especially if one hadn't bottomed in a while. Isaac didn't want to chance it, and Tim seemed reluctant too. Though Tim had promised they would fuck immediately after his last dive. "I'll take you in the locker room while I'm still wearing my gold medal, if it comes to that," he'd said.

And wasn't that an image to keep Isaac warm at night?

Isaac ran his hand down Tim's chest and grabbed his also-hardening cock. He gave it a squeeze.

"How is it possible either of us has anything left?" Tim asked.

"We're that hot together," Isaac said.

"What time is it?"

Isaac glanced back at the bedside clock. "Eight."

"Fuck. I have to be at practice in two hours."

"Me too. My first race is right at noon."

Tim pulled away and rolled over to face Isaac. "I just want to say, this has been the best meet of my entire life. And last night was a heck of a lot of fun."

Isaac smiled and kissed Tim softly. "I can't believe I want you again."

Tim laughed. "I know. But we should get up."

Tim rolled out of bed and stretched. Isaac got an eyeful of Tim's whole body, which was basically perfect. He was a smaller man than Isaac—narrower shoulders, smaller waist, shorter legs—but he was well proportioned. He had those round muscles on his arms, the well-defined pecs and abs, his half-hard cock hanging there as if waiting for something, and those powerful thighs. Isaac leaned over and ran a hand from Tim's hip to his knee. "God, your thighs. So amazing."

"It's from the springboard work. All springboard divers have huge thighs."

"Not huge. Strong. I like them."

"That's good. Not everyone does. Pat used to tell me I had fat thighs."

"No. Definitely not fat. Look at this muscle definition." Isaac ran his fingers along the ridge of muscle down the side of Tim's thigh. "Your legs are amazing."

"Thanks."

Isaac shifted his weight on the bed, missing having Tim next to him. "This Pat fellow. He sounds like a terrible human being."

Tim laughed. He sat back down on the bed, facing away from Isaac. "I don't know if I'd go that far."

"Can I ask what really happened? You've alluded to some things, but I feel like I don't have the whole picture."

Tim sighed. "I… well. We met at a bar, I think. I don't really remember it well. I think he must have known who I was at that point. It was shortly after I won my gold medal four years ago, so pictures of me were all over the internet. I don't know if he sought me out, but I didn't suspect anything at the time. And I thought we were happy, but apparently I'm a terrible judge of character."

"You like me, so…." Isaac meant it as a joke, but he couldn't deny there was a little truth to it; he still doubted sometimes he was worthy of Tim's attentions. Still, at least he wasn't a total asshole. This story Tim was about to tell seemed like it might reveal that Pat was indeed a total asshole.

Tim smiled ruefully. "Long story short, it took me longer than it should have to realize he'd manipulated me to benefit his own career. He was already publicly out when we started dating, or he told me he was, but 'publicly' is relative. He meant that he'd been outed on a gay gossip blog with a tiny readership. I think he thought getting outed would garner him more attention. His personal philosophy was that any publicity is good publicity, so his being gay would be newsworthy enough to get him the kind of attention he could parlay into more work, or so he thought. Which is so strange to me, because don't most actors stay in the closet because coming out would cost them jobs?"

"I thought so."

"Right. Anyway. We kept a low profile until he had the idea to do the coming-out video. Only it turned out that I was more famous than him. I mean, the headlines were things like *Gold Medalist Tim Swan Comes Out in Video with Actor Boyfriend*. That really bothered Pat. He has a small, devoted following online—all these girls who are fans of his show—so I think he thought he had a big enough platform. But we did the video, and then things got creepy."

"How?" Isaac lightly ran a hand along Tim's back. Tim was tense, which Isaac took to mean he found this upsetting to talk about. Isaac was glad he was willing to share, though.

"I started getting messages from people telling me how brave I was, which was nice, although I didn't feel especially brave. But then Pat's fans started making art. I wanted to ignore it, but Pat used to collect it. And some of it was really creepy. Like, drawings of us in bed together. Stories about our sex lives. And they used to send all these messages over social media about how cute we were. I started to feel like I was their pet. But that was nothing compared to the fact that, you know, we were engaged, so I let Pat have access to my bank accounts."

"Oh no." Isaac's heart sank; he knew exactly where this was going.

"He never loved me. He thought being with me was his ticket to fame. I didn't realize it because I was so head over heels for him and we were having fun together. And I guess the fan following for his show brought some cachet, because I started getting sponsorships from unexpected places. Like, places that wanted me to model their clothes, that kind of thing."

"You don't think you would have gotten those jobs without Pat? Cuz you're really hot. You could model a trash bag and people would buy it."

Tim sighed. "Being with Pat attracted a different kind of fan, I guess. And the extra money was nice, I can't complain about that. But then his show got canceled and everything went south. Instead of asking to borrow money from me, he just took it. When I finally confronted him about it, he showed his true colors."

Isaac felt a spike of jealousy at hearing Tim had been head over heels for this guy, but more than that, he wanted to hug Tim close and protect him from assholes like that. "God, I'm so sorry you went through that."

Tim nodded and looked down. Isaac realized his rapid blinking meant he was trying to keep the tears at bay. "The worst part is that I felt like such an idiot. I should have seen it, you know? I should have known he was manipulating me. He played me for a fool for a long time. When I figured it out, I was heartbroken. And I was mortified. How could I have let this happen?"

Isaac moved his hand in what he hoped were comforting circles along Tim's back. "You were in love." And wasn't that a kick in the teeth?

"Yeah. I did really love him once. But that's all over now."

A thousand clichés about love being blind ran through Isaac's head, but he was having a hard time keeping his jealousy in check. This asshole had received Tim's love for several years and he'd wasted it.

"I'm not.... Am I making a mistake like that with you?" Tim asked after Isaac took too long to respond.

"My gut says no, but I don't know if I trust my instincts anymore."

It was like an ice pick to Isaac's heart, but his own confidence in his ability to be a good partner was precarious. He cared about Tim and liked what they had together; he wanted it in his life for as long as he could have it. But could he stay on the wagon? "Honestly? I don't know. By that, I mean I won't steal your money. I won't use you to gain anything. I don't want anything from you except your affection, and that's the God's honest truth. But I'm an alcoholic. I'm probably not a good bet."

Tim nodded slowly. "I've been thinking about that. I keep telling myself that this ends when we fly home, so it doesn't matter. You respect your sport too much to relapse while you're competing, so I believe you won't drink while you're here, but after that…."

"That's true. And I swear I am going to fight my base nature and stay sober. I can't… I can't go back to where I was, how I was living. I was in such a dark place. I never want to see rock bottom again." And that was true. Staying sober was the hardest thing Isaac had to cope with, and he confronted temptation on a daily basis. But he vividly remembered the cop yanking him out of his car, followed by the moment he realized it had all spun too far out of control, that he'd put his life and the lives of many others in danger because of his own selfishness and addiction. He'd never in his entire life felt as awful as he had in that moment, and he never wanted to feel that again.

"I believe you," Tim said. "I believe you want sobriety. I know there's risk, but the thing is, I want to be with you. For more than just the Olympics."

Isaac breathed slowly for a long moment. Tim's faith squeezed Isaac's heart. "I want that too."

"You see me. You get me. That was never true for Pat."

"You have faith in me. So few of the people in my life do. I don't blame them, because I did a lot of shitty things when I was drunk, but I guess I've gotten used to everyone doubting me."

"What a pair we make."

Isaac laughed softly. "Yeah." He shook his head, feeling truly encouraged for the first time in a while. "I can't make any promises about my drinking. I have to control my impulses daily. I've been on the wagon for seventeen months, one week, and five days, but I've fallen off in the past, and I probably will again. I don't want to. I battle it constantly. But I can promise I never want to deliberately hurt you. And I could have died. I could have given up and sunk into that dark place and been lost there. But I clawed my way out of the bottle precisely so that I could live a full life, and I intend to do that." Because while Isaac missed the sweet oblivion of being drunk, the life he led now was so much better. Feeling strong and healthy, swimming to the best of his ability, spending time with people he cared about—all of that was a thousand times better than being drunk. He wanted this life, not his old one.

Tim turned around, propping his legs up on the bed. He looked down at where Isaac still lay. "I don't know how we make this work."

"One day at a time." Isaac reached over and took Tim's hand. "That's how I approach my sobriety. I take every day as it comes. So we live each day as if it's the last one. We spend as much time together as we can, we cheer each other on when we can, and we'll worry about everything else when the day arrives that we have to tackle it. All right?"

Tim nodded. "All right. One day at a time." He leaned down and kissed Isaac's forehead. Then he glanced at the clock. "Come on, let's go get breakfast. I'm starving."

"I'm under strict orders from my coach to up my calorie intake. Think they'll have bacon at the cafeteria today? And sausage? Ooh, what about that Spanish ham they had the other day. So salty and delicious." Isaac let his head fall back and made orgasm noises.

Tim laughed and got up.

CHAPTER 16

Day 5

DAY FIVE of swimming was a little rough. After the prelims and semis of the 200 breaststroke, Isaac had moved on to the finals, although he wasn't happy with his times. After the semi, Adam found him at the warm-up pool and asked to chat for a minute.

"What's up?" Adam said as Isaac hauled himself out of the pool.

"I don't know. You're the one who wants to talk."

Adam rolled his eyes. "I swear to Mark Spitz, kid. Twenty-nine years old, and sometimes you still act like the teenager you were when we first started training for the Olympics." Adam sighed. "You looked upset after the last race. What's going on?"

"I should have gone faster."

"You're in the final. Doesn't matter."

"I'm tired. And I have the 400 free tonight still."

Adam glanced at his watch. "In an hour and a half. Go see Bill."

Bill was the Chinese medicine specialist. "Are you fucking serious?"

"If you don't want to do any of the therapies, that's fine. But he might be able to massage any soreness or at least give you a space to lie down quietly for a while. I don't want you to cool down all the way, so wear your coat over there. You need to rest up somehow, and there isn't time for you to go back to your room. But you gotta do something to get some of your strength back if you're weak or hurting."

Isaac toweled off and shrugged into his coat. He could feel the fatigue in his muscles. He knew he should have spent more time sleeping last night instead of fooling around with Tim—that his lack of sleep was affecting him now—but he couldn't say he regretted it that much. Or at all. He just hated that he was paying for it now, especially since four years ago, he could have partied a lot harder and still coasted to a win. He couldn't tell if it was good or bad that he had to fight harder for it now.

When Isaac walked into the little curtained-off area where the American medical staff worked with the athletes, Bill was putting the cups on Conor, whose face lit up as Isaac approached. "You here for therapy?"

"No," Isaac said. "Look, I'm tired, but I have one more race tonight. Adam made me come back here. I don't want anything weird to happen to me, I'm just following Coach's orders."

Bill pointed to a massage table. "Take off the coat and lie on that facedown."

"Fine." Isaac climbed on the table.

"Which muscles are sore?" asked Bill, turning on a space heater.

"Arms," Isaac said. "Shoulders."

Bill nodded. "Conor, sit tight for a sec."

Isaac turned his head and watched as Conor sat there with the cups on his shoulders, making those weird circular hickeys like big polka dots across his skin. Isaac was willing to do a lot for his sport, but he was too vain to allow that.

"Does that really help?" Isaac asked.

"Yeah, it helps with blood flow," said Conor. "It eases some of the muscular tension."

"Okay," said Isaac. But Bill would put cups on Isaac over his dead body.

Bill said, "Put your head in the hole."

Isaac moved his head. "No cups," he said as he settled onto the table.

He was rewarded by Bill massaging his back and arms. It felt so good on his tired muscles that Isaac possibly moaned and definitely fell asleep. Bill had to wake him up a half hour before his race so that he could go warm up again.

Isaac dragged himself back to the warm-up pool, but the massage had definitely helped. He was still tired, but he had less soreness, and he thought he had enough gas left in the tank to swim another race.

Less than four minutes of swimming. Isaac could do it.

Thirty minutes later he stood up on the block to race the 400-meter freestyle final. Tim wasn't in the audience this time because he'd promised his diving teammates he'd watch whichever diving event was happening that day—women's springboard prelims, if Isaac was not mistaken. Isaac was kind of glad, because he would have hated to embarrass himself in front of Tim. And this race could very well be an embarrassment.

Luke was a few lanes away, swinging his arms, doing the prerace ritual. But Isaac didn't care about

Luke. He bent down and moved into starting position, focused only on his own race.

Deep breath. Set. Go.

The water felt good, at least, and it buoyed Isaac a little, both literally and figuratively. His arms didn't start to burn until about halfway through, but he knew he was at least ahead of the swimmers in the lanes on either side of him. So he wouldn't finish dead last.

For whatever crazy reason, he decided to all-out sprint the last length of the pool. His body screamed. His muscles were on fire. But he pushed through the fatigue and the pain, swimming with everything he had. By the twenty-five-meter mark, he thought he might throw up right there in the middle of the pool, but he kept pushing. He wanted to give this his all, to know that if he lost, it was because he was outperformed, not that he didn't try.

No regrets. To live each day as if it was his last.

He reached out and touched the side of the pool but stayed underwater for a second, not quite ready to face it yet. Then he popped up and looked at the screen.

He'd touched third. Somehow, by some miracle, he'd touched the wall third and won a bronze medal.

"Thank Mark Spitz," Isaac said, echoing Adam's favorite expression.

Luke had won the gold.

Isaac swam over to Luke and gave him a loose-armed hug.

"First," Luke said.

"Congrats, man."

"Thanks. Holy shit, that was incredible."

Isaac's limbs had turned to spaghetti, and Luke had to help him out of the pool, but he at least got to his obligatory postwin interview. Mindy Somers wore a sea-green polo today. Isaac didn't think he'd be able to say much because he still hadn't caught his breath. Luckily Mindy shoved the mic in Luke's face first.

Luke babbled about how honored he was to be representing America and how great that swim had felt. When Mindy got to Isaac, he mostly panted. But he managed to get out, "Hey, can't win them all," and "Couldn't have lost to a better guy," even though a Japanese swimmer Isaac didn't know had claimed the silver. Although he was probably a good guy too.

He held it together until he got back to the warm-up pool, at which time he basically collapsed into a chair. Bill ran over and checked his vitals, but Isaac waved him off.

"I'm fine. Just tapped out."

"Yeah. You might have overdone it a little. Your pulse is kind of thready."

"Can I just lie here forever?"

"No," said Adam, hovering over him. "You have to cool down properly or your muscles will seize up. Get in the pool."

Isaac swore a blue streak.

Adam helped him out of the chair and tapped his back. "You did good, kid. I'm really proud of you."

"I might throw up."

"Happens," said Adam. "Now get in the pool."

Isaac took a deep breath and hopped into the water.

WHEN TIM woke up from his afternoon nap, he looked around. Jason sat on the other bed, staring at his phone. Tim sat up, felt pretty well rested, and was about to get up to shower when he heard Jason say, "Oh no."

"What?"

Jason shot Tim a sidelong glance. "You are not going to like this."

"What is it?"

"There's an article on some news site. A straight reporter put a gay hookup app on his phone and turned it on in the Olympic Village. He found a bunch of guys looking to hook up and recognized a few of their profile pictures."

Tim's stomach flopped. "Oh no."

"Yup. He called out a bunch of athletes, although none by name. Still, you could read between the lines and guess who he's talking about. He says he messaged an American fencer and a Dutch gymnast, among others. And holy shit, an archer from Iran."

Tim broke out in a cold sweat. Not so much for himself, since he was out and didn't have any hookup apps on his phone, but for all the athletes in the village who only wanted a good time during their Olympic experience but didn't need to be in the center of a controversy. Then the fear flipped to anger. Tim sat up and said, "Fuck that guy. What an asshole. Does he not get that some of these people live in countries where being outed can get them arrested or killed? That even the American fencer has a lot to lose if he wasn't out publicly? I hate shit like this. Do you know why gay apps are even a thing? So we have a safe space to talk to each other without this bullshit. Goddamn, I can't believe that happened."

"I know. It gets worse. Because then he says, 'It's interesting that all these athletes are hiding on the app, but out athletes like Timothy Swan are nowhere to be seen on it.'"

Tim wanted to throw up. "He could have left my name out of it."

Jason sat quietly for a moment. "It's a brave thing you did," he said softly.

"I just want to dive," Tim said, getting out of bed, throwing his covers onto the floor with some force. The sheets fluttered down in an unsatisfying way.

"I'm sorry, Tim. I didn't mean to piss you off."

"No, it's not your fault. But this is why I didn't want to talk to that reporter who showed up at the pool. Nobody wants to talk to me about diving. That woman would have talked to you about platforms and spring-boards and back three-and-a-half pikes, but she only wanted to talk to me about my sex life, and I am fucking sick of it."

"I know. It's not fair. I wish it was different."

"Dave's wife came out here to see him dive. I caught part of the American broadcast of the semifinals. The camera kept panning to Dave's wife and daughter, and the kid is cute and all, but it was like Dave's worth was being determined by the fact that he'd succeeded in life. He has a bronze medal from the last Olympics and now he has a wife and daughter, and his life is complete." Tim sighed. "And it's the nature of the beast. Olympics coverage has been like this forever. They're trying to appeal to female viewers or whatever the fuck. But do you think that if I got married, they'd pan to the audience to show off my husband? Doubtful."

"I know. It sucks."

"And Isaac, poor crazy Isaac, doesn't really care who knows about us, and I guess I don't either, but what happens if it does get out? Are we gonna be able to do cutesy stories about our Olympic love during any of the broadcasts?"

"Tim, sorry, I shouldn't have mentioned it."

"No, it's okay." Tim sighed. He shook out his shoulders, trying to calm down. "I didn't mean to get so angry. This bullshit gets to me sometimes, but I'll shower and shake it off. You coming with me to watch the women's team dive tonight?"

"Yeah. I'll get dressed."

Chapter 17

Day 6

THE LAST hell day—a day in which Isaac had to swim in at least three races—dawned as the past few days had, with Tim in bed beside Isaac. Isaac had a bit of a swing in his step as he got to his preliminary race. He felt a million times better than he had the previous evening.

Luke raised an eyebrow as Isaac walked into the locker room. "You look… improved."

"I don't need PEDs. I don't need alternative medicine. All I need is a solid night's sleep." Isaac did feel pretty incredible. He jumped up and down a couple of times, shaking out his body, testing how he felt physically. "It's probably all adrenaline, but I feel great. I'm like a shark. I have to keep swimming or I'll die."

Luke guffawed. "That's a hell of a metaphor."

"This is the last terrible day. 200 IM prelims today, the 200 breast semi, relay tonight, then the IM relay tomorrow. Adam says I don't have to swim the relay prelims."

"Yeah. I'm on the relay tonight too. I might swim in the prelims for shits and giggles."

"Hell, maybe I should too. I feel good enough to do it."

"Slow down there, hotshot. You could barely move last night. Don't overdo it."

Isaac grinned. He wasn't sure why he felt so great—he had some theories and a lot of superstition—but he didn't want to question it.

When he walked into the warm-up room, someone was blasting Beyoncé, so Isaac did a little dance by the side of the pool.

"That might be the gayest thing I've ever seen you do," Luke said, laughing.

"Pretty sure giving my new boyfriend a blow job last night is gayer, but whatever." Isaac dove in the pool before Luke could respond. He felt too giddy to let Luke get his goat.

Of course, Tim had been upset last night by the story, which had now spread through the Athlete Village, that a reporter had scoped out athletes in a gay hookup app and outed a bunch of them. Not Isaac, since Isaac's phone still buzzed too much for him to do anything except text the people he actually wanted to speak with—limited mostly to his mother, sister, and Tim—but he supposed it could have been him if he hadn't met Tim. He didn't generally seek out that kind of companionship until after his events were over. But this was his fourth Olympics. He knew what an orgy the Athlete Village tended to devolve into the second week of the Games. And if an athlete finished his events early and wanted to get a little something? What was the harm? Thousands of athletes, all in one place, meant a plethora of beautiful people to choose from.

Tim was right, of course, that the article invaded the privacy of the athletes and the enclosed bubble of the Athlete Village. Although by the time Isaac read it, the identifying details had been removed from the article. Still, the damage had been done.

Isaac wanted to double down on their relationship, to be seen together somewhere in public, maybe with cameras around. But Tim told him he preferred to lie low for a few more days. Isaac agreed, recognizing the rebellious tendency in himself that wanted to go public to make trouble, not because it was the right time for them.

Luke caught up with Isaac when Isaac stopped at one end of the pool to rest for a moment. "You don't always have to be the asshole," Luke said.

"But I so enjoy it."

"I haven't seen you like this in... years, I think."

"Am I annoying you?"

"No. No, not at all. You used to love this sport. You had fun. You won races because you had fun. You remember your first Olympics? One of the youngest American swimmers to win a gold medal, and do you remember what you said during the interview when you got out of the pool?"

"That was fun." Isaac didn't have an actual memory of this happening, but the clip had aired on TV a zillion times.

Luke nodded. "I'll always remember that. I think about it whenever I compete. I do this because I love it, because it's fun. You used to also." He shook the water out of his hair and leaned on the pool wall. "You were so unhappy the last few years before your fake retirement. I always kind of thought that if you could remember how much fun this sport was, you'd be all right."

Isaac nodded. He'd been unhappy largely because he faced the end of his career. Well, and because he'd been drunk most of the time. He treaded water for a moment, ducking his head under the water and resurfacing again. "I have three more days of competition. I plan to make the most of them. I'll give it whatever I have. And then I can retire for real and feel good about it."

"You clawed your way back just to retire again?"

"I'm thinking about coaching."

Luke tilted his head. "Yeah?"

"Yeah. I think I have some unique experience I could share. You're right, you have to love something like this. Enjoy it, find it fun. Because otherwise what the hell is the point? I've pulled muscles. I've gotten banged up. After Worlds six years ago, I came home with a huge bruise on my thigh where that guy kicked me. It took forever to heal. Remember that?"

"Yeah. That guy had some kick."

Isaac smiled. "I want these kids coming up to know what it's really like. The temptations you face when you're successful. How not to let defeat crush you. It's something I thought about a lot in rehab. I love this sport, but my body will only allow me to do it for so long. My meets as an athlete are numbered, but I can stay involved with the sport in other ways."

Luke smiled. "You are absolutely right. I think you'd be a great coach."

"Thanks. I appreciate it."

"You're leaving Raleigh too, aren't you?"

"I don't know. I don't want to make any concrete plans until the Olympic bubble pops. I love my family and my friends. I'll keep training with Adam as long as my body lets me. Then maybe he'd take me on as an apprentice or something."

"Is that what you really want? To stay in Raleigh?"

"Maybe. I don't know. I guess if there are other opportunities out there, they might be worth thinking about."

"I'll miss you."

Yeah. Despite everything, Isaac had people at home who cared about him, and moving away from them would suck. But it felt like the next phase of his life was beginning, and Isaac needed to keep moving forward instead of treading water. Isaac grabbed Luke's head and pulled him in for a hug. "I'll visit and shit."

Luke laughed. "Come on, let's finish the warm-up."

TIM WAS very close to pulling out of the springboard event. After a day of training, his body felt like he'd been thrown in a blender.

"Selaya pulled out," Donnie said, his tablet in his hand as Tim approached him after the last dive.

"What, no 'hey, that was great' or 'you bent your body too much' or 'your legs were separated during the pike'?"

"No, you looked good. It was a solid dive. You're fine for competition. But the Australian team just announced Selaya hit his foot on the springboard during practice yesterday, and apparently he hit it hard enough to break a bone, so he's out. One less competitor to worry about."

"That sucks for him."

"Oh. Yeah. It does. Try not to hit *your* feet on the springboard."

"No, I won't. Are you sure I should do the spring-board competition, though? You don't think it's going to put too much strain on my body to do two competitions next week? If I make it to the finals of both spring-board and platform, that's three rounds of six dives for each competition. Thirty-six competition dives."

"Yup. And how many dives do you typically do in a week?"

Fair point. "You're certain I can do this?"

"Yes. Are you sore anywhere?"

He was sore everywhere, but not more than usual, so he said, "No, I'm all right."

"Kayla has really good things to say about that Ki-nesio tape she's been using. Apparently it helped stabi-lize her back."

"I'm not injured. My body feels good."

"Then you're fine. But Kayla has more tape if you need it. It's waterproof and stays on during competition pretty well."

Tim nodded. He did feel good, just tired. "I tossed my shammy from the springboard. Did you see where it went?"

Donnie handed it over, so apparently he had been paying attention. Tim had a lucky shammy that he carried around like a security blanket during competition. It was a little towel with unicorns and rainbows on it—he figured he might as well embrace his identity—and it was faded in parts from chlorine and too many washings. Every diver used this kind of fast-drying shammy, and there was a fair amount of superstition regarding them, but Tim needed his. He wiped his face with it now.

"Look, Timmy, you can do this. If ever there was a diver who could, it's you. And you probably *are* going to hurt come the platform final, but it's the Olympics."

Tim nodded and thought of what Isaac had said about pushing himself to his limits. Tim supposed it wasn't worth doing if he didn't put his all into it. "All right. I hope I don't regret this later."

"I think you'll regret it more if you don't try for both."

Tim nodded. That was probably true. "What time is it?"

Donnie looked at his watch. "Seven."

The evening swim session started in an hour, so the swimmers were likely in the building. Tim was tempted to stick around to watch Isaac again, but he felt worn out from a grueling practice and not getting enough sleep.

"Come on," Ginny said. "We'll go back to the Athlete Village. You look like you could use a nap or five."

Tim followed her out of the Aquatics Center. As they walked outside, Ginny looked at her phone. "Uh-oh," she murmured with a glance toward Tim.

"What now?"

"Don't get mad. It's probably not true. This gossip site is mostly just made-up shit."

Tim's heart raced. Was it an item about him and Isaac? "What is it?"

"Uh. There's a rumor Pat's in Madrid."

Tim's heart stopped. That could not be true. "Let me see."

Ginny reluctantly handed over her phone. "Again, just a rumor."

"He knows better than that. It's over. I was very clear about that. Why would he be in Madrid?"

Tim was so tired, he could barely focus on the words on the screen, but Ginny had a celebrity gossip website open on her browser. Tim swallowed and made himself focus on the text: Oak Hills *star Patterson Wood was spotted in Madrid. Could he be there to see ex Tim Swan dive at the Olympics? Does this mean a reunion is on the horizon?*

"It does *not*," said Tim aloud.

"Maybe he's got a doppelganger."

"He can't be here, Ginny. He *can't*."

"He probably isn't. I'm sorry. I shouldn't have shown you this."

"No, it's better to know. Do you think he'd show up at one of the competitions?"

"No. You're right, he knows better. It's probably not even him. How many tall, brown-haired, handsome actors are there in the world? What are the odds your ex would turn up in Madrid? Push it out of your mind, Timmy."

While they waited up for the bus, Tim tried to forget he knew there was a small chance Pat was in Madrid. He texted Isaac to wish him luck but explained he needed to sleep.

Isaac texted back a moment later: *I left my spare key under your door.*

Well. At least that would be a place to hide for a bit.

CHAPTER 18

THE 200 IM semifinal was kind of a trial, and Isaac's arms began to burn sooner than usual, so he swam a conservative race and made the final by the skin of his teeth. Which meant he had a shitty lane assignment, but he was in the final, and that was what mattered.

Because next he had to anchor—goddamned anchor—the 4 x 200 free relay.

The anchor job was a particular challenge, because either the anchor was gifted with a lead by his teammates and had to keep it, or he had a deficit to make up and had to push to close it. Isaac had anchored relays with those kinds of deficits and made up the time, but he'd been younger then, and better rested. That the American team was both the defending Olympic champion and the overwhelming favorite here didn't do much to ease the pressure. And, yes, he'd anchored the 4 x 100 meter relay, but that was a sprint and his part was over in less than a minute. Swimming two hundred meters when everyone depended on you was a different task entirely.

The team was full of heavyweights, at least. Luke had his gold medal in the 400 free, and Randy had also made a good showing so far. The first leg was a young guy named Nate who had won a silver in the 200 free. Luke thought he'd kill it, and Isaac trusted Luke's insights.

They did the prerace song and dance. The relays were popular with the crowd, and there were a lot of Americans here, including a lot of nonaquatics Olympians: half the women's basketball team, the beach volleyball pair that had already been eliminated, and a few fencers, according to Isaac's teammates who knew such things. There were American flags all over the Aquatics Center.

Nate dove into the pool for the first lap before Isaac felt ready, but he forced himself to focus on the race. Randy got them a decent lead, which Luke then compounded, so by the time Isaac got up on the block for the exchange, the US team had about a twenty-meter lead. Isaac could work with that.

He tried to pull from his joyful mood from earlier, thought about Tim maybe watching from the lounge back at the Athlete Village—if he wasn't sleeping—and listened to the crowd cheering for him. Well, a Spanish team swam in the final too, so in reality, the majority-Spanish crowd was probably rooting for them, but Isaac pretended the whole world was behind him.

For the last fifty meters, Isaac pushed past the pain until he had so much adrenaline in his system, he didn't feel anything anymore. He felt giddy, even, his skin numb and tingly, like he could do anything. He reached out and touched the wall and surfaced to see if he'd held on to the lead.

He had. The Americans had won the race by four seconds.

Two hours later, almost as soon as he stepped off the medal podium, Sheri handed him an interview itinerary for the next day. Five medals got you that kind of attention, he supposed. His only race the next day was the IM final, but he couldn't take the whole day off, because not getting in his morning practice would screw with his conditioning. He saw that the schedule gave him time in the pool as well.

The relay team wanted to party and talked about it the whole way back to the Athlete Village. They invited Isaac to come with them to America House, but Isaac begged off. "I have to be up early" was his first excuse. It wasn't a lie; Sheri and the USA Swimming car would be picking him up first thing. But he couldn't deny the pang in his chest as he thought about all the athletes and family members and assorted other personnel laughing and having fun at the bar. And drinking. Isaac could practically taste that cold beer, could feel the sweaty glass in his hand, feel the bubbles tingling in his mouth. No, it was too much. He couldn't go to a bar.

Luke nodded, but Randy nagged him. "Come on, you're not swimming until late tomorrow. At least have a drink with us."

"Well, I'm an alcoholic, so no, I won't be doing that," Isaac said. But Lord, it was tempting. Isaac was still buzzing too much with postrace adrenaline to trust himself with these guys. It would be so easy to just reach out and take that beer. And then all of his hard work would have been wasted.

"Oh, right," Randy said.

That effectively shut down the party conversation, so when the bus pulled up to their building, Isaac got out while his teammates went to drink themselves silly. He felt a pang of longing, wanting to hang out with those guys, wanting to celebrate a hard-fought-for victory. He wanted to party, with his whole soul he wanted it, but he knew he couldn't. Each step into the building, away from the bar where his teammates were about to have a great night, felt like he was pulling cement blocks.

Isaac could see the beer. He imagined cracking open a can, letting the cold liquid slide over his tongue. Cheap beer had been his drug of choice when he'd been controlled by alcohol, something he could buy a lot of with his limited savings but that also didn't taste strongly enough of anything to be a struggle to get down. But good beer was worth savoring: the bitterness of the hops, the tickle of carbonation, the smooth way it went down. He craved one of those now with his whole body. It would be so satisfying, and also so devastating.

So no, he wouldn't put himself in a position to be close enough to beer where it would be too easy to simply ask for one. Hell, five medals? The whole bar would probably buy him one. But he would not be partying with his teammates, no matter how much he wanted to.

Also, he really wanted to see Tim. He didn't want to rely on Tim. When he'd first begun training with Adam again, he'd talked with his doctor about not becoming reliant on any one thing to keep him sober—not Adam, not swimming, and now not Tim. But it wasn't just that seeing Tim would keep him sober. Seeing Tim made him happy, aroused him, excited him.

Isaac was tired now. The adrenaline was wearing off, leaving behind an ache that spread through his body. How great would it be to just lie down with Tim and fall asleep, to be warm and comfortable and safe?

He stuck his head in the lounge on the way to his room, because a lot of people were gathered around the TV.

"Here comes the Flood!" some guy said. "Fourth gold! You're a goddamn superhero."

This crowd looked a little rowdy. Isaac waved to them. "Thanks." He walked into the room and let people manhandle and congratulate him while he confirmed Tim was not there. The TV showed gymnastics—women's all-around, according to the caption—and it had most of the room riveted to the screen. They were passing around beers too. Isaac's mouth watered.

It would be so easy. It would take away the pain and fatigue that moved through his body in waves now.

"You know anything about gymnastics, Flood?" asked a blond guy Isaac thought might have been a pole vaulter. He was long and lanky and wore a USA Track & Field shirt.

"No, not really," Isaac said.

"The Americans have the team with the most depth. So there are two Americans in the all-around final, and they're currently one and two. This girl Chelsea is unbeatable. Like, thirty points ahead of everyone else. Crazy, right?"

That gymnast, Jake, would know what it must have been like to be a skilled athlete who choked in international competition and be constantly compared to those who raked up the medals. Isaac thought of him as a couple of people in the crowd explained the women's competition to him.

After all that, Isaac ducked out of the room; he couldn't be around beer. The smell called to him now. It was hard to pull away—he still wanted to celebrate, to party, to bask in the praise of the other athletes—but it was for the best. The assembled crowd booed when he announced he was leaving. He gave them a little wave, then went down the hall to his room. He opened the door and was delighted to see Tim passed out on his bed.

Isaac changed out of his official American warm-up suit and into a pair of boxer briefs and a T-shirt. He put his medal—the fifth one, God Almighty—into the special lockbox Adam had given him. Then he got into bed beside Tim.

Tim stirred and rolled to look up at Isaac. He smiled. "Hi."

"Hi. Bad news, babe."

"What's that?"

"I won another gold medal, so you're going to have to put out for me again."

Tim grinned. "Are you kidding?"

"Nope. We won the relay tonight."

"So you're the best swimmer currently racing, basically."

"I guess."

Tim put his arms around Isaac's neck and said, "How's about, 'You're the best swimmer currently in this bed'?"

"Well, that I'll believe." Isaac smiled. Then he leaned down and kissed Tim soundly.

He was safe here, away from temptation, and it occurred to him that Tim made him safe too. It wasn't reliance, it was that something in Tim soothed the part of Isaac that otherwise would have spent tonight beating himself up. His body hurt, a pain easy to dull with alcohol. He still felt in awe of that medal and wanted to celebrate. But more than anything, he wanted to be with Tim. He trusted Tim. He could be honest with Tim.

Another vestige of rehab was the suggestion that, when Isaac felt like he was in trouble, he needed to let someone know. He hated asking for help, he didn't want to talk about it, and he worried Tim would judge him, but for the sake of his own safety, Isaac knew he had to speak up. He took a deep breath, inhaling Tim's scent, and said, "I really want to drink right now."

Tim frowned. "Are you okay?"

"A little sore. Anxious about all the interviews I have tomorrow. I'm okay, but everyone wanted to celebrate winning the relay tonight, and I...." Isaac looked away, struggling to say what he knew he had to. "I'm telling you I'm tempted, not that I will do anything about it. I'm getting better at knowing when a situation will be too much for me, so I came here instead of partying with my teammates. But in the interest of full disclosure, I'm jonesing for a drink more than usual right now. I just wanted you to know."

Tim nodded slowly. "Thank you for trusting me with that." He threaded his fingers through Isaac's hair and pulled him into a kiss. "You still want to drink?"

"Yes. Always. Now that I'm here, away from athletes with beer, the urge is waning. But I gotta say, I really need the rest. USA Swimming set me up on a ton of interviews tomorrow, and I need to race in the IM final."

"All right." Tim stroked Isaac's hair. "So rest. That's important."

"Thank you, Tim." The words felt like a weak way to express the gratitude Isaac felt. Tim hadn't judged, he hadn't offered advice, he'd just looked at Isaac in that serious but kind way, and that was precisely what Isaac had needed. He could still practically taste cold beer on his tongue, but now that he was here with Tim, the need wasn't as strong. He'd be okay. He'd done the right thing. He'd stayed on the wagon. He realized quite suddenly that ever since he'd gotten off the bus, his anxiety had spiked and his heart had been pounding, but now his body's operations began to fall back to normal speed. He breathed slowly, calming down, thankful that Tim was here when Isaac needed him.

"You're lucky I'm more tired than horny," said Tim.

Isaac chuckled and settled back into the bed. He snaked his arm around Tim and pulled him close. It didn't take long to drift off to sleep.

CHAPTER 19

Day 7

TIM SAW Isaac off to his car to the broadcast center before joining his diving teammates for breakfast. Jason and Kayla flirted like wild, which was new, but Tim thought it all in good fun. Jason came with Tim to the gym afterward, where Donnie made Tim perform what felt like five thousand aerial somersaults while jumping on a trampoline. Tim was sore now, especially his abs, and coated in a gallon of sweat. Jason looked similarly drenched when they wrapped up their workout.

"I could use a shower and a cold drink," Tim said. "I'd kill for a lemonade."

"Oh yeah," said Jason, wiping his face with a towel. "You know where they have good lemonade? America House. The bartender makes it fresh-squeezed."

"Too much sugar."

Jason rolled his eyes. "I think they have unsweetened iced tea too."

"I guess that'd get the job done."

After quick showers, they walked together over to America House. Since only Olympians were allowed in the dorm buildings, it was the main place athletes went to meet with their families. Ginny was there having lunch with her parents; Tim and Jason waved to her as they walked to the bar.

Cold iced tea in hand—and a few jealous looks at Jason's lemonade—Tim found a booth near one of the TVs. It showed the American network's broadcast, which happened to be airing an interview with one Isaac Flood.

Everyone else in the room seemed to be watching the interview, so Tim could hear Isaac talk.

"I worked really hard for this," Isaac was saying. "You can't just wake up one morning and decide to go to another Olympics. I've been training for a year and a half. I radically changed my diet, and I'm in the best shape of my life."

"Do you think some athletes are naturally gifted?" asked Nikki Kenmore, the *Wake Up, America!* cohost. "I mean, you had so much raw talent when you were younger."

Isaac laughed. "That's true to a point. My mother basically tossed me in a pool when I was an infant, and I've been swimming ever since. After that, it's kind of a chicken and egg thing. Genetics might have given me my height and my long limbs, but the rest of it's all training."

Nikki grinned as if she didn't believe him. Isaac did have an incredible body that seemed designed specifically to move him quickly through water, but Tim understood exactly what he meant.

Nikki said, "So what's next?"

"Well, I've got at least one more race. Two if I do the IM relay on Saturday."

Nikki laughed. "And what about after that?"

Isaac shrugged. "Guess I'll go back to Raleigh."

"More swimming?"

"Yeah, maybe. I'm not a hundred percent on that yet, but I think I've got a few more world championship races in me."

"Do you have another Olympics in you?"

Isaac smiled but then shrugged. "We'll see. Four years is a long time in the life of an athlete."

The interview wrapped up soon after that. Tim sipped his iced tea and watched as the show went to commercial, letting himself dwell on the idea that Isaac would go back to Raleigh when the Games ended. Or sooner. Just that morning Tim had heard some of the swimmers talking in the locker room about getting flights home on Monday.

The very idea of losing Isaac so soon left Tim bereft. They'd only just found each other; it seemed cruel for Isaac to leave so soon. He knew intellectually that when the Games ended, they'd go back to their own home cities, but even contemplating that made Tim feel hollow. They had so much more to learn about each other, to explore together. There had to be more of a future for them than the end of the Olympics. Right?

Isaac intended to stick around past the end of swimming, Tim thought, but they hadn't talked about it. He thought he remembered Isaac saying his flight home wasn't until after the Closing Ceremony, but he couldn't swear to that.

Tim's phone chimed. He looked down and saw a new text from Isaac.

Miss u. TBC is making me do entertainment show interview.

That sounded like Isaac's nightmare. The American network, TBC, owned a half-dozen channels and had a lot of hours to fill. And that included their evening block of tabloid-esque shows that covered celebrity news. Tim had seen the *Hollywood Tonight* reporters talking to people after the incident during practice, so he knew they were still hanging around Madrid. But the idea of Isaac going on the show seemed so strange.

Tim texted back, *Sounds terrible.*

Isaac returned: *I've been warned I'll have to answer love life questions. Wouldn't it shock the hell out of the people back home if I told them I've been hooking up with a dude?*

Oh boy. Tim's stomach flopped. *I'd love that, but I don't want to go public about us until after the diving finals.*

It wasn't that Tim was ashamed of the relationship or even unsure about it anymore. He just didn't want the press attention to distract him from what he was there to do. He was pretty sure Isaac understood that, but he made a mental note to clarify with him later. He'd happily go public about dating Isaac Flood thirty seconds after his last dive.

Isaac texted back a smiley face, then: *Understood. I'll be vague. I'm off the market. Dating a nice young fella.*

Tim laughed, inadvertently snorting, which made Jason look at him with both eyebrows raised. "I'm texting with Isaac," Tim said.

"The guy who was just on TV?" Jason shook his head. "The Olympics are surreal."

IN 1972, Mark Spitz—Isaac's idol—won seven gold medals, then the record for most medals won in a single Olympics. Michael Phelps, probably the greatest swimmer of all time, came along later and won eight.

Isaac wouldn't be breaking those records—he hadn't qualified for enough races—but he walked out to the blocks for the 200 IM final with four golds and a bronze acquired only in this past week. If he medaled tonight and swam in the IM relay tomorrow night, he had the potential for seven medals this Olympics. Not a record, but still really fucking impressive.

He was pushing his body to the limit of what it could do. He was tired and sore, although his muscles hummed now with anticipation.

He excelled at middle-distance races, liked them more than sprints. He'd always had the balance of speed and endurance that was best suited to the 400. The 200 IM was more like a sprint, doing each stroke for only one length of the pool as fast as he could manage. The challenge with the IM was that every swimmer had a strong stroke—his was breaststroke—and a weak stroke—his was butterfly. The lead in the race would change hands four or five times, probably. The trick was to not fall too far back in the first two weaker strokes so that he could make up the time in the last two stronger laps.

He plotted out his strategy while one of the Australian swimmers with a goggle problem stalled the proceedings. Racing was as much about strategy as it was about strength, speed, and stamina. Swimmers had to calculate when to conserve energy and when to push it, and Isaac had made a lot of wrong guesses in his career that had cost him races.

He did not want to lose today.

Winning five medals was nothing to sneeze at, and the 200 IM was hardly his best event. He'd earned a shitty lane assignment thanks to his barely squeaking through the semifinal, so here he was at Lane Eight, all the way on the edge of the pool. It meant he couldn't take advantage of the wake of the swimmers on either side of him—strategy and physics—and he wouldn't be able to see the swimmers who would probably capture the lead. Harvey, a swimmer from the UK, did a fast butterfly lap, and he'd likely maintain some kind of lead for the first hundred meters, but Isaac wouldn't be able to see him.

Maybe that was ideal. Maybe it was better for Isaac to swim his own race.

He was better rested now, he reasoned as he got up on the blocks. He'd gotten a solid nine hours' sleep the night before. He'd done a workout with Adam earlier that day, but he hadn't raced, so his body felt good. Tired, but good.

The beep of the race starting spurred him into Pavlovian action, as he threw himself off the block and started to swim what felt like the butterfly lap of his life. His arms and shoulders burned as he got to the wall, making the backstroke feel like a fucking vacation. He followed the lines of the beams that ran the length of the Aquatics Center ceiling to make sure he was going straight, and he hugged the rope a little to get some of the kick from his neighboring swimmer, and then he saw the little flags that indicated it was time to turn.

Then it was the breaststroke lap.

For whatever reason, this combination of arm and leg movements was the one his body was ideally suited for, and he glided through the water. He sprinted, only surfacing to breathe once in fifty meters, though when he popped his head out of the water, he heard the crowd screaming their heads off. He imagined he could hear

Adam screaming too, and his mother and sister, and maybe even Tim.

So when he made the last turn, he wanted to win. He wanted his fifth gold medal of these Games for everyone who had believed in him when he'd been on the bottom, for his mother, who'd put him in swim lessons, for Adam, for seeing his potential and agreeing to train him even though he was an alcoholic, and for Tim, for making this week the best week of his whole fucking life.

For the first time in five years, probably, Isaac thought his life might have taken a turn in the right direction, and nothing would signal that better than a win here.

He told himself it didn't *really* matter as he reached for the wall. He'd already accomplished so much.

Except it fucking did matter. And when he finished the race and popped up to look at the scoreboard, there it fucking was: Gold: Isaac Flood.

He shouted. Just noise, nothing coherent, but he shouted and slapped at the water. He looked back at the scoreboard to make sure he hadn't imagined it. His body pulsed with adrenaline, with tingly giddiness, and he looked around, seeing other people bearing witness to this too. He accepted the congratulations of the swimmer in Lane Seven, still not completely convinced he'd done it.

He was out of the water before he even knew what he was doing. The officials were trying to clear the pool to get it ready for the next race. Isaac got pulled aside by Mindy Somers again but didn't hear her first question because his ears were ringing so much.

"What?" he asked.

"You just won your fifth gold medal, Isaac, and your sixth medal overall for these Games. That has to feel incredible."

"It does," Isaac said. "God, it feels amazing. I can't believe I pulled that off."

"You made up a lot of time in the last one hundred meters. Was that part of your strategy?"

Isaac wanted to laugh. "Well, I knew the first hundred were my weaker strokes." Isaac had to stop to pant because he hadn't gotten his breath back yet. "So I just tried to swim well, but I knew I could make up the time with the breast and the free. What was the time?"

"Uh. 1:56."

Isaac nodded. A sub-two-minute race was… really fucking good. "Oh. That's… that might be a personal best."

"It is, yes. Now's the time to have it, right? At the Olympic Games?"

"Yeah." Isaac wanted to curse, but the TV camera loomed large in front of him.

"We'll let you go, but congratulations again, Isaac."

"Yeah. Thanks."

After a couple of laps in the warm-up pool, Isaac was done for the night, so he got his things and went back to the locker room. He had to change into the official warm-up suit for the medal ceremony—God, he really had just done that—but more than anything, he wanted to get back to the Athlete Village so that he could be with Tim.

He knew the other swimmers would want to party again. A bunch of them were flying home Monday and were also done racing because Saturday's contests were limited to the long-distance races and the IM relay.

Which meant roughly three-quarters of the swim team wanted to spend the weekend in an alcohol-and-sex-fueled haze. Isaac had already been invited to three parties. But all he wanted was Tim.

Adam stopped him on his way into the locker room. He grinned. "Goddamn, Isaac." Adam bit his lip and shook his head, a rare show of emotion for him. Then he pulled Isaac into a hug. "Goddamn. I can't believe you had that in you."

"I wanted it," Isaac said.

"I know. And I know how hard you worked for it. You deserve it." After slapping Isaac's back, Adam backed up and said, "When we went to the Trials, I knew you'd win some races there, that you'd qualify for a bunch of things here. But when I got to Madrid, I thought you had a chance to medal in a couple of things, but I knew our odds were long. To see you swimming the way you have been...." Adam bit his lip again, clearly trying to keep whatever he was feeling at bay. But his voice broke when he said, "I'm so proud of you, Isaac. So proud. Of what you've done, of how far you've come. We... we thought we'd lost you for a while there, and I'm so glad you're back."

Isaac's chest seized, and tears prickled at his eyes. It meant a lot to hear that from Adam, who was always so stoic. Isaac said, "I'm glad to be back," and it sounded watery.

Adam hugged him again.

Isaac knew he wouldn't come to another Olympics. He might swim another year or two, maybe try for a few world champion medals, but this was the twilight of his career. It was a spectacular twilight, the kind that looked like someone on acid had painted it on the sky, but the sun was setting nonetheless. His body knew that, which was probably why he'd been able to pull so much from it this week. But it was definitely the end.

Adam had to get back to the pool to coach someone for the next race, so Isaac went to find his locker and change.

And there was Tim.

Tim stood leaning against Isaac's locker, casually examining his nails as if he just happened to be there, but Isaac knew better and wanted to whoop with joy.

"Did you see that?" Isaac asked.

Tim grinned. "My friend Ginny and I caught the races tonight. I got in here by lying to the security guard that I forgot something here earlier and flashing my pass."

"Smart guy."

Tim looked up and down the aisle, so Isaac followed his gaze, likely making the same mental calculations. The locker room was crawling with other swimmers, but in this little row of lockers, there was no one but Isaac and Tim. "I had to see you," Tim said softly.

"Thank God," Isaac said. Then he kissed Tim.

That felt amazing, because it was all Isaac wanted. He wanted to win swim races and kiss Tim. If he could have those things forever, his life might just turn out all right.

One of those things was not in the cards, but he held out hope for the other.

He was falling in love with Tim, wasn't he?

It didn't scare him the way it once might have, back when he was still drinking and living by the seat of his pants. Instead he embraced it, and embraced Tim. He put his arms around Tim, who in turn pressed his palms into Isaac's back, and they stood like that, kissing against Isaac's locker.

A clang on the other side of the row of lockers snatched Isaac's attention away, though, and he pulled away from Tim gently. "This feels like... I think this might be one of the greatest moments of my life," he said, his voice low.

Tim nodded. "I'll sing the national anthem extra loud during the medal ceremony. Just for you."

Isaac laughed. "You know, I never sing. I always forget the words when I'm up there."

"It's okay."

"I don't even think I know the words to the second verse on a good day. That probably makes me a bad American."

Now Tim laughed. "Your secret's safe with me."

Isaac sighed and said, "I have to change, but thank you, Tim. So much. It means... well." He shook his head. "It means a lot that you would come back here to see me."

"Say, when are you flying home?"

"Uh, week from Monday?"

"Really? You'll be here next week?"

"Yeah. I know a lot of the swimmers take off once swimming is over, but when I booked my trip, I thought it might be my last Olympics, so I wanted to take advantage of the experience. Figured I'd take in some of the events, do some tourism in Madrid, the whole nine."

"Come to see me dive."

Isaac smiled. "Yes. I will definitely do that. I want to see that."

Tim stood up on his tiptoes and kissed Isaac's nose. "Good. Now go get your medal. You've earned it."

CHAPTER 20

Day 8

"SO, OKAY," Ginny was saying, "it says here that the world record in this event stands from two Olympics ago. Isaac Flood swam the breaststroke lap in that race."

It was Saturday night, and although most of the divers had gone off to find parties after practice—well, except for the women competing in the springboard finals the next day—Ginny, Jason, and Tim had gotten tickets to the last night of swimming. The Aquatics Center was packed, likely with people there to see if Isaac would win his sixth gold medal. A bunch of other American athletes were there. A tennis star fresh off her gold medal in women's singles was seated in the adjacent section of the stands, and Tim recognized a bunch of basketball players and part of the women's soccer team.

Tim had spent the previous night with Isaac again. Isaac had been so high on adrenaline that he'd wanted to have sex as soon as they closed the door to his room, and Tim had accommodated him, stripping him naked and pushing him into bed, where they made out like teenagers for a while and then exchanged blow jobs.

Isaac passed out mere seconds after he came and then slept the sleep of the dead for the rest of the night, but Tim was content to lie next to him, phasing in and out of sleep as the night went on. It gave him time to fantasize about the kind of life they could build together if they could make this work once they got back to the real world.

Because Tim was determined now to make something work.

But for now, he was going to cheer Isaac on to victory in his last race.

He looked around the stands while Ginny babbled. Almost everyone in their section wore Team USA T-shirts—a good half of them were swimmers; Tim recognized them from seeing them around in training all week—and a handful of people had handmade *Here comes the Flood!* signs.

"The lineup for this race," Ginny said, looking at her phone, "is some kid named Dylan on backstroke—I guess he won bronze in the 100 backstroke a couple of days ago—Randy Manning on butterfly, Isaac on breast, and Luke Rogers on free. That's pretty killer."

"Yeah, I overheard someone say the Americans are favored to win, and everyone thinks it will be by a huge margin," said Jason.

"Takes some of the suspense out of it," said Ginny.

"It's the Olympics, though. Tom Daley didn't make the finals."

Ginny hissed. "Tom Daley didn't make the finals" had become their code for "expect the unexpected." Because sometimes the best diver in the world could qualify in first place in the prelims and then have a bad day and not make it out of the semifinals.

Jason waved his hand. "The race is starting."

The race started with the backstroke. The American, Dylan Raines according to the scoreboard, kept up with the pace of the leaders. The tricky thing with the IM relay was that each country put up their best racer for each stroke, so it went by fast. Dylan was going against the gold and silver medalists from the 100 backstroke race earlier in the week. He got to the exchange in fifth, but within two seconds of the top four swimmers. Randy Quinn had won a silver in the butterfly, but he was young and didn't have the elite training of the other swimmers on the relay team. A lot of people hailed Randy as the next potential Michael Phelps, and he did look good in the water, pulling ahead of the third- and second-place swimmers, putting the US team in second place by the time he got to the exchange with Isaac.

Tim sat forward, anxious for Isaac.

"It's on now," shouted Ginny.

A well-rested but still well-conditioned Isaac was lethal. Tim knew Isaac was tired, that his muscles were probably sore, that Isaac had pushed himself hoping to make his body go beyond its limits. That was the thing with being an elite athlete; one was always pushing himself to go faster, be stronger, push harder.

And Isaac did here. The first-place team when Isaac dove into the water was the team from South Africa, but the swimmer on the breaststroke leg was clearly not as good as Isaac, and the lead they'd gained evaporated. Then Isaac pulled ahead. Then he kept pulling. The audience screamed and shouted for him. It felt for a moment like the whole world was behind Isaac, was pushing him forward. Likely Isaac couldn't even hear them—he didn't seem to be surfacing for breath often, if at all—but by the time he got to the exchange with Luke, he'd gained a substantial lead.

All Luke really had to do was maintain the lead. Instead, he increased it.

Tim's eyes were riveted on Isaac, though, who had gotten out of the pool and stood on the sidelines, his breathing so hard, Tim could see his chest heave from thirty yards away. As Isaac's breathing calmed, he got closer to the edge of the pool and started cheering for Luke with his teammates.

The Americans won by almost four seconds.

"That wasn't even close!" said Jason while everyone in their section of the stands went crazy.

Dylan, Randy, and Isaac hugged each other, then helped Luke out of the water, then hugged Luke.

And there it was. Isaac Flood had won six gold medals and one bronze during these Games. Having gotten to know Isaac this week, Tim understood just how significant that was, in a way maybe not everyone did. He wanted to get close to Isaac, to hug and congratulate him, but knew it would impossible now. He'd hook up with Isaac that night, though. They'd have to have some celebratory sex.

Isaac got herded into an interview off to one side of the pool. When that was over, he ran over to the stands, where his mother stood against the railing. He reached up to touch her hand, but she reached through the railing and hugged him. The image was broadcast on the huge screen next to the scoreboard. Isaac's mother cried as she hugged his head to her chest, something she could only do because the stands were elevated—she didn't look like a tall woman.

Would Tim ever get to meet her? Did he mean enough to Isaac for that?

As Isaac pulled away from his mother, he started scanning the stands. He knew Tim was there; Tim had told him he planned to sneak into the race. Isaac found Tim and they made eye contact. Isaac smiled, waved to the crowd, and then ran back to grab his stuff from the pool.

"He looked at us," Ginny said, sounding breathless.

"He looked at Tim," said Jason.

Ginny turned to Tim. "So it's, like, a real thing. You're dating Isaac Flood."

"Shh. But yes. Kind of. I guess. I don't know. It could be one of those temporary event-specific romances that burns hard and fast. I'll go back to Colorado after the Games and my old life will be waiting for me without Isaac."

"No, I don't think that's how it's going to go," said Ginny.

"No?"

"Nope. It's too good. You'll show up for the next Olympics married and have to do those fluffy news pieces about your epic romance and it will be super adorable."

"Doubtful," said Tim, though he smiled and wished that would turn out to be the case. "In order for that to happen, I'd have to marry Isaac, who I've only known for, like, nine days, and I'd have to make the Olympic team four years from now, which who even knows if I'll be able to do." He spoke softly. The crowd around them jumped and cheered, so he didn't think they'd be overheard, but he was hyperconscious of the fact that the wrong person would report what he said to the media.

"How old are you, Timmy?" asked Ginny.

"Twenty-four."

"Well, I'm twenty-eight, and as the older and wiser of us, I can say that you, my dear, will most definitely be able to make the next Olympic team, barring injury. Knock on wood." She looked around as if she were trying to find wood to knock on, but there were only the plastic benches of the stands, so she knocked on Jason's head.

"Ow," said Jason.

"Well, from your lips to God's ears," said Tim. "I mean, you realize he's going to have to do a ton of press now, so I may not even get to see him much."

"Like you haven't been spending every night together," said Jason.

Ginny grinned triumphantly.

Heat flooded Tim's face. "Fine. Whatever, guys. Plan our wedding. But, again, Tom Daley didn't make the finals."

"Nah." Ginny grinned and threw an arm around Tim. "It's too perfect. It will work out."

CHAPTER 21

Day 11

Transcript: Men's Three-Meter Springboard Final

HOLLAND: Who are your favorites going into this final?

BELL: Well, the Chinese divers, of course. Wao Yan has looked fantastic through all of the preliminary rounds. Near perfect. His countryman He Qian less so. He had a rough semifinal and barely made this final, but it doesn't matter. All of the previous scores are thrown out. If he dives cleanly today, he has an excellent shot at a medal. Other favorites are Kevin O'Roarke from Australia, who is tremendously strong. He's the reigning Olympic champion in this event. And we've got divers from Italy, Portugal, Canada, and Russia who are in this mix.

HOLLAND: And we can't forget the Americans.

BELL: No, we definitely should not count them out. Lance Steele is the current American champion, and he looked good through the prelims, qualifying in fifth. But, of course, there's Timothy Swan.

HOLLAND: It's rare for divers to do both the springboard and platform events these days, right?

BELL: It's true, divers today tend to specialize. Jumping off the platform is a different skill than jumping off the springboard. And now that synchronized diving is in the mix, doing three events is too much for a lot of athletes. But Timmy Swan is not just any athlete. He's stronger off the platform, but he's a solid springboard diver too, and he qualified for both at the Olympic Trials, so he's doing both here. But three events can be pretty hard on the body. I half expected Swan to scratch this event, but no, here he is.

HOLLAND: What do you think his chances are?

BELL: I like him better for a medal in platform diving, but if he keeps his dives clean, he's got some of the hardest difficulty-level dives we'll see today, so he can get big scores. If he keeps it clean.

HOLLAND: Looks like we've got some familiar faces in the audience too. There are a few members of USA Swimming sitting in the stands. There are a pile of medals between them. Luke Rogers, Katie Santiago, and Isaac Flood practically need a wheelbarrow for all the hardware they will be bringing home.

BELL: Nice to see them coming out to support their Team USA colleagues.

HOLLAND: And there's Greg Louganis. He's become something of a mentor to the US divers. Tim Swan in particular has called Louganis his hero.

BELL: That might be part of why he's doing platform and springboard here. Louganis did both in his day.

HOLLAND: Swan will get a few days' rest between events, at least.

BELL: That is true, and he's not even the only diver entered in both. Roberto Jimenez of Mexico is also doing both and is a diver not to be overlooked. Mexico has a long tradition of sending excellent divers to the Olympics, and Roberto is pretty great. The difficulty level of his dives is not as high as the Chinese divers' or even Timothy Swan's, but if he dives well, he's in contention.

HOLLAND: Guess we'll have to wait and see.

TIM KNEW Isaac sat in the audience. As in the swimming finals, USA Diving had a section reserved for noncompeting divers, friends, and family, so Isaac, Luke, and Katie had snuck in. Or, more likely, no one would tell a man with seven Olympic medals no.

So Isaac was there, but Tim wasn't looking at him, because he needed to focus on his dives.

The first dive was easy. It was a low difficulty-level dive meant to show off his form and precision, so he did an easy one-and-a-half pike and landed it vertically. He scored nines, probably only because he didn't have the same superpower the Chinese divers had that allowed them to enter the water without creating a splash.

The finals required him to complete six dives, so he had five more chances to fuck this all up. He knew from a hundred competitions that sometimes it only took one dive to take an athlete out of the running. He'd been a little shaky during the semis the previous day, entering the water less than vertical a few times. He'd spent the morning reviewing video with Donnie, trying to work out how to correct his mistakes. He felt better now, more stable and less nervous.

He wasn't as strong a springboard diver as he was a platform diver, though. He liked the platform better, liked having more space to fly and complete somersaults. Springboard had so many variables: you had to compress the springboard enough for it to give you the push into the air you needed to get up high enough to complete whatever the trick was—a somersault, a twist, a pike. Then you only had three meters to get that trick done and get vertical again. Tim found competing springboard stressful, and had almost stopped entirely, but Donnie still thought he had a chance to medal, so here he was.

The second dive had a higher degree of difficulty. As he dried off with his lucky shammy, he mentally practiced it. He tossed the shammy over the side of the springboard and saw it land near the base of the stairs. Then left leg up, right, hop, and he threw himself forward into a two-and-a-half tuck, which he straightened out quickly. He felt his feet slap the water in a way that indicated he hadn't been perfectly vertical, but he'd been close.

Most of the judges rated that an 8.5. Enough to keep him in second place.

Tim didn't want to obsess over scores. A lot of the other divers spent the times between dives under the showers or in the hot tubs, staying warm and loose. And even more of them had waterproof headphones on—like Jason usually did—ignoring the noise in the stadium and the glowing allure of the scoreboard. But Tim always had to know what he was up against. One of the Chinese divers had missed his second dive, apparently, because his scores were shockingly low. The other was diving flawlessly, and if he kept it up, he'd be unbeatable.

Tim's third dive was solid but not perfect, pushing him into third place behind the top-ranking Chinese diver and Perez from Mexico, whom Isaac thought was a beautiful springboard diver.

He returned to the waiting area and ducked under a hot shower spray. Then, curiosity getting the better of him, he peeked toward the stands, hoping to get a glimpse of Isaac. He knew approximately where the friends and family section was, and... there he was, talking with Luke and Katie. They seemed to be having an involved conversation, although a lighthearted one, because when Isaac said something, Luke threw his head back and laughed, and Isaac had that sheepish smile on his face he got when he didn't want it to seem like he was laughing at his own joke.

So Tim decided to look for his parents, who were predictably in the front row.

Then his gaze slid around to see who else was in the stands, and....

Pat.

Jesus Christ. Tim ducked behind a pillar, not wanting to be seen. Pat was here. He sat by himself in the section adjacent to where Isaac sat, and he seemed intent on reading his program. But it was definitely him. Tim had been with the man for long enough that he could pick him out of a crowd.

What the fuck was his ex doing here?

Tim couldn't worry about it now. He tried to pretend he hadn't seen Pat in the stands and instead returned to the shower, letting the hot water pour over him. He had to get his head back in the right space. The people in the stands didn't matter. All that mattered was Tim's feet on the springboard, his form in the air, and entering the water cleanly. Diving. He was here for diving.

For the fourth dive, Tim planned a back inward three-and-a-half tuck, the dive he struggled with the most on the springboard. He liked doing this dive off

the platform better, since he had more room and didn't
have to rotate as fast. He positioned himself at the end
of the springboard and started flexing his feet to get
the board to bounce. He focused on just this, on the
bounce of the board beneath him, on what he had to do
once he was in the air, on how he'd get himself into the
water. Then he launched himself backward, got his legs
up immediately into the tuck, spotted the water, rotated, spotted the water again, rotated, spotted the water
again, and kicked out his legs to go vertical.

He could tell by the sting of water on the back of
his legs that he was short of vertical. Fuck.

When he got out of the water, the scores were
sevens. Not a disaster, but he fell out of medal position now.

"It's fine," said Donnie, standing in the coaches'
area when Tim walked over that way. "You didn't quite
kick hard enough and never got completely vertical, but
the dive looked really good in the air. Maybe the best
I've seen you do that."

"Yeah?"

"Yeah. Your scores aren't low enough to take you
out of contention. If you do the last two perfectly, which
is within your ability to do, you might walk away with
a medal."

Tim took a deep breath. "Okay. I'm gonna go dunk
in the hot tub." And hopefully shake that off. And forget
Pat was here.

Why was Pat here? Tim had been very clear when
they broke up that he never wanted to see Pat again. But
there was no reason for Pat to be here... except to see
Tim. Did he want something? Did he want to get back
together? Because that was not happening. Shit. Tim
could not think about this right now.

"Stay warm. Remember for the twist to tighten here." Donnie patted his stomach. "Keep it really straight. These judges have been sticklers for form. They found some deductions for Wao's dive, which looked damn near perfect from here. I couldn't see room for deductions, but his feet must have been half an inch apart or something."

"Okay. Thanks."

The dive tower stood between the hot tubs and the stands, so Tim couldn't see the audience as he sat in the tub, trying to stay warm. He couldn't stand seeing any of the people in the audience. Even the thought of Isaac watching him made his heart pound.

"That's a bad break," said Perez in heavily accented English as he slid into the tub.

"My last dive?" Isaac asked.

"Yeah. I watched. Sorry."

"No, it's okay. You've looked really good all day."

"Thanks. It's just… how the wind blows."

"Yeah." *Tom Daley didn't make the finals.* "I don't think we can catch Wao, but we might be fighting it out for the silver the next two dives."

Perez smiled. "Yeah? I won silver at Worlds but never an Olympic medal. Four years ago…." He shook his head.

"Yeah, I remember," said Tim. Perez had basically belly flopped during a semifinal dive, which had taken him out of the running.

Perez nodded. "My wife is in the audience. I don't want to disappoint her. She's so patient."

"That's good. It's nice that she's here. You'll do well. Two more dives to go."

Before his fifth dive, Tim hung back for a second, toweling off but looking for Isaac in the stands.

Isaac faced Tim, probably looked right at him, though it was hard to tell from this distance. Luke and Katie sat next to Isaac, talking excitedly. Tim glanced at his parents but made a point of not looking for Pat. Tim nodded to himself, tossed the shammy, and got ready to do the twist dive. He followed Donnie's advice in the air, tightening his muscles to keep perfectly straight as he turned, placing his arms in the proper position until it was time to put them down, entering the water with very little splash. The water seemed to hug him that time, a good sign he'd done it well.

He stayed under water for a moment longer than he probably should have, to collect himself and because he wasn't quite ready to face the score yet.

But… nines. A couple of 9.5s. Tim was back in second place.

Pat had rarely come to see Tim dive when they'd been together, which had the effect of making Tim feel kind of alone at meets, despite having this high-profile relationship. Sure, his parents came to all his big meets, but it wasn't quite the same. Now Tim was secretly dating Isaac, who was right out there in the stands, supporting Tim, cheering for him. Tim knew in his gut that Isaac wouldn't think less of Tim if he didn't medal and that Isaac would be excited and proud if he did. It was a nice feeling, reassuring, like a warm hug even if Isaac was fifty feet away. Isaac would probably be proud as long as Tim put his all into the competition, no matter the outcome.

It made Tim realize how lonely he'd been when he and Pat had been together.

So why was Pat here *now*? Would Tim have to talk to him? Really, what Pat did with his time was none of Tim's business anymore. Tim could still refuse to talk to him, the same way he'd turned down that tabloid reporter who'd shown up at training. There was no reason Tim and Pat needed to have anything to do with each other.

He shook that off and stood under a shower for a few minutes, closing his eyes and mentally rehearsing his last dive. One more to go. That was all he needed.

The final dive was the showstopper. Tim jumped off the springboard and into a pike, which he rotated once before straightening out and twisting until vertical and entering the water. It had the highest degree of difficulty of his dives, and if he pulled it off, it was worth a lot of points.

The stakes were low, he told himself as he climbed the ladder to the springboard. His parents loved him no matter what, which he knew because he'd pushed them pretty hard the past couple of years through all the drama with Pat. Isaac was watching, but his affection was not contingent on Tim performing this dive flawlessly. Pat was here somewhere, for some reason, but fuck him. Sure, a medal was on the line, but Tim didn't care about this one as much as he did the platform final, which was still several days away. The springboard was a lark, something Donnie had wanted him to do, because no one had medaled in the springboard and the platform in the same Olympics in several decades.

The media called Tim the best diver since Greg Louganis, a compliment Tim treasured, but he knew it was his sexuality as much as his skill that invited comparisons. Greg sat in the coaches' area now—Tim still thought it surreal that he got to talk to his idol before Olympic competition—and had told Tim earlier that day that he had the potential to do something no one had done in a long time. But Tim didn't want to let that weigh on him. He was a skilled diver. He was a world and Olympic champion diver. The gold he wanted was the platform gold, though, so if he won a medal on springboard, it was gravy.

He caught sight of Isaac in the audience, and imagined they made eye contact. If Isaac felt half as much for Tim now as Tim had felt for Isaac during his last race, Tim and Isaac would be fine. Winning a medal would be amazing, but it wasn't everything.

Tim took a deep breath, reminded himself he could do this—but if he didn't it wasn't a big deal—and he launched off the end of the springboard.

He felt good as he entered the water.

Diving had so many variables. You had to get a good hurdle and take off from the end of the board; then you had to not just complete the elements of the dive, but you had to do so with perfect form; then you had to get vertical again so that you went into the water straight, and you had to place your hands in exactly the right position to push the water aside so that you entered with very little splash. You had to keep pulling once you were in the water to keep your legs vertical until you completed that dive. If any one of those things went wrong, you'd be penalized. If conditions were less than ideal, it could affect those things too. Keeping your muscles warm between dives was crucial, or you'd seize up. Nerves could make muscles tense, which could cause problems when completing somersaults. Wind tended to throw off divers, who had to move their bodies to compensate, but in the indoor Aquatics Center, there was no wind, at least. Divers had to get themselves as dry as possible before diving too—hence the shammies—because dry bodies turned in the air faster.

Tim had done everything right. He'd gotten a good push off the springboard, he kept every part of his body in the correct position as he rotated through the air, he held his muscles tight, he straightened out and got his body vertical when he needed it to be, and he pushed into the water with very little splash. He'd done everything he could do and he felt good about it.

He got nines on the last dive. He stared at the scoreboard as the rest of the divers completed their final dives. A slap on his back startled him, and he turned to see Donnie, who must have snuck out of the coaches' area. "Great job," Donnie said. "That last dive was your cleanest. The scores should have been higher, but like I said, the judges have been sticklers."

"Okay." Tim could hardly speak now. His body shook as everything hit him. He was done. He'd done all he could do. He'd dived with everything he had in him. Now he had to wait for the results. Isaac, his parents, and Pat were in the audience. Isaac was here. Pat was here.

"Do not beat yourself up. I know you're cataloging the things you did wrong, but I'm proud of you. No matter what happens."

Tim let out a breath. He opened his mouth to thank Donnie but couldn't. He nodded instead.

It was over now, and he'd made his body do some things he hadn't thought it could do. Now he wanted that reward. He wanted the medal. He could taste it. But he hadn't been flawless, and some of the other divers had been better.

Donnie was right. Tim now mentally listed all the things he'd done wrong. He hadn't pulled his tuck in hard enough in the fourth dive, hadn't used his core to control his second dive, his feet had been too far apart in the first dive, he hadn't gotten a strong enough push off the springboard in the fifth dive. A hundred things could have shaved points off, and now he was left with a score that was good by any measure but maybe not good enough to win a medal. Tim *could* have been better. Had he pushed hard enough? Had he really performed to the best of his abilities? Doubt began to creep in as he stared at the monitors.

Perez's last dive was nearly perfect, performed beautifully, everything positioned correctly, very little splash. Wao had a big enough lead over everyone else that he'd never be caught, even if he whiffed the last dive, which he definitely did not do.

So Tim knew even before that last score was posted that he'd fallen to third place. Bronze medal.

He couldn't help but feel a little disappointed by that. Tim hadn't realized how much he'd wanted the gold medal until he hadn't won it.

A wave of emotion suddenly consumed him. He'd done something amazing, but he hadn't been perfect—Greg Louganis had won gold in both disciplines, after all, and *had* been perfect—and the strange catharsis that came with the competition ending hit Tim hard.

He hadn't been perfect, he hadn't won gold, he'd fallen short. He could have done something else, could have tried harder, could have been better. The disappointment was crushing, but it shouldn't have been. A bronze medal was still an accomplishment. So why did Tim feel so shitty? And panicky? He had to get away from everyone before he completely lost it.

There were cameras everywhere, but Tim refused to cry in front of them, though he felt it coming. He wanted to duck into the locker room and hide his face, but he got stopped by Diane Bell—a gold-medal-winning diver in her own right—who wanted to know how winning bronze felt.

"It feels great," Tim said, hoping the audience at home would buy any tears or red eyes as a reaction to the chlorine in the pool or his joy at winning any medal. "That was… I mean, I've worked hard all week, I did those dives the best that I could, and, you know, Perez from Mexico, he's just an amazing diver, and Wao was basically perfect, so… I mean, this was great, I feel great."

Tim didn't think he sounded very convincing, but Diane nodded. "We'll see you again for the platform final later in the week. What do you think your chances are there?"

"I'll repeat my gold-medal performance there," Tim said, smiling, though he felt his control slipping.

"We can't wait for it. Congratulations!"

Tim nodded and then scurried to the locker room before anyone else could stop him.

ISAAC DIDN'T know a lot about diving. He knew the basic mechanics of it, sure. He knew the object was to take off from the board, do some tricks in the air, and then go into the water with as little splash as possible. But he didn't know much about the judging criteria. And the dives happened so fast, he didn't know how anyone *could* judge them.

Well, he could tell when a diver missed. The American diver who was not Tim, some guy named Lance Steele—which sure sounded like a gay porn star name to Isaac—had totally missed his entries on a couple of dives, creating huge splashes. The whole audience went "Ooof" when that happened.

"At least he's pretty," Katie said.

He *was* pretty, supporting Isaac's case that Lance could be a porn star. Lance was a tall blond guy who could not have been older than twenty. He had a boyish grin, which he flashed whenever a camera turned toward him, but his body was all man: defined pecs, a fucking eight pack, and really powerful thighs. The tiny bathing suit highlighted all of it.

He had nothing on Tim, though, who was a fucking marvel as far as Isaac was concerned. Every time Tim went out on the end of that platform, Isaac took it all in. Tim's proportions were a little off; he had a long torso but relatively short legs. He had thick thighs too, but they weren't as bulky as some of the other divers'. He had nice, round muscles on his arms, and his chest and back rippled as he walked. He was all strength, not an ounce of fat on him, and his body looked baked to a golden tan. Isaac knew what was beneath that tiny bathing suit now, and he liked the whole package immensely. So the rest of the world could have Lance Steele and his porn star looks; Isaac would keep Tim.

Between rounds five and six, Katie tried explaining the judging. "My sister's a diver," she said. "The judges can take off points for a lot of things. If a diver's form isn't perfect. If he doesn't get far enough from the board when they take off, if there's any splash."

"That Chinese guy Wao keeps getting tens," Luke said.

"Yeah. He's the world champion. He's basically unbeatable. Even if Tim Swan does this last dive perfectly, he's too far behind to earn a gold. Unless Wao misses, which I doubt."

"Tim said he's better at platform," Isaac said.

"That's probably true. My sister dove in the Trials, so I watched him dive then. He's really good. You can tell his form is amazing. He's strong but also graceful, which is not a combination every diver has. Like, take Perez." She gestured toward the diver currently on the board. "He's a strong diver, and he executes everything well, but he's not as pretty in the air as Swan, you know? So even though he gets vertical, there's still quite a bit of splash. He's not tightening up his form as much as he should. Not as much as Tim does, or the Chinese divers do."

Isaac nodded. "So you think Tim looks good?" He picked up his phone and used the zoom to try to see Tim, who lingered near the stairs up to the platform.

Katie peeked over his shoulder at the phone screen. "What's the obsession with Tim Swan about?" she asked in a whisper.

"Isaac's porking him," said Luke.

Katie's jaw dropped.

"I'm not.... That's gross, Luke, come on."

"So you're not sleeping with him?" Luke asked.

"No, I am, I just wouldn't have phrased it the way you did."

Katie put her hand on Isaac's knee. "Wait a sec. I saw you eating with Swan in the cafeteria a few times, so I knew you knew each other, but I didn't know you were, like, *together*."

"I just met him here in Madrid. We've been spending time together. And yes, some of that has been naked time, but it's not.... He doesn't want to go public yet, so you have to keep it down."

Katie nodded. "Sorry. I didn't realize."

"You think Isaac would want to see diving if he didn't have an... interest in one of the divers?" asked Luke.

"I don't know. He could like diving," said Katie. "I didn't know you were gay, Isaac. Weren't you hooking up with that girl Julia for a while?"

"I'm bi, and Luke's basically right. I don't think I'd want to come to diving if it wasn't for Tim. Who's about to dive, so shut up."

Luke looked around. "You know, if any of these people overheard this conversation...."

Isaac shook his head. "Tim said he wanted to wait to go public about our relationship until after he finishes competing so that any resulting media attention is not a distraction, which I get. I've been shaking hands with people for a fucking week, and they all look at me like they think I'm about to fall off the wagon, so I completely understand why Tim doesn't want the publicity. Not to mention, he used to date a TV star and now hates the media. I want to respect his wishes."

Luke looked chastened. "Yeah. Lips are sealed, dude."

Isaac let out a sight. "At the same time, I will not be that broken up if people find out. I mean, just for the record, I'm not ashamed of our relationship. It's the best thing that's happened to me during the Games, and that includes all the medals, you know?"

Katie poked at Isaac's bicep. "Who are you and what have you done with our Isaac? I've never seen you this sentimental."

"I like him," Isaac said.

"You *love* him," said Luke with a lot of eye rolling.

"Hey, man, you're the one who said I should go for it." But Isaac didn't bother to deny it.

Luke laughed. "I'm just giving you a hard time."

"He snuck into the locker room after I won the 200 IM final. I wonder if I could do the same now."

Katie elbowed him. "Six gold medals. They should let you do whatever you want."

"Stop talking."

Tim walked out to the end of the springboard. The dive looked beautiful in the air. Tim launched himself off the springboard, pulled himself into a tight pike, and rotated before kicking out into a straight position, pulling his arms into place to twist, and then straightening his arms to enter the water. It looked pretty dang flawless to Isaac, both powerful and graceful as Katie had said, and he entered the water with very little splash.

Isaac was on his feet cheering for it before Tim even surfaced from the water. So were a group of people a few rows in front of where Isaac, Luke, and Katie sat. These were presumably Tim's parents, a middle-aged couple wearing sweatshirts. Tim's mother glanced back at where Isaac was hollering, and Isaac saw her sweatshirt said *Team Swan*. Cute.

Isaac wanted to be on Team Swan.

He'd been thinking about introducing himself the whole competition, but he wasn't sure what he'd say. "Hi, Mrs. Swan, I'm the man currently banging your son" didn't seem to convey the right message.

But man, Isaac's desire to run out toward the pool to pull Tim into a tight hug was strong. He ached to put his arms around Tim, to congratulate him for diving so well, for... well, hell, for winning a medal. Isaac looked at the leader board and mentally did the math. Perez and Wao still had to dive, but that score guaranteed Tim at least a third-place finish. That would give him his second medal. Isaac's chest swelled with pride.

That's my man, he thought. *I'm with that beautiful man who defies gravity and physics to do something amazing, and he'll be getting his second medal of these Games, and he's mine.*

Perez dove next, and he looked great while doing it, a bit more elegant than he'd looked in the previous rounds. Wao's last dive was, of course, textbook, and he got the requisite high score because of it, securing himself the gold. The final scores went up on the big board, showing that Tim Swan had won the bronze. The crowd cheered wildly, most of the spectators on their feet, clapping and hooting for the winners.

Katie said, "Hey, isn't that guy that CW actor? What the hell is his name? Patterson Wood?"

Isaac's heart stopped. He followed Katie's gaze to a tall guy with his hands stuffed into the kangaroo pockets of his Team USA sweatshirt. Isaac didn't recognize him—not that he would—but if Katie was right, that was... alarming.

"Can't be," said Isaac.

"Do you even own a TV, Flood?"

"Yeah. I even turn it on sometimes. But... Patterson Wood is Tim's ex. What would he be doing here?"

Katie raised both eyebrows.

"No way," said Isaac, not even sure what conclusion she'd drawn. Tim had been pretty clear things were over with that scumbag, hadn't he? Could Patterson Wood be here to get Tim back? Would Tim go back? Tim had been in love with that douchebag once, and Isaac certainly knew the pull of something dangerous and completely wrong for him better than anyone. Not to mention, Pat could offer Tim things Isaac couldn't, such as reliable sobriety and the sort of fame that ensured better endorsement deals and sponsorships and modeling gigs.

He wondered if Tim knew if Pat was here. If that even was Pat. And if Tim *had* known, why hadn't he said anything?

He turned his attention back toward the event. After some fanfare at the edge of the pool, Isaac glanced up at the big screen, which showed a close-up of Tim's face, and he looked upset.

Oh fuck.

"Something's wrong," Isaac said.

"What makes you say that?" asked Katie.

"He looks like he's about to cry." Isaac gestured at the screen.

"Oh, yeah. He—well, he's gone now."

The screen showed Wao's coach and less-successful teammate hugging him as Wao laughed.

"He could be injured," Isaac said. "What if he's injured?"

"He looks fine, physically," said Luke, pointing to where Tim was hurrying toward the locker room. "He's not limping or anything."

"No, but… oh God. What if something's wrong?"

"Isaac, calm down," said Katie. "He looks okay. But even if he isn't, security won't let you down there, not when the competition is wrapping up. See those barriers they put up? Even Isaac Flood doesn't have the power to get past them. Hell, most of the media can't get past that barrier over there. You'll have to wait until later to talk to him."

Isaac knew she was right, but his heart pounded anyway. He pulled out his phone and texted Tim.

I know ur busy, but r u ok?

He didn't expect an answer. He lingered in the stands with Luke and Katie. They chatted for a few minutes about possibly going out for dinner somewhere in the city now that they could be a little more lax about their diets. Luke got out his phone and pulled up some Spanish restaurant app he'd downloaded.

Isaac recognized that he was starting to spiral. He'd long had these moments when his anxiety got the better of him and his thoughts began to swirl around and grow and fester until he was no longer rooted in reality. In the past, he drank to get those thoughts to stop. He'd worked with his doctor to come up with some strategies for when he caught himself in one of these patterns, and one of them was to focus on something else going on around him—making dinner plans, Tim's shiny new medal—and not on his impending panic that something was wrong with Tim and that Tim's ex was right fucking here in the stands, perhaps because he and Tim were not so broken up after all. Why else would this guy fly halfway around the world if not to see Tim?

He bit the inside of his cheek and looked at Luke. He took a few deep breaths. The stands started to thin out, but Tim's mother turned around again. "You're Isaac Flood," she shouted up at him.

"Yeah," Isaac said, swallowing. Had Tim told his parents about their relationship? Isaac had barely said anything to his own mother.

"Congratulations," Tim's mother said. "We couldn't get tickets to the last night of swimming, but we watched on TV from the hotel. That was a spectacular race. Timmy said he saw it in person." She was a striking woman with a heart-shaped face and black hair like Tim's pulled up into a bushy ponytail. She was clearly Tim's Filipino half. Tim's father was a good-looking white guy with salt-and-pepper hair and a mustache.

"He… yeah. Um. It was pretty great." Isaac never knew what to say when people congratulated him, and his heart was pounding from his near-spiral. "Thank you."

Tim's parents stepped up a couple of the risers to get closer to where Isaac stood. "That's our son Tim who just won the bronze."

"Yeah, I know. Team Swan." Isaac gestured toward the Swans' sweatshirts.

Tim's mom looked down. "Oh yeah. Have you ever seen Tim dive before?"

"No," said Isaac. He felt stymied, not knowing what he could say. If they felt it was necessary to explain who Tim was, they likely didn't know Isaac and Tim even knew each other. "Uh, he looked great."

"Yeah," said Luke. "Pass on our congratulations. I'm Luke and this is Katie. We're also swimmers."

"We decided to stick around and see some of the sports for ourselves," said Katie.

"That's great! It must be nice to do that now that the pressure is off you guys."

Isaac looked around for Tim. He was nowhere in sight. He'd probably gone to change into his official warm-up suit to accept his medal. Then Isaac's pocket buzzed. He grabbed his phone.

I'm ok. Emotions got the best of me. Did I cry on camera?

Isaac smiled. While half listening to Mrs. Swan, he texted back, *A little. I think I'm the only one who noticed.*

Then he added, *I'm talking to your parents right now.*

Tim sent back a shocked-face emoji. He added, *I didn't tell them about u.*

I gathered, texted Isaac.

Isaac smiled at the Swans. Mr. Swan said, "We're staying for the medal ceremony, of course."

"We couldn't be prouder," said Mrs. Swan. "He's diving again later in the week. The springboard isn't even his best event, and he won a bronze."

"Maybe we'll check that out too," said Isaac. He'd already bought a ticket to that event, in fact.

His phone buzzed then. Thinking it was Tim texting, he looked at it, but it was actually Adam calling. "I gotta take this. Sorry. Lovely to meet you, though!"

Isaac moved to the aisle, away from where people were chatting. "Adam. Hi."

"Do you have an agent or a lawyer?"

Oh shit. "No, not anymore." God, what had happened now?

"It's not bad, I promise. But USA Swimming has been getting phone calls almost nonstop for two days from various sponsors who want to get in touch with you."

Sponsors? Good Lord. Was endorsement money coming back in? "Well, gee. And all I had to do was win six gold medals."

"Don't be a smartass," said Adam. "Do you want to deal with these people directly, or should I get Sheri on it for now? She's been fielding requests for some of the other athletes too."

"If Sheri feels okay handling it, I'd prefer that. Until I can line up an agent again."

"Sheri can help you with that too. Or talk to Luke. I like his agent a lot. Maybe you guys can sort through all this mess. I hate this shit, as you know, but if it pays well enough to keep you in the pool, I'm all for it."

Wow, shit. Of course, endorsements were usually predicated on his continuing to swim for at least a little while. Speedo wouldn't want to pay him much if he couldn't model their swimsuits during competition... which threw a wrench in his fantasy plan of moving to Colorado. More swimming meant more Raleigh. Adam was the best coach in the biz, and they'd been working together for more than two decades. He'd be insane to switch now.

"Okay," said Isaac. "Yeah, let Sheri handle it, but tell her she can call me anytime if she needs me. I'll be in Madrid for another week."

"Good to know. And I... I'm proud of you, Isaac, if I haven't told you that enough. If all this keeps you out of a bottle, that's really the main thing, though. Where are you now? Not in a bar, I hope. It sounds noisy."

Isaac knew Adam was just looking out for him, but he hated the suspicion. Would they ever move past questions like that? Then again, Isaac supposed he deserved it. "No, I'm at the diving finals with Luke and Katie. It just ended."

"Oh. Interesting. Team USA do anything good?"

"Tim Swan won a bronze medal."

"Right on. Well, I'll talk to you later. I'm flying home Friday. My wife wants to see Madrid before I head home, so we're going on some insane tour tomorrow. Then I've got some interviews and shit to do the rest of the week."

"Thanks, Adam. I mean for all of it. For believing in me. For coaching me."

"Of course, kid. You're.... I mean, there will never be another one like you. I know you get the Phelps comparisons all the time, but you really are one in a million. Phelps was a phenom, but you have a strength

I've never seen in anyone else before. I don't think any other athlete on the planet could have done what you did at these Games."

God, what did one even say to that? Adam's words humbled Isaac, moved him. He'd spent a lot of time in the past few days thinking about what he'd done and how he'd done it, but he'd felt weak, as if he'd succeeded despite himself. Adam had called him strong; maybe he was. "Yeah. Um, thank you."

Isaac got off the phone and took a deep breath, trying to keep his emotions in check as he rejoined his friends. Luke and Katie were still chatting with the Swans. Isaac looked around and his gaze settled on the guy Katie thought was Patterson Wood. He seemed to be hovering.

Isaac kept an eye on him as he approached his friends. They seemed to be getting restaurant recommendations. Unfortunately, everything happening made him pine for a beer, so he said to Luke, "Let's not go somewhere with a noisy bar."

"Gotcha." Luke looked up from his phone and asked the Swans, "Is there some quiet spot not far from here you've been to? I'm starving, so I don't really want to go across the city."

"Oh, there's this marvelous place we went the other night," said Mrs. Swan. "Just a few blocks from here, pretty easy walking. Best seafood I've ever had. It should be quiet this time of day. You know the Spanish don't eat dinner until late into the night…."

That all seemed to be in order, so Isaac texted Tim: *I want to hold u now.*

Tim texted back. *If only. I gotta get a medal now, tho.* He texted a medal emoji.

Isaac wanted to cash in on that medal but thought better of saying anything now. *What a hardship*, he said instead. His therapist would probably have something to say about using sarcasm as a defense mechanism.

Tim deserved a far better man than Isaac.

But he had bigger problems because Patterson Wood finally stopped hovering and made his presence known. "Mr. and Mrs. Swan?"

Mrs. Swan looked startled. "Pat," she said with a wheeze. "What are you doing here?"

"I came to see Tim dive. Flew out here a few days ago."

Mrs. Swan shook her head. Her husband stood right behind her, glaring at Pat. It was nice to see where they stood, at least; neither seemed to like Pat much at all. "You shouldn't be here. It's very important for Tim to focus. You'll be a distraction."

"I want him back," Pat said.

Isaac opened his mouth to state that wouldn't be happening, but he realized quickly that letting the Swans and Pat know he was with Tim would only make this situation worse.

Tim had loved Pat once. Could he again? Pat was handsome and had a certain amount of charm. And if he begged Tim enough, Tim might decide someone familiar and close by might be a better bet than the alcoholic who lived on the other side of the country. Isaac had known plenty of Pats in his lifetime, guys who were douchebags but handsome and charming enough to hide it. He could easily appeal to Tim's sense of nostalgia, to the way their relationship used to be, to the earning potential of merging their collective star power, to being a better bet than the drunk swimmer.

"We should, uh, go," Luke said, hooking his thumb toward the exit.

Isaac nodded, not realizing he'd stepped toward Pat. "Uh, it was nice meeting you all."

He followed Luke out of the stands, but not before he heard Pat say, "I made a terrible mistake and I came to Madrid to make up for it." But Luke pulled him away before he could hear the Swans' response.

Chapter 22

Tim let himself into Isaac's room, completely out of sorts.

It had been one of the worst nights of his life.

He found Isaac lying on the bed, looking cool and casual, flipping through a book.

"I bought this at the America House gift shop tonight," Isaac said as Tim came in and put his bag down. "It's a history of the Olympic Games. But it's, like, the officially sanctioned IOC version, so it's all spit-shined and sanitized."

Tim sighed. "No scandals?"

"Well, they talked about the unavoidable scandals. The Nazi Games, the Black Power salute in Mexico City, the terrorism at Munich. There's one measly paragraph on doping. But take your man Louganis, for example."

Tim's heart sank as he sat next to Isaac on the bed. "Did they leave him out?"

"No. There's even a bit about how he hit his head but still came back to win a medal. Just no mention of homosexuality or HIV."

"Well, I guess I can't blame them for that."

Isaac looked up and met Tim's gaze. "No? You don't think it's important?"

"I think it's very important, but when it happened, nobody knew about Greg being gay or HIV-positive."

"Yeah. But, like, they also didn't talk at all about the antigay stuff in Russia during the Sochi Games or the pollution in Rio or any of that. We both know there's a lot of bullshit the public doesn't see. To read this account, everything having to do with the Olympics and its host cities has always been on the up-and-up."

"Of course."

Isaac put the book aside. "God, I'm glad to see you."

Tim smiled. He felt tired. After the medal ceremony, his family and most of the USA Diving staff had taken him out to dinner; then he'd had to put in some requisite time with the divers partying at America House. He'd been about to succumb to postcompetition fatigue when Pat had shown up.

"Did you party?" Isaac asked, pulling Tim into his arms.

"Yeah, a little." Not at all, because Pat had insisted on *speaking* to Tim. And Tim didn't know how to tell Isaac about that conversation. He knew he needed to. He had no idea what to say.

"Did you drink?"

"No. Too much sugar." The answer was automatic—Tim didn't drink during competition because alcoholic drinks had many unnecessary calories—but the enormity of the question hit him after he spoke. "Would it have been a problem if I had?"

"No," Isaac said. "I'm not quite strong enough to be out where people are drinking a lot in front of me. But I don't care if you drink."

"Is that why you keep skipping parties with your teammates?"

"Yeah, but I also would prefer to spend time with you."

Tim smiled and sank into Isaac's arms. Isaac was warm, and he wore a soft T-shirt and sweatpants. Tim loved sinking into this comfortable space with him. He laid his head on Isaac's shoulder and snuggled up close. "My parents talked about you a lot during dinner. Meeting you was the second-most-exciting thing that happened to them today."

Isaac laughed. "I hope their son winning an Olympic medal was the first."

"Yeah. It's going to make telling them we're together especially interesting. I guess that can wait until after the platform final."

Tim yawned. God, he was tired. He completely understood all those nights Isaac had fallen asleep before they'd gotten the opportunity to fool around much. Now that he was here, in Isaac's arms, surrounded by his scent and his warmth, Tim could easily close his eyes and sink into sleep.

"Seriously, though," Isaac said. "Are you okay? You looked upset after the last dive."

No. Things were not okay. But how to explain?

"It just…. Everything kind of hit me all at once. Like I'd been holding in all my emotions through the whole competition, and when we got to the end, I didn't have the strength to hold them in anymore." Tim paused to think about how to express what he felt. "First, I kept telling myself that it didn't matter whether I won or lost because I wanted to defend my platform title more. Springboard isn't my specialty, so making the final felt like a fluke. But I dove well today—really well. I guess I didn't know how much I wanted that medal until it ended, and then I was…. I felt so disappointed. I kept second-guessing myself. Like, if I'd had more faith, I could have done better. If I'd taken the competition more seriously, I could have at least beat Perez. I've beaten Perez a dozen times before. But he was good today, and I was less than perfect, and…." The tears came then; everything Tim had been holding on to all day leaked out and ran down his cheeks. "I was disappointed. In myself more than anything."

Isaac gave Tim a little squeeze. "You realize that you're still the third-best springboard diver in the whole goddamn world, right?"

"I know!" Tim felt his grip on his temper, on everything he felt, slipping away. He didn't want to yell at Isaac, but he felt so irritated and frustrated. "And I felt bad for feeling bad that I only won a bronze. I mean, I won an Olympic medal. I won my second Olympic medal in a week. And the gold was totally out of my grasp because Wao killed it today. I have it in me to dive like that on my best days, but I'm rarely that perfect in competition, and I just…. I don't know. Like I said, I'm disappointed in myself. I could have been better."

Isaac stroked Tim's back and made little comforting noises.

But Isaac wasn't getting it. "I feel so ungrateful," Tim went on, really crying now. He leaned against Isaac. "I don't know why I'm reacting this way. I should be happy. I've been handed this amazing opportunity that so few people get. I have a supportive family. I have the money to keep training. Only thirty-six male divers in the whole world qualified for this competition, and only a third of those made the final. I won a bronze medal, which is an incredibly difficult thing to do. I should be grateful." Tim pressed his face against Isaac's chest, Isaac's T-shirt absorbing the tears. He felt so melodramatic, but he needed to say this too. "And my parents were so proud. They were so happy for me. So I had to hide how disappointed I was, and how stupid I felt for being that disappointed, all through dinner." God. It was all one big knot that made Tim feel ridiculous. But he'd expressed himself honestly and was glad at least he had someone he could be that honest with.

Isaac was quiet for a few moments. He simply held Tim and stroked his back. Then he said, "I know that feeling."

"Yeah?" The word came out sounding watery.

"Yeah. Last Olympics. That silver I won while hungover. I mean, the circumstances were different, but I went through that same thing. If only I hadn't drunk so much the night before, if I hadn't taken my talent for granted the way I had, if I'd focused instead of being a cocky asshole, I would have won that gold medal. But I tied the Olympic record and swam the fourth-fastest time recorded that year. I still did something extraordinary. That whole Olympics, I swam really well. And I felt like complete shit afterwards."

Tim took a deep breath. Isaac was right, the circumstances were different, and Tim realized that Isaac's unease with his own behavior was partly what had probably driven him to drink more. But the fact that Isaac understood how Tim felt right now was amazing. Probably no one else on the planet would get it, but Tim believed that Isaac did.

"I hate this feeling," Tim said.

Isaac hugged him close. "I know. But here's the thing. You have another chance this week. Don't let it defeat you. Take it for what it is and go for redemption in your next final. Give that next series of dives everything you have. Even if you don't win the gold, even if the Chinese divers earn all 10s and you only earn 9.5s, it doesn't matter if you put all you have into it. The disappointment comes from knowing you could have done more but didn't, so do everything you can. Leave nothing behind." Isaac took a deep breath, and his chest rose and fell below Tim's cheek. "Be grateful you don't have the switch in you that makes you act out when things go like this."

"Drinking, you mean?"

"Yeah. What you feel right now? I've felt that a lot. Even when I won, I second-guessed myself. Like, if I'd pushed myself harder or, hell, been sober the whole meet, would I have won and also broken a world record? Could I have swum a personal best time if I'd given it my all? And why didn't I? Why did I assume that I should have won just because I'm Isaac fucking Flood?" Isaac sighed again. "Last week was my redemption, you know? I gave those races everything I had. In some of them, I felt like my body might fly apart, I pushed it so hard. After I won the 200 breast, I puked in the locker room. I've been sober for a year and a half and I trained my ass off and I put everything I had in me in that pool. And even if I hadn't won, I would have been okay with that, because I tried my hardest. Luke won the 400 free, and I'm okay with that, because I couldn't have given that race any more. That's what this Games has been for me."

Tim lifted his head and looked Isaac in the eyes. "You have no regrets about this week?"

"Nope. Not one. And I don't want to see you regret anything either. So give the platform competition your all, okay? And win a gold medal for me, would you?"

Tim laughed. "I'm glad you get it."

"I think there are only a handful of people in the world who do."

"I wish you'd been there with me today. It was hard to pretend to be happy with my parents."

Isaac pulled him close again. "I'm here now."

"Yeah. You're…. Thanks." Tim pressed his face into the space where Isaac's neck met his shoulders. Isaac smelled a little sweaty and a little like minty toothpaste, but Tim liked it. And he'd have to figure out a way to get Isaac to come with him to Colorado, because he could not give this up. "Thank you, Isaac."

"You're welcome." Isaac took another deep breath. "I figure, what's the use of going through what I did if I can't help others avoid the same fate?"

"Yeah?" Tim sensed Isaac wasn't just talking about the two of them.

"Yeah. I'm starting to think that's part of my purpose. Like, when I was drowning myself in cheap beer, I could have died. I almost did a few times. I did some incredibly stupid, dangerous things. And I think, you know, if there's some kind of higher power? I think he had a reason for rescuing me. I know that's some twelve-steps shit, but… I can't swim forever or my body *will* fall to pieces, but I *can* help people. Coach, maybe. Become a mentor. I don't know. But my experience has value, I think."

"It does, you're right." Tim yawned again. "Before I fall back to sleep, I have something to tell you."

"Pat's in Madrid."

Tim jerked away, fully awake now. "How do you know that?"

"He was in the stands. He came up to talk to your parents just before Luke dragged me away. I still think I could have taken him."

Tim laughed despite how tense he felt. "He came to see me at America House tonight."

Isaac pressed his lips together and nodded. "What did he say? No, you don't have to tell me."

"Isaac, I *do* have to tell you." Tim wrapped his hand around Isaac's forearm. "He showed up all apologies. He said he came to see me at the Olympics to make up for all the times he missed my meets in the past, because he wants to be with me again." He rolled his eyes.

"Oh," Isaac said. He seemed disappointed in that. "Do you think he meant it?"

"He seemed sincere, but I—oh, Isaac, no." Tim shook his head. "I'm not getting back together with him. There's a reason I'm here with you now and not with him. So banish whatever you're thinking from your mind."

Isaac smiled faintly. "That dickbag really came to Madrid to try to win you back?"

"Apparently. I told him to go home. He's too much of a distraction here."

"Will he?"

"Remains to be seen." Tim sighed and sank down beside Isaac. Seeing Pat had been horrific. He'd waited somewhere until Tim's parents had left to return to their hotel; then he'd swooped into America House, signed a few autographs, and gone right to Tim to plead his case.

"I'm so sorry, Timmy. I know you're mad about the money, but I needed to get to this audition in LA. See, they were filming a movie near Boulder. Wouldn't that have been perfect? I did it for us, don't you realize that? I wanted for us to be together. I love you so much. I still want to marry you."

Tim believed Pat was being earnest. He didn't trust Pat and sensed he still had an ulterior motive somewhere, but flying to Spain at his own expense seemed like a grand gesture, even for Pat, who generally spoke in grand gestures.

Still, Tim had no intention of taking him back. And now that they'd confronted each other and Tim had told Pat where he could stick his apologies, he felt a lot better. The anxiety of facing Pat had been worse than actually facing him, and Tim realized quickly he didn't love Pat anymore—if he ever had—and he would not be letting Pat's presence do anything to compromise his chance at the platform medal.

"I don't love him, Isaac."

Isaac nodded slowly. Tim wanted to protest, to say he was falling in love with *Isaac*, that it felt completely different from being with Pat, that he never wanted to be with Pat again, but he felt the pull of fatigue like something heavy dragging him under water.

"You're exhausted," Isaac said.

"I am."

Isaac opened his mouth as if he was going to say something, but instead he pressed his lips together and shook his head. "Here, let me get you out of some of these clothes. Then you can sleep."

"No, tell me what you were going to say."

Isaac kissed Tim's forehead. "I will later. We have all the time in the world."

ISAAC HELPED Tim out of his warm-up suit and stripped him down to briefs and a T-shirt; then he tucked Tim into bed. Isaac wanted to lie down with him, but his mind buzzed now. He paced instead.

He'd just figured it all out.

He pulled out his phone and called up the results of men's gymnastics. He smiled to himself, remembering the pep talk he'd given to Jake Mirakovitch. Whether he'd influenced the results was an open question, but he couldn't get over the idea that if he'd had someone like himself to talk to when he'd made the national swim team, his life might have taken an entirely different track.

That coaching might be a part of his future was an idea he'd been flirting with for a while, but it had really gelled as he'd talked to Tim tonight. He knew everything there was to know about swimming; he knew how to teach the strokes, knew how to train, how to build speed and endurance. He knew the workouts required for conditioning out of the pool, knew about diets and calorie intake, knew about warm-ups and cool-downs. He could teach someone to swim at the elite level—he had faith in himself about that at least. But more to the point, he had a depth of knowledge about what being an elite athlete was like that Adam didn't have. Adam had swum competitively at the NCAA level when he'd been in college, but hadn't ever made it to a World Championship or an Olympics. He was an amazing coach, but he lacked firsthand elite athlete experience.

But Isaac had it. He knew what it felt like to rise to the highest places and fall to the lowest. He could use that knowledge to help athletes who struggled not just with the physical tolls of elite sports, but the mental and emotional ones.

He could see his whole future before him, and he liked it.

He stopped pacing and looked down at Tim. Tim was dead to the world, curled onto his side and fast asleep. A little stream of drool leaked down the side of his chin. Isaac smiled.

He felt happy.

It struck him as a little odd. He'd been unhappy for so goddamn long. Five years, probably. Depression over the end of his swimming career, caused by listlessness and boredom, had driven him to drink to begin with, and he was determined not to let himself go to that place again. He needed a purpose, and he thought he'd found one. He'd talk to Adam after he flew home about what kind of training he needed. He'd....

Well, what if the University of Colorado needed an assistant swim coach?

Isaac sat on the side of the bed, careful not to jostle Tim too much. What if... what if Isaac moved into Tim's pretty house in the mountains, and he came home from a day of coaching a college swim team, and Tim came home from a long day of training, and they fell into bed together, exhausted but happy? What if they spent their days off together, hiking or skiing or just fooling around in bed? What if Isaac sat in the stands at Tim's dive meets, and Tim came with Isaac to important swim competitions? What if they had each other? What if Isaac wasn't alone anymore?

The thought of uprooting his life in Raleigh, as shitty as his apartment was, terrified Isaac. He'd never lived farther than an hour's drive from his mother, and now he could see her, or Abby and her husband and his little nephew, in ten or fifteen minutes if he wanted. Having his mother nearby had been crucial to surviving his return from rehab. She'd been his rock, his support system, and her faith in him had never wavered. Tears sprang to his eyes as he thought about being so far away that he couldn't just drive over to her house for a pep talk and a hug anymore. Could he really live without that? He felt a pang at the thought of his nephew growing up without Uncle Isaac around too, because he loved that kid to pieces. He loved his whole family, and Luke and his other friends, and even Adam. Could he really leave them?

He'd come to Madrid and done what he'd intended to do—he'd competed the right way, with his whole being, and he'd been handsomely rewarded for it—so maybe it was time to turn the page and start the next chapter of his life. He hated to leave Adam and Luke and his family, but it wasn't like he'd be moving to China. And he couldn't leave right away anyway, not if he wanted the endorsement money. He'd have to swim competitively for another year or two. He'd talked to Sheri about that after dinner. He had the potential to make enough money from endorsement deals to fly cross-country once a month if he wanted, though. And he wanted to.

It was probably better not to make any rash decisions until after the Olympics, until after the bubble popped. The Olympics were magic; could he and Tim really make a relationship in the real world, with all their other obligations and responsibilities, truly work?

He looked at Tim again. He hadn't moved. Isaac reached down and wiped the drool from Tim's chin, and Tim stirred but didn't wake up.

What if Isaac loved this man?

Because he was pretty sure he did. He'd never really been in love before, but every time he looked at Tim, he thought, *This is it. He's the one for me.*

But what about Pat? How did Tim feel? He'd said he didn't love Pat, but he'd been half out of it with exhaustion. What if Pat charmed Tim back? Tim had loved the man once. If Pat was here, he was probably planning some kind of siege campaign to win back Tim's heart. What if Isaac couldn't compete with that? What if Tim didn't return Isaac's feelings?

Then again, Tim was here. And Isaac was having a hard time distinguishing between the distorted thoughts his old demons made him think and what was real and in front of him.

Isaac lay down next to Tim and smoothed Tim's hair away from his face, then kissed his forehead. "I love you," he whispered experimentally, to see how it fit. He liked it. Tim stirred and settled again against Isaac's arm, so Isaac pulled him into a hug and lay back against the pillows.

It was probably the post-gold-medal excitement and adrenaline or whatever that was making him feel this way. Probably as soon as he got on the plane home, it would fade. But Isaac thought that *this*? Forever? Sounded pretty damn awesome.

The trick now would be to hold on to it.

CHAPTER 23

Day 12

TIM TOSSED his unicorn shammy off the side of the dive tower and clapped his hands a couple of times. He shook out his body and did a little dance toward the edge of the platform.

Donnie shouted from the base of the platform, probably to tell Tim to knock it off, but this was a practice dive. It didn't count. It should be fun. He danced harder before he took a deep breath and got into an armstand. Then he shifted his weight and propelled off the top of the platform.

He nailed the entry. The dive *felt* perfect. When he got out of the water, Donnie was shaking his head. "Stop grandstanding."

"I feel good, Donnie. I got this."

"Do you want me to bolster your strange happy mood, or do you want me to tear you down?"

Tim laughed. "Give me the bad news."

"The Australian judge has been really tough on form. During the springboard, she docked the Chinese divers half a point or more on almost every dive. I got the official results and rewatched the video to try to figure out what she was criticizing them for. It has to be form. Legs not perfectly together, hands in the wrong place, that kind of thing. So that's something you have to think about. That dive?" Donnie pointed at the platform. "It was great! In any other competition, that would get you a nine or a ten easily. But your feet were just slightly apart in the tuck and your left hand wasn't in quite the right place during the twist. You kind of had it here." Donnie demonstrated.

"Oof," said Tim. "Did I really do that?"

"Yeah. Bottom line is that the details matter. I don't know if the same judge will be watching the platform competition, but I can tell you, the judges have been equally harsh on the women."

Donnie handed over a page full of notes, meticulous details on every practice dive Tim had done that day. Tim looked it over. Some of the notes were helpful—misplaced hands during twists, a habit Tim didn't realize he'd picked up; not getting enough height out of the armstand dives—but some of it seemed petty and nitpicky. Then again, maybe those nits needed to be picked for the sake of Olympic competition. He'd just have to put his all into it, that was what Isaac had said.

"Seriously, though? You're in fine form," said Donnie. "I'm only being hard on you because I think you have a solid shot at the gold medal. But remember, you can't control the other divers. You can't control how perfect or terrible the other eleven men in the final will be. You can only control yourself. You're capable of doing all six of these dives flawlessly, you've gotten a lot of practice in over the last week and a half, and you're ready for competition. Yeah?"

"Yeah."

Donnie clapped a hand on Tim's shoulder. "That gold medal is yours. Let's show the world your winning four years ago was *not* a fluke."

"It wasn't," said Tim with conviction.

Tim thought he saw a glimmer of tears in Donnie's eyes, but Donnie blinked a few times and it was gone. He glanced at his watch. "Go change, big guy. I have to go make Jason stop goofing around and concentrate, and then I have a meeting with the other coaches tonight."

Tim nodded, found his discarded shammy, and walked into the locker room.

Isaac was leaning against Tim's locker when Tim walked to it. "You win a few gold medals and they just let you go anywhere, huh?" Tim said.

"Fun story," Isaac said. "A Hungarian swimmer tested positive for PEDs and the Anti-Doping Agency is cracking down on everyone, so I had to come in for another drug test, even though I finished swimming four days ago."

"Ugh, really?"

"Double-fun story is they did a blood alcohol test too, and I think the doctor thought he got me. He was all, 'You've been partying for three days, haven't you?' Well, joke's on them."

Tim shooed Isaac out of the way so he could put his stuff away in his locker. "They're really cracking down?"

"Yeah, especially on swimmers and runners. Runners are getting the brunt of it, actually. I've heard the Olympic Stadium has more people in white doctor's coats than a hospital. But since I'm still in Madrid...." Isaac sighed. "As much as I enjoy peeing in a cup while some dude watches, I had better plans for my afternoon."

"Such as?"

Isaac gave Tim a long appraising look, sweeping his gaze from Tim's head to his toes. Tim became acutely aware of how little he was wearing—just his dive suit. He felt heat rise to his face and chest.

"That blush is adorable," Isaac said.

Tim rolled his eyes. "Shut up."

"I saw you practicing. You're…. You amaze me. How you jump from that height and do all those somersaults without injuring yourself, I will never know."

"I've injured myself plenty over the years."

"You make it look easy. I don't love heights like that, but you make me think I could just climb to the top of that tower and hurl myself off it."

"Don't. They upped security around the dive pool since that reporter got into practice. They'll probably arrest you." Tim nudged Isaac out of the way again, because he kept shifting back in front of Tim's open locker.

Isaac put a hand on the back of Tim's neck. "I did want to mention one other thing."

Isaac's tone had grown so serious, Tim turned to give his full attention. "What?"

"I called Marcus Holt to see if he still wants me to do the interview. Swimming is over, so I thought I might have missed my window, but I thought about it, and I decided that it might be worth talking about my alcoholism."

"Are you sure?" Tim asked, aware suddenly that he was in a locker room and other men were around. A couple of water polo teams were trickling in to get ready for their match in an hour. How many of these guys spoke English was an open question, and Tim's little aisle was still empty, but Tim was suddenly very conscious of the fact that they could be overheard.

"I am," Isaac said, keeping his voice low. "Holt still wants to talk to me. I'm meeting with him this afternoon."

"Are you sure?"

Isaac looked pensively into the distance. "Being frank about my alcoholism will cost some endorsement money. Big corporations want to sponsor athletes with stories of triumph over adversity, not those of us who struggle daily. But...."

"What?"

"I didn't sleep much last night and kept thinking about my purpose. And I think the glossy sheen everyone always puts on the Olympics is actually doing a disservice. Because we, as athletes, put ourselves through a blender of training and injuries and triumph and shame. There's so much pressure to be the best—that's why these athletes turn to things like doping. I needed to take my pain away, so I turned to alcohol. And I think if we talk about that, if I talk about it, maybe I can help some other athletes out there who, just like you did last night, are beating themselves up for being less than perfect. I want to tell those athletes that they don't have to be perfect, and tell the public that this pressure we put on athletes to perform like monkeys for an adoring public can do real damage."

Tim stared at Isaac for a long moment. That was one of the reasons Tim had no regrets about being out publicly. If he could show someone struggling that being gay was okay, that there was no reason he or she couldn't reach for the stars, then everything was worth it. "That's... that's amazing, Isaac. I think that's a really worthwhile message. But I think you also have to be sure. If you say all that out loud, a lot of people will be angry."

"Maybe it's time to muddy up the glossy sheen on the Games. We're not all machines. There are athletes here who struggle with all kinds of things. They have addictions, they have a hard time making ends meet, they have injuries that will never heal completely or chronic illnesses, they've dealt with racism or homophobia or any number of things."

Tim nodded. "Do you plan to talk about me?"

"No. I mean, I thought about that too, because I think you're a part of the story now, but I can leave you out, if you'd prefer."

"I would. Just because I don't need the distraction right now." Tim exhaled sharply, suddenly picturing the platform final crowded with reporters who wanted to talk not about tucks and pikes but rather about Isaac, about their relationship and what it all meant and…. Not to mention, if Pat was still around and somebody recognized him…. Tim didn't want that to overshadow everything.

Because there'd been a time when it had. He and Pat had been in the midst of one of the most vicious arguments they'd ever had, and things had been unresolved when Tim had gotten on a plane to Helsinki for Worlds. They'd been arguing about money too; Pat wanted access to Tim's bank accounts, but Tim had been reluctant and yet still unable to say out loud that he didn't trust Pat, not entirely. Tim had successfully pushed the whole matter out of his mind to focus on the preliminary rounds, but then, right before finals, Pat appeared.

Of all the times for Pat to get over himself. There had been a hundred meets at which Tim had looked longingly into the stands, hoping the man who supposedly loved him would be there, cheering him on. But Pat never came—he was always busy—so Tim had resigned himself to do this alone. So it figured that when Pat did finally show up at a meet, he did it with what looked like an entourage, waltzing into the city with a bunch of reporters and photographers on his heels. In fact, he talked to reporters before saying a word to Tim, so the reporters hounded Tim on his way into the finals. Pat then made a big show of being the supportive boyfriend, waving and cheering from the stands. It was bad enough that nothing between them had been resolved, but on top of that, Tim was so thrown off, he'd missed most of his dives and finished a dismal eleventh out of twelve. Afterward Pat had said, "But I thought this was what you wanted." And Tim had said nothing because he couldn't figure out how to tell Pat that he wanted the support, but not like this. He didn't think Pat would understand the distinction.

He didn't need any of that here. No Pat, no reporters, no photographers, nobody wanting to ask him about his relationship or his sexuality or any of it. He was in great physical shape, he felt prepared, and he was in a good place mentally. That medal was his to lose, like Donnie kept saying. The last thing he needed was that cloud of microphones and cameras in his face.

Except that Pat was still here in the city. He hadn't shown up with the whole entourage—he'd seemed quite alone in the stands, according to his parents, and he'd been alone at America House last night—but he was here. Did that mean he'd learned something? That he wanted Tim back for more than just fame and

magazine covers? Not that it mattered, because Tim
was not going back to him.

He shook his head and looked at Isaac, who gazed
at him warmly. It killed Tim to say it, but he whispered,
"Please don't say anything about us. At your interview,
I mean."

"I won't." Isaac kissed Tim's forehead. "I completely understand. But I wanted to let you know I'm
going to do this interview. Do you think it's a terrible
mistake?"

Tim put a hand on Isaac's waist and looked into
his eyes. He knew Isaac wanted to do the interview and
was moved by that desire, even if he wasn't confident
it was a good idea.

"You said," Isaac said softly, "that telling your story to the public meant kids had a role model. That they
could see a successful gay man and know that good
things were possible for them too. What if I said, you
know, you can sink into some dark places, but you can
also fight your way back out? Do you think that would
be an inspirational message?"

Tim's heart squeezed. Had he actually inspired
Isaac to make this choice? He could see the question
in Isaac's eyes, the struggle he'd probably had mentally for the past few days while he wrestled with the
decision.

Tim realized that somewhere in the past two weeks,
he'd fallen in love with Isaac Flood. Warmth spread
across Tim's chest as he looked at Isaac; this was a man
he'd come to care about deeply in a short amount of
time. And Isaac had done something incredible, both by
getting sober and by using his sobriety as motivation to
become one of the best athletes in the world.

How had this happened? How had Tim fallen for a man so fast? Was he making a terrible mistake, like he had with Pat? They'd known each other for such a short amount of time, and Tim clearly wasn't the best judge of character. He didn't completely trust his feelings yet.

Well, he figured, they'd made no decisions yet. As far as things stood right now, Tim would fly back to Boulder on Monday, and Isaac would fly back to North Carolina. Nothing had really changed. But everything had changed.

Still, Isaac was waiting for Tim to say something, concern etched all over his face, probably wondering if he was making a horrific mistake by talking about his struggle so publicly.

Tim looked around, then leaned forward and kissed Isaac. "I think it's an important message."

"Yeah?"

"Yeah. And I hate to be a jerk about going public with our relationship. I'd love to go public. But can you imagine how many gawkers and cameras would show up at the platform final if we did?"

"I understand. I won't say anything."

"I've been through this before and I can't... not before the final."

"Tim. I get it. I swear, it's our secret until you say otherwise."

"The minute diving is over, we can tell anyone you want."

Isaac shrugged. "The world doesn't need to know yet. I'm happy with this being between us. And our closest friends, I guess."

Tim smiled, relieved. "When is the interview?"

Isaac pulled his phone out of his pocket and glanced at the screen. "In an hour. Sheri from USA

Swimming is arranging for a car to take me from here to the broadcast center in about ten minutes. So I'm really glad I caught you."

"You watched me practice."

"I did. Is that creepy?"

"No, I think it's sweet." Tim kissed Isaac again.

Isaac lowered his eyelids and smiled slowly. "Good. What are you up to now?"

"I was going to put in an hour at the gym. Then I might take a nap in your room."

Isaac grinned. "Sounds good to me. I'll see you when I get back."

Isaac bounded out of the locker room, so Tim changed into his gym clothes. He hummed a little to himself, feeling content for now, buzzy from realizing how much he cared about Isaac. He smiled to himself as he shouldered his gym bag and left the locker room. He nodded at the security guard on the way out, glad that he was there, keeping out anyone who didn't belong.

Because Pat did not belong. And yet there he was, standing just outside the police barrier. He grinned like an idiot when he saw Tim.

"Didn't I tell you to go home?" Tim asked, pushing past him.

"Can we talk? Somewhere less public? Like your room maybe?"

"No." Fury rose up in Tim's belly. How dare Pat be here like this? How dare he interrupt whatever was growing between him and Isaac? How could Pat be so presumptuous as to think Tim would just dump everything to be back with him? "First of all, only athletes are allowed in the dorms. Second, I have nothing to say to you."

"I've changed, Timmy. I made a terrible mistake. I never should have treated you the way I did, and I'm here to make up for that now."

"Your timing is terrible. I'm due at the gym. Because, you know, I'm here to compete and fulfill a lifelong ambition, not to sort through my old dirty laundry."

"Timmy."

"Fuck off, Pat. I have things to do."

"I flew all the way here for you. Doesn't that mean something?"

What would it take to make Pat go away?

Well, if he wanted to talk, they could talk, but not here, not with the media setting up to film the next competition, and not with so many onlookers. Tim kept walking, Pat on his heels, toward the athlete exit. A bus idled outside. Tim started to calculate whether they could have it out on the back of an empty bus if the driver didn't speak English, but then Pat said, "I rented a car. You want a ride back to the Athlete Village, at least?"

He didn't, but at least the car was a place they could argue out of the public eye. "Yeah, all right."

Luke Rogers, of all people, strolled out of the Aquatics Center then. "Hey, Tim," he said.

"Hi, Luke. You just missed Isaac."

"I know. He told me he had to go do some big interview. We both got called here for drug testing, which is dumb now that the competition is over. Whatever, nature of the beast." Luke glared at Pat.

Pat stepped forward and thrust his hand out aggressively. "I'm Patterson Wood." His tone indicated that Luke should have understood who Pat was.

Luke just stared at his hand.

Pat withdrew it and threw it around Tim instead. "I'm Tim's boyfriend."

Tim ducked out from under the arm. "*Ex*-boyfriend."

"And hopefully boyfriend again. I'm here to win him back. We're gonna go talk now, sort things out, you know?"

Luke tilted his head. "You okay, Tim? Need me to rough this guy up a little?"

Tim laughed, trying to sound lighter than he felt. "No, that's all right. Pat offered me a ride to the gym, so we're gonna talk, and then he's *going back home* like I told him to."

Pat shrugged.

Luke stepped toward the bus. "All right. See you later."

"Who was *that*?" Pat asked as they walked toward the car.

"A gold-medal-winning swimmer. And a friend. Not that it's any of your business."

Pat led Tim to a car, a fairly nondescript black sedan. Tim tossed his bag into the back seat and got into the passenger seat. God, what a mess.

After Pat slid into the driver's seat and was about to put the key in the ignition, Tim said, "What the hell are you doing here, Pat?"

"There's no pleasing you, is there? You spent so much time during our relationship moping about how I never came to meets, so I finally came to one and then you were mad I brought the press. So I came without the press this time."

Tim took a deep breath, determined to make this as clear as possible. "Patterson. Hear me, okay? I don't love you anymore. You spent all those years of our relationship treating me more like a prop than a boyfriend.

You didn't love me, you loved what I could get you. And you stole money from me. Explain to me why I would ever want to get back together with you."

"It's different now. Okay? It's different. Yeah, I did those things, but I realized how wrong I was to let you go. I love you, Timmy. I really do. And I want for us to be together. No pretenses this time. Just you and me and love. I'll move to Colorado if you want. I'll still have to travel back to LA, of course, but I'm also in talks to be a lead on a TV show that will be filming in Vancouver. I know you hate LA, but Vancouver is pretty."

"Pat...."

"You're mad and I deserve that, but our time apart has made me realize how wrong I was."

There was no sense trying to talk to him—Pat wouldn't be listening. All right. Tim pointed in the general direction of the Athlete Village and said, "Drive me to the gym." His fury was a tangible thing, sitting like a fire in his chest, burning and making him want jump out of the car. But the bus was pulling out of the parking lot, so if he didn't want to wait around another half hour for the next one, he'd have to go back with Pat.

Pat started the car. "All right."

"It's over, okay? The answer is no. We will not be getting back together. Get that through your fucking skull."

"Language, Timmy."

"I don't care. I'm furious, okay? I've never been this angry. I can't believe you have the fucking nerve to come here and think that I would *ever* forgive you. Just drive me back, okay?"

"Fine." Pat stomped on the accelerator and veered out of the parking lot.

MARCUS HOLT had been a morning show host for as long as Isaac could remember. His name might not have stuck in Isaac's head, but he definitely looked familiar now that Isaac sat across from him. Holt had silver-flecked black hair and a deep tan, and for the interview he wore a yellow shirt with a navy blue tie, looking ready for the summer weather in Madrid.

The camera guys were still fiddling with their equipment, so Isaac asked, "Can I decline to answer a question?"

"We'll edit this later."

That was not an answer. "I just mean, there's some stuff in my personal life I'm not willing to talk about on TV, so if you happen to ask about it, I want the right to say, 'No comment.'"

Marcus seemed intrigued by that, making Isaac think he shouldn't have said anything. "We can edit out parts you're uncomfortable with."

Right.

They'd already discussed that Isaac wanted this interview to be candid as far as his alcoholism and his Olympic experience went. Holt had argued at first that he wanted to keep things positive, but probably the part of him that had delivered hard news before cohosting a show that was mostly segments about cooking and pop culture had been snared by the idea of doing an in-depth interview with a guy like Isaac.

Isaac knew he had to put most of his energy into thinking through what he said before he said it. He felt a bit like he'd walked into a trap. The set was supposed

wanted to come back this year. I felt like crap the whole week of competition four years ago. I drank because I felt like crap and I felt like crap because I drank. By some miracle, I won some races anyway, but it was the wrong way to do it."

Holt leaned forward. Maybe wanted to ask about that. He looked down at his notes—which Isaac had thought were probably a prop, but apparently not—and then he said, "You never swam drunk?" like a father asking a child.

"No. I respect the sport. I genuinely do. But, like, after a race? I'd have a few too many beers. Everyone always wants to celebrate when you win. Then I'd show up for the afternoon races still hungover. And that felt just awful."

"Wait, you're telling me that you won several medals at the Olympics when you were hungover?"

"For at least one of those races, yeah. Not the world record, but one of the others."

"So you took your gifts for granted."

"I did, yeah. I thought I was the best, you know? Those gold medals were mine. I should have just been able to win. Or that's what I thought. And I didn't win all of my races, probably because I wasn't in top condition."

"So what happened when you went home?"

"I drank more." Isaac shook his head. This was harder to talk about than he'd expected. It was important to talk about, and he could help someone maybe, but Lord, this was hard to confess. "My career was over, right? I didn't put together that drinking was affecting my conditioning, so I thought my age made me swim slower. And, you know, I'd been swimming my whole life, so facing the end of my career was tough. I didn't know what to do with my life. I got depressed, which made me drink even more."

"And then you had the DUI."

"Yeah. It was a stupid mistake, but it was also a wake-up call. I didn't think I had a problem, you know? But I put people's lives in danger. I put my own life in danger. That night I got absurdly drunk, and then I got into a tiff with the officer who pulled me over. So I got arrested. I spent the night in the drunk tank, and at some point I sobered up and thought, 'What the hell am I doing?' It finally hit me that I was addicted, that I wasn't having fun. That moment inspired me to go to rehab."

"Did you stop swimming?"

"For a couple of years, yeah. I mean, I got in a pool every now and then, but I wasn't actively training. My, uh, doctor in rehab encouraged me to give it a shot again, though. I went back to Adam because I wanted to see if I could do it. But once I got sober, I felt better. Adam hired a nutritionist, who put me on this insane diet for a while. I lost weight, got my old body back, kind of."

"And started racing again."

"I honestly didn't know if I'd make a team again. I just knew I wanted to give it an honest try. Do it right this time. Sober up, get healthy, and swim as hard as I could."

"It seems to have worked."

"Yeah. I didn't know it was possible."

"So what happens for Isaac Flood now?"

Isaac nodded. "I plan to swim as long as my body lets me. Then I don't know. I've got a few things I'm feeling out. Now that I'm sober, I feel like there are a lot more possibilities."

"And personally? A family? Kids?"

"Yeah, that's all possible too. I mean, nothing is set right now, but I'd like a family someday."

"Gotta meet the right girl, right?"

Isaac had to work not to roll his eyes. "Sure, something like that."

"You are something of a sex symbol, you know. All those magazine covers. *Sports Illustrated.* The Wheaties box. There are photos of you all over the internet."

Isaac didn't know what to do with that. He knew intellectually that it was true, that he'd been spotlighted in media coverage of the last Olympics and done an *ESPN Magazine* body issue or two, but knowing there were other people who looked at his picture and lusted was surreal. "I... sure."

"Just curious if the ladies at home should give up hope."

"Well." Isaac didn't know how to handle the question. He settled on, "I'll keep you posted."

Holt maybe realized he'd stumbled into one of the things Isaac didn't want to discuss publicly. He looked like he wanted to press the issue, but one of the camera guys started gesturing. Holt nodded. "That may be enough, so let's do some parting questions. How does it feel to win so many medals at these Olympics?"

"It's wild. It feels amazing. I worked really hard for this, and I'm proud. My body feels good. Part of me still can't believe I pulled it off."

Holt wound down the discussion, conferring with the cameramen about whether they needed to reshoot anything. Then he turned back to Isaac and said, "One more question. Why did you agree to do this interview?"

Isaac smiled, thinking of Tim. "A friend of mine pointed out to me recently that we, as Olympic athletes, are role models. Millions of people all over the world are watching. I didn't want to talk about all this publicly at first, but I thought that if maybe one person who is trapped in what feels like a hopeless situation sees my story, he might be inspired to work to get out. I know what the claws of alcoholism feel like, what depression feels like, how hard it is to climb out of all of that. It's bleak, it really is, and it feels hopeless when you're at the bottom. But I'm here to tell you it's possible to get out. That's the message I want to send. It's possible to get your life back from alcohol. It's hard. Lord knows I struggled for a long time. I still struggle. But it's possible."

Holt nodded. "That's.... It's a good message." He looked at his notes again. "Let's talk about that a little more. Anyone who knows an alcoholic knows that you never stop being an alcoholic. Do you still struggle with wanting to drink?"

Isaac took a deep breath. "Daily. But the message I took from rehab is to take each moment as it comes. I stay on the wagon by telling myself I just have to get through this hour, this day. If I feel overwhelmed, I talk to someone I trust, like my mom or one of my friends. I have a support network now that I didn't have before rehab. And they are so valuable to me."

"Your mother has been your biggest cheerleader."

"She's... she's the best. I couldn't have done any of this without her. Not swimming, not winning medals, not getting sober, none of it. I will never be able to thank her enough."

"Do you think a lot of athletes struggle with problems like yours?"

Well, that was really the question, wasn't it? "I'm sure they do. Maybe not alcoholism, but other things.

Athletes feel a lot of pressure from coaches and families and the media and even ourselves to be successful, to be the best we can be. I coped with that pressure by turning to alcohol, but some turn to other drugs, including those that help with performance. I think every elite athlete probably knows someone who has done something extreme to be successful. Of course, that doesn't excuse any of it, and I certainly don't deserve anyone's forgiveness. I just think we're doing everyone a disservice by not talking about it."

Phew. Isaac had just said a lot. Probably more than he should have. Part of him wanted to take it all back, but on the other hand, it was good to have it out there. And, well, if it cost him some money, so be it.

"I appreciate your honesty," said Holt.

"I'm not even saying that, like, doping is rampant, or whatever. Just pointing out, you know, that we all have things we deal with. Every athlete has fought through a significant challenge to get here. I think overcoming those challenges make us better athletes."

Holt nodded. "Thanks, Isaac. I'll recut this a little before it airs, and I'll have to trim it for time, but I do appreciate your coming to sit down with me."

"Thank you for the opportunity."

And that was it. It was over. Isaac let out a breath. He'd discussed the worst period of his life frankly to a reporter, and it would air on TV. He'd felt oddly distanced from it while he'd spoken, but now that it was over, it hit him suddenly.

He thought of Tim crying after the springboard final. A sudden wave of emotion hit Isaac. It stole his breath. He asked Holt where the restroom was, and then speed-walked there and made it in time to throw up in a toilet.

Had he really done that? Did he regret it? Because the whole world was about to find out not only that he was an alcoholic but that he'd done some supremely stupid things. His mother had implied the DUI had been a major story of the Olympics when they'd talked the other day before she flew home. It was a good narrative, for sure—a media darling goes bad, wrecks his life, but manages to come back. But now everyone would know the bigger story: Isaac was a drunk, he definitely wasn't a saint, and he probably wasn't the only athlete in Madrid who had struggled with such things.

Then he started to wonder if he'd said enough, if he'd really gotten the message across.

He sat on the cold tile floor of the men's room in the TBC offices within the Olympic Broadcast Center, and though he still felt nauseous, he thought he was done vomiting. He flushed but didn't move, willing his head to stop spinning and his stomach to stop churning. He took long, deep breaths until it felt like he was out of danger. Then he stood, walked to the sink, and splashed cold water on his face.

The first step toward living a good, honest life was to tell the truth. He'd just done that, or as much of the truth as he could right now. Now he just had to talk to Tim and let him know what he was thinking.

Isaac managed to heave himself up off the floor and walked back to the green room. There was a little TV on in the corner. It seemed to be showing that dumb gossip show. Isaac poured himself a cup of coffee and was about to go back out to find Sheri when a headline snagged his attention.

"Is diver Tim Swan back with his hunky ex-boyfriend? We caught up with Patterson Wood here in Madrid this afternoon." There were some colorful graphics and then the camera landed on Patterson Wood's stupid face. "I'm here in Madrid to see Timmy. He's the love of my life."

"Over my dead body," Isaac muttered.

But then the camera showed footage of Tim and Pat walking through the public area of the Athlete Village, near the gym. Tim smiled and waved at the camera; then Pat threw his arm around Tim.

When had this been filmed? Tim was wearing the same T-shirt and warm-up pants he'd worn to dive practice that morning. Hadn't Pat gone home? What was he doing with Tim?

The image flashed back to Pat's face. "We're talking," he said. "I came to Madrid to win him back. He's the best diver in the world, you know that? I bet he'll win another medal—a gold one this time."

The screen flashed again, and there was footage of Tim and Pat walking into America House, Pat with his hand possessively on the small of Tim's back.

Were they back together? No! Tim had said a few times he had no interest in Pat anymore. But then, why were they together now? What did that mean?

Of course, it could have been a weird coincidence. Or garbage gossip reporting. And Pat was not the most trustworthy person, so he could have been lying about them getting back together.

But was he?

Tim had admitted he wasn't the best judge of character, and maybe that charming asshole had managed to persuade Tim that he was a better man than Isaac. He probably was, actually; he'd been on a popular television show and wasn't an alcoholic. Not to mention those magical endorsement deals that Pat had helped Tim get. That could all add up to a really appealing package to someone like Tim. Or at least, a more appealing package than a broke alcoholic swimmer.

Before Isaac could contemplate that much more, Sheri burst into the green room. "Car's out front."

Isaac nodded and followed her back to the elevator.

His mind spun as he sat in the back of the limo. He answered Sheri's questions about how the interview had gone and tried to be pleasant about it, but all of his old anxieties suddenly came rushing back. How could he think he was good enough for a man like Tim? He was a washed-up alcoholic with no particular prospects. He'd probably just pissed away all of his earning potential by doing that interview. He had nothing to offer Tim. Of course it made sense for Tim to go back to that douchebag Pat, because Isaac wasn't much better, not really.

Or was that Isaac's depression getting the better of him? Was this the cost of talking about his experiences? He'd just dredged a lot of stuff back up, as evidenced by that stint in the men's room. His therapist at rehab had told him the same miswiring in his brain that caused him to lose control around alcohol also disrupted his thoughts, lied to him even. Maybe Isaac was experiencing some kind of postcompetition down that made everything worse. Just a few hours ago he'd been convinced he loved Tim, and he'd thought Tim had reciprocated at least some of those feelings. This gossip story that Tim and Pat were getting back together must have been just that. Gossip.

He texted Tim: *I did the interview. On the way back now. Want to get dinner?*

He and Sheri rode in silence for a few moments while Isaac waited for a response.

It never came.

CHAPTER 24

ISAAC WANTED a drink.

Tim had said he planned to take a nap in Isaac's room, but Tim wasn't there when Isaac returned. He wasn't in his own room either. Jason was there, though, and had no idea where Tim had gone.

Isaac had felt so happy just a few hours ago. Why was he reeling now?

And what did it really say about him that what was probably a minor setback—some television footage that really meant nothing; they might have just been talking—had sent Isaac on this spiral?

The time indicated it was too early to call his doctor during his office hours back home, so he went to Luke's room instead.

Luke and Katie were there, both in sweats, as if they'd been napping instead of fooling around, which made Isaac feel slightly less guilty. Only slightly.

"Isaac. What is it?" Luke's facial expression indicated he knew something was wrong. He gestured Isaac into the room.

Isaac said in one long breath, "I can't find Tim and he's not answering his texts and I saw a news story this afternoon that he might be getting back together with that Pat asshole, and even though that's probably not true, I can't stop thinking about it, and I want a beer so badly right now I can almost taste it."

Luke shut the door and exhaled loudly. "All right. That's a lot, right there."

"Wait, *are* they back together?" asked Katie.

Isaac made a big show of shrugging.

"I saw that Pat guy today. He came to the Aquatics Center and offered Tim a ride back to the Athlete Village. I guess Tim took it. He said something about wanting Tim back. But I gotta say, Tim seemed pretty annoyed at him."

"What if they talked and he said the right thing and Tim is all charmed and they're off in his hotel room right now? Huh?"

"Isaac." Luke's tone was stern. "That's insane."

"I know. I *know*. But I can't get these thoughts out of my head. It's probably nothing and I'm overreacting. But it's too late on the East Coast to talk to my therapist, so I needed to tell someone that I want to drink, because I'm starting to spiral. I can't seem to control my thoughts or myself."

"What do you normally do when this happens?" Katie asked.

"Drink," Isaac said.

"You did the right thing coming here," Luke said. He guided Isaac over to a chair and made him sit down. "What's really going on? You and Tim?"

"I think I'm in love with him."

"Wow," said Katie.

"And I thought he cared about me too, but how can he, if he's with Pat?" Isaac looked at the door, mindful of Luke's and Katie's gazes on him. "How easy would it be to walk outside, to walk to America House, to order a goddamned beer and have that be the end of it? Because I don't feel this way when I'm drunk."

"No, but you *do* feel like shit. You've worked so hard, Isaac. This thing with Tim, maybe nothing is happening and he's just at the gym or he turned his phone off or something. I can't believe he'd go back to Pat, especially not without saying something to you."

"But you saw them together."

"They did get in Pat's car," Luke said, glancing at Katie. "But it looked like they were arguing."

Isaac felt an anxiety attack coming. God, he hadn't felt like this in a long time. Not since before the last time he fell off the wagon. He'd developed so many coping mechanisms, and they were all failing him now, because this was stupid. It was probably nothing. Luke was probably right—Tim was just at the gym and his phone was in his locker. He wasn't with Pat.

But what did it say about Isaac that he could fly off the handle so easily?

"Why am I like this?" Isaac asked. He was aware of Katie staring at him, but, well, she'd just have to witness his nervous breakdown. "I should be happy. I'm the best swimmer at these Games, you know? I've won gold medals. I met this amazing guy, and he seems to like me back. But it's like my brain won't even let me have that, because here I am, freaking out about what is probably nothing." Isaac bent forward and put his head in his hands. "I don't deserve him."

"Isaac." Luke's voice took on that stern tone again, though there was softness around the edges. "You deserve everything. Don't you know that? I've never known anyone who works as hard as you do, who fights for things the way you do. You've told me your sobriety is a daily battle, but it's one you keep winning.

Don't let this break you." Luke exhaled loudly again. "I won't lie and say this is nothing, because it's clearly got you out of sorts. I don't see Tim betraying you this way, but I don't know him, and I did see him and Pat together today. But you know that even if he did, you'll get through it and live to swim another day."

"That's not helpful, Luke," said Katie. "I'm sure it's nothing. Tim probably needed to tell Pat off one more time."

Isaac had to make these feelings stop. His anxiety over Tim, his anxiety over his anxiety—it was all threatening to pull him under. There was only one way he knew of to make these things stop.

"I need some air," Isaac said, standing.

"You aren't going to do something stupid, are you?" Luke asked.

"I can't make any promises." Isaac ran out the door before Luke could protest more.

"If YOU don't leave right now," Tim said to Pat, "I'm going to call over that security guard and have you escorted back to your hotel. And then I'm filing a restraining order. Because I never want you within fifty feet of me ever again. Is that clear?"

Pat had been shadowing him since they got back to the Athlete Village. He'd followed Tim to the gym and watched him work out like a creep—which was supremely distracting, so Tim cut the workout short—then trailed after him as he walked back toward the dorms. So Tim made the decision to steer him into America House, a public enough place. And on the way, he'd spotted the cameras, so he'd schooled his face to make sure he was not scowling and waved to make it look like he was a good sport about the press coverage. But once they were inside, he steered Pat into a corner booth and did his best to make Pat see the truth. So far he'd been failing miserably.

"So that's it," Pat said simply, easily. Too easily.

Then something occurred to Tim. He sat back in the booth. "Oh my God. You orchestrated all of this, didn't you? You tipped off that camera guy that you'd be here with me and tried to get us filmed together. I bet that gossip show is doing a story right now on how we're getting back together."

Pat ducked his head, indicating it was the truth. He'd probably already done an interview with one of those reporters. God *damn* him.

Tim pointed to the door. Through clenched teeth, he said, "Get the hell out of here. I never want to see you again. You hear me? I. Never. Want. To. See. You. Again. It's over. I don't know how I can be any more clear about it."

"I did do the interview, but just because I thought it would be nice to make my intentions public. You always said you wanted to be honest with everyone about who you are, so I didn't think you'd mind."

"You never change." Tim shook his head, anger and disbelief running through him. "Well, if you're not leaving, I am. I'm done, Pat. Finished. *Finito*. Do not ever contact me again. Don't show up at my meets. I'm going to give your picture to security at the Aquatics Center to make sure you're denied entry. And while you're at it, go fuck yourself."

Tim stood, grabbed his gym bag, and stormed out of the bar. He speed-walked all the way back to the dorm building, because he was furious, and it pulsed in him like a living thing. All he wanted right now was to find Isaac, who was probably back from the interview by now, and sleep until he had to dive again.

Tim went to his own room first to drop off his gym bag. Jason was there, reading a book.

"Isaac came by looking for you," Jason said. "He seemed a little anxious. Said you weren't answering your texts."

Tim hadn't looked at his phone all day. He fished it out of his gym bag and saw he had a half-dozen texts and a voicemail from Isaac. He was overcome by a sinking feeling. "Oh no," he whispered.

"You're not back together with Pat, are you?"

"God, no. In fact, I just told him to go fuck himself. I never want to see that piece of crap ever again. Why would you think we were back together?"

"Uh, it's all over the internet that you are."

Oh no. An anxious Isaac had come by looking for Tim, meaning he'd likely seen the stories. And Pat *had* orchestrated for that camera guy to be there, to capture them together, so that it would be all over the web that they were back together and Pat could get his goddamn press.

What must Isaac have thought? But Isaac couldn't really believe Tim would betray him like that, would he?

Fuck Pat. "I have to find Isaac."

As he climbed the steps to Isaac's floor, he looked at his texts. Isaac asking him to dinner… then asking where he was… then an *I'm really worried now lol*, but there wasn't really anything funny about this. Tim pressed the voicemail button and listened.

"Hey, Tim, I just… I need to talk to you right now. Please give me a call when you get this."

His tone reminded Tim of the night Isaac confessed that he wanted a drink more than usual. This was really bad. And Tim was not about to let Isaac throw away his hard work and sobriety on Pat's account.

Tim pounded on Isaac's door but was greeted with silence. There was no light under the door. No movement inside. He wasn't here.

Tim called Isaac. It went straight to voicemail, so Tim said, "I'm trying to find you. Where are you?" and hung up.

Where was there alcohol? Well, everywhere, probably.

Tim checked every lounge in the building. He thought to check Luke's room but didn't know which one that was, and in a building with a few hundred rooms, he'd lose more time knocking on every one than it was worth.

He took the elevator down to the lobby and figured he'd head back to America House and see if Isaac was there. He'd check all the other international houses if he had to. He'd go to every bar in Madrid if that was what it took to keep Isaac from falling off the wagon.

The elevator doors opened and Luke was there in the lobby, standing beside Katie. Tim called his name.

"Oh, Tim, thank God."

"What's going on? Where's Isaac?"

Luke glanced at Katie. "Well, I'm not sure exactly, but he was in a bad way. I've been trying to call him, but he's not answering his phone. He's…. You're not back together with Pat, are you?"

"No. And I'm going to murder Pat for making so many people think that."

Luke nodded. "I'm glad of that. I don't think Isaac really believes you are either, but he's beating himself up a lot for getting worked up about it. We need to find him before he does something he'll regret later."

"Then let's go find him. He might have gone to America House. He's not in any of the public areas in this building."

Luke nodded. "That was my thought too."

Tim, Luke, and Katie walked quickly out of the building and toward America House. Luke tried calling Isaac again, with no luck.

But when they all got to America House, there was Isaac, sitting alone at the bar, a full pint of beer in front of him. He was clearly lost in his own thoughts and didn't move as Tim and Luke approached slowly.

Tim's instinct was to run over there and take that beer away from him. But he thought more delicacy was called for. To Luke, he whispered, "What should we do?"

"I think you should talk to him. Try to be understanding. He spends all his days fighting his demons, and usually he wins, but I think today, they might be winning."

"He did that interview with Marcus Holt today. They were supposed to talk about his alcoholism. Maybe it dredged something up."

"Yeah. I don't think this is really about you and Pat. But I think you should be the one to talk to him."

"Okay." Tim took a deep breath and walked forward slowly, not wanting to spook Isaac.

Was this the future he was signing on for? Would he have to rescue Isaac from himself more? Likely yes; alcoholism didn't get magically cured and go away. Maybe it would get easier with time, but Isaac hadn't even been sober for two years. Probably there would be hard times like this ahead. Was Tim prepared for that?

No. But he'd take Isaac with all his flaws in a heartbeat anyway.

He sat on the stool next to Isaac and said, "Hi."

Isaac swallowed. He stared at his glass. "Hi."

"I'm sorry for not answering my phone. I had a really terrible afternoon and wasn't looking at it."

"You shouldn't have to be at my beck and call."

"No, but I could have texted you back. I'm... I'm not back together with Pat, in case you were thinking that."

"I wasn't... well. I knew that was true on some level, but part of me kept thinking about it anyway."

Tim took a deep breath. "He, ah, followed me around all afternoon. I told him off about eight times. I think he may even have heard me that last time. I never want to see him again, Isaac. He orchestrated the whole day so that we'd been seen together."

"I saw you on that fucking gossip show. When I was at the broadcast center. It was on TV."

"I know. All Pat's doing. If I had known at the time that was what he was up to, I would never have spoken to him at all." Tim leaned forward and cautiously put a hand on Isaac's shoulder. "I'm so sorry."

Isaac shook his head. "It's not you. It's not your fault. I didn't really think you were stupid enough to get back together with him. But sometimes I.... It's my fucked-up brain, it gets the better of me. I'm usually better at coping with it, but today all of my emotions are turned up to eleven, and I just... I freaked the fuck out is what I did." Isaac sighed. He pressed a hand to his forehead. "And I felt like such an idiot. I trust you. I do, I promise. I just got all up in my own head. And all I kept thinking was that I knew a surefire way to make it stop." He lowered his hand and gestured toward his glass.

"Did you drink any of that?"

"No. I haven't. Truthfully. I ordered it about ten minutes ago and I've just been watching the bubbles."

Isaac's sadness radiated off him, and Tim felt it in his gut. He wanted to cure it, to take it away, but he knew that wasn't possible. "It's not too late, then."

Isaac reached for the glass but pulled his hand back again. "How could you possibly want to be with someone as fucked-up as I am? One setback and here I am, ready to drown my sorrows."

Tim found some comfort in the fact that Isaac didn't really believe him capable of getting back together with Pat, but the larger problem of Isaac's thoughts getting the better of him, and that full pint of beer, felt like a pretty steep mountain to climb. Tim considered the situation and tried to figure out how best to find a path up and over the mountain. He glanced back at Luke, who stood a few feet away with his arm around Katie. Luke gave him a thumbs-up.

Tim was out of his depth. It felt like cliff diving. At least in a pool, he knew what to expect when he dove. Diving outdoors, into a natural body of water, had any number of hazards, from shallow water to rocks. One didn't truly know what to expect until one went for it.

Tim put his hand on Isaac's arm, and Isaac turned toward him slightly.

"I don't have a magic wand that will take your pain away. If I did, I would wave it in a heartbeat, because I hate seeing you like this." Isaac winced, so Tim said, "Not because I'm ashamed of you or I think any less of you, but because I know you're struggling a lot right now and I want to make it better. But I don't know how, except to say that I'm here for you now. And that you, Isaac, might be the best man I know."

Isaac shook his head. "I'm really not. I don't... I don't know how to handle all these compliments, because I know you all mean well." He glanced at Luke. "But they don't feel like me. I mean, I know I've done some incredible things since I've been in Madrid, and I worked really hard to get here, but at the end, I'm still Isaac, an alcoholic who can't even hold it together enough to get through one stupid stumbling block with a guy I really like."

Tim rubbed Isaac's arm. "You're stronger than you think. And I'm glad you really like me, because I really like you too. And I feel terrible for ignoring your texts. I could have at least responded to let you know I'd get back to you later."

"No, I shouldn't.... I mean, we're not together, are we? You're not, like, my boyfriend. We met two weeks ago."

Tim balked, trying not to be offended by that, but it felt a bit like a punch in the chest, because he'd thought they were. "Aren't we together? We've spent all of our free time together for two weeks. We care about each other. I got the impression we were going to try to make something happen when we got home. Was I wrong?"

Isaac looked miserable. His face melted as he stared at his glass. "I want to, but this... this is me."

"I don't believe that. This is part of you, yes, but the real you is the man I've spent the last week with. A strong man who can beat this, who can get past it. And you, Isaac, you *see* me in a way no one else does, and I think I see you. Today I told a man I once thought I loved to go fuck himself because he's more selfish than

I ever realized. But partly, it was for you too, because I want to be with you, Isaac."

Isaac pursed his lips for a long moment, glancing at Tim, but mostly looking at his glass. "I want to be with you too. But I can't be so dependent on you. I can't rely on any one person to keep me sober. I have to do the work on that myself."

"But you can accept help, right? I *want* to help you. I want to be with *you*, Isaac, warts and all. I know you're not perfect. I know you battle demons. But I know you have it in you to fight those demons too. You have it in you to do amazing things. A weaker man would have let the demons win, but you won't. I know you won't. I have faith in you."

Isaac looked at Tim, tears in his eyes. He blinked a few times and they were gone, but Tim had seen them. He'd gotten through somehow.

"You have faith in me," Isaac said softly.

"I do. And if you need to talk about things tonight, I'm here for you. Or if you just want to go back to your room and go to sleep, we can do that too. Or if you want to be left alone, I'll leave you alone. Whatever you need, I'll do it."

Isaac nodded. He put a hand on Tim's shoulder and leaned forward until their foreheads touched. "Thank you."

"So what do you want to do?" Tim asked softly.

"Get out of here," Isaac said.

Tim smiled. "That we can do." He gently leaned away from Isaac and stood up. Then he offered Isaac his hand.

Isaac took it and slid off his tool. He gave one last, longing glance at the pint of beer; then he nodded to himself and turned toward Tim. Tim opened his arms for a hug, and Isaac stepped into them and let himself be hugged.

Luke and Katie walked over. "You okay, Flood?" Luke asked.

"Yeah. I'm sorry for freaking out on you before. This day, this whole month, it all kind of hit me and I didn't handle it well."

"You still on the wagon?"

"Barely. I ordered the beer but didn't drink it."

"That's what matters. How long you been sober?"

"Eighteen months, two weeks."

"You got this," Luke said.

Isaac nodded, a faint smile on his face. Katie reached over and patted his shoulder. Tim took Isaac's hand, and then they all walked back to the dorm together.

CHAPTER 25

Day 15

Transcript: Men's Ten-Meter Platform Final

BELL: We had some exciting preliminary rounds.

HOLLAND: Goes to show, nothing is a given at the Olympics.

BELL: Australian diver Andrew McKinnon dove exceptionally well in the preliminary round, but then this happened in the semifinal. This dive looked so great in the air, but it was a total miss when he hit the water. He never recovered after that.

HOLLAND: Yes, he finished just out of the top twelve who made the final.

BELL: The Chinese divers also both looked off their game. Liu is usually such a beautiful diver, and he does things in the air that nobody else can do, but so many of his entries were just short of vertical.

HOLLAND: He qualified for the final in eighth place.

BELL: But he did make the final. The good news is that all of the previous round scores are thrown out, so if he dives well in this final, he's got a good shot at a medal. The trick for Liu will be to shake any residual nerves from the previous rounds. We see this all the time. It's these athletes' first Olympics, and nerves make them tighten up.

HOLLAND: What do you think about our returning Olympic champion, Timothy Swan?

BELL: Well, I'll tell ya, Swan looked fantastic all through the preliminary rounds. All of his dives looked good in the air, and he entered the water very well. Let's take a look at this third-round dive from the semifinal. See, he gets out from the platform fast so he can pull into his tuck. Then, as he rotates, he sights the water here, and here again, and here again, and then he kicks out. He always knows where he is in the air and how far he is from the pool, so he can straighten out and enter the water perfectly vertical. His entry is smooth with hardly any splash.

HOLLAND: You think he looks good to repeat his gold-medal win?

BELL: If he keeps diving like this? Almost certainly. He's an entirely different diver from what we saw in the springboard finals. He seemed a little uncertain there. But here, he's diving very well. He's in top form. Again, all of the previous round scores go away, so everyone is diving with a clean slate. Swan has looked great, but Liu has several world champion medals, so he's a contender. I wouldn't count out Schmidt from Germany either. Or the Italians, who were the bronze medalists in the synchro competition. Both divers have been diving very well in individual competition. And Timmy Swan's synchro partner, Jason Evans, made the finals as well....

TIM MIRACULOUSLY held on to first place going into the third round of diving. He'd given his all to the prelims, following Donnie's advice to be mindful of his form, thinking through everything but not tightening up. He'd trained hard all week, he'd gotten a good night's sleep the night before, he'd eaten well and felt focused and ready to defend his title.

One thing that had made him feel better was the fact that Pat had flown back to the States. He'd called Tim the day before prelims to say he was giving up and going home. Tim had pushed him right out of his mind.

Donnie always said that when Tim was on his game, anything was possible. And Tim was on his game today.

He took a deep breath before ascending the platform for his third dive. When he got to the top, he looked out at the audience and toward Isaac, who sat with Luke and Katie in the stands again. Isaac was too far away for Tim to see more than his fuzzy face, but he imagined they made eye contact. Tim didn't know why, but seeing Isaac there reassured him and reminded Tim that he needed to put his all into this, that he needed to focus and dive and execute it the way he knew he could.

Isaac kept fighting. Tim could too.

This was an arm stand dive. Not Tim's favorite, but a way to show off how athletic and strong he was. He put his hands down and slowly lifted his legs into position, which showed the judges he had control over his movements.

He pushed off the platform, the same way he had a thousand times in practice, and immediately pulled into his tuck. He did four and a half somersaults before straightening out and hitting the water. He knew intellectually that he traveled toward the water at close to thirty miles per hour—Donnie had gotten his hands on a radar gun once to test this—and rather than being a nice cushion, the water felt a lot like pushing through a brick wall. He already had bruises from practice and competition. But he slid into the water, no sting on his legs to indicate he'd missed going in vertically, and Donnie was jumping up and down when he surfaced, so he must have done well.

He had this. That gold medal was his. Tim still had three more dives and three chances to fuck this up, but he could practically reach out and touch that medal.

An hour later Tim pushed himself out of one of the hot tubs and toweled off. Donnie was standing in the coaches' area, trying to get his attention. Tim walked over.

"I assume you know your scores?"

Tim nodded. After five dives, he had accumulated 465.5 points. He was also two points out of first place, behind Liu, who had apparently shaken off whatever had caused him to flounder in the semifinal. Tim's sixth and final dive could easily earn him 125 points, but so could Liu's.

"I don't want to give you some bullshit about how this is yours to lose, but it's you or Liu for the gold medal. The guy in third… ah, Schmidt, I guess? He's thirty points behind you. Unless you really blow this last dive, that's too much of a deficit to take either you or Liu out of medal contention."

Tim nodded. He'd made the same calculation. A handful of points meant gold or silver, and his heart raced as he thought about it. He wanted this, God he wanted this, and it was within his power to get it.

Donnie said, "I *am* going to tell you that I know you can do this last dive well enough to earn tens. You've looked fantastic through the whole competition. So, basically, you've got a medal. Don't tense up and blow it."

Tim laughed despite himself. Donnie had never quite mastered the art of giving a pep talk. Donnie laughed with him, likely recognizing that laughter helped. Anything to keep from tensing up.

Jason sat in eighth place, well out of medal contention, not that he probably even knew that. He had his waterproof headphones on and bobbed his head while he danced in and out of one of the showers. His eyes were shut.

Tim had to wait a while to do his last dive, since he'd qualified near the top of the rankings. He tried to stay warm, but mostly he fidgeted through ten other dives, hopping under showers, dunking himself in the hot tub, toweling off and then getting wet again.

It was the most nerve-racking part of diving: knowing that even if he did everything to the best of his abilities, he could still lose if someone else was better.

His last dive was also the trickiest, at least in terms of the difficulty score. It was a reverse four-and-a-half somersault dive, which had a high difficulty level but which Tim found easier than dives in which he had to transition between somersaults and twists. That had been his fourth-round dive, his lowest-scoring dive, the one that had allowed Liu to pull ahead. But Tim's worst—which, as he'd seen on the video Donnie had taken on his phone, was a hair short of vertical but otherwise a pretty solid dive—was a lot better than many divers' best, so Tim felt okay with it.

And now: four and a half somersaults, starting from the arm stand position.

When he got to the top of the platform, Tim looked out at the audience. Isaac's head was turned in his direction, so Tim imagined they made eye contact again.

Tim didn't have anything to prove, he realized. He'd won this event four years ago and performed very well here. He was one of the best divers in the world and had been for five years. He was young enough that he probably had another Olympics in him, barring injury. He loved this sport, loved hurling himself through the air. But this wasn't redemption. He wanted to show he was still good, but he'd done that. So if he won gold or silver, it didn't matter. He wanted the gold, yes—he wanted it more than anything in the world right then— but he didn't necessarily have control over whether he won it. Diving wasn't a race; there was no objective indicator of who was the best. Just a group of flawed humans giving numerical values to each athlete.

All Tim could do was dive to the best of his ability.

He took a deep breath, tossed his shammy toward where Donnie stood, and walked to the end of the platform. He got into the arm stand, slowly lifting his legs into the air. He held the arm stand for a long moment. Then he bent at the waist and threw himself off the platform. He got into his tuck quickly, somersaulting through the air. He sighted the water, knew he had control over this dive, and when it was time, he kicked out and straightened. Hitting his hands on the water hurt like a bitch, but he knew he'd gotten his body position right, that he went into the water vertically.

And there it was. The best dive he could have executed.

He swam to the side of the pool and pulled himself out. The audience roared. Tim liked that, though he knew better than to think the volume of cheers would be reflected in the scoring. But then the score flashed on the scoreboard: all nines and tens. Final score: 134.4.

Tim walked by the coaches' area. Donnie grinned and said, "That'll do, pig."

Tim rolled his eyes.

He was done now, so he didn't bother with the showers or hot tub. Instead he found his shammy and stood near Donnie to wait for the last dive.

Liu was performing a back four-and-a-half, according to the scoreboard, which had a degree of difficulty 0.3 below the dive Tim had just done. Tim did the math. If Liu got all tens, he'd score a 135, which would be enough to win. And Liu could get tens across the board; Tim had seen him do it before. Even if he didn't, the two-point lead Liu already enjoyed might be enough.

It would be close.

Liu got into position at the end of the platform. Then he jumped in the air, his body position perfect, his somersaulting clean. He kicked out, straightened his body, and went in straight but... splash.

A lot of splash.

Physics dictated that splashes like that could only happen if Liu had done something wrong—if his entry position hadn't been quite right, if he'd moved his feet at the last second, if he'd failed to enter vertically. It was hard to tell what had happened, even in the replay on the screen, but what it meant was that Liu's final dive was not perfect. Liu needed 133 points to win gold.

His score: 121.5.

Tim had won the gold medal.

Holy shit.

Donnie hugged Tim before Tim even really knew what was happening.

He wasn't a fluke. He'd won that gold medal fairly at the last Olympics, even though everyone tried to talk him down—he was cute, he'd had a good day, the wind had thrown off everyone else. But Tim had just proved he'd belonged in the diving finals four years ago, and he belonged in the final now. He was the best platform diver in the world, and no one could take that from him. He'd worked his ass off, he'd thought through every part of the competition, and he'd put everything he had into his six dives today. This was his. He'd earned it.

Isaac was in the audience. Tim tried to see him, but he was at a bad angle in relation to the stands and couldn't really see anybody, including his own family. But his parents had been there to see this. And Isaac had been too.

"Amazing." Donnie slapped his ass. "Go change, kid. I want to sing the national anthem with you."

ISAAC'S MOTHER was already back in Raleigh, but she'd called him that night anyway. When Isaac joked, "Ma, do you know how much this call is costing me?" she'd replied, "Oh, hush. You've got endorsement deals from here to Neptune. You can afford to talk to your old mother."

She'd been calling to get his flight information so she could pick him up from the airport on Monday. Isaac felt some sadness at that; he, Luke, and Katie had been all over Madrid together in the days since Isaac's little breakdown. Isaac and Luke had even done a filler segment for TBC where they toured some Madrid landmarks with a camera crew, including El Rastro, an open-air market where they found all manner of weird stuff. Isaac's favorite site had been the Prado, but then, he'd always liked art museums.

They'd also taken in a lot of Olympic events; on top of the diving, they'd gone to see a bunch of track-and-field competitions, including cheering on American sprinter Jason Jones Jr. in the 100-meter sprint.

And he'd spent every night with Tim.

He was a bit embarrassed about his overreaction to Pat and that night at America House; he'd come very close to falling. Staring at that pint of beer, a battle had waged in Isaac's head. He still thirsted for that beer, but he'd worked so hard. He and Tim had talked about it quite a bit in the intervening days. Tim seemed to understand that Isaac would have bad days, and Isaac promised to recommit to therapy when he got home so he didn't fall into the trap of depending too much on Tim to help him on those days, especially since they'd be separated by geography.

And even with that one rough night, these had been the best two weeks of Isaac's life, and he didn't want them to end. He didn't want to fly home to Raleigh and face the real world. He'd have to deal with the financial nonsense of his endorsement deals, for one thing, and how many of them were contingent on his continuing to swim. He'd have to decide if he wanted to stick around for another couple of World Cup seasons or if he wanted to retire. And then there was the big question: Would he stay in Raleigh?

The sun had gone down. Luke and Katie were probably doing it like rabbits and Tim was out with his family and the dive team, so Isaac was alone in his room. He hit the email icon on his phone, immediately regretting it as several hundred messages loaded. He scanned the names and subject lines, wondering which emails were worth his time.

He stopped on *Re: Coaching positions at CU.*

He held his breath.

He'd emailed the staff at the University of Colorado one night while waiting for Tim to return from training. It had been an impulse, although not one that he particularly regretted.

The reply said: *Actually, one of our coaches is retiring at the end of this season, so we're starting to think about replacements. Let's talk when you return from Madrid.*

So there it was.

Isaac held his breath for a moment, imagining his life beyond Madrid. Could he see himself ensconced in some mountain retreat with Tim? Could he coach? Could he see a way forward?

He could.

He let out the breath and smiled to himself.

A moment later there was a tap at the door. "It's open," Isaac called.

Tim opened the door and slid inside. "I think I've escaped them." His gold medal still hung around his neck, and he was still wearing the official warm-up suit. He looked good, but tired.

"Yeah?" Isaac said.

"My parents went back to the hotel a half hour ago, but I was with Jason and the rest of my team at America House, but then I got really tired? So I told them I had to call it a night and we could party more tomorrow, but a bunch of people followed me back to the building. I had to get a security escort up here." He sighed. "I lied to the security guard and told him I was on this floor and I could get to my room alone."

"Okay."

Tim flopped down next to Isaac on the bed. Then he slipped his gold medal off and handed it to Isaac. "I think you know what this means."

Isaac laughed. "You want to have sex?"

Tim stood and pulled off parts of the warm-up suit. "Yep. How well supplied are you?"

"Well, they give out condoms like they're energy bars around here, so pretty well. Are you serious?"

"Yup." Tim had stripped down to a USA Diving T-shirt and his briefs, which were turquoise. "I have two more nights with you before we fly home, and I intend to make the most of them. I don't have to train anymore, so if we fuck and I'm sore tomorrow, it's all good. Get naked."

Isaac laughed. "Tim, I—"

"Look, I'm riding a pretty intense wave of adrenaline right now, but I'm going to crash really hard soon, so I'd like to have sex with you while I'm still awake enough to participate. And as you'll recall, we had a sex-for-medals agreement."

"Well, I mean, by that measure, we should fuck... um, a bunch. How many medals did I win?" It was hard to concentrate when Tim was so naked. Because now he was. Naked. And standing at the side of the bed stroking his cock.

"Who cares? I won a gold medal today. That's all that matters. Get naked, Isaac."

Isaac slid off the bed and went into the bathroom. There was a bottle of lube in his toiletries bag, and he had the condoms from his welcome bag, so he grabbed those too and headed back to the bed. Tim lounged there, sprawled out on the skinny mattress, looking completely beautiful.

"I loved watching you today," Isaac said. He dropped his supplies on the corner of the bed and then pulled his shirt off. He decided not to bother with stripping gracefully or putting on much of a show, because Tim was hard and his skin was flushed, so he was clearly ready to go. In fact, he picked up the bottle of lube, looked at it for a second, and then poured some on his hands.

Isaac's heart pounded.

"That was some of the best diving I've done in... wow, years, maybe. I kept thinking about what you said. About just doing everything I had in me to do. So that's what I did."

"You were nearly perfect."

"Yes. That's... me at my best. I can do that."

It wasn't arrogance in Tim's voice but rather awe, like he'd surprised himself today. Isaac knew the feeling. He pushed his sweats down his hips and hopped a little to get them off, until he was naked too. He slid on top of Tim.

"You *can* do amazing things," Isaac said. "I'm not even saying that to stroke your ego. I had a lot of fun watching you today, and so did Luke and Katie. You earned that medal."

Tim put his arms around Isaac. "Thanks. But honestly, I'm happy about it, but I really want to fuck right now, so maybe you could do that instead of talking?"

Isaac grinned. God, he wanted Tim. He'd been trying not to think too much about what it might be like to be inside Tim, because it was off the table until the competition ended. But now they were both finished with their respective events, and they could spend all night fucking.

Well, probably Tim would conk out after this first bout, but that was okay.

Isaac kissed Tim's shoulder and reached for the lube. They worked together to prepare Tim. Their fingers kept tangling at the entrance to Tim's body, and Isaac watched it up close while also kissing and licking Tim's hard cock. Tim threw his head back and groaned.

"I've wanted this for two weeks," Tim said.

"God, me too."

"Kiss me, Isaac."

Isaac granted the request, sneaking up Tim's body and planting his lips on Tim's. Tim spread his legs wide, inviting Isaac between them. So Isaac rolled on a condom and then positioned himself.

"Not much foreplay going on here," Isaac said.

"The last two weeks have been foreplay. Do you know how sexy you are?"

"Do you know how sexy *you* are? I kept secretly hoping the impact on the water would pull your suit off."

Tim smiled. "We use a special glue that keeps that from happening and also prevents wedgies, but I appreciate the thought."

"Don't tell me things like that. It ruins the illusion."

Tim laughed. "Isaac? Please fuck me."

Isaac bent his head and kissed Tim thoroughly while he shifted his hips and pressed the head of his cock against Tim's hole. His pulse raced as he did it, his anticipation at high, prerace levels, not to mention the fact that this man beneath him, *this man* could make him laugh, could make him feel pride and affection, had shown him things he hadn't seen in himself before, had woken up all these things in Isaac that Isaac had thought died the moment a cop had yanked him out of his car.

He had his life back.

he curled his body around Tim's and said, "I can't wait until we can do this in a decent-sized bed."

Tim murmured something that might have been "Hmmm?"

"Sleep, my gold-medal winner. Just sleep. We'll worry about it tomorrow."

TIM WOKE up slowly. When he was conscious enough to form rational thoughts, he noticed the room was dark but for the white glow of Isaac's cell phone screen, which illuminated his face.

"What are you doing?" Tim asked.

Isaac hit the button on his phone that made the screen go dark. "Just checking my email."

"Trouble sleeping?"

Isaac mumbled an assent. "Sorry if I woke you."

"You didn't. Anything good in your email?"

"Mostly fan mail. I'm trying to clean out my inbox to focus on the messages that are actually important. Although even then, it's mostly my mother forwarding articles about me."

"Good press?" Tim rolled slightly to better cuddle up against Isaac.

"Yeah, but through the filter of my mother. She won't send me the articles that say mean things."

Isaac put his phone on the side table and slid over into Tim's space. Tim adjusted his hold on Isaac, snaking his hand around Isaac's midsection.

"I want to thank you," Tim said.

"For?"

"For not saying anything about our relationship. I could just focus on diving today."

"Of course." Isaac stroked Tim's back. "Although the security guards had a role there."

That was true. Tim and Donnie had met with security at the Aquatics Center a few days before to give them photos of Pat before Tim felt confident Pat had actually gone home. Only approved reporters would be let in during the competition. Whether others snuck in or not, Tim didn't know about it, and he'd felt safe enough to push it out of his mind.

And once Pat flew back home, the tabloid media seemed to have lost interest in Tim.

Tim understood that media coverage was part of being an elite athlete, but there was a line between doing puff pieces for TBC or the occasional *Sports Illustrated* story and the kind of media attention Pat had brought into Tim's life.

"I try not to dwell," Tim said, tracing patterns along Isaac's skin with his fingers. "Pat was bad for me. Our relationship went sour before I ended it. I see clearly now what kind of man he is. I don't miss him, and I don't regret telling him to go home."

"That's good," said Isaac.

"I never want that particular media spotlight on me again. If I get press coverage, I want it to be for diving, not for who I date."

Isaac was silent for a long moment. He exhaled loudly, shifted his weight a little on the bed. "You do realize that if we go public with our relationship, we're in for some of that, right? I just did that big interview with Marcus Holt. They edited out some of what I said, but the bottom line is that half the world knows about my alcoholism right now. I did lose a couple of sponsorships over it, but not as many as I expected, probably because of my medals. And because of those, I'm in the spotlight. You know, one of those emails I just checked? It was *Sports Illustrated* trying to get in touch with my new agent because they want me to do a photo spread or maybe even a cover."

And Tim did know that, at least in the back of his mind. He didn't love the idea of his sex life being so public, but it would be, with someone like Isaac.

But Isaac would never show up at one of Tim's meets with a camera crew. He'd never call a photographer he knew to tip them off that he and Tim would be in a certain place that day. And he would never use Tim, not the way Pat had.

"I'll be honest," Tim said. "I'm not looking forward to that. I don't want to hide, but I don't want to talk to reporters about us either. I want what we have to be between us. Which I guess is not possible."

"Fuck 'em," said Isaac. "We can say as much or as little as we want. You don't want to talk about our relationship with the press? I don't either. But maybe I want to, I don't know, hold your hand sometimes."

Warmth spread through Tim's chest. He laid his head on Isaac's shoulder. Isaac could be so heartbreakingly sweet sometimes. "There are some important differences between you and Pat. First, if we go public, it will be on our terms. It will be on my terms. You and I will decide what's right or wrong for us to say."

"That's true."

"Second, I know you're not using me for your own gain. We're just… together."

"I am really gonna kill that guy."

Tim sighed, happiness bubbling up through him. He propped himself up on his elbows and looked down at Isaac. He wanted to see Isaac's eyes when he said this last thing. "Here's the most important thing, though.

After Pat and I had been together for a while, my gut started telling me something wasn't right. Those feelings all turned out to be correct. When I broke up with Pat, I promised myself I would trust my instincts from then on."

Isaac bit his lip. "I see where you're going with this, but are you sure? Because if I ever fall of the wagon...."

"I'll help you get back on. Because my gut tells me that you are a good man, Isaac, one with some flaws and some demons, but a good man in your heart." Tim placed a hand on Isaac's chest. "And you care about me genuinely, just as I care about you. Somehow I just *know* that. Probably we weren't destined to be together or anything like that, and I'm sure once the bubble of the Olympics pops, we'll have problems and arguments and, I don't know, couple stuff. But I also think we'll have something really great together."

Isaac closed his eyes and tilted his head away. He brought a hand up to his mouth. He looked back at Tim and said, "You'll help me."

"And not because you depend on me, but because I want to, because I care about you, and because I know that even if you are an alcoholic, and even though I know vodka and beer call to you, I also know that you want so much more from life than that. You didn't even sip that beer. I know you want to be sober, to live your life the way you swim. Right?"

"Yeah. Yeah, that's true." Isaac swallowed. "God, how you get me. You see right through me."

Tim was on a roll now, convinced more than anything that this was right, that this would be good. He knew they'd struggle. He knew putting up with post-Olympics media attention would be the worst. But he also knew that he and Isaac could weather the storm. His gut told him that it would be worth it in the long run. "You've said a dozen times since I've met you that the key to being an elite athlete is pushing your body to its limit, and I think that's how you approach life. You partied like there was no tomorrow, then you drank like it, and now you live like it. You pushed yourself to do the impossible last week, and you did it, you pulled it off. That's how I know we'll be okay, even if you're an alcoholic. Because you, Isaac, can do anything."

Isaac nodded slowly. "That's not true, but I'll go along with it. You're pretty fucking amazing too, by the way."

"Well."

Isaac lifted his hand and smoothed the fringe of Tim's short hair away from his forehead. "I know that I'm a better man than your ex, for the record, but I'm glad you can see that too. And I'm glad that today, you have no regrets, that you got up on that ridiculously tall platform and made your body do things no human body should do, and that you were rewarded for it. I don't have the words to express how great you are. How sweet and smart and talented."

Tim flushed and ducked his head, feeling suddenly bashful in the face of all this praise.

But Isaac put his hand on the side of Tim's face and moved him until Tim was looking right at Isaac's eyes again.

"I don't believe in destiny," Isaac said. "I think you make your own way in the world. I don't really understand all the science behind alcoholism, but part of it is probably genetic, and I suppose you could argue I was destined to have a problem with booze. But I can choose being sober over being drunk now. And I am so glad I did, because it meant that I met you."

Tears stung Tim's eyes. He leaned down and kissed Isaac.

This man.

If Tim had been given free rein to choose his mate, he wasn't sure Isaac would have been the man he'd pick, but now that he'd gotten to know Isaac, he couldn't imagine being with anyone else.

"The media attention is going to suck," Tim said.

"Fuck 'em."

"Eh. It'll be worth it."

CHAPTER 26

Day 16

THE USOC had furnished everyone with official Closing Ceremony outfits. Isaac's Opening Ceremony uniform still hung in the plastic he'd received it in, but he looked at the Closing Ceremony uniform—a crisp navy blue collared shirt to be worn over a red-and-white-striped T-shirt and tucked into white shorts—and shrugged, figuring it could be worse.

As he slid the official belt through its loops on the shorts, there was a knock at the door, so he hollered for the knocker to come in.

It was Tim. He wore the same outfit, except his shirt was red and his undershirt had blue-and-white stripes.

As they walked down the hall together, Isaac said, "Not for nothing, but I feel like we're one of those tourist couples who wear matching outfits."

"Well, it's you, me, and several hundred other American athletes stuck in this getup."

Indeed, as they reached the lobby, they got pulled into a mob of other athletes looking to board the buses to the Olympic Stadium. Luke and Katie were there holding hands, as were Jason and Ginny—not holding hands—so they all formed their own sub-mob and managed to get seats together on one of the buses.

"I can't believe it's over," said Luke.

"Do you think they'll let us mingle?" asked Jason. "With the other countries, I mean. I want to try to catch my new friend April before she flies out in the morning."

"Your new *lady* friend?" asked Ginny.

"Yes, if you must know. She's a rhythmic gymnast from the UK."

"Did you do any rhythmic gymnastics with her?" Luke asked.

Jason ducked his head in response.

The USOC had asked Isaac to be the Closing Ceremony flag bearer, but Isaac had passed because he wanted to maximize the amount of time he could spend with his friends—especially Tim—before he had to fly home. He'd heard one of the gymnasts had gotten the honor instead. Tim hadn't heard if his replacement was a male or female gymnast—he spared a thought for Jake Mirakovitch, although his sister had apparently cleaned up the women's gymnastics medals, so it might have been her—but he supposed it didn't matter much. He just wanted to hang out with these people and find a way to say goodbye to an incredible Olympic Games.

When they got to the stadium, they were led underground, and the athletes were all corralled onto the practice track. Flag bearers would go into the stadium first and then the athletes would follow. There was some pomp and circumstance that had to happen before that, but once the athletes got into their designated part of the stadium, a bunch of Spanish pop stars started putting on a concert. So that had some potential to be fun.

They didn't enter the stadium until almost an hour later, at which point they were kind of herded into a pen where, yes, the athletes were given space to mingle with their former opponents from other countries. Jason took off to find his rhythmic gymnast, and Ginny got pulled into a conversation with a Mexican diver. Luke and Katie made eyes at each other, which effectively left Isaac and Tim alone together in this big mob of people.

Fireworks exploded overhead.

And then, improbably, it started to rain. It had been sunny and gorgeous for sixteen straight days, but now at the end of the Olympics, big fat raindrops fell into the stadium. Isaac didn't even care. He and Tim stood in a mélange of athletes, the countries all mixed together, and they held hands as the Madrid Olympics came to a close.

"I can't believe it's ending," Tim said.

"It's not ending. This is just the beginning."

Tim turned to face Isaac. "What are you saying?"

Suddenly the heavens opened and it started to pour. Some of the athletes seemed to embrace it, squealing with joy as it poured, though a lot of people ran for the cover of the inner corridors of the stadium. Isaac didn't move, because he had to say this.

"Tim, I love you. I know it's only been, like, two and a half weeks, but I do. I love you. You're the one for me. So I can't let this end. I won't. I've turned my life around, and I want to be a good man. I think, with you at my side, I can do fucking anything."

Tim met his gaze. He looked like he might be crying, but it was hard to tell in the rain. His hair was matted to his head and his clothes were starting to cling to his body. But he said, "I love you too. Oh my God, I love you too. I don't know how it's possible, but it's true."

Isaac grinned. "You and I can do anything!" he shouted because the rain was hammering against the track.

Tim nodded. "No matter what, we'll figure it out."

Isaac lunged forward and kissed Tim, sealing the promise. Because they would figure this out.

And so they stood there kissing in the rain, and probably the press caught them and would have things to say about it the next day, but Isaac did not fucking care, because he loved Tim and they were both Olympic champions and he wanted this moment to go on forever.

comfortable life for many years to come. But Isaac didn't like idle time, so after he'd retired and moved into Tim's house for good, he'd taken that coaching job at Colorado and seemed to genuinely love it. He still flew back to Raleigh every few months to see his family, but he seemed happy up in the mountains. He said the setting suited him better.

Isaac wasn't on the official Team USA coaching staff, but as the coach of one of its stars, he had some privileges and had been spending a lot of time by the pool. Still, Isaac kept swearing to Tim that he was really here to support him more than anything else. He wasn't allowed in the athletes' dorms, though, so Tim had to settle for nightly phone calls, something that annoyed his roommate, Jason.

Well, whatever. Tim would cope. He could limit his spousal visits to dinners at the America House like everybody else. How was that for equality?

"Okay, we're ready," the official said.

Jason and Tim toweled off again and got ready to climb the dive tower. "You ready?" Tim asked.

"Are you?"

Tim rolled his eyes. He gave Jason a fist bump; then they climbed the tower. When they got to the top, Tim sought out his family. They were all sitting in the second row wearing matching Team Swan T-shirts, which Isaac hated but gamely went along with. They were bright yellow at Tim's mother's insistence, which made them all easy to find.

Tim reflected that it didn't matter if he did well today. He planned to retire after this Olympics and had a job waiting for him at the newly opened USOC Aquatics Training Center in Boulder. He and Isaac had been talking about adopting a baby in the near future, something Tim was ready for now that his diving career was waning. He liked the idea of Isaac as a father immensely and knew Isaac would excel at it, even if Isaac himself had doubts. They had their house and their life together in the mountains outside of Boulder and Tim had never been happier, so what happened here was immaterial. If he won, great, but if he didn't, that was okay too. He'd put his all into this, although age and a back injury the previous season meant he didn't dive as well as he once did. He and Isaac joked about Tim needing to win a medal in order to have spousal privileges with Isaac, but Tim knew it didn't really matter to Isaac as long as Tim went out there and put everything he had on the platform.

Tim glanced at Jason. They walked to the edge of the platform. Their first dive was the lowest in difficulty, a way to ease into competition. Tim took a moment to push his thoughts aside in favor of mentally picturing the dive and how it needed to go. He got into position and, as agreed, would count the lead-up to the dive.

Jason nodded, so Tim counted.

"One, two, three, go!"

KEEP READING FOR AN EXCERPT
FROM THE NEXT IN THE SERIES

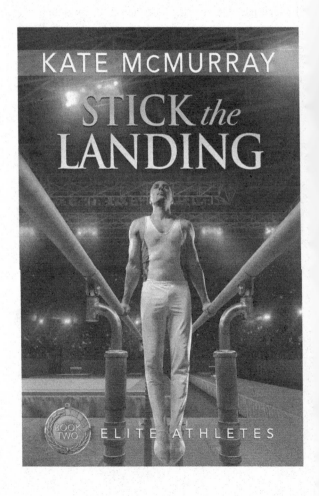

KATE McMURRAY

STICK *the*
LANDING

BOOK TWO · ELITE ATHLETES

An Elite Athletes Novel

Jake Mirakovitch might be the best gymnast in the world, but there's one big problem: he chokes in international competition. The least successful of a family of world-class gymnasts, he has struggled to shake off nerves in the past. This time he's determined to bring home the gold no matter what.

Retired figure skater Topher Caldwell wants a job as a commentator for the American network that covers the Olympics, and at the Summer Olympics in Madrid, he has a chance to prove himself with a few live features. He can't afford to stumble.

Olympic victories eluded Topher, so he knows about tripping when it really counts. When he interviews Jake, the two bond over the weight of all that pressure. The flamboyant reporter attracts the kind of attention Jake—stuck in a glass closet—doesn't want, but Jake can't stay away. Topher doesn't want to jeopardize his potential new job, and fooling around with a high-profile athlete seems like a surefire way to do just that. Yet Topher can't stay away either....

Coming in Summer 2020
www.dreamspinnerpress.com

thus prevented the beleaguered American men's gymnastics team from qualifying for the Olympics....

Alexei, Jake's coach, and Brian, one of the other coaches, helped Jake to his feet. Jake wasn't hurt so much as stunned. "Do I vault again?" Jake asked, confused again.

"No," said Alexei. "You get down and let Doctor Ruiz look at you."

"Am I supposed to vault again? Like, if I'd stuck that landing, would I?"

"No. It's the team competition. You only vault once."

"Okay."

Jake heard clapping, but it could have been a herd of bees buzzing, the way it sounded in his ears. All sound was tinny and distant.

He'd fucked up, big time.

"Score gets erased," said Alexei.

Well, yeah. Landing on his back was sure to earn Jake a zillion deductions. "What happened?"

"Over-rotated." Alexei guided Jake into a chair. "When you came out of tuck, you should have kicked your legs harder, but instead, you kept rotating."

"Ah," said Jake.

Dr. Ruiz, the team medic, swooped over and started asking questions. Did Jake hit his head (he didn't know, but probably), had he hurt anything else (his pride; otherwise, no) and did he know where they were (yes, Beijing). Really, he felt stunned more than anything else. This was like all the times he'd gotten the wind knocked out of him when he hit the mat too hard during practice; now he felt like he'd just got his breath back. Surprised, but okay. Not nauseous. No obvious pain.

"I'm fine," Jake insisted, though it started to sink in now how badly he'd fucked up. Sure, they'd toss out his score if it was indeed the lowest vault score for the American team. But fucking up in international competition—again—did not make his chances of making the American Olympic team much better.

"You sure?" asked Alexei.

"Yeah. Just stunned. I thought I'd land that." Jake tried for a self-deprecating smile. Probably he looked crazy.

Alexei patted him on the back. Dr. Ruiz finished taking his vitals and ruled him okay to keep competing. Up on the scoreboard, his score flashed up: 13.333. Jake grimaced. Not embarrassing, but definitely not good, especially on a vault that he routinely scored better than 15 points on.

"You didn't quite push off table hard enough," Alexei said, rewatching the vault on his phone. "You would have landed it if you got higher off table."

"Okay." Jake pretended to absorb that criticism, even though he was thinking, *Too fucking late now*.

"It's fine," said Brian. "As long as you're okay?"

Jake nodded.

"We're in second place right now." Brian pointed at the scoreboard. "One more event to go. We should podium, at least."

"No thanks to me."

"Your high bar routine was brilliant," said Brian.

"Good on parallel bars," said Alexei.

"Pommel horse not so much," said Jake, who'd biffed a skill there, too.

Alexei shook his head. "When we get back to States, we change training. I've seen you do that vault a hundred times, no problem. Now, people watching, you land on your back. Why?"

"Oh, Alexei, if I could answer that question...." Jake shook his head. "Forget it. I'm all right. We'll qualify a full team to the Olympics, which is all that matters."

"You'll be on that team," said Alexei.

But Jake was not so sure.

On the other side of the world....

"YOU WANT me to do what?"

Topher stood in his kitchen with his cell phone wedged between his chin and his shoulder. It was very likely going to end up in the pot of boiling water below. The smart thing would be to fetch his headset from the other room and finish the call that way, but suddenly Angela, his agent, was saying strange words, and Topher felt dumbfounded.

"They want you to walk at Fashion Week. As a model. See, Jennifer Cole has a new collection—"

"She's a womenswear designer." Topher did not like where this was going.

"Yes, she is, but she collaborated on a menswear collection that is being put out under her label, and they want a couple of splashy stars to walk as models."

"It's insane, isn't it?" Topher stepped away from the boiling water. An onion sat half-chopped on his cutting board, next to the still-unopened package of pasta and a tomato that seemed to be shriveling up as it sat, still whole and unblemished, mocking Topher. His dinner date would be here any minute, and he'd miss out on the pre-dinner flirtation if he didn't get this meal going. He sighed. "The collection, I mean. Hot pink feathers and, like, rainbows and whatever. I saw Cole's collection last year. She designs for teenage girls."

"I've seen some of the drawings," said Angela. "The collection certainly couldn't be called subdued, but I've seen crazier men's fashion. Hell, I've seen you wear crazier men's fashion. This could be a really good opportunity for you, Toph. You'd get the kind of positive press that would win over the TBC execs."

Topher harrumphed. TBC was the television network that had an exclusive contract to air the Olympics in the United States. Topher had been hired during the last World Championships as a figure skating correspondent—because who better than a two-time Olympic figure skater and World Champion to comment on the sport—but because the old guard wasn't ready to retire, mostly he just interviewed the athletes off the ice. There had been rumors swirling that TBC liked Topher enough to have him replace one of their regular commentators, and Topher wanted that job more than he wanted his next meal. The ancient man who'd won his gold medal in 1960, when all one really had to do was spin around a couple of times somehow still did the primetime commentary. Topher kept hearing that the old man could barely walk these days, let alone muster up the energy to say anything informative about figure skating, so that spot was Topher's.

If he didn't blow it.

Or, not even blow it. More than one TBC employee had implied they wanted him to be less flamboyantly gay. Which, sorry, but no.

"I don't know if Fashion Week is the kind of thing the network executives really want me to do. Play football or hunt for wild game, sure, but prance around that he couldn't make it up in the long program when everyone else skated flawlessly. He ended up in fourth place, which was basically the worst. The second time, he was still expected to win, but expectations seemed more tempered, and by then, there were all these other rising stars, and Topher was kind of the old man—at the ripe-old age of twenty-five. Still, after a near-flawless short program that had landed him in first place going into the long program, something had happened, and he'd choked. Actually, he'd fallen on his ass executing a jump he'd done without incident hundreds, if not thousands, of times.

Topher had won three World Championships, but something about the Olympics' stage was like a curse. He'd been hoping to try one more time, but fatigue and an old injury prevented him from doing so, and now he had bad knees that ached on rainy days and zero Olympic medals.

TBC generally hired retired athletes to comment on Olympic sports, but they got the guy who won a gold medal in Seoul or the woman who won a silver in Albertville. Not knowledgeable, albeit flamboyant, also-rans. Because Topher had been skating almost since the time he'd learned to walk, but he'd never won an Olympic medal. So what kind of expert could he be?

He shook off his shame spiral and said instead, "Hey, if Jennifer Cole wants me to dress like a unicorn, and that's what I need to do to persuade TBC to send me to Madrid, then I'm already practicing my runway walk."

"Attaboy." Angela laughed. "I'll let the Cole people know."

DON'T MISS THE REST
OF THE SERIES

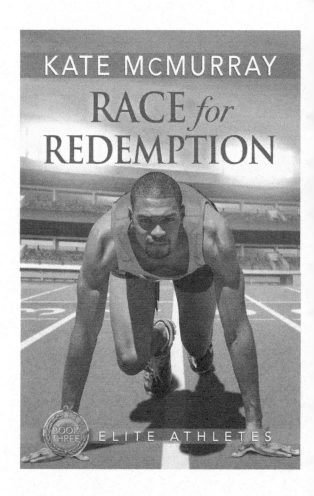

KATE McMURRAY

RACE *for*
REDEMPTION

BOOK THREE

ELITE ATHLETES

An Elite Athletes Novel

Sprinter Jason Jones Jr., known around the world as JJ, is America's hope to take the title of Fastest Man in the World, the champion of the Olympic 100-meter sprint. Two years before, a doping scandal brought his winning streak to a crashing end, and even though he's been cleared of wrongdoing, he's finding it hard to escape the damage to his reputation. At the Games in Madrid, no one believes he's innocent, and officials from the doping agency follow him everywhere.

It just fuels JJ's determination to show them he's clean and still the fastest man on earth.

If only he wasn't tempted by foxy hurdler Brandon Stanton, an engineering student and math prodigy who views each race like a complicated equation. His analytical approach helps him win races, and he wants to help JJ do the same. But JJ's been burned too many times before and doesn't trust anyone who has all the answers. No matter how sexy and charming JJ finds Brandon, the Olympics is no place for romance. Or is it?

Coming in Fall 2020
www.dreamspinnerpress.com

KATE MCMURRAY writes smart romantic fiction. She likes creating stories that are brainy, funny, and, of course, sexy with regular-guy characters and urban sensibilities. She advocates for romance stories by and for everyone. When she's not writing, she edits textbooks, watches baseball, plays violin, crafts things out of yarn, and wears a lot of cute dresses. She's active in Romance Writers of America, serving for two years on the board of Rainbow Romance Writers, the LGBT romance chapter, and three—including two as president—on the board of the New York City chapter. She lives in Brooklyn, NY, with two cats and too many books.

Website: www.katemcmurray.com

Twitter: @katemcmwriter

Facebook: www.facebook.com/katemcmurraywriter